I0604297

BE THOU
MY BRILLIANT

BE THOU MY BRILLIANT

The Devil's Foundry • Book 2

JOSEPH MARCIA
AKA ARGENTORUM

Podium

To Felisa and Oscar, who knew I was an author before I did

All rights reserved. No part of this publication may be reproduced, stored in a retrieval system, or transmitted in any form or by any means electronic, mechanical, photocopying, recording, or otherwise without prior written permission from Podium Publishing.

This is a work of fiction. Names, characters, places, and incidents are either products of the author's imagination or used fictitiously. Any resemblance to actual events, locales, or persons, living, dead, or undead, is entirely coincidental.

Copyright © 2023 Joseph Marcia

Cover design by Podium Publishing

ISBN: 978-1-0394-3324-3

Published in 2023 by Podium Publishing, ULC
www.podiumaudio.com

BE THOU
MY BRILLIANT

CHAPTER 1

Once More, with Feeling

Over there!" I pointed, voice almost lost in the din of the construction site. "No, over *there,* dammit."

I shook my head as the two men stumbled, almost spilling the pallet of metal onto the ground. We were working with spools mostly, so it was no great loss, but winding them all again would be such a fucking chore. Still, even having metal *wire* would be a massive boon, we had the infrastructure in place to do something with it.

I pinched my nose, trying to suppress the headache growing behind my eyes. "Where's my fucking coffee?" Joke's on me, there's no such thing as coffee in this world! Think, Via. Think! Why would you invent electricity before the French press?

"Get the carts back to the dock." I sighed. "We're running out of daylight."

"Yeah, boss."

I waved him off. I hadn't asked to be called *boss,* but it had kinda stuck. Well, more like my gang was all calling me that, and the local villagers didn't want to offend the new petty tyrant too much. At the very least, commanding demons to help build so many houses provided a steady stream of experience pushing me towards my second class.

Well, maybe bringing in food and money to a growing village of refugees had something to do with all of that as well, especially when

I told my boys (and girls) to keep their hands to themselves or so help me god.

"Lady Via."

I let out a long breath, smiling slightly as Rel pressed an earthenware cup of something herbal into my hands. "Thanks, Rel. You're a lifesaver."

The young woman ducked her head, tugging on the rim of her fedora. "It's nothing, my lady."

And yes, I *did* invent fedoras before I invented coffee. Cursing my own demented genius, I threw back the tea. "What's the progress at the dock?"

I started walking, and Rel fell in step beside me. "It's proceeding within accepted limits. I'm not a shipwright, nor was anyone else that came with us . . . but we're making do."

We had a few people who knew how to hammer a pier together if nothing else, she meant. But really, that was all I needed.

"And the village?"

She paused, looking off to the side. ". . . Still tense." Rel shrugged. "But less than they were the first week? You've been good on your word, Lady Via. That means a lot."

I nodded. "I keep my promises." Till all my debts were paid. I'd been racking up a fair few of those the last few months on this world.

I stepped to the side as a group of children rushed down the street, giggling playfully. One of the boys sketched a little bow, and I waved him off—more gently than I'd sent the workmen going. I always had a soft spot for kids.

"This school system . . ."

"I won't budge on it," I said. "If nothing else, universal education, universal *opportunity* to excel is a human right as far as I'm concerned."

Rel nodded.

"Look at me, preaching to the choir." I sighed. "You had it even worse than I did."

It really drove home how, despite the flaws I'd battled against for years, Earth was a post-scarcity society in so many ways compared to this world. But then, if I were *unwilling* to kill the good to save the perfect, I never would have become a villain in the first place.

"Tell the people worried about it that we will speak on the subject at the next town hall meeting."

"It will be added to the list of topics for your next audience," Rel said.

I growled. "Now *that* I thought we'd talked about already."

Rel smiled. It was a sly one that she'd picked up from Electra no doubt, the kind of half-smirk that said 'I know more than you nen-ernernener.' "Yes, my lady, we've talked about it."

"And there's a *reason* we're calling them town halls, dammit. There has to be a velvet glove to go with the iron fist here, Rel."

Relia shrugged. "You told me to, ah, focus group it? My lady." She shrugged. "People responded best to public audiences."

I grumbled, finishing off my tea. "Never should have called myself Empress."

Rel blinked. "What else would you be?"

"Oh, I had a bunch of ideas." I waved my hand in the air. Around us, the once-small village of Ineir bustled with activity. I'd had plans, I'd had money, and, most importantly, I'd had food enough to see us all through the winter, and so people got to work. "Black Cipher, Mechan-ess, the Techno Qu—" I pulled up short, just before a cart rolled across the intersection in front of us. "Gotta get those stupid traffic lights installed, and the roads paved before it snows."

I groaned, pressing a hand to my face. "This is why I don't *do* minions." I spun, pointing at my ever-reliable right hand. "You did this to me."

Rel simply bowed. "I am yours to command."

"You're such a sap." I clapped her on the shoulder. "Now come on. We have places to be tonight."

"Yes, Mistress."

"And I told you not to call me that."

"Of course, Mistress."

I held back another groan.

"You reward a girl for going above and beyond the call of duty *one time . . .*" I pretended not to notice Rel preening at my side, her fingers ghosting over the ornate silver bracelet I'd given her.

Some would call it a waste of silver. Me? I called it an investment into the most valuable coin of all.

Still, no matter how much I griped about the workload, there was something . . . captivating about watching the city spin to my will. Around me, there were work crews—mostly women, as the men were still needed to tend to the fields as winter approached—digging holes, putting up posts, and, as ever, running more and more wire through the air.

Let me tell you, finding something to use for insulation had been a bitch and a *half*, but luckily there was this demon with some strangely useful intestinal physiology—and no, I *didn't* just cut up my demons for parts. That wouldn't be economical.

At last, we made it to the river. The village, now quickly growing into the *town* of Ineir if I had anything to say about it, boasted a single river that ran along its southern border. Honestly, the river was probably the sole reason for its survival, cutting off the thick jungle and putting them on a trade route between Silverwall to the north and the capital city of Corvandyr on the opposite side of the island's isthmus.

Of course, just because it was a source of fish and irrigation for the city didn't mean it couldn't be used for so much more. Hell, they'd already had a water wheel when I got here.

"It's come a long way." Rel looked up at the much larger wheelhouse. The newly installed overshot wheel spun round merrily as the river gushed out to sea.

"Not hard." I shrugged. "It was practically falling apart when we got here." Really, reforming this entire village in less than a month would have looked like an impossible task, but many hands made light work.

Two Slythids, snakelike demons that loved nothing more than to lounge next to warm stones, opened the doors for us as we approached. I smiled.

I had the most hands of all.

Inside, of course, the water wheel couldn't have looked more different. Gone was the millstone (though we'd set it up elsewhere for the time being), along with the half rotted supports and drafty wooden walls.

In their place were stone walls, with masonry. The floor was tiled and leveled. The beams were varnished, and their connections sheathed in strong steel.

And of course, the *pièce de résistance*, a massive spool of wire in the middle of the room, set around the world's first, greatest, and grandest artificial magnet.

If we were being honest, this is what had taken most of my time.

"Okay, flip the connection!"

Luckily, I hadn't been alone on this either.

Electra grinned from one of the catwalks, uncaring of the bare wire she held in her hand as two burly men manually spun a series of gears leading to a smaller 'backup' generator.

She lit up like a livewire, before diverting the current to another series of wires. I felt myself smile as another series of crude lightbulbs began to glow.

Electra, for all her flaws as a person, *did* possess at least a rudimentary understanding of electricity, even if it was only because the PR team had forced her to take classes after she blew out an entire skyscraper's power grid that one time.

I cupped my hands around my mouth. "We ready up there?"

Electra leaned against the railing as the generator whirred to a stop. "Empress! Yeah, we're about done!" She looked back over her shoulder. "Whaddaya think, guys?"

"Looks good to me, ma'am." The workman shifted. "Er, uh, yer majesty."

I held back the urge to snap at him.

They'll think it was because he didn't address you properly, Via. And then they'll all *be calling you 'your majesty,' and that would be even worse than* 'boss.'

"*Hay que pena*," I muttered.

Rel leaned forward. "What was that, my lady?"

"Nothing." I straightened with a grin. "Good work! Why don't you join us up on the balcony?"

"Er, uh." The first man glanced at his friend as Rel and I made our way up the stairs. "We couldn't im-impose like—"

"Hey, don't sweat it!" Electra put one of them in a playful headlock. "Now c'mon, don't you want to see what all the big fuss was about?"

The two looked torn, but it was clear they were curious. I'd only given basic explanations of what I was doing, after all. Enough to show its value, but still, to see it in person?

I waved them after me. "It's a special occasion, after all."

We emerged onto the stone balcony overlooking the village of Ineir just as the sun began to sink below the horizon. On this, the western shores of the island republic of Vecorvia, the sunset painted the ocean in brilliant chromas of purple and scarlet.

Below, the shadows had begun to lengthen, the air just now starting to cool. I picked out Dee and Dum at the edge of the town square, herding people into it. I quirked my lip when I saw that more or less the entire village had turned out to the mill.

"I said it wasn't mandatory."

"Gimme a break, Em'." Electra socked me in the shoulder. "Everyone wants to see what's up with this giant brick house you built instead of a palace."

"Who needs a palace?" I tilted my head back. "Too many rooms."

Electra just laughed.

I waited for the rest of the crowd to filter in, and they waited below, a sea of upturned faces waiting in the growing twilight.

Waiting for me to change the world.

"Everything ready below?" I asked.

"Yep!" Electra popped her lips. "We just did the last batch of tests, and General Tock was in charge of getting the wires together after."

I smiled. "And my little robot is nothing if not punctual."

"Yep."

I nodded once, taking a deep breath. Usually, for occasions like this, I would go out of my way to prepare a speech. But this time, in this place, I decided that actions would speak far louder than words.

I turned to look at the two workmen who had accompanied us. Evandr and . . . Merz, if I remembered correctly. "Would you two like to do the honors?"

They shared a glance, and I waved at the sturdy wooden lever just inside the door of the balcony. "Well, go on." I smiled. "Let's not keep everyone waiting."

With one last nervous glance, they pulled the lever. A massive *clunk* echoed up through the soles of my feet. The great gears behind me strained, taking up slack, before slowly, ponderously, beginning to turn. A *whirr* filled the air, something that you felt more as a prickling on your skin than heard. It grew louder and louder, into a hum that seemed to sing of a future we'd long since forgotten.

And then the night turned back into day.

The wires, the streetlamps, simple crude lightbulbs sitting on simple crude wooden poles . . . they were electrified.

First the square lit up, as voices started rising through the air. The darkness of the main road was peeled back by a wave of gentle golden light. Even though it was only one square and one road, it bathed the entire village in warmth.

The sun set on Vecorvia, but in the tiny village of Ineir, a new day had only just dawned.

CHAPTER 2

Ah Yes, the Plot

Now that's a sight."

I smiled at Electra's words. "It's a start."

She huffed. "Never satisfied, are you?"

"No." My smile grew. "I will *never* be satisfied."

She gave me a complicated glance before shrugging. "I mean, better than settling, I guess."

The two workmen were a bit more shocked by the way I'd lit up the night, of course. This was . . . still just something small for me and Electra. Practically more a proof of concept than an actual electric grid. But to people who were used to living by candlelight, suddenly having morning in the middle of the night was sure to be a surprise.

There were mage lights of course, but as I'd learned from my enchanter back in Silverwall, such things were the domain of the rich.

"It's beautiful, my lady."

I looked over at Rel. She had her hands pressed to her chest, eyes sparkling.

"Oh?"

She nodded. "It's like a sea of light."

I tilted my head, remembering how on our first outing together, Rel had never been afraid of the waves, only the monsters on shore. It was a distant memory, but it sparked a connection. "Do you like the ocean, Relia?"

Rel gave a little start, glancing over at me in surprise. Then her features softened into a smile of her own. "Yes. My mother . . . she was a ship captain." Rel turned back to the lights below. "She would tell me stories of her voyages when I was a little girl."

I blinked. "The compass. Rel, you didn't have to—"

"I know I didn't." She ducked her head. "But you needed it more than I did, and . . ." She reached into her vest, pulling out the compass I'd retooled into an elaborate pocket watch. ". . . I think my mother would have liked what you did with it."

I gave a quiet laugh. "I'll show you more oceans than this," I said, in lieu of anything else. "This is just a puddle in comparison to what I have planned." I smiled, both at my minion and at the people below. "Ineir will be so much more."

"I believe you."

Of course, that was when the eastern palisade exploded.

My head snapped up, tracking the fireball that erupted from beyond the outer wall. With the streetlights, I could just make out a scorched section, where logs were sagging inward.

Well, it was about time to tear down the ad-hoc thing anyway.

"Empress."

I nodded at Electra. "Go."

She sank into a crouch before leaping from the balcony, arcs of electricity streaming from her heels. Her newest skill.

I hadn't been idle either, though.

I waved a hand, and a winged demon, shaped like a long blue pterodactyl, formed at my side. He was twice the size of Blue and, before, would have been far beyond my ability to sustain with my mana pool. But now, that was much less of a problem.

I leapt onto his back, raising a fist for the people below to see as I took off into the air. At the last second, Rel jumped up behind me, holding on to my shoulder with one hand.

A cheer went up, starting with my own men, before swelling to encompass everyone in the village.

System Message

Your skill Crowd Sourcing has increased to level 5.

I huffed. It made things too easy sometimes. Granted, I'd learned how to play a crowd from the best of them.

I tore through the night on Pterry's back. She was a good girl, easily my favorite of the flying demons I'd contracted, and even with Electra's head start, we found the source of the explosion at the same time.

There was a group of bandits on the road, pursuing a fleeing caravan.

I frowned, leaning over. Rel's hand on my back kept me steady on my perch.

No, not just bandits. I huffed. "Another group of guildies."

Rel's grip tightened. "You would think they would all be gone by now."

I shrugged. "Yeah, well, they all got kicked out of Silverwall, so of course they'd all end up here eventually." I was sure it was Arlo just making more trouble for me after I ditched. My fellow gang leader was spiteful and pragmatic like that.

"There's still an Adventurer's Guild in Silverwall," Rel reminded me.

I snorted. We'd heard the same rumors after all. "A gutted corpse completely under the control of the City Guard."

This is where the rest of the surviving guildies had turned.

As I watched, one of the men in the back hurled another fireball. The first one had missed the caravan, but they were closing distance.

A spear of lightning tore through the knight, shattering the other's skull. Electra slid to a stop next to the caravan, waving them onward to Ineir. The group of raiders-cum-adventurers slowed. I counted seven, half mounted, the rest on foot. No doubt they'd laid the ambush for the caravan.

My eyes flicked to them, noting the arrows sticking out of the wood and the way the horses heaved from where they'd sprinted down the road.

I said caravan, but really, it was just two carts. If they'd had someone give them a warning, they could have outrun the initial attack. Well, for a bit at least.

It looked like the group of bandits wasn't going to wait on Electra forever, though. So I kicked my heels into Pterry's flanks and we dived.

Even in this world, people rarely looked up.

Rel and I landed behind the group in a gust of wind. Rel slid off my demon, slinking into the shadows. She was no rogue, but she was the next best thing.

Meanwhile, I pressed my hands together into a single fist, and the wrist-mounted laser lit up with a whine. Without a power core, I had enough juice for two shots, and then I'd be walking home in a tin can.

Fortunately, so far, I'd never needed more than one.

"And who the hell are you people?" My voice rang across the road. The group shifted slightly, pinned between two people of a higher level. No one here was above level 10. Meanwhile, Electra and I were nearing in on our tier-two classes.

And, you know, there was also a giant flying lizard, grinning at them toothily.

Unsurprisingly, none of them were willing to step forward.

I aimed my wrist laser. "Well, if none of you are willing to talk."

"Scatter!" the mage shouted.

I clicked my tongue, holding my shot as the rogue tossed a handful of smoke bombs to the ground. Actual, factual smoke bombs. Were we in one of Electra's anime or something?

At my mental command, Pterry took off again, pushing off the ground with a massive beat of her wings. It cleared the smoke as well, revealing the fleeing figures in the fading light. I dove after one.

The figure in leather armor must have heard the whistling of the wind; he dove to the side just as we cut through the air behind him. I let out a hiss of frustration as they vanished into the jungle.

From the air, I was in a commanding position, but the canopy was thick, and with the sun fully beyond the horizon now, there was no way I could pick out anything.

I circled for a moment more before returning to the road.

Electra and Rel likewise returned empty-handed.

"I'm sorry, my lady." Rel gave a bow. "I was too far away when they ran."

I waved her off, raising an eyebrow at Electra. She was fast enough to take them down with her new Lightning Sprint ability.

"I stayed to make sure no one went after the caravan." She shrugged. "Figured we can probably get the story from them just as easy."

I sighed. "You're probably right. Still, it would have been nice to handle the problem before it can crop up again."

Electra ran a hand through her hair. She had it pulled back into a ponytail now, but even that couldn't contain its inherent spikiness.

"We've already taken care of all the dumb ones. Makes sense only the smart guys are left."

I rolled my eyes. "This is why I prefer to have a monopoly."

Electra snorted. "What, on intelligence?"

"Well, why do you think I never tried to flip you?"

"Rude." She sniffed, turning away. "See if I help you when we get back to Earth."

I rolled my eyes, noting how Rel stiffened slightly at my side. "Whatever. Let's go deal with the people showing up at our door." I gave a small frown. "Last I checked, we hadn't sent anyone to Silverwall in the past week."

"Nope." Electra started walking, with Pterry padding after her. My girl wasn't the fastest on the ground, but she was certainly the most eye-catching. Too bad Blue wasn't big enough to ride. "Everyone's been heading south to Corvandyr."

"How odd."

We made it back to Ineir quickly enough. There were a few people standing around the new palisade, more specifically the *newer* hole in it, and Electra waved them off. It was late enough, and today had been busy for everyone, putting the finishing touches on the streetlights.

Now how was I going to sell running them all underground? Maybe if I made something that could dig trenches for the wires first.

I shook my head.

Dee and Dum had the two wagons stopped next to what was generously called the gate. Really, it was just an opening in the palisade that we could drag another section of wall in front of if we needed to. I took in the people riding with it in a glance.

They were the same as my people.

Tired and hungry, young and old. There was a weariness in their eyes, so tired that no one even flinched as Pterry came to a stop in front of them. But there was a spark of hope as well, one that had not yet been extinguished.

And that's what made them my people.

"Why have you come to Ineir?" I asked. My voice carried, and at that the travelers shifted. Finally, an old woman came forward, slipping off the first cart.

She was stooped, wrapped in rough homespun. I tried to ignore how she'd still be taller than me if I was standing on the ground. "Heard things were good out here." She gave a slow shrug, her voice low and raspy. "Better than in Silverwall."

Electra tilted her head. "What's happening in Silverwall?"

"Nothing good." The old woman bobbed her head. "Guilds've been driving up the price o' everything, guard won't do anything 'bout it. No work either, less you sign up with one of the guilds now. Went and drove everyone else out of business."

I sighed. "Rank protectionism." I turned to Electra. "What do you think?"

She gave me a look. Yes, yes, I knew what she was going to say. I just wanted her to be the one to say it. "We can always use more hands. Lots of new things that need doing 'round here." She grinned. "If you're all willing to learn."

The woman nodded, the tension easing from her shoulders.

"We have communal dormitories for the work crews," I said. "We'll get you settled there for the night and figure out more permanent residence in the morning. Any news from Silverwall would be appreciated." I paused. "And also, we will need to know why you were ambushed."

The crowd shifted again at that, muttering.

I continued. "That was hardly some random group of bandits. Guild Remnants, this far south? They looked like they were doing well for themselves, too. Hardly the type of living you can afford off of knocking over starving caravans."

I looked them over, face firm.

To be clear, I wasn't going to turn them away. Even if we *didn't* need more hands, more eyes, more *everything*, Electra and Rel would have gutted me in my sleep if I'd sent them packing.

But I liked to get out in front of my problems when I could. Which, in case you haven't been keeping track, was always.

We stayed there in silence for a handful of moments, then the crowd shifted again, parting to let a younger woman to the front. She wore a headscarf and kept her head bowed, but even at first glance I could tell that her clothing was nicer than that of the people surrounding her.

She came to a stop in front of Pterry, hands rising up to her shawl. "It's me." She lowered the wrappings, revealing silver hair and golden eyes that seemed to glisten in the lights of Ineir. Beside me, Rel sucked in a sharp gasp. "They are after me."

I stared at her for a long moment. God, I *hated* missing the context. That shit was for other people.

Then I sighed. "Might as well get you all inside then. It's been a long night."

And it wasn't over yet.

CHAPTER 3

The Princess and the Proles

So, you're the heir to the throne?"

The young woman in front of me tried to hide a wince. "Seventeenth in the line of succession, yes." She gripped her teacup with a fragile decorum, raising the simple brew to her lips. "This is quite fresh. My compliments to the chef."

Electra put a hand to her mouth, holding back a giddy laugh. She was getting off on this whole thing.

"I shall ensure he knows." Rel removed the teacup as . . . *Princess* Ishanti set it back down. Somehow, she was doing better in this whole meeting than I was.

I blamed her stupid skills. I wasn't specced to deal with people of higher social status than me, in this life or the last one.

I sighed, running a hand through my hair. We were in the house I'd commandeered for the three of us. Well, I say commandeered—the thing had been abandoned for more than a season, and it was close to the docks. Getting it back into livable condition was an ongoing project.

At least we'd fixed all the leaks.

"Ostensibly, the Adventurer's Guild works for you." We didn't have many spies in Silverwall. I couldn't afford to have too many magic mirrors floating around yet, so at the moment I was working off of woefully outdated information. "There's no reason for them to be chasing you."

Ishanti shook her head, silvery hair glinting in the overhead lamp.

Okay, so maybe I abused my authority *a bit* to get interior lighting installed here. It's not like anyone else wanted it at first. Fortunately, that meant we could have meetings after dark, and I could impress people with the value of electric lighting.

But back to the matter at hand.

"The Adventurer's Guild," Ishanti said, "or what remains of it, now works for Seneschal Hawkwright, as do the guard and other ancillary institutions of Silverwall. My aunt, the Duchess Ivey, has limited control over the household staff and her own personal retainers, which is how I managed to escape the city to begin with."

"Wait, wait, hold up." Electra waved her hands. "So, what, you were just a prisoner inside your palace?"

The woman hesitated, glancing off to the side slightly, before nodding. "It was nothing odious, for the most part . . . but my freedoms, and that of any member of the royal family in Silverwall, are severely diminished." She folded her hands in her lap. "In the capital city of Corvandyr things are different, but even there, the influence of the monarch is fiercely curtailed."

I rested my chin on the back of my hands. "Well, that's a surprise. You'd think the king and queen would have something to say about it."

"Queen of Vecorvia is a ceremonial position that exercises little in the way of outright power." Ishanti recited that little tidbit as if she were reading from a book. "We are a republic, after all."

"Coulda fooled me." I leaned back, turning to look at Rel. "Did you know anything about that?"

Rel shrugged. "I wasn't really educated, Mistress." She scratched her cheek. "I believe I occasionally heard about the Senate during one of my apprenticeships?"

Ishanti nodded. "The Royal Senate is the *de facto* and *de jure* governing body of Vecorvia. Though, likewise, they allow most of the cities to attend to their own affairs."

"Well, aren't you a delightful little info dump," I muttered. "So. What does this Seneschal . . . *Hawkwright* of yours keep you and your aunt locked up in that ivory tower for? What was so important that he'd pay good money to hunt you down and drag you back?"

The princess's eyes tightened. "I . . . do not know."

I blinked. "Really? That's what you're going with?"

"It is the truth." Ishanti looked at me, gold eyes flashing for a moment, before she glanced back down at her lap. "There is . . . a procedure."

Electra tilted her head. "A what now?"

"A procedure." Ishanti tucked a strand of hair behind her ear. "I have not witnessed it myself, nor have I been made privy to the details. But my aunt undergoes it over the course of a moon's turn. I know that it wears on her, leaving her listless and feverish by the end. A month of rest is prescribed by the royal physicians, before she is required to submit to the procedure again."

"Required to?" I raised an eyebrow. "So that's just one more thing that you don't have any control over."

"I have surmised it is the reason that Vecorvia still has a royal family at all," Ishanti said.

"Well, that's not ominous," I said.

She glanced up warily at my words. I waved a hand. "Relax, I'm not about to dump you at Hawkwright's feet or anything. Silverwall hasn't done anything to endear itself to me."

Ishanti's eyes fluttered with relief. "They will . . . continue attempting to retrieve me, you are aware?"

This time, Electra did laugh. "Girl, you have no idea how to bargain, do ya?"

Ishanti looked away. "Barter is crass trade of the lower classes."

I rolled my eyes. "And I wonder why the Vecorvians would want to do away with their royalty."

"Honestly, I'm kind of surprised they still have any at all." Electra rubbed the back of her head. "Don't most of these sorts of revolution things end up with people beheaded or shot, or something awful like that?"

"Don't be an idiot, Electra." I leaned back in my chair. "You can hardly apply Earth history to a world with magic. Really, it's somewhat surprising that they still have monarchies at all, but I guess the addition of magic wouldn't really change feudalism, would it?" I gave a wry grin. "Just the definition of who has the biggest stick."

"It is true then." Ishanti leaned forward. "The two of you are, indeed, outworlders?"

I raised an eyebrow at her. "Do we look like we're from around here?"

She sat back in her chair, looking relieved. My other eyebrow rose to join the first. "Is there something special about us being outworlders?"

She demurred, looking down as her cheeks grew a light red. Christ, even her blushes were delicate. "Merely that they don't follow the same logic as the people of this world. In truth, I scarcely believed you would shelter me otherwise."

Even still, wasn't she way too trusting?

I wouldn't have had an issue selling her back to Hawkwright, but I knew how these sorts of deals went down. First, he would play all nice, and then the moment he had the girl back in his clutches, all of the loose ends would just start to . . . *disappear.* The whole situation reeked of a coverup, after all. Whatever the true rulers of this tiny island kingdom—excuse me, *republic*—did with their 'royalty,' they didn't want the common people to know.

When someone shows you who they are, believe them.

I sighed. "What a mess you've dumped on our lap."

"My sincerest apologies. If I had anything that could ease your burden, were it simply in my power to offer it—"

"You know writing and arithmetic, don't you?" I asked.

Ishanti blinked once at my interruption. "They were both a . . . part of my tutelage, yes."

"Well, in fact there is something you can do then." I smiled. "We need more accountants. I've tried to teach the people here how to read and write, but it's slow going." I waved a hand. "Whatever translation magic that's on us doesn't help."

"You want me to . . . notate documents for you?" Her mouth pursed slightly. "As if I were some sort of barrister?"

"It's either that or schoolmarm." I grinned. "Somehow, you don't strike me as great with kids."

"I see." She nodded once. "And if I were to say that such things were . . . beyond my capabilities?"

"Well, first off, you might have had more luck with that *before* you told me you'd gotten an actual education."

She gave a faint grimace. "And second?"

I jerked my thumb over my shoulder. "It'll cost me less to carry you back to Silverwall than to carry your ass here."

"There is no need to be crass." The young woman sniffed, turning her head. "Very well, you drive a hard bargain, but I see no other option. I shall serve as your personal notary, provided that I am not tasked with unnecessary trivialities."

"How generous." I waved a hand. "Dee, go show her the guest room. Knew I had it installed for a reason."

Dee nodded. "Yeah, boss." He stepped away from the wall. "Thissa way, princess."

"My thanks, good sir."

He chuckled. "I'm not a sir, lady." Still, he didn't protest as she laid her hand on his beefy arm to lead her up the stairs.

And people said that chivalry was dead.

Electra perched on the table next to my shoulder. It was a roughly lacquered thing cut into a rectangle. It was large enough that I could meet with various family heads over a meal, and much less ostentatious than the 'audience hall' that Rel had set up in the water mill.

I felt like I was in a bad drama, with the massive stone chair and the gears turning over my head . . .

Ugh, you had to be there to really appreciate it. I'm sure I'd be suitably annoyed with it later on. For now, I had more than enough trouble on my plate without borrowing more.

"So."

I glanced up at Electra, raising an eyebrow.

"You weren't really gonna kick her out, were you?"

I chuckled. "Would you rather wait on her hand and foot yourself? I have enough work to do."

Electra opened her mouth, then paused, tapping her chin. "Well, maybe for a day?"

"Oh, my god, is this another novel thing?"

She blushed. "No!"

I rested my head in my hands with a groan. "If you show up to work in a maid uniform, I'll ship *you* back to Silverwall."

"Puh-lease." Electra leaned back on her palms. "You need me here. No one else can do any of the wiring work at all."

"Yes, well, I apparently have a personal secretary now, so maybe I'll have more free time to handle that myself." I glared up at her. "Or do you think you can handle that as well?"

"Mistress . . ."

We paused, glancing over at Rel.

"Yes?" I asked.

"Why is . . . that woman your secretary?"

I paused for a moment as Rel shifted awkwardly in front of me. I sighed, getting to my feet and walking over to my minion. "Rel, you'd be wasted on a desk job like that."

"Still, my lady, I could do it."

"Rel." I reached up, placing a hand on her shoulder. "I need you exactly where you are, trouble shooting for the rest of the town." I sighed. "A secretary is useful, but *you're* the one who lets me handle two projects at once. All of this would be impossible otherwise."

She eyed me suspiciously, but for once it was nothing but the truth. While I couldn't assign her any technological work—what little of it there currently was—Rel was the *only* person I could put in charge of a work crew and *know* that she'd oversee them to my every specification, often without me even needing to specify.

And when setting up a power grid, a port, an iron refinery, and literally everything else I needed in about half the time it would normally take, that sort of skill was worth its weight in gold.

She sighed. "I understand."

I gave a laugh. "I don't know what you're so upset over, Rel." I shook my head. "Just because this Princess Ishanti is going to be my 'notary' doesn't mean we'll get along."

Rel tilted her head, but Electra just snorted.

"Oh, you'll get along." She grinned. "Like a house on fire."

I sighed. "You can already tell, can't you?"

"You *bet* I can."

CHAPTER 4

Meat Cute, Meeting Cute, Mote Cute?

The reward for good work was always more work.

"I have the census data compiled, Lady Via."

And that was only more true now that I'd unveiled the 'miracle' of electricity.

"Thanks." I took the sheaf of papers from Ishanti. "Christ, I've had these numbers for days and haven't had a chance to compile them." The woman dipped into a smooth curtsy at my words, accepting the compliment.

We were in my office, a small room in the water mill. The mill itself was the biggest building in town, even after all the machinery had been installed. Really, though, I'd set up here because I was too used to the sound of my inventions lumbering along in the background to get any work done anywhere else.

"I fear that the numbering of households may already be outdated." Ishanti folded her hands in front of her, smoothing out the fabric of her plain dress. "There has been an influx of new families from several nearby villages."

I clicked my tongue. "Long as we have a starting point. Still, I didn't expect so many new people just because I turned the lights on . . ."

I'd actually expected people to start clamoring for indoor lighting and do whatever they could to keep the influx of new people out, but that never materialized. No one even understood the possibilities that electricity offered.

Ishanti nodded her head. "I have done my best to rectify the errors, but my efforts were based completely upon hearsay. As such, there are limits to what I have managed to compile." Did I see a hint of worry on her normally placid face? "The sudden migration stems from the collapse of the Adventurer's Guild in Silverwall."

"So, that explains the lack of people controlling the local monster population and the sudden uptick in bandits." I hummed, fanning the sheaf of papers.

"It is just so."

"Got it." I nodded, flicking through the report. "Good work on getting things up to date." The village of Ineir hadn't taken a population census in ages. At this point, *any* numbers were better than no numbers.

At best guess, the village had just over a hundred households, at least a dozen of which were new. An elegant hand made a note in the margin that prior to the influx, the village had been on the verge of splintering into disconnected homesteads and disappearing entirely.

I glanced at Ishanti. "Your own analysis?"

Her shoulders tightened slightly. "Yes, my lady." She straightened with an effort of will. ". . . Members of the royal family are expected to be well versed in matters of statecraft."

"Despite never being expected to actually use it?"

She winced. "It is . . . just so," she said again.

I hummed, flicking through the next two pages and looking over her notes. "Seems solid to me." I was no sociologist or city planner, so hell if I knew about half of this shit. At least someone in this mess knew what they were doing.

I pretended not to notice how Ishanti's shoulders dipped slightly in relief.

"Anyway," I said, "if that's everything—"

"As a matter of course, my lady, it is nearing the appointed hour of your daily audience."

I paused, before letting out a long sigh as I checked the clock on my wrist panel. Noon on the dot.

"This is why I always fucking work alone . . ." I huffed, pushing myself up from my desk. "Cook's all done?"

Ishanti nodded. "The hall is being set as we speak."

"Alright, alright, you don't need to drag me." I combed my fingers through my hair a few times before rising and exiting my office.

Rel was already waiting at the door. "Mistress."

"Rel." I rolled my eyes. "I told you I'd do the stupid audience already, didn't I?"

"You said as much last week as well." Rel's lips quirked upwards.

"It was one time!" Still, I couldn't keep the smile off my face as we proceeded to the throne room.

Now, I was a 'handle your own shit and let me handle mine' kinda girl. I would have been perfectly fine leaving Ineir to its own system of governance, as long as they didn't get in my way. Unfortunately, both Rel and Ishanti told me that things didn't really work that way. Folks were very big on absolute rule here.

The banquet was my own addition, because if a girl was gonna handle all these people's problems, then at least she was gonna do it over a good meal.

Now, you might wonder how we were getting enough food for everyone, considering that this was a tiny village in the middle of nowhere that was already struggling to feed itself. If you'd been listening closely, you would also have realized that there were a bunch of monsters in the countryside made of delicious, delicious meat, and that I had a shit ton (yes, that is the scientific unit) of demons at my disposal.

What, did you think I started a vegetable garden?

I ran my hand along the slightly more ornate chair at the head of the room. Behind me, the gears and shafts turning the generators hummed in a giant clockwork masterpiece. It was a fitting backdrop for the high table where I and my trusted lieutenants sat. The floors were stone, the walls were bare, and ad-hoc wires and ancillary gears framed my throne like a mechanist's wet dream.

I should know.

I slipped into the throne, tucking up one leg to hide how the stupid chair left my toes brushing the floor. Rel took her place at my right hand, with Ishanti one seat farther down. Meanwhile, I had chairs for Electra and the boys to my left. I had expected Ishanti to raise a fuss about her spot at the table, but she seemed to realize exactly what kind of position she was in.

Or maybe she just wasn't another entitled self-important bitch like I was used to dealing with. I'm sure it was possible to be born rich and still possess a moral compass, I'd just yet to meet anyone who did.

My father's entire family included.

"There's the lady of the hour!"

I glanced over, giving the cook a smile. "Ma'am." She was a large woman, and apparently the adoptive mother of Dee and Dum, and dozens of other children besides.

"None of that." The woman smiled, brushing a strand of gray-blonde hair behind her ear. "I told you to call me Mama—whole city did!"

"Most of the village as well . . ." I ran a hand through my hair. "How were the ranger eels?" My demons hunted the surrounding jungle and sea both for extra food, and thus far 'Mama' had yet to find something she couldn't cook.

"Oh, those." She waved a hand, *floomph*ing into the nearest chair. "Elaine is a wonder with that little filleting knife you made, and Ferrio loves seasoning fish."

"Just soak it in brine!" a cute little black-haired boy called from the kitchen door. He and a few others were carrying out the last two plates of eel and assorted other bits from my larder. At least we had plenty of steelware.

"How are the kids liking their work study?" We didn't have nearly enough teachers to have everyone at school at the same time, and families still needed hands to work the fields. Never mind that someone had to teach the teachers what to teach, as if that wasn't confusing enough just to think about.

It looked like I'd be waiting a while to get that college program up and running.

"It's fine, fine." Mama waved her hand. "I appreciate it, you know, givin' these kids a chance to make something better of themselves."

I bit my lip, looking away. "It's the least I can do."

"Well, I think I'll be the judge of that."

I shrugged, sitting back in my chair while the rest of the tables were set.

I remained seated as the villagers and my own people, looking more and more like one group with every passing day, started to filter in from their daily tasks. "Just over one hundred families, huh?" I ran my fingers against my chin.

Rel glanced over at me. "What was that, Mistress?"

I shook my head. "I have never in my life been responsible for so many people."

"But they still call you 'Empress.'" I could hear the question in Ishanti's voice.

"An empire of steel." I chuckled, stroking General Tock as he skittered over to his customary place at my side. "Robots are easier. You can just put them back together if they break."

The princess didn't seem to know what to say to that.

In any case, the village was still small enough in absolute terms. It didn't take long for the four long tables that made the rest of the hall to fill up with the men, women, and children under my care.

If there was one good thing about the feudal system, it was that no one else in the damn republic seemed to care that I'd sniped a village out from under their noses. Hell, I hadn't even seen the tax-man yet.

Once everyone was seated, I waved my hand to begin. Rel and Ishanti both made to stand, and I held back a wince. Both women—intentionally or not—seemed to be vying for the position of my herald. Today, it was Rel who won the impromptu stare-down. "The audience hall is now open," she declared.

Fucking finally. At least I talked them down from me making a speech every single day. I liked to keep my dramatic flair in my back pocket for special occasions.

I picked up my fork and knife, cutting myself a bit of the smoked eel to my left. At that, everyone else began eating as well, a low murmur of casual conversation filling the room. Now, you'd think that since I held audiences every flipping day, I'd be able to eat in peace at least half of the time.

In reality, the first petitioner was lined up before I had finished chewing my first *bite*.

"Dulhan, boss," Dum called from the floor. An older farmer came before the high table. Dee was happily munching away on my left, but the boys would switch off about halfway through.

"Dulhan." I took a sip of the (boiled) water I had at my side. I'd need it. "What would you ask of me?"

"Your ladyship." Dulhan sketched a messy bow, and for the *n*th time I had to refrain from telling him that I was not a lady.

Christ, but I'd had enough bowing and scraping for a lifetime.

"It's about the big old fence you got put around the village." He tugged on the sleeve of his jerkin. "I know it's to keep those monsters out, but it makes a mess of getting to the fields in the morning, not leastwise if we need to bring the livestock in or out of that gate. I'm here on behalf of . . . a few others—and meself o'course—asking for the gate to be widened there summat to make it easier for us to get to our fields."

I set down my fork, swallowing another morsel of fish. "There are already plans being drafted to push the walls out to enclose the nearest fields, and all of the barns." I pretended not to notice that the room quieted down as I began to speak. At least this way I don't have to bang a gong. "If you and any other farmers want to speed that process up, we always need more lumber, or more hands to finish the clear cutting."

My kingdom for a bulldozer, and this was one place my demons couldn't help, because I had yet to find one that could chop down trees instead of tearing them apart into unusable splinters.

The man tried to hide his wince. "That'll be helpful . . . ladyship."

I hummed, using the moment to cover for another bite of eel. "How bad is it in the mornings?"

He shrugged nervously. "Betimes it can take an extra bell to get to the fields, ladyship."

I sighed. What, a whole extra hour then? "I'll draft a work crew to knock out additional gates in the north and south walls. A bridge over the river will have to wait, but we'll see what we can do in the meantime. Next!"

The man gave another bow, a happier one this time, as Rel quickly pulled out a map of the village.

I gave a light chuckle as I looked over the walls. Ineir sat only a short way from the sea to the west. The river ran along the village's northwest flank, with a rough wooden palisade surrounding the rest. I'd had a lone gate put in the east wall, trying to split the difference between the northern and southern fields.

Well, nuts to that. I quickly marked two sections of the wall for work crews to look over and find the best spots for the extra gates.

As Dulhan walked back to his cheerfully waving table, I took a moment to scarf down some more food.

Dum announced the next petitioner all too soon. A severe-looking woman, Carnenn, stepped forward. I despaired at the queue already forming behind her as more and more people finished their meals.

"Your ladyship." Carnenn folded her arms. "I have a problem with these schools of yours."

Here we go. I set down my fork again. "Your concern is noted. School attendance is mandatory for children three days a week."

"Three days!" the woman threw her hands up. "Do you know how hard it is running a home when your children are up and gone near half the week? It's hard enough to get the crops and animals tended when—"

I cut her off with a slice of my hand. "Schooling is mandatory, and that is final." Hell, I'd have classes more than every other day if there were enough teachers, but that was just one more thing on the pile. "In the meantime, we are doing all we can to balance out the distribution of labor around the village while the next generation learns the skills and the knowledge that will reshape the—"

"And that's another thing!" the woman pointed a finger at me. "Forcing this wrongheaded 'knowledge' down our children's throats! Why I—just the other day my own daughter called me a liar! I'm not sure what you're teaching those kids, but it's not the gods' honest truth." I held back a frown as I saw several other people at the tables nodding along. Oh, goodie, I'd knocked over a protectionist syndicate just in time to butt heads with the PTA.

I took a deep breath. Publicly destroying this woman would defeat the entire point of having these audiences in the first place. Not that I was *against* striking these meetings from my calendar, but Rel would be disappointed with me.

The things I did for people.

"If you have a problem with what the children are learning, you're more than welcome to sit in on their lessons to see for yourself," I said instead. "The freedom to learn is a fundamental right of all people."

And one I wholeheartedly believed in, for once.

The woman glared at me. "Well, maybe I will! In fact—"

"Good." I clapped my hands. "Next!"

She sputtered. "Now listen here, I wasn't . . ."

. . . Able to stop Dum as he bodily removed you from the floor? No, I suppose you weren't.

But the annoyance drained out of me as the next person shouldered past the petitioners to the front of the room. She was a short woman in armor, an axe hanging from her side.

I leaned back idly in my chair. "There's a line for a reason, you know."

The short woman gave a smarmy grin. "What, can't make an exception for an old friend?"

I blinked. "I'm sorry, who are you again?"

She stopped, frowning. "Oi! I'm the one who helped take you down?"

I tilted my head, before glancing out around my throne room with tables full of food and the overturning edifice of gears behind me. "Are you sure about that?"

She glared, crossing her arms. "Not my fault you escaped."

I waved a hand, and a few of my higher-level enforcers rose to their feet, weapons in hand. "Maybe I should make sure *you don't* escape, then?"

"Woah, woah, woah! Let's not be so hasty here!" The woman waved a hand back and forth in front of her. Of course, that didn't hide her other hand as it went to the weapon at her waist. "Come on, I'm practically here to help you! I mean, you can't really think you're gonna get away with kidnapping a princess!"

A low murmur swept through the room at that, more than a few gazes turning towards Ishanti as she shrunk back into her seat.

I mean, not that her identity was a secret we could keep. The royal family was pretty eye-catching, with their silver hair and golden eyes.

"Kidnapped?" I raised an eyebrow. "Do you see any chains? She's as free to leave as anyone else here."

"Oh, that's a—"

"Meanwhile, I do see some metal on you." I leaned forward. "That axe. You were one of the bandits who raided Ineir less than a week ago. You almost burned down half a dozen fields." I smirked as the focus of the room shifted. "Or was that also just something you were doing to . . . *help*?"

"She's done it before, too," Electra chimed in. "Last time she and her party were here, they threatened to ransack the inn and who knows what else."

The blonde adventurer scowled, but she knew when she was beat. "Fine. I was just gonna offer you an easy way to get rid of the girl, but we can do things the hard way."

"Now who's trying to kidnap a princess . . ." I smirked. "Why don't you run along now, tell whomever is holding your leash to back. The fuck. *Off.*" I would have preferred to keep her as a prisoner, but we didn't have the capabilities to imprison someone with a combat class. "Or don't, because making an enemy of me worked out so well for you the last time."

Her scowl deepened, before she turned and exited the room, sending the doors slamming shut behind her. I sent Dee with a few others to make sure she didn't get lost on her way out of the village.

After the conversation in the hall started up again, Electra leaned over. "Did you really recognize her axe?" she whispered.

I blinked. "What? Of course not, idiot."

CHAPTER 5

Hope for the Best

We need to get hustling," Electra said.

"No shit." I rolled my eyes, pacing back and forth in front of my desk.

"Geez, no more fish for Empress." Electra folded her hands behind her head. She was leaning against the wall. "Guess it didn't sit right with your *delicate constitution.*"

"You're a delicate constitution."

She rolled her eyes. I continued pacing.

Rel stood next to my desk, silent, but ever ready to offer her support. I appreciated it, I really did, but unfortunately, she was only one person, and we were dealing with something a lot bigger than that.

Ishanti was here as well, lingering by the door. I thought it only fair, all things considered.

I came to a stop in the middle of the room. "The problem isn't the guild remnants." I planted a fist on my hip. "I don't think whatever riffraff they've picked up will be enough to make a difference either."

"Then why are you losing your dang head, Em'?"

I sighed. "Simple, my dear Elenore." I waved off her annoyed 'hey!' with a wan smile. She still hated when I used her real name. "After we clear out the bandits, do you really think Silverwall is going to just let Ishanti go about her life? Hell, what about the entire rest of the island? We're only a few days north of the *capital city* of Corvandyr. We've been sending caravans there to trade steel for food, coin, and everything else we need to keep this place running!"

I could make tools and I could make plans, but I *could not* make seeds appear out of thin air, or fashion harnesses for plows, or nets, or sailcloth, or anything else that I didn't yet have the industrial base for.

Electra frowned as the situation started to hit home. "Would be, uh, kinda rough if they marched an army on us."

"Rather." I turned towards Ishanti. "Unless you're going to give me some good news like 'we don't have a standing army'?"

She flicked her eyes to the side. "Vecorvia does not maintain a standing army."

"Well, there we go!" Electra grinned. "Problem solved."

"However," the princess continued, "most of the noble families maintain house troops of comparable training and higher levels. The Senate also maintains a strong navy, capable of enforcing control of the surrounding waters. Silverwall is the most pressing concern. As Seneschal Hawkwright is not a noble, he does not have his own troops, but as I said before, the guard is bought and paid for, functioning like his personal army."

"And then, I'm sure there are people who are worth an army by themselves."

Ishanti nodded, clasping her hands in front of her. "It is just so. Every fighting force contains at least a few tier-three individuals at its head, though in Silverwall, only Seneschal Hawkwright has distinction, and his abilities are not suited for direct combat."

"Tier three? Ah nuts." Electra rubbed the back of her head. "We haven't even hit tier two yet."

"Not for lack of trying." I shrugged, looking at my stats.

Between grinding my demon-summoning skills and running this place, my abilities were rising nicely. I'd put most of my stat points into Soul for more mana, but I made sure to keep my dexterity high as well. Sometimes, you just had to get out of the way.

"Are there tier-four individuals?" Electra asked.

Ishanti paused, glancing to the side. "The High Warlock, Supreme Chancellor of the Senate, is currently tier four." Electra and I shared a laugh at that.

I waved off Ishanti's confused look. "Don't mind us, just outworlder things. Anyone else?"

She shrugged. "It is said that the Master of the Watch is at least tier four, but he hasn't stirred from the Watch's stronghold on the northern shores of Vecorvia since well before I came into this world."

"Right, and I'm sure this 'Watch' is some mythical organization that will be trouble for us sooner or later."

"Not . . . as such." Ishanti paused. "While they do at times concern themselves with outworlders who enter our shores, their mandate is to protect the strait from the forces of Old Mulmyn and the other barbaric kingdoms of the continent."

I rolled my eyes at the 'barbaric kingdoms' bit. Next thing we'd be talking about expeditionary forces and how the sun never set on the British Empire. "At least that explains why they had my armor."

"Indeed." She nodded. "Unless we go out of our way to antagonize them, it is likely that the Watch will not involve itself in the affairs of the republic, unless we threaten their sacred duty."

"I'll be sure to keep my demons to the south," I said dryly.

"Well." Electra clapped her hands. "One thing at a time, yeah? Betcha we can deal with the bandits easily enough, and we make plans to deal with these house troops or whatever while we're at it."

I huffed. "We don't have enough *people*, Electra. Not to mention that, my gang aside, most of them are farmers."

"Well, how many guys do ya got?"

I waved a hand. "A few dozen or so." I cast a gaze around my office. "Where did I put those reports . . . I had a list of everyone who came with us from the city."

"Right here, Mistress."

"It is in the third drawer, my lady."

Rel and Ishanti both paused, sharing an inscrutable look. I pinched my nose, even as Electra waggled her eyebrows at me.

"Right. Thank you both." I took a sheaf of papers from Rel. "We had thirty or so come with us, not counting children," I read. "A few had thug or cutthroat classes, and the rest still haven't reclassed."

"Ah, Mistress." Rel raised her hand. "Several have changed their classes since arriving here. Work boss is the most common, but we have a fair few runners and even a technologist."

I blinked. "Excuse me, we have a what?"

"Technologist." Rel spread her arms in a shrug. "One of the boys who helped Electra with the wiring discovered he has a bit of a knack for it. It's only an uncommon class, but it's been helpful."

From the corner of my eye, I saw Ishanti frown. "That would have been useful to know when I was compiling reports."

Rel raised her chin. "You didn't ask."

The silver-haired woman scoffed. "Didn't ask? You—"

I snapped my fingers twice. "Enough. We have bigger problems, namely the people after *your* pretty little head."

"Well, pretty little something, anyway."

"Shut *up*, Elenore." I glared. She laughed, raising her hands in surrender. I rolled the sheaf of papers into a tube, tapping it against my palm. "We'll need more new classes. Combat classes are important." I still remembered how Delia had shattered Electra's magic with her spear. We needed people who had the necessary abilities to tip the scales back in our favor.

"Well, I can probably start training a few people." Electra rubbed her chin. "Not sure if they'll get anything special from me, but I can get 'em into shape."

"I can't spare you from the work crews," I said.

Electra fluttered her hand at the papers. "Didn't Rel just say we had a technologist or something? He can help cover for me."

I paused, rubbing my head. "I'm not sure I trust someone else with my tech."

"Via, he's got, like, a magic system telling him what to do. He'll probably do a better job than me, y'know?"

I bit back an instinctive retort. "I'll have to find time to check his work." I turned to Rel. "And the crews? Can we spare anyone and keep the docks on schedule? By the sound of it, we're going to need at least a few ships, never mind getting the walls up sooner rather than later."

Rel crossed her arms. "There should be a few . . ."

"There are ample men and women in search of work." Ishanti stepped forward. "The last band of refugees contained three new families; the patriarch of one is a tier-two warrior, if nothing else."

I pointed at her. "Get him then. And anyone else who doesn't fit into a work crew." I shook my head. "We need more raw materials, too, then. And we're going to have to start stockpiling some of my weapons . . . spears, maybe. Arrowheads definitely."

"What about the bandits, Em'?"

I glanced over at Electra.

She shrugged. "I mean, I get why you're thinking about the bigger players, but we kinda have to deal with the people hitting our trade caravans and making more refugees."

I rubbed my forehead. "At the rate we're going, we could use a few more refugees."

"That's cold." Electra frowned. "Real cold."

I waved a hand. "We don't have the time to play world police. Still"— I met her eyes—"they'll make good fodder to cut our teeth on."

Electra grinned. "Now that's what I like to hear!"

I huffed. "You always did have a bloodthirsty side."

"You know it!"

"Ishanti." The princess perked up at my words. "Get Rel a list of those people with useful classes; she'll organize people with combat classes and get the ball rolling with them." I turned. "Rel, in addition, you'll be on the lookout for anyone with uncommon or rare classes like yours."

"Yes, Mistress." Rel bowed.

"And me, boss?"

I ignored Electra's smug smile. "We probably have a few farmers' sons and daughters who dreamed of being adventurers." I shrugged. "Beat them into shape. Maybe we'll get something useful out of it."

She laughed, her smile growing. "One hero boot camp, coming right up."

"Try not to make an *actual* hero." I quirked my lip. "I'm contractually obligated to humiliate them."

"Yeah, yeah." Electra waved her hand. "We even have a magic sword for them." She pointed towards the sword mounted on the wall behind my desk.

I glanced at the old blade, one of the first things I'd fished out of the ocean in this world. I'd used the ruby set in its pommel to make General Tock's power core. Maybe it was a bit sentimental, but I didn't want to just melt it down for metal.

Even if I might have to.

I waved my hand. "It's rusted into its sheath."

"So, anyone who can pull it out will be crowned King of England, right?" Electra grinned.

I blinked. "I'm surprised that you, wait . . ." My eyes narrowed at her. She shifted, looking off to the side. "There was an anime about King Arthur, wasn't there?"

"Well, uh, I'm not sure what *that* has to do with anything." Electra rubbed the back of her neck. "Don't we have more important things to worry about?"

"Electra," I said. "You're a fucking weeb."

"H-hey!" She cringed back, arms crossing over her protectively. "That's just rude!"

I sighed, sinking into my seat. "It's alright. We all have our foibles."

Electra huffed, glancing away. "I'll get you one day."

"I'm sure." I nodded once. "Right, you all have your jobs. We don't have time to lose." I glanced out the window, where the sun had only just begun its long trek down to the horizon. "And miles to go before we sleep."

"There was an anime about that, too!" Electra chimed in.

"Was there?" I tilted my head. "After we rule the world, you'll have to tell me about it . . ."

"You got it."

I stayed looking out the window as the three women left my office. As the door clicked shut behind Rel, I let out a breath. I leaned forward, resting my face in my palms. My shoulders trembled slightly.

I was . . . no stranger to struggle. I was used to throwing myself into danger. Hell, I'd thrown *other* people into danger nearly as often.

This was different.

This village, these people, they hadn't *asked* for me to come in here and upend their lives. They hadn't come tugging at my cape for scraps. They hadn't even put themselves in my path for me to crush with reckless abandon.

Instead, I just found myself responsible for them.

I tightened my fingers against my scalp, as if I could crush the pounding headache growing within my skull.

Sometimes, it felt like I'd spent my whole life walking a tightrope. Now, suddenly, I had a hundred more lives resting on my back: a number that was only set to grow.

I stayed like that for a long moment, breath coming in short, almost painful gasps. Then I sucked in a deep lungful of air, lowering my hands.

I nodded sharply. "No way out but through."

I got to work.

CHAPTER 6

Prepare for the Worst

And . . . *heave!*"

The ropes creaked as scores of men pulled in unison.

"And . . . *heave!*"

Slowly, the mass of the ship began to shift, moving forward in its drydock.

"And . . . *heave!*"

For a moment it seemed balanced, and then with a soft groan, it slid out of its cradle, down the channel they'd cut for it and into the water with a massive splash. Whoops and cheers rose into the air as men scrambled out of the way, some swimming as the boat, the first produced by this tiny little village, slid forward in the water.

From the dock (because there was only one at the moment) Rel watched with a small smile. It reminded her of when she was a kid, and the sailors and dockhands would pull galleys into the water. This one only had a single mast; barely a sloop, even.

But even still.

She walked towards the burgeoning port as the men clambered up the dock, grinning and slapping each other on the back. There were enough hands to crew a single sloop, and to train more men to crew the next. The manifest for this vessel was already determined, bringing the goods highest in demand from their trade caravan, and enough coin for the materials for another two ships and more than that besides.

"Well done, dockmaster!" Rel smiled.

"Feh, dockmaster." The grizzled old shipwright who'd come with Lady Via from Silverwall waved his hand. Still, Rel could see the pride shining in his stormy eyes. "It's barely a ship, my lady. The next one will be grander still."

Rel felt her smile grow. "I know." She turned towards the sea again, watching as the work crew hauled the ship abreast of the pier. It still had to be rigged and sails hoisted.

And, of course, a flag christened. That was the most important part.

Rel had even swallowed her pride and asked the *princess* to make sure Lady Via's schedule was clear.

"It's finished ahead of schedule, too."

The man chucked, stroking his bushy white beard. "The lads were eager to see it put to water. For a lot of us, it's the first time we've put out a ship in over a decade."

Rel smiled, nodding. It reminded her so much of home. True, Silverwall had never been as large—or had as *many* ships—as the capital city Corvandyr, but it *had* ships.

And now, they would have ships here as well. Just one, but more coming soon.

"If it pleases you, my lady, I've yet to see that the hold is filled and made ready for the voyage."

"Right, best get that sorted." She nodded. "And tell everyone who helped make the ship to take a day off."

"There's still work to be done."

Rel raised an eyebrow at him. "We're a full two days ahead of schedule; give the men one."

He chuffed one last laugh and doffed his hat. "If the lady wishes." It was only then, on the third time he said it, that the words finally penetrated Rel's brain.

"Oh, no—I'm—" She raised her hand, but the man was already gone, swept off into the bustle of the port, where even on a day off there was more work to be done. Rel's 'I'm not a lady' died on her lips.

She stared for a moment longer before shaking her head. "Still have more work to do." She'd see to that misunderstanding later; for now, she still had to check to see that the outer walls were going up on pace.

There had been some trouble with raiders in the woods, but so far they were only about half a day behind schedule.

Rel knew Lady Via had all sorts of plans for the new space, once they finished expanding and knocked down the inner palisade.

With a sharp nod to herself, Rel turned and marched back into the village proper. And it *was* a proper village now. Before, it had been barely more than a few hutches clustered together for mutual protection. Now, after nearly a month, the first set of new houses were well and finished, and another set was currently being built.

More and more people continued to stream in from the surrounding countryside, and both of the trade caravans to Corvandyr had brought back able-bodied men and women as well, people looking for steady employment, even if it only meant guarding a stretch of wall and hauling lumber every third day.

Rel felt her heart swell with pride. It was—

She paused, hairs on the back of her neck standing up. Rel turned, catching sight of a small face peering out at her from behind a stack of building materials. The child's eyes widened before they ducked back out of sight.

Rel felt a small smile break out over her face. "Hello there." She sank into a crouch, leaning halfway around the side of the pile. It was stacks of lumber and rope, either bound for houses or for the docks. "Do you have something for me?"

Most recently, Lady Via had enlisted several of the children as runners and administrative assistants on their days off from class. Now that they'd started learning their letters, Mistress could entrust them with notes, knowing that they'd be able to read the recipient's name and get it where it needed to go.

Rel herself usually received several such notes every day, and while she wished she could get her orders in person, things were moving too swiftly, and the currents too deep, for Rel to run back to the Lightning Mill after every job.

That's what the locals were calling Lady Via's new headquarters in the village, and Rel found she liked the name. After all, if a sawmill produces cut wood, what else should they call a mill that produced *electricity*?

In any case, after a moment, the girl peeked out again. She was one of the kitchen helpers, Rel realized. The one who was good with a knife.

"I—I do, Lady Rel."

Rel blinked again. "Ah, I'm no lady. The Lady is my Mistress."

The girl looked at her for a long moment before shrugging and holding out the missive.

Lady Rel stared back at her from the parchment.

"It's on the paper." The girl proffered it. "I just take it where it needs to go."

Rel opened her mouth, before closing it, unsure what to say. After a second, she just shook her head, taking the piece of paper with a mumbled 'thank you.' She'd have to talk to Lady Via about this later. It wouldn't do for people to start getting the wrong idea.

Rel flicked open the message, scanning it quickly. She'd been literate before—first from her mother, and later her myriad of apprenticeships—and she recognized the elegant hand as Ishanti's almost immediately.

After a moment, Rel sighed, tucking the parchment into the pocket of her pants.

She didn't like the princess, still.

"It's a good idea." She gave the girl a smile. "Can you tell Ishanti I said as much? I'll take care of things on my end."

The girl tilted her head the other way. "Can I come instead?"

"What?"

The girl nodded. "I'll get Mattew to tell the silver lady."

Rel blinked as she waved another boy over. "Go tell the silver lady that Rel said . . ." She cleared her throat. ". . . 'It's a good idea, I'll take care of things on my end.'"

Rel could only watch as the boy nodded. "Thank you, Lady Rel!" Then he dipped into a brief bow, sandy blond hair flopping, before dashing off.

"But I'm not . . ." Rel stopped; he'd already gone around the corner.

There was no way he would have heard her anyway. The street was full of people. In fact, in the time it took to have this conversation, two men had come and carried away the bundle of building materials the girl had been originally hiding behind.

"Don't you have somewhere to be?" Rel asked.

The girl shook her head. "'M done."

"Then . . ." Rel grasped around for something else to say. For once, her Dream Sequence skill had nothing to help her. "Shouldn't you be back home?"

"Don't wanna." The girl pulled a face. "Mama gave me to an uncle I didn't know 'bout."

Rel opened her mouth again, before pausing.

"Ah."

The girl looked up at her with big red eyes beneath her black fringe. Rel knew that there were lots of orphans who'd come with Lady Via, and that Mama still took care of many of them. There had been a concerted effort to find family for the children where possible.

All well and good, but most of the people who'd fled the city with Lady Via had been poor, criminals, or poor criminals.

Rel had never wanted to go back home, either.

She opened her mouth; to say what, she did not quite know.

Then there was a rush of heat and light to the east of the village. A moment later, the alarm bell started to ring.

"*Shit.*" The curse felt like a razor against her lips, but she held in the cutting word. She'd need it soon enough. "Get to the Lightning Mill," she told the girl, before turning and running towards the wall.

She met up with Electra and a band of combat classers at the gates. The women shared a look, before nodding. There wasn't time for anything more.

So far, no one had come back from the farms.

They set out from the village at a brisk jog.

The cause of the light became apparent almost immediately. Nearly a mile from the village itself, one of the farmsteads had gone up in flames.

"Round up everyone!" Rel called as they ran. "Keep away from the flames! Anyone with water magic, with us!"

They'd gathered a few—water magic was a useful skill on an island—by the time they'd made it to the barn. Electra organized the water brigade, spraying down the grounds around the blaze and working their way inward, trying to quench the flames. Electra took a team of her own and rounded the property, searching.

They found a few survivors, two men and a woman who had been far enough away to run when the barn had gone up, and they were still covered in soot.

"The animals all ran," the man managed after a moment and a cup of water. "Someone—" He coughed, doubling over for a long moment as his lungs spasmed. "Someone opened the doors before they set fire to it."

Rel frowned. "Isn't that a good thing?"

"One of the horses caught fire." The woman choked back a sob. "It's what caught the fields. I tried to catch her, but . . ."

Rel looked over towards the fields, where even now most of the crops were still burning. Electra's team had managed to put out the buildings, but all they could do was hope to contain the grass fire.

There was a rush of air, and Rel looked up just in time to see Lady Via land her demon bird. The woman jumped off, striding forward. Her black cloak and hair whipped around her, and it took the woman only a moment to pinpoint Rel.

As always, Relia knelt before her Mistress. "My lady."

"Up and attem, Rel." Lady Via crossed her arms. "We don't have time to waste." She looked over the scene. "Any sign of who did this?"

Rel paused for a moment, then shook her head. "No. We don't . . . know if someone did this on purpose."

Via drummed her fingers against her bicep. "Did any of you set your own farm on fire?"

The three survivors shook their heads vehemently.

"Yeah, didn't think so." Via glared at the flames. With a wave of her hand, she summoned a massive demon made almost entirely of water. "Devour the flames, and nothing more."

The demon burbled happily at her command, launching itself into an arc like a waterfall in reverse, before crashing down onto the burning field.

A moment later, all that remained was steam.

"Coordinate with Electra; she has the most experience with crime scenes," Lady Via said. "It's too much to hope anyone will still be here, but maybe we can figure out how they set it all up."

"Yes, my lady." Rel ducked her head. "You're sure then, that it was intentional."

Via snorted. "Of course it was. It's what I would do, in their situation." She glanced over at Rel, before finally cracking a smile. "Cute kid. About time you picked up an assistant."

Rel blinked in surprise. Her head whipped around to see the red-eyed girl from earlier just a few steps behind her.

By the time she turned back, Lady Via had already returned to her mount. "I'll trust you to handle things here. I need to head back and make sure no one tried to sneak in while we were distracted!"

Rel opened her mouth, before nodding. "Yes, Mistress!"

Via snorted. "Didn't I tell you to stop calling me that in public?" Then she was in the air, and Relia was left with three sooty farmers, a burnt-out farm, and a little girl. She decided to do the reasonable thing and deal with these problems in order of least to most difficult.

Rel turned towards the girl.

"So," the child said, kicking a foot against the ashy ground. "Can I come?"

Rel turned towards the farm.

CHAPTER 7

The Best Defense

Anything?"

Electra shook her head as she came through the door. We were in my office; I'd rushed back after the fire, but luckily no one made a play for Ishanti. Either it just hadn't occurred to them, or they were still testing our defenses.

Really, I should just be glad they didn't have the *cajónes* to go for the gold.

"Nothing." Electra spread her arms. "They weren't subtle; there were plenty of boot prints near the barn, and I saw a place where they might have moved a bale of hay so it went up better."

"But?" I prompted.

"But the moment they went back into the jungle, they started covering their tracks." She snorted. "So yeah, it was arson, but that's not a lot of good without a police database and sh—and stuff."

I nodded, steepling my fingers. Electra gave me a few moments of silence, and Rel and Ishanti came into the room.

"How were they?" I asked.

Rel stepped forward. "No one died, fortunately, but several livestock were lost, as well as the farmstead.

I waved a hand. "They'll have the next available house within the walls. Hopefully we'll be able to find work for them."

"That should not be a problem, my lady." Ishanti dipped into a brief curtsey as I looked over at her. "At present, we are still running short of hands to do the work required. That is only likely to increase if you intend to push forward with your plans for the shipyard."

I rolled my eyes. "We've invested too much to turn back now. I can only prop up my entire economy on salvage for so long before I actually need to get on with things."

"On that note, it should please you to know that the foundry was unaffected." Ishanti pulled out a thin missive from her sleeve, looking it over. "Indeed, the scouting demons you sent out have reported, inasmuch as they are capable of reporting anything, that there is a bounty of scrap metal well beyond our local waters. With a few more ships on hand to more readily harvest that bounty, we could keep our steel works in production for quite some time."

"Why's that, anyway?" Electra scratched the back of her head. "Like, don't get me wrong, we have other problems to deal with, but why is the ocean just carpeted with weapons and armor for us to use?"

Ishanti gave an airy laugh. "The Empire of Mulmyn has waged more wars upon Vecorvia than any historian cares to count."

"Would be the first time they gave up on *counting*," I muttered.

Ishanti continued unimpeded. "Of course, even after it fractured, Mulmyn has had a great deal more men of much higher level than Vecorvia. Should they make landfall, it would spell the doom of the republic."

I let out an 'ah' of realization. "The solution: drown them at sea."

"It is so." Ishanti nodded. "The Vecorvian navy is the jewel of the seas, though there is much less call for it these days. Old Mulmyn has greater concerns than the colony that never was."

"Didn't know the whole island was the tutorial zone." Electra rubbed her chin.

I clapped my hands. "Focus, Sherlock. You're our detective."

Electra jumped, before shaking her head once. "Right, right. So yeah, we know who did it." She shrugged. "From what we've picked up, all of the remnants of the Adventurer's Guild in Silverwall have more or less formed a bandit guild in the surrounding jungle. There's a point, at the isthmus or something, where they don't mess with anything because the capital city will come down on them like a ton of bricks, but we're north of that."

I turned my gaze towards Ishanti. "A remarkably laissez faire approach to governance."

Ishanti bowed her head. "The Senate knows that as long as the cities remain under control, any such group is doomed to sputter out and die."

"There's plenty of food out here." Electra waved her hand. "We're doing okay."

"*We* are also cheating off of a thousand-plus years of technological development." I rolled my eyes. "Even still, elaborate."

"There is food aplenty," Ishanti said, "but as you've no doubt discovered, other resources are scarce. Of wood, there is no shortage, but workable stone? Metals? Other such resources as a band of cutthroats or revolutionaries may require?" She shook her head. "Those are in vanishingly short supply. Silverwall itself owes its prominence not only to the fact that it sits on the only known silver vein on the island, but also that it has claimed control of the lava mines, where most of the iron is mined from."

"And those lava mines are no doubt fortified," I mused.

"Better guarded than the city." Rel tugged on her hat. "Da—my father works the mines. They have nearly half the guard on rotation there each day, to make up for the lack of walls."

I hummed. "So all the material goods come from the cities, or else the ports."

Ishanti nodded. "Just so. Corvandyr has maintained a stranglehold on maritime trade since the fracturing of Mulmyn. No other coastal power has had the resources or the experience to challenge her dominance of the sea, and that dominance has made the Senate very rich, and very powerful."

I laughed. "And when you're rich and powerful, why waste your time swatting gadflies? The idiots."

"Via?" Electra tilted her head.

"They're making the classic blunder, El." I shot her a grin. "Ignoring the plucky underdog."

A look of dawning realization crossed her face. "It never works out well for them, does it?"

I snorted. "Why do you think I always took you so seriously?"

"Awww, you *do* care."

"Don't get sappy on me." I leaned forward on my desk, pulling over a map of the island. "That still means we have to deal with this mess ourselves. And I doubt Silverwall is going to help, least of all because they're paying this bandit guild to get you back, princess."

Ishanti dipped into another curtsy. She'd slipped back into her court etiquette as she found her balance here, but it wasn't like I was gonna punish her for being *too* deferential or anything. "Indeed. Though, that is the very same reason that Silverwall will not move against us directly."

"Even though we're only a day's march away?" Electra asked.

"Two." Ishanti came over, drawing her finger down the map, along the road from Silverwall to our little village. "Men on the march move slower, and they would need to bring more than a few guards, knowing that you've already given them a black eye."

I drummed my fingers against the map, glancing back up towards the lava mines. "And they *can't* bring that many, can they?" I glanced over at Electra. "How many guards do you remember seeing in Silverwall?"

She blinked, shrugging. "Not many; they mainly stayed near the gates and other hard points." She blinked. "Heck, now that you mention it, I don't think I saw a single patrol the whole time we were there."

I nodded. Leave it to a hero to understand the importance of manpower. Well, after I rubbed her face in it. "They don't have that many men." I glanced over towards Ishanti. "Surprising since they have to guard those mines *and* keep the royals from running away."

The princess inclined her head silently.

"Alright." I clapped my hands again. "So, we know our enemy, and we know who's propping them up. Next we need a plan."

I curled my fingers into a fist. "First and foremost, they attacked my people. That is not acceptable. There will be recompense."

"Whoa, there." Electra gave a nervous smile. "Your supervillain is showing."

I grinned in reply. "We all need a bit more supervillain in our lives."

She huffed. "Speak for yourself."

I waved her off. "What's the status of your irregulars?" Irregulars, of course, was the term for people with supernatural abilities who assisted the heroes but weren't full time themselves. In this day and age, Aegis and the other hero organizations had almost never needed to call up and train irregulars.

Of course, if we had all the resources of Aegis Corp, we wouldn't be having this conversation.

"They're still green." Electra shrugged. "We're seeing some okay skill growth, and they've all managed to swap over to combat classes, but right now I'm worried they'll fall apart if we force them into a scrap."

"Noted." I turned to Rel. "Our infrastructure?"

"My lady." Rel bowed, hand folded across her chest. "The first sloop was put to sea today. It will be ready for its maiden voyage tomorrow."

"Excellent, we'll need the money." I turned.

"Lady Via."

I paused at Rel's voice. "Yes?"

"There is also the matter of christening the flag," she said.

I shared a confused glance with Electra. "The flag?"

Rel nodded, a nostalgic smile flicking across her face. "It's a tradition for the ruler of the port to hoist the flag showing the ship's port of call. Of course, it's something that most monarchs ignore for normal construction, but for flag ships or the first ship laid down at a new port . . ."

Ah, so christening was different here, but our magic translator didn't change the word to 'flag of port raising ceremony' or some kludge. Good to know.

"We're really busy this week." I waved a hand. "We need to hit this problem hard before we can worry about stuff like that."

"If I may, my lady." Ishanti stepped forward. "The ceremony itself is only a short affair, requiring you to stop by the docks. It could be slipped into your itinerary later this week.

I narrowed my eyes at the both of them. Rel and Ishanti got along like cats and dogs, and yet here they were saying I should go glad-hand people and kiss babies?

I looked back towards Rel. "And you agree with Ishanti on this one?"

Rel quirked her lip, before nodding. "I do, Mistress."

I sighed, massaging my forehead. "Right, sure, pencil it in." I pretended to ignore the triumphant look the two of them shared. Whatever. I'd leave them to their little plans. If they thought it was a good idea, then I'm sure there was a reason for that.

"Beyond that, what does our infrastructure look like?"

"Ah, of course." Rel took a moment to gather herself. "The construction of the outer wall will be delayed."

"We'll have to increase the number of guards, too." Electra raised her hand. What a goody two-shoes. "It'll take a bit to put a rotation together."

I turned towards the window. My office—which by now had been shuffled around more than a few times as we made space—was set on the second floor of the Lightning Mill.

As an aside, can I just say, in the privacy of my own thoughts, that I wish *I'd* come up with that name? Oh well, even a villain as fabulous and intelligent as me couldn't be right a *hundred* percent of the time.

"So, we're stable right now, but a stiff breeze away from collapse." That was more due to the nature of our expansion than any sort of bandits. The population had more than tripled in the past few weeks, and my days were full of scheduling work crews and setting up power lines just to get everything in place. "Growing pains are never easy, huh?"

"Indeed." I heard more than saw Ishanti's nod. "Though with the sloops, we might countenance closing some of the farms and importing more food from the southern side of the isle."

"That will slow us down in more ways than one." I leaned against the windowsill, looking out over the village I was responsible for.

But when I closed my eyes, I could see the shape of the *city* I had only begun to build.

"No," I said.

"Uh . . ." Electra shifted on her feet. "No?"

"We're fragile right now, but so are our opponents." I turned back to face my three most trusted lieutenants. "Our fighting force is green, but theirs is poorly supplied and still demoralized from their beating at

Silverwall." I waved a hand. "If we take a defensive stance, not only do we slow down our own growth, but we give them more time to organize, to consolidate, to prop themselves up with money and supplies from this Seneschal Hawkwright of yours." I smirked.

"So, what do we do?"

I leaned forward.

"We *attack.*"

CHAPTER 8

Shell Game

With supervillainy came a certain amount of subterfuge.

Oh, sure, everyone talked about the lying, the grand schemes, the moments of 'you've fallen for my trap!,' but cloak-and-dagger games were usually far less . . . romantic.

And when you were my size, more often than not they involved being smuggled somewhere in a container that was far too small for me to fit into comfortably.

Case in point, I jolted as I felt the bale of hay I'd been rolled up inside of being set down. I couldn't really open my eyes; not only was hay pokey and dusty, but my face was also pressed against my knees. I didn't really know how farmers made bales of hay without equipment—hell, I didn't know how they make them *with* modern-day farm equipment—but suffice it to say, I'd been carried through more dangerous places in even more obvious containers.

I waited until there was a large bang that told me the barn door was closed.

Once the cows started to munch on the hay, I pulled the string I'd been holding on to this whole time. It released the knot, and I burst (silently) out of my erstwhile tomb and sucked in a big breath of air.

"Ugh." I stared back at the cows. They gave me unimpressed looks. Well, that was only to be expected, considering we'd done this trick a couple of times in the last few days. "Remind me to come up with something more glamorous next time."

"Empress! There you are." I glanced up at the sound of Electra's voice. She was up in the loft, peeking through a narrow crack in the barn's roof that had been covered from the inside with a piece of thin cloth.

Thin enough to see through from this side.

I stood up, brushing myself off, and moved to the ladder. I nodded at the handful of other people we had smuggled in. I reached out, grasping Rel's hand and giving it a squeeze. She smiled back. She'd been here the longest, hiding in a dusty old barn.

We had picked this one because it was roomy enough to hold a small army, not because it was comfortable. It'd only been about three days, and already the hastily dug latrine in the corner almost stank worse than the cows.

There were multiple reasons I waited until today to smuggle myself out.

"Anything?" I asked as I pulled myself up into the loft next to Electra. She shifted to the side, and I pushed my eye up against the cloth, looking out at the woods. Right now I couldn't make out anything. It was already nearing dusk.

"I caught a flicker of something moving out there when the guards came through." Electra jerked her head back towards town, where our guards would be heading now that they'd 'fed' the cows with the hay bale I'd been hiding inside of. There wasn't another soul left on this farm.

Well, except for the small army I'd smuggled into the barn, of course.

"Looks like they've noticed the bait," I said.

Electra huffed. "Gotta say, I like you a lot more now that I'm on *this* side of your schemes, Em'."

"You would." I rolled my eyes. "At least you're not afraid of getting dirty."

"Heck no!" Electra gave a quiet laugh. "If anything, I'm relieved that the PR team isn't riding me to try to be more ladylike when I take down a villain." Her smile grew a bit wider. "So, do you think it'll be tonight?"

"I honestly thought it would be earlier." I shrugged. "But yes, it will be tonight. That's why I'm here."

"Good." She rubbed her hands together. "Oh, this is gonna be so cool."

I couldn't hold back my answering smile. "Just keep watch."

"I will."

She was right, though. If it all went to plan, it would be *epic*.

Over the past few days, we'd been smuggling men from Electra's new combat training out to the barn, along with a few heavy hitters like Electra herself, Rel, and now *me*. Of course, there were a lot of farms, so really, turning one into a booby trap was a crap shoot at best.

But that's the thing about subterfuge: it's always the little details that go into selling it.

The farm was a small one, to the south side. It was one of the farthest from the river. To the north, one of the larger farms was now playing host to all the other animals that we'd been slowly moving there over the week.

Slow enough for any enterprising bandit to notice what we were doing, but fast enough to look like we were still in a hurry. As of today, this was the last farm we hadn't moved yet.

And, as the *piéce de résistance*, 'Via' would be 'sneaking' herself and her demons into that heavily defended farm to the north, as I'd done every night since we had picked it as the anchor for our northern defenses.

This would just be the first night it wasn't actually me. Rel had her cute little assistant Elaine put on a pair of stilts, and I'd given the raptor demon carrying her *very* specific instructions.

That was how you did subterfuge. Set an obvious trap, then dangle the hint of opportunity in your other hand. There wasn't a mark in the world who wouldn't feel clever when they attacked your exposed weakness.

Only to realize that they'd walked right into the *real* trap.

I admitted, there was an element of chance to these things. There always was, when you needed someone other than Electra to play the fool. That being said, I was confident in this plan. If the bandits attacked, it would be here, not the northern farm, and certainly not the town.

The reason being that they'd already as much as told me their plans.

After the first encounter at the edge of the village, they'd sent a representative to bargain. When I'd turned them down, the bandit guild didn't do anything. Instead, they'd let me grow my support base far more than they should have, before attacking an isolated farm and vanishing before I could show up.

Then, instead of pushing their advantage, they'd gone back to hiding in the jungle.

Those weren't the moves of someone who had an army of trained Adventurers at their beck and call.

It marked the leader as someone timid, or else someone who didn't have a large support base. Either way, they wouldn't have the resources to hit either of the hard targets. With the window of opportunity slowly closing, they'd almost certainly go for a quick win, trying to snatch a victory from right under my nose

I'd been wrong before, when I'd played these games, but this time I wouldn't be. I could feel it.

All that remained was the waiting.

With one last nod to Electra, I climbed back down the ladder as the light slowly faded. We had a single hooded lantern, kept well away from our peephole, and the rest of the cracks in the barn's walls had been painstakingly plugged with mud and black cloth.

I moved over to the lantern and began my part in this whole affair: summoning demons.

A real shocker, I know.

For this, I'd decided to go back to my old standby, the humble hobblefiend.

They were small, obeyed simple orders, and attacked with reckless abandon. Plus, they could see in the dark.

All in all, they were the perfect little monster to throw into the meat grinder for our counter ambush, and then my troops would form a second wave, pouncing on disoriented foes. I called them troops because that's what they were; Electra's training was apparently more regimented than people usually went through, leading to a large number of soldier class unlocks.

On one hand, more rare classes were always a plus. On the other, though, I could work some magic of my own with standardized classes.

I was a tech villain. Give me a warehouse and a long enough assembly line, and I could rule the world.

"My lady."

I smiled at Rel as she came to my side. "Rel. Good work keeping everything under control here."

She dipped into a short bow. "It was nothing, Mistress." She shared a quiet grin with the fifteen soldiers we'd smuggled out here. "We're all eager for some action."

"Well, with any luck, we'll get it tonight." I summoned another wave of demons, the last I could support without giving up all of my mana regeneration. I smiled at the men and women who were my vanguard, my soldiers. "And then you can show both me and the world everything you've learned."

The grins I saw were answer enough.

Well and good that they should be so eager. Electra was no slouch of a drill sergeant; no one from Aegis pushed themselves harder than my old rival, and she'd demanded everything and more from those who wanted to fight.

As for myself, I hadn't been idle either.

Full plate was still beyond me, but each man and woman had a solid spear with a good steel tip and a short sword of the same. For armor, we'd managed to get padded gambesons and bucklers, smuggled in as barrel lids with the water. They were hardly a legion of doom, but with a pinch of luck—and a *lot* of demons—I thought we should be able to get through the night without anyone dying.

"So"—I turned to Rel—"how's your little buddy liking her new job?"

Rel flushed lightly. "She wants to be fighting . . ."

I chuckled. A diplomatic way of saying 'she hates it like only a child can.' "Just like another little guttersnipe I found." I patted her on the shoulder. "I know I've asked this before, but why didn't you run away? I gave you so many chances to."

Rel twitched away from my hand, eyes fluttering. "Well, my lady, that's . . ."

It was a shared exhale, more than a laugh, that ran through the crowd of soldiers, and Rel flushed even deeper. I smirked. Ah, I'd been so busy, I'd forgotten how much fun it was to tease my favorite minion.

"In truth . . ." She shrugged. "It didn't seem so much worse than any other apprenticeship I'd tried." She gave a shy smile. "And it has turned out so much the better."

"True words, that," a woman murmured. "We ain't have nothing to do out here but tells stories. To 'ear Lady Rel tell it, ya damn near took over all of Silverwall."

I smiled, seeing a familiar glimmer of interest in the crowd. Everyone wanted to know about the villain that pulled it off.

"Well, I wouldn't say the *whole* city." I waved a hand. "And I hardly conquered it. Just . . . turned it upside down for a day."

"Woulda been a sight to see," the woman replied.

"Indeed it was." I smiled. There's nothing like a successful scheme. "And it all would have been impossible without Relia." I reached out, tracing my fingers down the side of her face again. This time she didn't pull away. "I asked a great deal of her, but she performed beyond my expectation. And in return?" I shrugged. "We broke the corrupt Adventurer's Guild and slipped out of the city with a wealth of resources both magical and not." My smile turned sharp. "This time, let's see if we can't finish the job."

Another murmur ran through the group. It was no secret that the remnants of Silverwall's Adventurer's Guild had turned to banditry. They were brave enough to attack small villages without a combat classer to their name, but so far they hadn't been able to pose a real threat to *my* village.

With this trap, I hoped to make sure they never would.

I nodded, letting go of my evil smirk™. "Still, I bet you'll all be glad to go back to your own beds once this is done."

"In the house you built me?" A man said as he rubbed the back of his head. "Course we are."

"You're not the only one who's looking forward to sleeping in Lady Via's beds . . ." one murmured.

Rel jerked next to me, and I smiled wide. "Oh my . . . do you—"

There was a sharp rap of knuckles on wood behind me.

I turned to see Electra leaning down from the loft, eyes sharp.

"Empress. They're coming."

I sucked in a breath. "Well then," I said. "Let's give them a *proper welcome.*"

CHAPTER 9

Good Offense

The wall of the barn exploded outward in a hail of stone and burning timber.

I'd installed a circuit with a deliberate fault, insulating it from the ground, and then Electra did the rest. I covered my eyes with one hand as the last burst of lightning arced out, lighting up the night for a brief instant. It showed me the fear and terror in my enemies' eyes.

I knew I could leave it up to her.

Then the darkness came. Before, the half-moon above would have been more than enough to see by. Now the attackers were half blind, but my demons shared no such limitation.

"Go!"

With a chittering screech, the hobblefiends darted forward in a wave. A man screamed. I saw a flash of light as a woman tried to use a skill before she was smothered, swarmed under by a pack of demons with sharp fangs and wicked claws.

I heard her body hit the ground with a wet *splat*. A mace came down on the demons swarming over her. But there were always more.

"It's a trap!"

I grinned. "Light us up!" I loved it when a plan came together.

In the loft, still supported by pillars *detached* from the wall, Electra shouted, "Buzzer bolt!" A lance of lightning hit a pile of hay soaked in pitch. It lit, and a circle of fire raced around the farm. It lit up our foes, half of them still with weapons in their sheaths. I'd prepared my battlefield well.

My soldiers knew the plan. With a battle cry, I raced forward. I fired an inky black *Demon-itize*, catching a surprised mercenary. He exploded and a new demon bounded into the fray. Meanwhile, the kill notifications continued to roll in as my hobblefiends pulled the bandits down by sheer weight of numbers.

Then the first group of soldiers hit them like a shit ton of bricks.

They broke.

A screaming man was the first. I caught sight of his back as he barreled through the flames, but I lost sight of him. But once someone turned tail, the rest were only a few seconds behind. In moments, the entire raid disintegrated. I caught sight of a woman throwing her spear towards the flames, a patch of ice flash-freezing the pitch and hay beneath.

Most just braved the flames, rolling frantically on the ground on the other side before sprinting into the woods.

I walked forward from the ruins of the barn. "Check for survivors."

"Got one here, my lady!"

I turned and saw two men, spears in hand, pinning a pale woman to the ground. She glared at me from beneath her fringe.

"Excellent. Take her weapons and get her back to the town. Make sure she's under guard constantly."

"Yes, my lady!" The man thumped his fist into his chest before he and his cohort hauled the woman up and stripped the bow from unresisting fingers. I surveyed the rest of the battlefield as two more mercenaries-turned-bandits were recovered and given the same treatment.

Electra jumped down, landing next to me with a *thump*. "Not a bad haul."

I nudged her. "Still not a fan of the bodies, huh?"

She winced, looking away from the . . . remains of a man who'd met just one too many hobblefiends. "It's . . . a bit much."

I shrugged, dismissing the remaining demons with a wave of my hand. "I don't start fights, 'Lectra."

"I know, I know." She ran a hand through her hair. "You end them. Still frickin' sucks."

I placed my hands on my hips, letting the heat from the fire soak into the black folds of my cloak. It was already starting to sputter; really, it had been more for the shock value than anything else. "I know, but put on your game face for the kids. This was their first scrap, and they did well."

"For you, maybe."

I patted her on the shoulder. "I'm not the one who trained them."

She shot a quick look in my direction before going around to congratulate the rest of the soldiers. I spent a few more minutes glad-handing as well—I may not have been a corporate hero, but I knew how to play a crowd—before I heard the sound of hoofbeats.

Two men rode into the farm from the town just as the ring of fire sputtered out.

"Lady Empress!"

I waved them down. Heh, Lady Empress. Now *that* was a bit egotistical, if I did say so myself.

"We saw the signal fire." The first man dropped from his horse's saddle, dipping into a rough bow. "Seems like you handled it well."

I nodded, smirking. "And without a drop of blood spilled on our side."

A cheer went up from the crowd, and the man in front of me cracked a smile. He was older, from one of the nearby villages, with orange hair going auburn and gray. "That's good to hear, my lady."

"Ready to go then, Wulgar?"

He gave a sharp grin. "Caught a bit of sleep before coming out. I'll be ready to go all night, if you need, my lady."

I cocked an eyebrow at him. "I'm sure your wife will be happy to hear it."

He smiled wider, joining the answering laughter. I waved my hand, and a gryphon formed from the ether at my side.

It was a newer demon, bigger than a horse, and with a darkly striped coat instead of the normal lion pelt you usually saw in mythology. Still had the head of an eagle and a *wicked* beak, though. Better for night flying than my raptor demons, and better in a fight as well.

It was also too tall for me to mount unassisted.

I pointed at the ground next to the demon. "Since I have your *tireless* aid, Wulgar . . ."

He gave another good-natured chuckle, before half-crouching and making a step with his hands. I swung myself up onto the gryphon's back, and it ruffled its wings.

"Eager to hunt, huh?" I stroked its feathered ruff as the beast squawked in agreement. With a 'hyup,' Wulgar vaulted up into the saddle of his own gryphon. The demons were powerful and versatile, but they weren't strong enough to carry more than a single person, and even with a single rider they were slow.

How fortunate that none of those factors mattered tonight. I grinned. "Now, let's go see just where our enemies are hiding."

A loud whoop went up from the rest of my men, along with a smattering of 'good luck's and 'hunt 'em down's. I kicked my heels into the gryphon's sides—more for show, but I'd always wanted to do that—and we rushed off into the sky.

I took a few moments to let my gryphon gain height, circling the farm. Then, once we were high enough that the air started to nip at my fingers, I banked towards the jungle. I waved Wulgar to take the lead, falling in right behind him as he began directing my demon away from the lights of my little town.

It still caught me by surprise sometimes, when I realized that the Republic of Vecorvia was a *tropical* island. The jungles were thick and lush green, and they'd had to clear-cut roads from city to city. It was part of what made our port so valuable.

Of course, at this time of night, the only thing I could make out was a blanket of pure blackness, the lights of my town sparkling dimly behind us. Luckily, I wasn't alone.

"What do you see?" I had to shout to be heard over the wind, but Wulgar was already leaning forward, eyes glimmering green as he used his *Hunter's Sight skill.*

After a moment, he pointed. "There." He banked his gryphon, my own only a second behind, and took us deeper over the canopy. "Seems like they grouped back up, lots of movement."

"How can you see them through the foliage?"

"Breaks." His eyes narrowed. "And I can see the evidence of their passing. Trees are smaller here, but they still shake."

I chuckled. "Good old-fashioned experience, then."

He nodded. "Looks like they're headed towards the river. Bank left."

I angled that direction. "How will I know when I'm over it?"

"You'll see the moon reflected on the surface."

Sure enough, I did, a pale half-circle rippling like a penlight down below. I started to circle, tailing Wulgar as he tracked the routed bandits slowly picking their way along the river. In the dark, even if they looked up they could never have spotted us without skills over their own. It would have been child's play to swoop down on them and finish the job. If my memory served correctly, only five or six got away from the ambush.

Of course, that wasn't my goal tonight.

It was slow going. Certainly made sense—we were waiting for a group of demoralized mercenaries to lug their asses through the jungle at night—but even still, the moon was starting to set by the time they reached their campsite.

"Found them." I could barely hear Wulgar's voice over the wind as he urged his mount to glide lower.

I followed in his wake, peering down into the darkness. If I squinted hard, I could *just* make out what might have been a clearing in the trees from where the moonlight cut shapes out of shades of gray. And here I'd thought *I* had excellent night vision.

But hey, what's the point of being the boss if you can't have your minions do the hard part for you?

"What do we have?"

Wulgar paused for a moment, taking in what I couldn't even begin to make out. "Only a few tents. I see a single firepit. Tracks, maybe, going deeper into the trees."

"And tracks don't make the trees rustle, do they?"

He shook his head, wind pulling at his hair.

"They must be spread out some." I bit my thumb. "It makes sense. Would be hard to keep everyone in the same place; not enough hunting, or water."

"Not that; it's the monsters." He looked back at me, our gryphons gliding almost abreast, dead serious expression on his face. "They come out of the deep jungle at night."

I raised an eyebrow. Sure, I remember that night a big monster chased Rel and I back to Silverwall, but, "Wouldn't it make more sense to keep everyone together, then?"

Wulgar shook his head. "Big monsters in the deep," he said. "Make too much noise, and they think maybe it's a meal worth their time."

I blinked. "So, the ones that come near cities?"

"Too small to run with the deep jungle packs."

I hummed. Maybe I'd been a bit . . . luckier with my jungle expeditions than I thought.

I glanced back towards the river. "What are the odds they make it through the night unscathed?"

"Oh, there's already something sniffing their trail." Wulgar pointed farther into the darkness. "But it doesn't look that big. If they've lasted this long, they'll be able to ride out one more monster."

"Well then. We've got what we came for—let's head back." With a mental nudge, I banked around. From this height, I could make out a glimmer of electric lighting on the horizon. "Let's make sure we have a nice surprise waiting for them in the morning. You'll be able to make your way back there?"

He grinned, teeth flashing white in the moonlight. "Just follow the river. Easiest trick in the book."

I grinned in reply. "Excellent." Then I leaned over the neck of my Gryphon and let the lights mark my way home.

CHAPTER 10

Lady's Port

We found them."

"Whoop, whoop!" Electra punched a fist into the air. "Not gonna lie, Em', it's nice to be on this side of your schemes for a change."

"I aim to please." I gave my trademark signature smirk, pretending not to notice how my erstwhile nemesis still shivered at the sight of it. What could I say, I was just the best. "Now all that's left is to root them out like the rats they are."

Did you get all of them?" Ralph glanced towards the hunter who'd accompanied me, still standing next to my gryphon. "Not that I doubt Wulgar's skill, but if there was such a large group of them in the nearby jungle, surely we would have heard of them already."

Wulgar shook his head. "Not all, just one batch. Seems like they're spread out 'cross several camps."

"Even still, any loss of manpower at this point will be devastating." I waved a hand. "And I've never been one to wait."

Electra hummed. "Normally I'd agree, but, like, if they're just a bunch of separate cells, taking out one will just make the rest harder to find, wouldn't it?"

I opened my mouth, then I paused. "Hmm." I folded my arms. "I guess them being so disorganized actually does work against us this time."

I paused for a moment, taking stock. My thoughts were a bit sluggish, which is why I missed the obvious consequences of stomping on the lone group of mercenaries. It was early morning, and Wulgar and I had just flown back in from our reconnaissance mission. My eyes felt heavy, but it was necessary to set a few things into motion before I caught a quick nap and then, presumably, set more things into motion.

The five of us—Electra, Rel, Ishanti, Wulgar, and I—were standing on the third-floor balcony of the Lightning Mill as the light rose slowly over the eastern part of the island. Below, the streetlights had just been extinguished and the farmers and morning shift workers were beginning to rise. There was always so much to be done, a never-ending stream of people bringing my dream into reality.

I was nothing if not prideful, but even still, it was a humbling sight.

"Separate cells?" Electra shrugged. "Back on Earth, I was usually taking out tiny groups of villains 'n' stuff."

"And I *was* the tiny group of villains and ''n' stuff.'" I smirked.

"High five!" Electra held out her hand. I rolled my eyes, but I slapped my palm against hers all the same.

Ishanti blinked at our byplay, though it really caught my attention when Rel tried to hide a frown. I had a sudden jolt of realization, thinking back to when I'd pretended to replace her with Electra in my little gang back in Silverwall. I should probably do something to make sure she didn't think I was doing something so stupid for real this time or—

"Then, would you both not be versed in the methods of such small groups, operating under the auspices of a larger power?" Ishanti's voice drew me back to the conversation at hand. "As well as the methods of best effect against such a disorganized foe?"

This time it was my turn to blink. Electra and I shared a glance, and I felt my thoughts kicking back into gear through the fog of sleep.

No, I'd been in situations like this before. It just took me a minute because usually I was the one hiding out in the middle of enemy territory.

"You know, now that you mention it, I did have that one job in the Amazon." Electra tapped her chin. "Buzzkill was running some cuckoo slash and burn or something."

I hummed. "Well, I've never been camped out in a jungle, but I certainly know a thing or two about small-unit tactics." I bit my lip. "Though, usually, I benefit from instant communication." Last I checked, we were the only ones who had cell phones in this world. I hadn't yet had the opportunity to set up a bigger operation for them; I didn't have an enchanter, and Maarin was still back in Silverwall.

"Would that make them all easier to track down?"

I looked over at Electra. "Not quite. Rogue cells already operate independently, but they have some amount of communication. Without that, it's even harder to predict how any individual group will react to outside pressure." I frowned. "Normally news of a huge defeat like the one we just dealt to them would be all throughout a network within a day."

Electra smacked a fist into her palm. "But instead, we won't even know when they all know that we know . . . about . . . them."

"Yes, Electra, how eloquently put." I shook my head as a wave of light laughter swept the balcony. "Still, you know more about anti-terrorism operations than I do. You're in charge of that; get me a workable plan for you and your men ASAP." I turned to the hunter. "As for you, your help was invaluable. We're going to need more hunters and trackers; we're going to take the fight to the bandits hiding in the jungle."

The man nodded. "Always a few lads interested in learning a thing or two from the old man." He scratched his beard. "I'll see if anyone has the aptitude to take a new job." I nodded before dismissing him.

"Well, if that's everything . . ." I stretched my hands up over my head. "I need to catch up on my sleep." I moved towards the door, only for Rel to remain standing in my way. I cocked an eyebrow.

"Actually, my lady, there is one more thing," my right-hand woman said. "Today is the christening of the first ship, after all."

I came up short, before huffing. "Shit, is that really today?"

Electra nodded. "Now that you mention it, I think you said somethin' about 'they'll probably attack before then anyway,' but, yanno . . ."

I stared at her for a moment, before she blushed, shrugging.

"I forgot my scheduled events a few too many times, so I started working harder at it."

I sighed. "I guess that makes sense." I rubbed my brow for a moment. I'd been up about a full day at this point, but it wasn't the first time I'd burned the candle at both ends. "Rel, dear, can you get me a stiff cup of . . . tea?"

Curse my arrogance for not discovering a coffee demon yet.

"I'll have Mama make something strong."

I patted her on the hip. "Oh, honey, you don't know the meaning of the word."

I stepped past her, smirking at Rel's blush. She really was too cute at times.

Behind me, I heard Electra say. "Your lady there izza 'I like my coffee black, like my soul' type of person." I could hear the smirk in her voice. "She likes most things sharp and to the point, yanno? Just some friendly advice."

I heard Rel choking on nothing as I stepped back into the Lightning Mill. As always, I didn't have the time to follow up on things like that. There was always too much to do.

Ishanti was waiting demurely inside, hands folded in front of her. On my desk was a folded flag. "That'll be for the new ship?" I nodded towards it.

Ishanti nodded. "It is so. Tradition dictates that the ruler of the settlement carries the flag to the port for the first christening. It is oft a fiercely contested role."

I ran a finger over the fabric, brow crinkling in thought. "Back when Silverwall had a port, did your family christen the new ships?"

Her eyebrows rose slightly before she nodded. After a moment, she added. "When the port was destroyed, Seneschal Hawkwright deemed the expense of rebuilding it too great, as Vecorvia has had uncontested dominance of the surrounding waters for nigh on half a century."

"And thus stripped another bit of power away from the royal family . . ."

Ishanti bowed her head, but said nothing. In any case I was beginning to see how the royalty here seemed to have lost almost all control of the country. And while this obviously wasn't the French Revolution, well . . . they clearly hadn't signed a Magna Carta.

Not with ink at least. There was still the unanswered question of *why* the Senate and other administrators of the republic kept such a large number of royals . . . around.

"Walk with me to the port," I said.

Ishanti's head snapped back up at that.

I met her confused gaze evenly. "Everyone here already knows that you're important, even if they haven't quite put two and two together. I won't have you hiding away, since you and Rel put this whole show on in the first place."

Her lips curled into a faint smile. "It would be an honor."

I nodded, gathering the flag up into my arms. "You'll be at my left, and Rel at my right." I cocked an eyebrow. "Unless there are any problems or unstated implications of such things?"

"The right hand is the higher position." Ishanti dipped into a curtsey. "As it seems in your own world. Ah, traditionally, the head of the guard would also be present."

"You hear that, 'Lectra?" I called over my shoulder. "Wanna come along?"

She groaned as she and Rel rejoined us in my office. "Do I have to?"

I gestured to her. "Off you go. You and the soldiers can get some sleep instead. We'll have another parade tomorrow."

"Deal."

We shook on it.

"Well, let's get this over with." I left the office, Rel and Ishanti trailing in my wake. At the first floor, I saw Rel give a quick signal to her own little helper. As the tiny slip of a girl rushed off to take care of some task, I leaned over to Rel. "If you're going to keep her, make sure she has everything she needs."

Rel blushed again. "Yes, my lady."

I smiled. It was nice to see my little duckling come into her own. I took one last breath.

Showtime.

I walked out of the Lightning Mill to see a small crowd already gathering. A cheer went up as I raised my hand and waved. Ishanti and Rel had briefed me on what I was supposed to do, and I quickly started walking towards the port.

On the way, we gathered more and more people behind us, almost like a parade, and when I finally came out around the corner and caught sight of the ocean, it felt like nearly half the town was behind me.

The other half was already waiting at the dock.

A bigger cheer went up as the sound of music filled the air. A mish-mash of people sat on a raised platform, playing an array of simple strings and pipes. I blinked in surprise, smiling wider. "You didn't tell me we had *music.*"

"Only because we had so long to prepare." Rel flicked a concerned glance towards me. "A few of them have even taken music classes."

"Good." I nodded. I began walking again, stepping in time with the beat. "Specialization is necessary in any complex society." I gave a little laugh. "Besides, I might have been evil back on my world, but I'd never stoop so low as to ban *music*!"

There was a set of steps leading up the deck of the sloop, a pair of beaming sailors next to its mast. With a salute, one hand pressed in a fist over my chest, I handed them the flag.

"Captain, what is the name of this fine vessel?"

The crowd cheered at my words, almost swallowing up his reply.

"*The Little Mistress of Lady's Port.*"

I blinked, head snapping over to Rel and Ishanti. They shared a sly smile.

"It was decided upon by the people, Lady Via," Ishanti said.

Rel nodded. "Most of the newcomers don't even know the old name of the village. Everything belongs to the Lady now."

I huffed, but I couldn't cover up the surge of warmth that rushed through my chest. "Well, I've always been a woman of the people." I managed to hold back the laughing sob threatening to escape my throat. I turned back to the captain and his first mate. "It's a fine name, and I shall christen the vessel with pride."

They smiled even wider, which I hadn't thought possible.

I walked towards the prow of the ship, overlooking the roaring crowd. When I raised my hand, they only cheered louder. I had to wait for nearly a minute for them to quiet down. I lowered my hand, look-ing over the port with something akin to shock.

I'd seen the numbers on scraps of paper and piles of reports, but . . . I hadn't quite believed it until I saw this port, with its three docks, packed from shore all the way up to the closest houses. There were over a thou-sand people who now called *Lady's Port* home. Nearly two.

I'd never been responsible for so many people in my life.

And I'd certainly never been cheered by so many.

Still, I was nothing if not dramatic. With a flourish, a flicked my cloak out behind me. "You built this ship!" I declared.

My voice rang out over the docks and over the houses, over the waves and crowd both pressing tight against the shore.

"You cut the lumber and wove the sails. You built the roads and cut the thread." I looked over them, a sea of faces. "You built houses and cooked meals for us; you carried messages and organized the work. You came from miles around and lent your hands to this, our first undertaking as a town."

I smiled; I couldn't help myself. "It is said, back in my homeland, that it takes a village to raise a child. It seems it takes even more to christen a ship." I raised my hand again, a fist rising up in the air. "And so it is with the *utmost* pride that I name this vessel the *Little Mistress of Lady's Port.*" I let my lips curl into a smile as the crowd cheered again, pumping their fists in the air.

And to myself, I whispered, "Long may she reign."

CHAPTER 11

Shadowed Wings

Seneschal Hawkwright of Silverwall stood in the sealed gardens.

The gardens stood high in the north tower, behind two barred doors and rows of trusted guards. He had opened them this day, with the head lepidopterist and their newest charge.

The Seneschal said nothing as the other man gently took the cage he was holding and undid the latch in front of a stand of nightdust lilies.

Within, the golden moth shifted slightly.

It was small, wings still wet from emerging from its cocoon. But the smell of the flowers enticed it from the cage, and soon enough it fluttered up to the flowers, perching with its golden wings. In time, those wings would dry, and the dust sprinkled would contain all the positive benefits of the nightdust lilies, without the poison that could take a man's life, regardless of level.

Well, without *almost* all the poison.

The newest moth was one of eleven in the sealed garden, and it was Hawkwright's duty to see them well maintained. The Seneschal turned towards the lepidopterist. "How go the rest of the eclipse?"

The man bowed. "The other moths are performing well, your grace. As I have long maintained, Silverwall is an optimal climate for them. The cool winters are beneficial for their longevity, as opposed to the sweltering arboretums of the south."

Seneschal Hawkwright nodded, dismissing the man. Alone in the secret garden, he watched the eleven moths flutter from stand to stand before returning to their perches. Over time, they would flap their wings, and a small sprinkling of dust would fall onto the carefully positioned trays. It was a bare handful, but the Republic of Vecorvia had learned well that you could shear a sheep many times, and skin it only once.

It was, in fact, the same principle that they applied to the royal family and its *carefully* pruned branches.

Of course, for a tree so lovingly tended, the loss of a single blossom could spell the end of Hawkwright's control of Silverwall.

He stood in silence for long minutes before his other agent arrived.

"You're late," he said.

"Tell the guards to let me in next time," the woman replied.

As Seneschal Hawkwright turned to the new arrival, he could not help but think of them as a study in contrasts. He was old, his hair gone, and his beard cropped tight against his cheeks. For all that, he stood unbowed, his eyes sharp as the hawk that was his namesake.

Mornia was young, pretty, perhaps, for a year or two more with her strawberry blond hair and blue eyes. But the Breath of Gold was already taking its toll on her body. Her eyes were clouded, and they kept darting to the moths, but Hawkwright and his guards still deterred her. The two men at her back were not there for her protection, and everyone in the room knew it. For now, that was enough to stay her hand.

Hawkwright liked to meet with his assets here, to see when they would no longer be controlled.

The Ash of Creation, the dust of the royal moth's wings, was a powerful tool. It allowed the Hawkwright control of the northern provinces of Vecorvia. The Senate cared little for the backwater that was the northern part of the island. They left it to Hawkwright and his line, as long as he supplied them with small 'gifts' of a substance the royal family had declared forbidden.

What use was silver, after all, when you could have gold?

"How goes the retrieval of the princess?"

Mornia winced. "They botched it, boss."

Hawkwright raised an eyebrow. "They? I told you to take those fools in hand."

"You also told me not to get caught!" Her voice came in a sharp hiss. "So I broke them up into cells, and good thing I did too! That 'Lady' down there has turned the little nowhere village into a right fortress. She smacked around one of my best groups a week ago. If they'd all been in one place, I've no doubt she'd have found the damn camp by now, too!"

Hawkwright hummed, stroking his chin with a single gloved hand.

"You know, I could handle this myself, if you . . ." Mornia's eyes glanced significantly towards the moths. "Me and one other, tops. I swear it."

He fixed her with a sharp glare, pinning the girl in place with his gaze. "Your ability has not shown promising results thus far." He slashed a hand through the air as she went to reply. "Besides that, I have other reports. How much Ash would you need to take that fortress of hers? Three vials, *four*? We have other concerns, you halfwit!"

She looked down, working her lip mulishly. "You said you wanted her back."

"And I do." He shook his head. "But *without* the Watch realizing what we're up to. Damn blithering fools in their northern fortress. Or worse, if the Senate gets involved, you can say goodbye to tasting the Ash ever again."

The Senate liked *control.* Thus far, he had maintained control by keeping beneath their notice while they played more important games in the capital city. The moment they turned their eyes north, he was done for.

"That must be avoided at all costs."

"Fine. Then what do you want me to do about it?" Mornia spread her arms. "I'm down to half a vial—" Hawkwright shot her a thunderous glare, and she immediately backpedaled. "I've been careful. I've been careful! But it took some doing to get all damn adventurers singing my tune, alright?"

He let out an explosive breath, folding his hands behind his back. That was the conundrum, wasn't it. Not for the first time, he wished that he'd been more proactive with the criminal element of Silverwall, but it had all been beneath his notice.

Even the silly little gang war the old Adventurer's Guild had kicked off wouldn't have phased him, if Duchess Ivey hadn't used that opportunity to slip Princess Ishanti out of the city.

If the princess hadn't had the wits to ingratiate herself to the outworlder *witch*.

"Perhaps I should just send the guard and be done with it," he muttered, even though that idea was a nonstarter. If he brought armed men south, towards Corvandyr, the Senate would want to know why. No, he had to solve this through other means. He shook his head. "Clearly, the time for delicate work is long past. Rally your little band of malcontents and storm the walls."

"Uh, they won't much like that, Seneschal, sir." Mornia wrung her hands. "Most adventurers aren't really the heroic type to begin with. Asking them to attack a fortified position? I'd lose half my force the night before, and the other half the next morning."

"What do I pay you people for?" He shook his head.

She shrugged. "Tier-two combat classers don't grow on trees."

Hawkwright knew she was right. Deniable assets were not easy to acquire, and Mornia had proven valuable in the past. Even if it was clear that she was quickly *outliving* that value.

"Figure something out, then." He waved his hand. "I've heard that even rats will bite, when backed into a corner."

"That's the problem." Mornia shrugged. "Hard to feel backed-in when you're attacking a hard target. If I had their number in trained guardsmen, maybe a couple of ballistae to crack that palisade, I could do it. With a demoralized band of would-be bandits? You'd have better luck writing a letter."

"I sent you because you can crack walls yourself, Mornia." Hawkwright let a hint of venom creep into his tone.

It didn't affect the younger woman. "Sure, once, maybe twice, then I'm outta juice." She shrugged. "If you've been keeping up with my reports, you know that the Lady has those farmers singing her praises. It'll take more than two holes in the wall to force a breach. You gotta take the fight out of people like that first." She pulled a face. "S'what I was trying to do, till she pulled one over on me."

"Then I suggest you look into getting even." Hawkwright glowered, and here he'd been a fool hoping for good news. "I stand by what I said: the time for soft power is long past."

"Give me a real *hammer* then, Seneschal."

He grunted, stroking his chin again. It's true, throwing men with no discipline at a wall would only lose resources. Still, Seneschal Hawkwright knew a thing or two about squeezing blood from a stone.

He did it every day with the duchess.

"I will turn out the rest of the adventurers from the city, as well as the fledgling 'Exploration Guild' that's tried to take its place. That should get you a few more men to replace your losses."

"And as for lighting a fire under them?" Mornia asked.

"I suppose the guard should proactively see to this year's monster migration." Hawkwright picked at his nails. "The miners are always asking for more protection, and the Watch is always so irate when we drive the monsters north towards the coast. I think this year, a southern push will be in order." He smiled. "I shall inform the Senate to have men posted on that little wall they have over the isthmus. I'm sure they'll make sure no vagrants slip away into the more *civilized* parts of the country."

Mornia whistled, an answering smile slipping over her own features. "*That'll* get 'em moving for sure."

"If the only way to be behind a set of strong walls is to storm them yourself, well . . ." Hawkwright waved a hand. "I trust you will be able to bring the riffraff around to our way of thinking."

"The monsters'll prove helpful, too." Mornia was grinning now. "There's a river, see, and if we can drive the monsters cross it to that little Lady's Port of theirs . . ."

"An excellent idea." Hawkwright nodded once. "See it done, but try not to lose too many of your men in the process." His eyes narrowed. "And remember, I need the princess alive."

"And the rest?"

"They are no concern of ours." Hawkwright shrugged.

"Oh? Don't you need some of them farmers to grow your crops?" Mornia asked.

"With another royal, we shall have twice the amount of Ash of Creation." Hawkwright looked back towards the sealed garden. "There are always plenty of eager buyers to the south, more than enough to cover the cost of grain." He turned his gaze back to Mornia. "Do well, and perhaps some of that Ash may find its way to your own pockets, for more . . . recreational use."

"Well don't you know how to talk to a girl!" Mornia reached out to clap him on the shoulder, before clearly thinking better of it. She cleared her throat, taking a step back. "I'll have those farmers cleared out and the princess back where she belongs by the end of the season."

"See that you do." Hawkwright turned back towards the garden in a clear dismissal. A moment later, there was a shuffle as one of the guardsmen escorted Mornia from the inner sanctum. Only the captain remained.

"Is there anything else you need, Seneschal?" the woman asked.

Hawkwright heard a small note of discomfort in her voice, perhaps misplaced concern for the farmers who had thrown their lot in with the Lady of this newly minted Lady's Port.

"It is times like these that I question the wisdom of investing solely in city guard, as opposed to a standing army." Hawkwright shook his head. "Truly, the navy guards our borders, but what about threats from within?"

"Sir!" From the corner of his eye, he saw the woman snap off a sharp salute. "You know that the guard could rout a rebel camp no matter how well fortified."

"Yes, but what if they're hardly rebels?" He shook his head. "By all accounts, the damn woman even paid her *taxes*." Hawkwright waved his hand. "Ah, but forgive the musings of an old man; I did have something important to add."

"Yes, your grace."

Hawkwright nodded. "See to it that Agent Mornia is not allowed back into the palace without my express permission, and ensure that every guardsman knows such by the end of the day." He paused, taking in the sight of the garden for one last moment.

"I fear after this assignment, she will have outlived her use."

CHAPTER 12

Level Up!

The last thing to deal with was my class up.

Over the course of setting up the newly renamed Lady's Port (and setting its first ship *The Little Mistress* out to sea), I'd finally maxed out all five of my skills. Ever since then, I'd felt a sort of pressure on the back of my neck, like I could finally push beyond the level 10 barrier I'd been sitting at for so long.

No one from my crew in Silverwall really knew much about the class-up process. The Northern part of Vecorvia was kind of a backwater, I'd realized. Everyone who had a bit of potential either went south or one of the two big groups snapped them up.

Silverwall itself certainly wasn't going to help me with the process, and all I knew about the Watch was that they stole my armor.

How lucky that I'd stolen a princess who'd been taught about such things as a matter of her education.

"It is as you say." Ishanti and I were seated in my office, I behind the desk and she in front of it. "Raising your level and all attendant skills to level 10 is what allows you to class up and unlock a new class. It is said that in the south, training to such an end is more readily available, but here, most are farmers or miners."

"Not exactly conducive to level grinding, I take it."

"Just so." Ishanti nodded. "It is normally recommended to not class up immediately, but instead, upon reaching level cap, attempt to accomplish a great deed, so as to meet the requirements for a better second class. But of course, there is also the chance that one will simply perish in the attempt."

"So most people take boring classes?"

Ishanti gave a demure shrug. "Rather, one accepts the best class that they have unlocked before reaching level 10. There is near always something interesting there."

I hummed. That seemed to track with my anecdotal evidence. Delia had possessed a mage hunter class or something, and she didn't seem like the type to risk her neck for power and glory before unlocking her next class.

If she'd been more driven, she'd be here, and I'd be a headless corpse rotting beneath the gallows.

"So what can I expect once I do class up?" I asked.

"The process is said to comprise two parts." Just another bit of proof that Ishanti had been kept from getting stronger. Why else would they teach her about this but not let her actually reach level 10? "First, you will be asked if you wish to reset your first class. This will not disallow you from taking another, and it is oft useful for those who rose to level 10 very slowly with a common class and wish for another chance at an uncommon class."

"Prestiging, huh?"

I rolled my eyes. "Electra, you promised you'd behave yourself."

Electra shrugged where she was leaning against the wall. She hadn't quite maxed her stats, but she wasn't far off. "Just saying."

"No one else here knows what 'prestiging' is." I waved a hand. "Anyway, I don't suppose you can see the other potential options beforehand?"

"You cannot," Ishanti said.

"Not going to bother with that then." I steepled my fingers. "My demons are far too useful, and now that I don't need to use up all of my mana regeneration clearing trees, I can actually put more projects into action. Getting rid of my biggest force multiplier would be a waste."

"Just so." Ishanti folded her fingers in her lap. "Most who unlock an uncommon class arrive at the same decision."

I tilted my head, looking at her for a moment. I realized that I'd never bothered looking at her class. I focused.

<Lady-in-Waiting lvl 10>

I blinked. "Are you also near your class up?"

She looked slowly to the side. "I have not been allowed to gain a fifth skill, my lady."

I sighed. Of course it was something like that. "Take whatever skill you like. You'll be more able to defend yourself if you're not stuck at level 10."

Electra chuckled. "What, not doing the classic villain thing where you're worried about your minions getting stronger than you?"

"I only have one minion," I said. "And she's perfect."

Electra coughed to cover a laugh. "If you keep raising those flags, people are gonna start expecting you to do something about it."

I sniffed, looking away. "Anyway, you're allowed to do whatever you want with your class, since most of your aid has been organization. I don't imagine Lady-in-Waiting has done much for your job as my secretary."

She gave a little dip of her head. "Nothing I am unable to replicate with my own ability."

"Good." I nodded. "The sooner you class up the better, then. We need more specialists around here, if we're gonna hold our own in the long term." Right now, a small handful of fighters was enough, but if any of the bigger powers in the area turned their attention to us in earnest? I'd want all the help I can get. "So, the first part of classing up doesn't really apply to the two of us, but what about the second part?"

"It is much like unlocking your first class, only instead of it occurring one at a time, all the classes you qualify for are listed at once. You must simply pick one."

"No descriptions?" I raised an eyebrow.

Ishanti shook her head. "Just the same unlock information as all other classes."

"What an annoying system," I huffed.

"Like whoever came up with this setting didn't want to bother." Electra laughed. "That's cool, though. The Isekai that're just numbers all the time are *way* more boring in my opinion."

I sighed. "That's nice."

"No, for real!" Electra waved her hands. "It's like they try to serve up a working man's dopamine rush from *ding* monkey brain progress, but completely forget about the characters and the story."

"Then why do you read them, Electra?"

She blushed. "Just because I know something's bad doesn't mean I don't enjoy it."

"And there we go." I pinched the bridge of my nose. "Is there anything else about the class-up process, Ishanti?"

"Not to my knowledge, my lady."

"Welp." I stood, brushing off my legs. "Nothing to do but pick out my new class, then. It's not like we really have time to wait."

"Sure you don't want to go hunt down a big-huge-o-saur or something?" Electra giggled at her own joke.

"Tell you what, you wrap it up for me, and I'll take a swing at it." With that, I took a deep breath, and pressed *back* against that feeling of pressure.

System Message

Would you like to class up?
<Y/N>

I picked yes, and immediately another, much longer box popped up on my screen.

System Message

You have qualified for the following classes!
For leading men into battle, you have unlocked the Captain class.
For establishing your own settlement in the Republic of Vecorvia, you have unlocked the Noble class.

There were a bunch of other common ones like that. I skimmed past most of them, since the rest weren't even as interesting as those two. Normally, I'd take a closer look, but after talking with so many people in this new world, it was pretty clear that rare classes were the way to go.

So I started looking for puns.

For establishing a port city in your name, you have unlocked the Port Lady class.

I snorted at that. So I'd be Lady Via, the Port Lady of Lady's Port? Not bad, system. Still, while it would be no doubt very useful for running Lady's Port, it probably wouldn't give much help beyond that.

Well, unless all the active skills had to do with boats, there would definitely be something there. But it wasn't quite what I was looking for.

For defeating a tenth of your foes in a single engagement, you have earned the Decimator class.

I raised an eyebrow at that. Was this about the ambush at the farm? Still, that gave me a number for the total amount of bandits. Seventy or eighty was more than I was happy with, but nothing we couldn't handle.

Well, it might also be forty or fifty, depending on how the system defined 'defeated.' Either way, nice Latin pun. Love those.

My only concern was that it would have some weird percentage limitations, but even then, if I started each battle by taking out a tenth of my enemy's force?

Armies in these kinds of engagements would route at about that many casualties. I'm sure leadership classes like Captain or General changed the math, but still, from the description, it was probably a very powerful ability.

Last, I found:

For commanding powerful servants to victory despite your diminutive size, you have earned the Little Mistress class.

I wasn't sure this was a pun, but really, with a class named after my de facto flagship, and with the allusions to 'commanding' and stuff, well, it was definitely a rare class.

The only question was if it would be some weird BDSM thing, just like Decimator would be some weird count-to-ten nonsense.

Beyond that, from the description, Little Mistress clearly had something to do with commanding people and offered much less by way of actual attack options. Hopefully I'd get skills like 'do this but better' instead of 'bondage etiquette,' though. For a moment, I was tempted to take a more normal class, just so I knew what I was getting into.

Unfortunately, I didn't have anything cool like Mage Slayer. It was all stuff like City Planner and Hunter and things that wouldn't be very useful to me.

So I was left with one of two mystery boxes.

"If I don't like my class, can I just select another one?"

"After picking a new class, if you discard it, you must unlock any new classes again as normal," Ishanti said.

I clicked my tongue. "No wonder no one swaps if they can help it."

One and done then. The only question was what did I need more: Direct Power, or Command and Control?

When put like that, the answer was pretty clear. The most useful part of my current class was the ability to summon demons. If I could buff them, my actual combat power would compound on itself anyway. On top of that, it was versatility that had gotten me this far. I didn't need to smite hosts arrayed against me, I needed to get this city off the ground before any great host showed up to take it from me.

I selected Little Mistress.

System Message

Congratulations! You have reached level 11 with Demogogue!
You have unlocked a new class: Little Mistress lvl 1!
You have unlocked a new skill: Safe Words!

I smacked my palm against my face. "God dammit."

CHAPTER 13

The Lady and the Lacky

System Message

Safe Words
Your words cannot be overheard unless you want them to be. If this effect
is penetrated, you will be immediately aware of it. In addition, your orders
will be conveyed immutably through 2 intermediaries.

I raised my eyebrow at the description of the skill. Usually, I had to use the skill a few times, work things out on my own, before the description would update.

"Maybe it's something to do with my second class." I'd have to ask Ishanti about that, but as always, the direct effect of the skill was less useful than what I could accomplish with it.

Sending secure messages, for instance, meant I could finally do something I'd been putting off for a while. Rel was off handling work distribution for the first true set of walls now that we had some breathing room, and I wanted to talk to her but didn't expect her back for another hour at least.

So, I was surprised to step out of my office just in time to see her crest the top flight of stairs.

I shook my head, letting out a laugh. "I thought you were still busy. Any problems?"

Rel smiled, coming to bow before me. "None. I simply felt that you'd need me soon, Mistress."

I raised an eyebrow at that. "I guess I am actually your *Mistress* now, aren't I?"

If anything, her smile grew even wider. "You always were, my lady."

I laughed, gesturing for her to follow me. "What happened to that shy little girl I almost killed on my first day in Silverwall?" Relia fell in step at my side, the fabric of her sleeve brushing past my shoulder.

"She found you, Mistress."

I laughed again, but Rel's smile stayed constant. She looked happy to be at my side. Really, my adorable little minion had bloomed since we'd arrived at Lady's Port. Rel had taken to her new duties like a fish to water, often taking care of issues for me before I even became aware of them.

She was invaluable.

I decided that we weren't in such a rush that I couldn't tell her as much.

I turned, stepping closer so that I looked directly up at my minion. Rel blinked down at me, breath catching in her throat. It seemed that I could still get a reaction from her.

"I'd be lost without your help," I told her. "I don't say that enough." Rel sucked in a breath, long eyelashes fluttering. God, but when did she get so *tall*. When we'd first met, she'd been barely a few inches taller than me. Since then, she'd stopped slouching and sprouted like a beanpole.

I hadn't realized that I had to look so far *up* to meet her soft brown gaze.

Her hand came up, catching mine between us. "And I, you."

I swallowed. "What happened," I said again, "to that shy girl who couldn't even meet my eyes?"

"You did."

That startled a laugh from me. "I suppose I should take credit for my work." I stepped closer still, pulling the tall woman into a tight hug, before moving back. I cleared my throat. I had stuff to do, after all. I just wanted to let a girl know I appreciated her.

I started down the stairs. "Anyway—"

Rel caught my wrist. "I mean it nonetheless, my lady. You have changed me in ways I did not think possible."

I swallowed. "Duly noted." I nodded once, then again. I was torn. I wanted to . . . explore that statement, maybe selfishly. I wasn't known for having a *good* impact on people. On the other hand, we were still on a tight schedule. In the end, that won out. "I need you to get a messenger back to Silverwall, preferably one who can get in and out again without raising any questions."

Rel let herself be pulled along down the stairs. "What are you looking for? I have a few that shouldn't be known to the guard."

"Good." I released a breath, but not Rel's hand. Instead, my fingers wrapped around hers as we made it to the first floor. "Good. It's important, so I need it to go to someone you trust."

"The message?" Rel asked.

I squeezed her hand. "I'll tell both you and the messenger at the same time. A new skill will keep people from overhearing, but it doesn't work unless I tell people directly." In time, I'd be able to pass on commands, through multiple intermediaries, but even now, the value of secure communications could not be overstated.

She nodded. At the bottom of the Lightning Mill, she slowly, almost regretfully, slipped her hand from mine. Outside, the town was bustling. I waved at the group of men laying flagstones for the main road up to the mill itself.

Rel whistled, two sharp notes. I took a breath, putting the earlier encounter out of my mind. I wasn't some romance novel protagonist; even I could see such blatant interest. I suppose it was only what I deserved for feeding her crush on me.

But she just looked so cute!

I brushed a hand through my hair. "How goes it?" I waved at the work crew. "It's Stenvin, isn't it?"

Stenvin laughed. He waved on the rest of his men to keep working. They were pounding the ground flat and laying gravel for the eventual flagstones themselves. "Didn't think you'd remember just another nobody like me, Lady."

I allowed a self-deprecating smile to cross my face. "I do my best."

Though the daily audiences at lunch had acquainted me with some of the people working under my command, it was clear that the town was growing faster than even my incredible intellect could manage.

That gave me an idea.

I glanced over to see one of the runners, a young girl with straight black hair, finally jog out of the crowd up to Rel.

<Mini-Me lvl 5>

I caught sight of her hat, a copy of Rel's that was still a size and a half too big for her head, and laughed. Still, it was good to see that Rel was building her own support network. It was time for me to work on mine.

"How has it been, hopping between crews?" I asked Stenvin. That was the other reason I remembered him. He was one of the few stone-masons we had, and even with him taking a few apprentices, we still needed him for nearly everything.

"Ah, well, 'tis a bit different from the work I'm used to." He patted his hands against the fabric of his pants. "But I get ta see the . . . bigger picture, yeah?"

I nodded. "You like seeing how it all fits together?"

He chuckled. "I s'pose I do, at that. Why I got into cutting stone in the first place."

And really, with this level of technology, he and his apprentices were a lot better at cutting rocks than I'd expected. Apparently, there were ways you could use water to make stone split more easily? To say nothing of the skills that came with his class.

"That's good." I clapped him on the shoulder, a feat only possible because I was standing on the front steps of the Lightning Mill. "In that case, I think I have a job you'll like."

"Oh? If it's working with stone, Lady, I'm your man."

I nodded. "I think it's pretty clear that you are more or less running the stone production in my town."

"You tell me where it goes, I'll put it down." He laughed, rubbing the back of his neck. "S'always been like that. Though, most nobles are a bit less forgivin' if things take longer."

"That's the point." I gestured out toward the road they were laying down. "I need someone like you who has a better idea of what it takes to get stone quarried and put in place. Especially now that we're starting on the walls."

"Ah, well, a lot of the other crews have been coming to me asking for help, it's true."

We had about five, going on six, work crews that were working on stone: quarrying, transporting, all of it. I was planning on growing the crews, now that the first ship had finally been put out to sea, but there was a limit to how many hours I had in a day.

"I want you running the whole project."

"The whole . . . wall?"

"Everything to do with stone, from the walls to the roads, I want you to organize it. I'll get you some help to manage the crews, but it's become clear just from the main road that you know more about what it takes to get things built out of rocks than I do." I gave him an encouraging smile. "Don't worry, I'm not asking you to take over planning the whole town, just to take a more active role in projects you'd practically be running anyway."

He blinked in surprise. "I . . . ah, don't know what to say, Lady."

My smile turned sharp. "Well, since people keep telling me I rule this little town, I imagine you could say, 'Yes, my lady, thank you.'" I clapped him on the shoulder and he laughed.

"Yes, Lady, thank you," he said.

"Good man. After tomorrow's audience, we'll get you settled. For now, think about who you want replacing you on the work crews."

He nodded, and I let him get back to his job.

"What was that about, my lady?" Rel asked when I came back to her side. I caught sight of the Mini-Me making her way across the square with a nondescript-looking man.

I grinned at Rel. "You may have shoved this town on me, but if it's going to survive, it will need more than just me." I pointed to the man just now coming across the road to the Lightning Mill. "He's part of it."

"What do you need, my lady?" the man asked. At his side, Rel's Mini-Me bounced in place, looking at my minion with an expectant expression.

"Good job." Rel patted her on the head and the girl beamed.

Was that a knife I saw strapped to her back? Kids these days.

But then, I'd never been the type to micromanage my subordinates. Instead, I turned back to the man and activated my Safe Words skill. "I have a message for Maarin the enchanter, in Silverwall."

He nodded. "I can get in. Hope your man is still there, though. Last I heard the Enchanter's Guild got eviscerated."

"Good thing he's not in the guild then." I crossed my arms, feeling Safe Words prickling at the back of my neck. "Tell him there's a place for him here, if he wants to create more wonders."

I smiled. "A place for him to make his own mark on the world."

CHAPTER 14

Here There Be Monsters

With Lady's Port well in hand and my enchanter on the way, next I needed to procure raw materials.

The original communication mirrors that had proved so vital in taking out the Adventurer's Guild had been . . . sidelined in lieu of setting up my powerbase. The original pair had eventually worn out and broken, as fitting for a rush job.

This time, since I had the time, I'd be building a much more comprehensive infrastructure.

I smiled at the thought, looking over at Rel. We stood at the end of the main road, at the edge of the streetlights. Light, hours before dawn, available to everyone.

Once, I'd promised to show a young woman the internet.

It might have been the best choice I'd ever made.

Rel noticed my gaze. "I am at your disposal, Mistress."

"Flattery will get you nowhere." I tossed my head. "Now, do we have everyone ready?"

"Yes, Mistress." Rel stepped to the side, gesturing to a few men and women who'd volunteered for this mission. They all had the soldier class, and Electra had taken to calling them our 'regulars.' The name fit. There were plenty of people in this world who had a taste for violence.

How fitting then, that we had need of them.

"This is first squad," Rel said. "Sergeant Tervis is in charge of them."

"Sarge." I grasped the man's hand, and he dipped his head in respect.

"Honor to help, my lady."

I waved a hand. "Save the niceties. Today, we've got work to do."

I got answering grins from the crowd of regulars. They were all on the younger side, maybe even all younger than me. Teens and fresh-faced adults eager to make their marks on the world. But Electra had assured me that this batch was made up of her best, and that they were loyal.

"Maybe too loyal," she'd said.

Please, as if anyone could be too loyal to *me*.

"This morning," I said. "We're going to be hunting hummingbirds."

That got me a ring of shocked faces.

I'd been rather unsurprised to learn that hummingbird glades, that is the circles of poisonous flowers filled with venomous birds that flew faster than the eye could see, were a well-known danger of the jungles. So well known, in fact, that no one thought to inform Electra or me of the danger we were walking into the first time we went to collect some feathers.

Go figure.

"There's a reason we're doing this right now." I waved a hand at the sky. No one wanted to go tromping through the jungle at night, after all. "At this time, most of the biggest monsters will already have returned to their dens. Our goal is *not* to fight them right now. Rather, our goal is to take advantage of a peculiar trait of hummingbirds." I grinned. "Tell me, does anyone wonder how something so small can fly so devilishly fast?"

My men exchanged confused glances. After a moment, one of them raised a hand. "Yes, what's your name, private?"

"Llen, my lady!" He snapped off a salute. My grin widened, and I waved at them to continue. "Is it magic, ma'am?"

"No." I slashed my hand through the air. "There's some good old biology at play, you see. They move fast because they live fast. They're constantly burning energy." Parts of this were bound to be different between worlds, but also, I imagine that blood of magical beasts was even *more* energy intensive than nectar. "They have to eat constantly, whether from the flowers that make them so deadly, or the other victims of the glade. If they stop eating, their body will start starving to death in less than an hour."

Llen blinked at that, before frowning. "Then . . . how do they sleep, ma'am?"

"That's the trick." I grinned, pulling out a an enchanted glow-stone. "At night, they go into a state that's more like suspended animation. In this situation, not only are they dead to the world around them, but they can take several minutes to wake back up again. A process that will leave them slow and groggy if they have to do it unexpectedly."

At that, I saw a look of comprehension flicker across Llen's face. "We'll hit 'em when they're asleep!"

I snapped my fingers. "Exactly."

And that was why I wasn't bringing Electra along this time.

Well, that, and she'd expressed rather strongly that if I ever brought her hummingbird hunting again, she'd throw *me* into the glade.

"What about the poisonous flowers?" a young woman with sooty black hair asked. "Private Haxes, ma'am!"

"Good question." I nodded towards their shoes. "That's why you all got new boots. It's actually a question that people around here have had the answer to for a very long time."

"We . . . have?" Llen asked.

"The poison from the flowers doesn't rise very high. It just irritates the skin. Unless it gets into your lungs—or your blood, you know, after the hummingbirds peck you open. You should all have simple cloth masks." I lifted my own. "Dip it in water and it will be annoying as sin to breathe through, but it will also protect you from the poison. One of the gatherers from a nearby village used this trick to harvest other herbs from the edge of the grove."

"Crazy . . ." Llen grinned. "That's nuts!"

They were an adrenalin junky type, huh? I could use more of those.

I nodded. "We've brought together the skills and the knowledge to make it happen. What I contributed is no more or less important than any other piece, it just so happens to be the last." I grinned. "So, who wants to hunt a hummingbird?"

The squad punched the air as one. "OOS!"

I raised my eyebrow at that. I guess every military, no matter how small, needed a chant.

"Let's move, then." I turned towards the recently disassembled palisade. "We're moving fast and quiet through the jungle. My demons will scout ahead, but be ready." I glanced over my shoulder. "There are more monsters than just mine running through those trees."

With that, I led the way from Lady's Port, out into the darkness.

It was, I'll admit, mostly a symbolic gesture. I let Llen take point once we hit the tree line. Leader or not, frontline demons or no, these people knew the jungle better than I did. And we were navigating it at night.

Rel fell in step behind me, a pair of her knives already in hand. I felt better, knowing that she was at my back.

Once we were in motion, the regulars were much less relaxed. They stayed quiet, using their own glowstones as little as possible. My own demons raced ahead on quiet wings, a new strand I'd discovered called blightbats. I could tell that I had lost several bats during scouting, but that just let me point our group away from whatever had killed them.

I wasn't in a hurry to confront whatever real monsters lurked in the shadows.

Of course, real life is rarely so kind.

"Stop!" Everyone froze at my sharp hiss. A moment later, a blightbat darted out of the gloom, landing on my raised arm.

It was an ugly thing, in the way most demons were, with two pairs of tattered wings that looked far too small to bear its lumpy naked mole rat body. It squeaked once, flapping its top pair of wings rapidly.

They were still smarter than hobblefiends.

I cursed softly, before casting the bat back off into the night. "Something big, coming right this way. It's not letting itself get distracted."

Sergeant Tervis responded quickly. "This way, out of its path." We immediately changed direction. "Llen, how far's the river?"

"Shouldn't be far."

"Then let's pick up the pace."

I fell in step with the rest of them, holding back a grumble at once again being the shortest person running for my life. Why did it always happen to me?

At least this time I was much more in shape, not that it helped much in the darkness.

Rel was the only thing stopping me from taking a nasty fall. After the third time it happened, I caught her hand with my own and gave it a squeeze.

There wasn't time for anything more than that.

By the time we could feel the vibrations in the ground, we were all running at a full sprint through the darkness. I slammed into more trees than I dodged, only catching sight of the river by the moon's reflection on its surface.

Fortunately for me, there was a demon for this situation, and I already had a bunch of them.

"Keep running!" I shouted. "Jump right before you hit the water!"

Then I took my own advice.

Half a dozen blightbats swooped out of the darkness, grabbing me by my arms. Even as they carried me over the river, I summoned up another group.

My mana dropped precipitously.

It was enough to get us all to the other side of the river.

There, Sergeant Tervis called a halt. "We're not going to outrun it if the thing decides to cross," he said. "This is as good a place to fight it as any."

"I'm out of mana." I pushed myself to my feet. "The bats will help buy time, but it will be a while before I can wind up for any big spells."

He nodded grimly, and then the regulars got into position on the bank of the river.

As always, Rel stood at my back, ready to protect me.

I quirked my lip. I could always have just summoned a gryphon, but they were expensive. It would be enough for Rel and I, and maybe two others. The blightbats wouldn't cut it over long distances.

Instead, I dismissed several of my bats, forming a handful of hobblefiends that trundled to the front of the formation. If nothing else, maybe they'd help break a charge.

Then across the river, a massive shape broke out of the tree line, and I realized that they really, *really* wouldn't.

The monster dug its massive claws into the far shore, carving gouges in the earth. It reared up, spines rippling across its back, and *roared.*

I flinched back at the sound.

Even in the darkness, I could see light glinting in its too-large eyes.

"Well," I found myself saying, "at least it only has two eyes this time."

Dimly, I registered someone out of the corner of my eye looking at me with concern. Ah, that would be Rel.

Reaching out, I grasped her hand again. Maybe I really should have just run away.

Then the giant, hulking, spined monstrosity took one last huff, slitted nostrils flaring. It turned slamming its tail into the riverbank, once, twice. Like it was forming a line.

Then it moved back into the shadows of the jungle, barely rustling the trees.

I took a deep breath, before letting go of Rel's hand and stepping forward to, ah, rally the troops.

"Sergeant Travis," I said.

He turned towards me, face pale. "Yes, ma'am?"

"You still have the map of glade locations?"

He nodded. "Yes, ma'am."

"Excellent." I tapped a finger against my chin. "I think that we shall go looking for one on *this* side of the river, instead."

He swallowed. "That sounds like an excellent idea."

CHAPTER 15

Here There Be Men

If Rel had been watching my back before, after the monster chased us across the river, she was practically glued to my side.

On one hand, it was nice to know I was appreciated. On the other, she really wasn't making it easier to walk in the darkness. Every few steps her leg would bump mine, almost sending me stumbling.

I gave her a *look* after the third time it happened, but even with the moonlight, I didn't know if she could see me. She certainly didn't change her behavior. I swear, the whole lost duckling thing was much cuter when she wasn't stepping on my heels.

In the end, I gave the order to light torches. Everything in this jungle probably knew where we were anyway, after the giant spinomonster thing chased us across the river.

"We need to move faster," I said as Llen and two others pulled out simple torches. "We're running out of time before dawn, and the last thing we need is the venomous hummingbirds to wake up while we're grabbing them out of the tree."

That certainly got them moving and bought me enough time to look over my shoulder at Rel. The woman looked completely unapologetic about practically walking on my calves the way here. Her eyes weren't even on me; instead, she was still staring out into the darkness, hand on a long knife.

"Hey." She didn't turn when I spoke. I snapped my fingers in front of her face. "Hey!"

Rel blinked, eyes flashing in the firelight as she turned that gaze to me. "Yes, Mistress?"

I grabbed her by the collar, pulling her close. "Stop standing on my heels." I took a step back as she blinked rapidly, cheeks coloring. "I appreciate it, really, but be a bit more aware of the situation at hand."

She nodded quickly.

I turned, raising an eyebrow at the rest of the group. "And why aren't we moving, people?" I clapped my hands once, the sound echoing sharply through the darkness. "You think I'm leaving without some feathers just because we got there after sunrise?"

Llen and the others picked up the pace, even as Llen himself leaned towards me with a concerned look on his face. "You, uh, know they'll attack us, right, Lady?"

I raised an eyebrow at him. "You know, Electra and I hunted our first batch of hummingbirds in the middle of the day." And didn't that sound ridiculous to say, even though I knew that they were venomous little bastards in this dimension. "I wonder if you lot can live up to her standards."

Llen's eyes widened slightly, before he nodded. After that, there was a bit of a fire in his movements. I smiled to myself.

I wasn't going to tell them that we'd only ended up in that situation because of my own mistake.

In under a minute, the torches were lit, and we struck out into the darkness once more. This time, I was able to see the ground beneath my feet, so even though we were heading farther away than initially planned, we made much better time.

"Llen." I fell in step beside the scout, helping him beat back the underbrush.

Well, I *tried* to help, anyway. For some reason, even in this new world with magical creatures and substandard nutrition, I was the shortest person around. It just wasn't fair, I tell you. Where were the dwarves?

"Yes, my lady?"

We kept our voices quiet, and I didn't distract him from picking out our path more than necessary. "Are the monsters near the village normally this aggressive?" I asked. My sole encounter with something that large had been over a month ago, back when I was first getting my footing in Silverwall. In a city with well, *walls,* I hadn't been too concerned about the monsters of the jungle.

The recent bandit attacks had shown that my own walls were much more fallible.

"Depends." Llen shrugged. "Usually they don't like coming round people, Lady. Da never told me why."

"But?" I prompted.

"Sometimes they get a bit more . . . angry." He rubbed the back of his head. "Round this season, actually. Every year, like sunrise and sunset. Lots a' moving and fighting."

I frowned. "They migrate?" I asked.

"What's a migrate?" Llen turned towards me, eyes lighting up. "Is that some new kinda beast from the outworld?"

I blinked, before shaking my head at the local name for foreign realities. "No, nothing like that." I chuckled. "We don't have big monsters like that spiny beast we ran across. Migrate just means that the entire population moves, usually from season to season."

"Migrate." He tasted the word. "Yes, Lady, think they probably all 'migrate' round this time."

I nodded, rubbing my chin. That could put a damper on my plans. I'd seen a TV special about elephants migrating from a preserve recently and tearing through a dozen farms. I liked to put on the news while I was tinkering around with my robots.

"Write me up a summary of how things usually go around here." If this world had poisonous elephants too, things might get a bit . . . tricky.

"Course!" He nodded, then paused. "Ah, my lady."

I turned back towards him.

"Why aren't there any big monsters in the outworld?"

"Hmm?" I rolled my eyes, turning back to the jungle. "We killed them all, or something." I smacked him on the back. "And if you don't pick up the pace, maybe 'Lectra and I will do the same thing here. So double time it, soldier!"

"Yes, ma'am!" He darted off into the jungle. "You don't need to kill no monsters here, Lady!"

"Wait for the rest of us!" I shouted, shaking my head. "Honestly." I glanced over my shoulder at Rel. "He reminds me of you."

She stumbled and I caught her wrist. "You okay?"

"M-me?" she asked. I squinted. "He reminds you of me?"

I huffed playfully, helping my favorite minion back to her feet. "Of course, you're both cute." By then, Llen had gone maybe twenty feet into the jungle and beat us a trail to follow. "Hard workers, too."

I gave her arm a squeeze. Wouldn't want her thinking I was going to replace her or anything, but really, a girl could get used to having good help. It was such a *refreshing* change of pace.

Speaking of changes of pace, with our newly motivated guide, we managed to make it to the secondary clearing with an hour or so before dawn. The men carrying torches stayed farther back as I made my way to the too-clean ring of trees in the middle of the dense jungle.

It was hard to see in the darkness, but it looked much the same as the clearing that I'd thrown Electra into to get our first batch of hummingbird feathers: a carpet of lush flowers and a single twisted tree in the middle.

And on that tree sat the birds.

Their feathers were so bright that they reflected the torchlight as though slick with oil. I shook my head. "How'd I ever mistake you for a normal hummingbird?"

"My lady," Rel said. "We're ready."

I nodded, stepping back. "Let's get it done, then."

I watched as my men split into two groups. The first, with Llen at the head, pulled on thick leather gloves and wrapped scarves, dampened from their own canteens, around their faces.

Those were the bird catchers, and they carefully picked their way across the clearing. I drew back from the puffs of glittering *poisonous* pollen that drifted up through the air, but we'd done our research. As long as we walked carefully, most of the stuff wouldn't reach our faces, and what little did was easily blocked by some . . . personal protective equipment.

Lessons learned from Earth, at least in part.

I watched as the three of them went up to the tree without the hummingbirds so much as stirring. Quickly, like picking apples, Llen and the others plucked the birds from the branches, stuffing them into the bags.

"No more than one per pouch!" I called. "We don't want them pecking each other to death after all this trouble."

After all, why buy the milk when you could get the whole cow?

At that thought, the second group, wrapped up much more tightly, started cutting into the carpet of flowers with a set of long-handled shovels. The bed was separated into neat squares, each one packaged back in the chests we'd brought with us.

I sighed. "It's almost a shame."

"What is, Mistress?" Rel leaned against my shoulder.

I opened my mouth, before snapping it shut. "Nothing." I shook my head. "I was just feeling maudlin for a moment, I mean really." I pressed a hand against my brow. "When it comes to broken eggs and omelets, I've done far worse than rip up an ecosystem for my own benefit."

I turned away from the jungle. They were just birds, after all. "That should be enough!" I called over my shoulder. "We're moving out before any of the rest start waking up."

"Think some of them are." Llen lifted up one of the small baggies when he came out of the clearing. It wriggled slightly. As if there were a bird inside, beating its wings weakly against the fabric.

I stared for longer than I should have, before letting out a sigh. "Be gentle with them," I said. "If they spend too much energy, they could die before we get them back." I snapped my fingers twice. "Good work people, now let's get back home before anything else big and spiky tries to take a bite out of us."

"Mistress?" Rel's hand came down on my shoulder.

I paused for a moment, before wrapping my fingers over her own. "Don't worry about it," I said in response to the silent question. "Just memories." I shook my head, making sure to keep my thoughts firmly in the present. "It's not important." I had a job to do, after all.

Just like always.

Thus, flowers potted and birds gotted, we set course back for Lady's Port.

Fortunately, the way back was much easier, and the sun crested the horizon just as we made it back to the stables. For obvious reasons, I didn't plan to bring venomous birds and their poisonous flowers into my town.

I nodded to Llen and the others. "Good work everyone. I'll handle getting Electra up to speed."

"Ah, Mistress." Rel stepped forward. "I can handle that, if you would like."

I raised an eyebrow. "Oh?"

Rel gave me a look, her brown eyes tracing over my face with an inscrutable expression. "Yes, my lady. I need to speak with her about some other things."

A second eyebrow joined the first. I laughed. "I must have been busier than I'd thought." Still, I trusted Rel to handle things. She'd never let me down.

I just had to return the favor.

With a nod, I went around, clapping the shoulders of the men and women under my command. "Good work today." I dug deep—it had been a long night—and put on a real smile. "I know it's not glamorous, like kicking the shit out of marauders and bandits."

They laughed. "Ah, it's the least we can do, Lady. We owe you."

"Hear, hear!" A woman wrapped her arm around Llen's shoulders. "We trust you, Lady."

They gave a cheer.

Ah, another responsibility. Of course.

I was starting to . . . remember why I didn't work with people.

I couldn't stop from . . .

I turned, throwing a careless wave over my shoulder.

"I won't let you down."

CHAPTER 16

*Rel*ationships 1

Rel wanted to get the soldiers sorted quickly so she could deal with her main concern.

Still, she took the time to watch Lady Via stride down the broad, airy road that was quickly becoming the town's main thoroughfare. Exhausted as she was, the woman still held herself as tall as her diminutive frame would allow, black cloak and black hair trailing behind her like paired banners. Each step was marked with a flash of the strange metal that made up her armor, black greaves coming down hard on the newly cobbled road.

Rel knew from experience that the armor was far too heavy for its size, that it gave Lady Via strength far beyond her stature. Still, the woman seemed so small, and Rel had to fight the urge to run after her.

Rel swallowed heavily. She hadn't had so much time with her Mistress in weeks now. That must be the reason why she was so affected, why she felt like she was being left behind yet again.

I-I wish we c-c-could spend more time with her . . .

The voice in her head, Rel's Dream Sequence skill, agreed with her.

But they were both so busy. Even the time she'd spent staring after Lady Via was time that she was *not* handing out the work assignments for the rest of the week. Nearly every person in Lady's Port looked to Rel and Lady Via for direction, and without them, things would quickly grind to a halt.

This time a runner who'd been tasked to bring over the information had gotten started on work assignments without her, but that was no excuse for such flights of distraction. Rel swallowed, even if the distraction was Lady Via herself?

With a shake of her head, Relia returned to the group of men and women just as they began looking over the sheets that outlined their duties after handing off the hummingbirds and poisonous flowers.

"Only guard duty for the rest of the week!" Llen complained. "And I'm on a farm?" He pulled a face. "Not exactly the beasts I'm interested in, Lady Rel."

Rel still didn't know how to react to people calling her 'Lady' anything. In her eyes, there was only one Lady in Lady's Port. Still, she couldn't just close up anymore, not when Via relied on her. "*You* have a report to write on monster migrations." She placed a hand on her hip. "The Lady is counting on it."

"Ah, Lady did say that." He nodded, rubbing the back of his neck sheepishly. "I'm, ah, not the best with my letters."

Rel nodded, many villagers were not, which was why Lady Via continued to place such an emphasis on teaching her people how to read and write if nothing else. Still, they needed that report quickly, and learning letters took time. "I'll have someone help you," Rel said. Many children attending the school were learning to read incredibly quickly, and they always wanted something more exciting to do than running messages or helping with farm work. "The rest of you, you have today off, of course, but we will need you back in training or guard rotations tomorrow."

Her words were met with nods all around. Everyone understood that they were short on hands: hands to build, hands to guide, hands to hold the myriad gifts Lady Via bestowed on them all.

Maybe the last one was just Rel. She had to stop herself from looking over her shoulder in concern, the direction that her Mistress had so swiftly departed.

I-is she s-s-sleeping enough? Rel's special skill tingled at the back of her mind. She added that to the list of things to check. Mistress would lie of course, but if she checked with the kitchen staff first about her tea consumption, perhaps?

"And what about them birds?"

Rel jolted back to the present. "The birds!" She nodded, slapping her pants once, twice. The sleek black fabric didn't hold the answers, just more knives. "The birds are . . ."

"Fear not." Ishanti breezed around the corner, nearly gliding across the rough cobbles. "That was my assignment; we have brought blood to keep them alive until we can finish planting their grove as well. Quickly now, quickly." She waved her hand, impatiently. "I was informed that they would not live long without nourishment—was I misinformed?"

"Whoop, nope!" Llen hopped to his feet. "Gotta get moving, Lady Rel! Talk about that report later."

Rel sighed as the young man dashed off with a crate of the flowers. They'd be set up in a glade that had already been selected to the northeast of the town, essentially between Lady's Port and Silverwall. It wasn't expected to prevent travel between the two, but perhaps it would be a stumbling block to any organized aggression that attempted to cut through the jungle.

"Come," Ishanti said to her helpers. "Put on the gloves, as you were instructed. We shall distribute the cow blood. The hummingbirds should be in a weakened state from hunger, but be cautious."

Rel took a step back as the other women took the protective gear from the soldiers. They didn't have an infinite amount of leather to make into thick gloves and face masks. For her part, Rel was just glad that the entire operation had gone over without a hitch.

Well, as much as any of Lady Via's plans did, that is.

Sh-she makes good plans! Dream Sequence said in her head. *Th-they just n-n-need some help, sometimes . . . right?*

Rel smiled. At least the little voice in the back of her mind was unequivocally on Mistress's side.

O-of course!

Rel nodded, all of her supported Lady Via all of the time. She marched forward, coming to a stop next to the princess. "How do the birds look?"

Ishanti glanced up over her shoulder. "Most of them survived the trip. A few did not." Ishanti sighed. "We've sorted the dead ones out from the rest." She looked down at the bird in her hands. "This one has a wounded wing."

Rel looked over the other woman's shoulder. The bird was a pale green, scales flashing like tiny gems in the morning light. Its wing was stretched out across Ishanti's gloved palms, bent at an odd angle.

"I do not think it will be able to fly." A note of lingering melancholy filled Ishanti's voice at those words. "Poor broken bird, the cage broke you before you could escape it."

Rel opened her mouth, then closed it. She did not know much about broken birds.

She knew much more about the tightly wound pain in Ishanti's voice. Rel's Mistress did very much like collecting her strays.

"Lady Via only demanded the dead hummingbirds be delivered to her workshop."

Ishanti blinked once, her silvery lashes brushing against her cheeks. She turned to look at Rel. "I do not understand what you are insinuating."

Rel shrugged, glancing off to the side awkwardly. "It is only an observation . . ."

Ishanti rose, eyes narrowing. She did not return the bird to its box, though; it remained trembling weakly in her hands. "If placed with the others, it will starve."

"It will." Rel nodded. "Sometimes . . . I think . . ." She didn't know what she was saying, but the words kept spilling out regardless. "Sometimes birds need a tender hand to heal them. Some . . . *someone* to keep them safe, before they're ready to fly."

Ishanti blinked again, golden eyes drifting slowly shut, before returning back to the bird in her grip. "They eat blood, it is said?" she asked.

"Yes." Rel nodded again. "And nectar."

Ishanti said nothing more for a moment, then she lifted her head. "Girls, transport the birds to their assigned glade. I shall handle the delivery of the ones that did not survive transit." She looked towards Rel. "And if I should also need to commission a cage?"

"Scrap metal will be enough for bars. Lady Via's soot imps should be able to help you quickly." Rel jerked her head towards the artisan's district that had sprung up next to the port. The two imps had a whole shop to themselves, and all the metal they could ask for. Rel pulled a face. "I need to tour the place, actually . . ."

Princess Ishanti, for her part, did seem to sense her hesitation. "If you inform me what it is I am to inspect, I could perhaps manage that task for you," the silver-haired woman said.

Rel shifted. On one hand, it was a task that Via had given to her, and she was loath to part with those, especially to Ishanti.

On the other . . .

Sh-she did tell us to d-delegate? Dream Sequence added. *A-a-and to . . . get along?*

Rel sighed. "That would be very helpful." She sucked on her lip for a moment before adding, "Thank you."

"It is of no import." Ishanti rose, the wounded bird still cradled gently in one hand as she held out a small rag soaked with cow's blood, dripping it into the hummingbird's waiting beak.

Rel thought it looked disturbingly like feeding a baby, only nothing like that at all.

"I'll give you the specifics of the task?"

Ishanti nodded. "Just so."

"It *is* simple. Ask the workers if they have any complaints, or if any of the equipment looks like it needs to be replaced." Rel glanced off to the side. "Also . . . make sure that Coaline and Mr. Burns haven't killed each other."

Ishanti raised an eyebrow. "Is this likely to be the case?"

Rel shrugged helplessly. "They don't . . . like each other? Lady Via ordered two different forges built to keep them farther apart."

"And now she visits only rarely . . ." Ishanti mused.

Rel bit her lip at the potential parallels between their own situation. "Thank you, again, for helping," she said at length.

Ishanti sank into a brief curtsey, making her simple green and brown dress look like something far more elegant. "Let us endeavor to escape our own cages, then," she said.

Rel's lips turned into a smile, looking down at the ground. "Before they start sending people to make sure we haven't killed each other."

"It is just so."

Th-that wasn't so b-bad . . .

Rel nodded to herself as Ishanti walked away. If only she could be certain that the princess was completely in Lady Via's camp. Even if Silverwall was closed to the woman, Ishanti still had connections in the capital that she could potentially leverage.

Yet here she remained, playing secretary to Rel's mistress.

Was she just another bird with a broken wing, waiting for the right moment to fly away?

Maybe . . . she hasn't m-made her choice? Dream Sequence asked.

"Then she'd best decide quickly," Relia murmured.

A small hand tugged at her elbow.

Rel blinked, looking down to see her own minion standing at her elbow.

Rel held back a sigh. So much for getting back to Lady Via in any reasonable amount of time.

"Hello again." She lowered one knee to the cobble. "What do you have for me, Elaine?"

Elaine looked up at her, bright green eyes peeking out from beneath her brown hair. The girl had light brown skin to match her hair and a solemn expression that turned utterly terrifying when she held a knife.

She'd taken to blades nearly as quickly as Rel had herself, and Relia had a skill for helping her out.

After a moment, Elaine reached into the small satchel she had, pulling out a sheaf of papers. She held it out to Rel with one hand, the other pointing towards the Lightning Mill.

Rel nodded. "Daily reports for Lady Via?" Perhaps she'd get to see her faster than she thought.

Then Elaine shook her head, making a jagged chopping motion with her hand.

"For . . . Electra?" Rel asked. Elaine nodded. "I see, these are the sketches then, for the forge, docks, and other public spaces?" Rel flicked through them, revealing diagrams and other important information that Electra and Via said they needed to expand the *lights*.

Elaine nodded.

Rel pushed herself back to her feet, tucking the papers into her jacket. Still, the little girl stood at her feet, looking up at her expectantly.

Rel still wasn't sure what to do with the girl. Elaine *could* speak, she just chose not to most of the time. At the same time, having a personal runner and helper really did streamline Rel's own tasks.

And yes, maybe she recognized a little bit of a kindred spirit in the small, quiet girl.

"Good work," Rel said. Then, slowly, consciously, she reached out and ruffled the girl's hair. Elaine tilted her head, blinking up at Rel. Rel took back her hand. "How are your letters? I need someone to write up a report for Lady Via."

Elaine looked at her for a moment longer, before nodding. "'Kay."

Rel smiled. "Go look for Private Llen at the northern farm, let him know that you'll write down his report on monster migrations for him."

Elaine nodded one more time before setting off, leaving Rel with yet another task to do.

She ran a hand through her own brown hair. "When did things become so busy?"

I bet Mistress feels like this . . . a-all the time.

Rel shook her head as her thoughts drifted to Lady Via once again. It had become a theme, and she didn't know how she felt, thoughts so often drifting in such a way, only that she misliked it when they were so often apart. Still, there was work to be done, and Rel set off to find Electra and complete her own tasks.

CHAPTER 17

Relationships 2

It was a testament to just how *big* Lady's Port had become that Rel almost got lost on the way to find her.

She *knew* where the blonde woman would be; Lady knew that Rel was the one who wrote the other woman's schedules most days. Expanding the electrical coverage was 'domestic priority number one.' While Rel didn't understand the exact meaning of the words, she understood the importance it held to Via, and to Lady's Port as a whole.

It was why she was running herself almost as ragged as Lady Via, making sure that new lighting bulbs rolled out of the glassworks and copper wire out of the smithy, why the beaches near Lady's Port had been dredged almost completely dry of sand, and why the *Little Mistress* came back with her hold nearly as full of copper ingots as everything else.

It was why she found Electra and her work crew deep in the guts of a second lightning mill. She and Lady Via had already began implementing plans for bringing light to the new homes currently being built, but that, plus the light and power needed for the smithy, was 'projected to outstrip' the Lightning Mill.

Rel did not yet understand the near-arcane equations behind it, but she was learning. Just one more reason she was constantly busy.

"Run that wire there, no there! Over *there*!"

Rel stepped into the foundation of the mill, quickly dodging to the side as a man and a woman rolled another spool of copper wire to the banks of the water.

They were going through a distressingly large number of those.

"Over there." Rel pointed. An electrician nodded to her, eyes lighting up in understanding.

"Ah, that's what she meant. My thanks, Lady Rel!"

"Eh, Rel?" Electra's head popped out of a hole in the stone wall. Her blonde hair was messy, coming down to her shoulders as the humidity of the coming spring seemed to have finally let it overcome its natural spikiness. "What's up?"

Rel glanced to the side. She'd been trying to have this conversation all morning, but now that she was here . . .

Well, she'd never been good at having conversations with people like Electra.

"Hey." The woman walked out onto the scaffolding that made up the second story, leaning against the massive wooden spoke that would form the center of the second water wheel. "Something wrong? The whole bird job went good, right?"

"Yes, of course." Rel nodded. "I just, wanted to talk to you about . . . Lady Via."

"Aaaah." Electra gave a knowing smile. "It's one of *those* talks, huh? Don't worry, girl, I got'chu!"

Rel blinked as the blonde woman hopped down to the ground floor, putting a hand on Rel's shoulder as she pulled the both of them away from the entrance to the mill. "So, spill. Did she finally say something? Jeez, I've been waiting for an effing *year* for one of you two boneheads to make a move."

Rel blinked again. "A move?"

"You know, on your nature walk." Electra waved a hand. "I mean, it's not really my idea of a romantic date, but I bet you got to get *real* close with her, yeah?"

Rel blinked a third time.

Sh-sh-she means . . . like . . . k-kissing, Dream Sequence stated.

Rel's cheeks slowly reddened, ears burning beneath her hat. "I—I—I . . ."

Electra leaned forward, staring at Rel awkwardly. "Oh, uh, hadn't ripped the Band-Aid off yet?"

"No!" Rel shook her head, hugging her middle. "Why should she be interested in someone like me, anyway? I-I-I'm only worried that she has been working too hard!"

"Oh." Electra crossed her arms, cupping her chin with one hand. "I maybe jumped the gun a bit. You . . . do like her, though?"

Rel sighed, running her hand down her face. "I . . . she . . ." She shook her head. "You're making this very difficult."

"Right, right, sorry." Electra waved her hands in front of her. "I, uh, forget I said anything, and uh, about Via, I mean, you know how she—"

"Of course I like her," Rel said quietly. "She saw me when I was nothing and made me valuable." She gave a quiet laugh. "Now when I walk down the street, all of these people call me 'Lady' as if I was even a fraction as important as my lady."

"Well, crud." Electra rubbed the back of her head. "So, maybe we can roll this conversation back a bit and I can give you some . . . advice?"

"I . . ." Rel began, "am not sure I want your advice anymore."

"Okay, harsh," Electra said. "Understandable, but a little harsh. I mean, I called that you're into her, right?"

"Apparently it's quite obvious."

"Well, probs not to Via." Electra shrugged. "I don't think she ever really dated, actually."

"I . . . don't need to have this information."

"Sure you do." Electra wrapped an arm around Rel's shoulder. "She's always been *super* focused. Hah, get it? Super?"

"Please let me go now," Rel said. "I'd like to forget that we had this conversation. And maybe I can figure out on my own some way to stop Mistress Via from working herself to death." Rel stepped out from under Electra's grip. "I think you should get back to work; the second mill is already behind schedule."

Electra blew out a huff of air. "Okay, harsh again. I get that's kind of the theme of this conversation, but we're kinda rediscovering electrical engineering here, and if you want the overshot wheel done so bad you can always pitch in some more work crews, you know, as a favor to a friend."

"I am going to go now." Rel took another step away, tugging the hat down farther on her head. "This was not . . . a good idea."

"Wait, wait, wait, wait, wait!" Electra waved her hands. "Okay, we're not doing favors, but about your *actual* question. I mean, Via . . . she kinda gets obsessed, you know? She works harder than anyone I've ever known, and really, that's only got more true now that I work with her. That's not, you know, something that just goes away."

"Look, I . . ." Rel shook her head. "Miss Electra, can you get to the point? Every time you talk, I feel the urge to go throw myself in the ocean."

"Don't do *that.*" Electra blew out a breath. "I mean, that would just double Empress's workload, you know? At minimum."

Rel scrunched her eyes shut. She was beginning to understand *exactly* why Lady Via was so incredibly *frustrated* with Electra all the time.

"Get to the point."

"Oof, that's, like, peak Empress right there." Electra laughed. "Keep doing that and she'll fall for you for sure."

Rel ducked her head, unable to formulate a response. The thought rattled around in her brain.

"Anyway," Electra continued. "My *point* is that, if you're so worried about Empress being hyperfocused on work, maybe you should give her something else to focus on, huh?"

Rel's head snapped up, and she stared at Electra, mouth working uselessly.

"Alright, off you go!" Electra spun Rel around, pushing her gently out the door. "Go say hi to Via for me. I recommend the direct approach!"

"Wait!" Rel spun around just as Electra pushed her out the door. "What are you talking about? I—I can't just. I . . . and Lady . . . and—!"

"Sorry, can't talk any longer!" Electra grinned. "Someone important told me I was behind schedule on Lightning Mill *numero dos!*"

Then she slammed the door shut, forcing Rel to step back as a pair of unmortared bricks fell out from above the lintel.

She stared silently at the shut door, thoughts frozen in place.

"What," she managed, "am I supposed to do with *that?*"

A hand tugged on her sleeve.

Rel spun, dagger falling into her hands.

Her helper Elaine stared up at her with big brown eyes.

"Lady Via," Elaine said.

Rel stood frozen for a second before stuffing the knife back down her sleeve. "Yes, of course. The Lightning Mill?"

The girl nodded.

"The report?" Rel asked.

She nodded again, holding out a small sheaf of papers.

"Yes . . ." Rel took a deep breath, taking the hastily written report before patting down her suit pockets in a gesture she'd seen Via and Electra do many times. "I should go then."

The girl nodded a third time.

Rel saved them both a few more words and started down the street, rubbing at her face. She'd also been up for most of the night, after all.

Running all over the town in a day had stolen the breath from her lungs, and that conversation with Electra—if it even deserved to be called such—had . . . well, Rel was a bit ashamed to realize she was yawning when she walked into her mistress's office.

She was so tired that she walked into a wall of muscle.

Rel took a half step back, holding her nose and looking up at the massive bald man who was standing in the door. "Dee?"

Dee grinned. "Little Rel!" He swept her up in a hug, her feet kicking frantically in the air. "Wasn't sure you'd last without us!"

"Put me down." Her one free hand smacked the big lug upside the head, for all the good it did. "Put me down!"

Laughing, he dropped her, and Rel landed deftly. "You . . . you *oaf.*" She struggled to hold back her laugher. "You're back?"

The big man nodded. "Him, too." He jerked his head, and Rel peeked around his arm to see Maarin, the enchanter from Silverwall, standing somewhat awkwardly in front of Lady Via's desk, Dum's hand on his shoulder.

"A-ah, hello again?" He gave her a little wave. "I-I hope you liked those mirrors of-of mine?"

"They were excellent," Lady Via said from the balcony door. "In fact, I want to make a whole bunch more of them." She gave Maarin a sharp grin. "I hear that business wasn't all that great back in Silverwall?"

"Aha-haaa . . ." He shrugged. "Not quite . . . no."

"The boys told me a lot," Via said, kicking her feet up on her desk. "Most they've talked in weeks."

"We just missed ya, boss," Dum said.

"Aww, I missed you two as well." Via grinned. "I've been knocking heads together myself while you were gone."

Dee clutched at his chest. "Say it ain't so, boss!"

Rel found herself smiling despite her growing exhaustion. It was nice to have at least one thing go right in this whole mess.

"Well then," Lady Via said. "It seems I have some job openings. Tell me, Maarin, how would you like to work for me in a more . . . complete capacity?"

The enchanter looked over his shoulder at the much bigger man holding him in place. "I gather I don't have . . . much of a choice?"

"Of *course* you do!" Via grinned. "I just can't have anyone in town who might be working for the Seneschal of Silverwall, you know."

"Ah, well, yes, of course." Maarin nodded. "Completely understandable."

"If you don't want to work for me you can stay the night; I'm not a barbarian, after all," Via said. "I'm sure we can find somewhere to put you up, you'll just have to find your own way back tomorrow."

"Ah. My . . . own way?"

Via shrugged. "It's not too far, is it? A day and a half at most?"

"Y-yes but you see." Maarin scratched his neck. "The monsters are a bit more active this time of . . . of year."

"True, boss," Dee said. "Beat off a couple ourselves."

"Hmm." Via examined her nails. "Well, that really is a shame." She pushed herself to her feet, clapping Maarin on the shoulder. "Hope you have a good night's rest! I've recently been informed that it's a bit of a dangerous trek back to the big city and all of that."

She brushed past him, and Rel stilled as her mistress came to a stop in front of her. "Rel, you should get some sleep."

Rel felt her cheeks start to heat up again, and she looked away. "So should you, Mistress."

"I'll sleep when I'm dead." Via glanced over her shoulder. "I hear it's quite restful."

Maarin gave a little jerk, working his thin fingers over each other.

"Well, I think that's all I have to take care of here," Via said. "Have a good night, boys! We'll talk more tomorrow" She turned, taking Rel's arm, completely oblivious to the thudding of Rel's heart in her breast. "A cat nap actually sounds great. Never been a fan of the long sleep, you know."

They took two steps.

"And, and, and if I decided I did want to work for you?" Maarin nearly shouted. "P-p-pending some conditions."

Rel watched, heart fluttering in her chest, as Via's lips curled into a massive, face-splitting grin. Then the diminutive woman shifted her expression into a calm, confident smirk, and turned around.

"Then let's talk business."

CHAPTER 18

Backfoot

Jeez, Em', you were supposed to sleep last night."

With a mumbled curse, I pushed myself up from my desk, rubbing at my eyes. They felt puffy, and my mouth tasted like something had crawled into it and died.

"I did." My voice was raspy, grating like sandpaper in my throat. "For a few hours."

Electra pushed into my office. She looked tired too, but more from all the wiring and electric work I'd had her doing. "It's been two weeks since you did that hummingbird raid thing."

I chuckled, rubbing at my face. "Once I fuck up my sleep schedule, it takes me forever to fix it."

"Yeah, well, you kinda need to get on that," Electra said. "We're all counting on you here." Behind her, Rel, Ishanti, the boys, and my pet enchanter Maarin filed into the office as well. My 'inner council,' as it were.

"When did you start talking back to me?" I pushed myself upright. "In any case, it's fine. I got the work done before taking my nap. I *am* a super genius, you know." I picked up the pieces of paper on my desk. I handed out the week's work schedules and allotments, then I paused.

"Ishanti," I said.

The white-blonde princess tilted her head. "Yes, my lady?"

"The fuck is that?" I pointed.

"Hmm?" She tilted her head, looking down at the cage attached to her waist. Inside of it was, unless I was *very much* mistaken, one of the venomous hummingbirds I'd gone through the trouble of capturing. "Ah, the new cage I ordered was finally finished."

I watched, eyes wide, as she stuck a finger through the bars. The hummingbird hopped over, flapping its wings pitifully, and pecked at her finger, slurping at Ishanti's blood.

"Are you immune to that now, too?" I asked.

"Members of the royal family have been known to heal much faster than the average person. It is part of what makes our bodies—still living—so valuable to the true rulers of Vecorvia," Ishanti said. "In this, though, according to the bestiary you had hunter Llen compile, the hummingbirds are only venomous because they imbibe the nectar of the blood lilies. This one has subsided on naught but sugar water and my own blood for near on two weeks now."

I leaned closer, handing off Ishanti's own orders as I examined the little bird. It held its left wing awkwardly—probably broken, which was interesting—but . . . "Is it just me, or is it going gold?"

Ishanti tried to hold back a wince, but failed. "I believe my blood is having beneficial properties on the monster."

I sighed. The more I learned about the girl's apparently magical bloodline, the worse it sounded. "Keep an eye on that for me."

Were I still simply Empress, villainess extraordinaire, I also would have ordered a sample of her blood sent to my labs for testing. Of course, I didn't have labs to do any testing. And I needed Ishanti more than I cared about whatever magic blood she had.

Finally, it looked like the Seneschal of Silverwall, and this mysterious Senate, had all the answers when it came to royal blood anyway. I'd get the answers when I came to grips with them.

We would be coming to grips with each other.

"I will keep you appraised, my lady." Ishanti flipped through the documents. "In addition . . . pardon me if I am mistaken, but did you forget to allot materials needed to build the next sloop of Lady's Port?"

"What?" I stood up. "No, I *distinctly* remember assigning all the work crews you needed."

"Crews, yes." A delicate finger scrolled down the line of . . . admittedly somewhat smudged ink. "But what of the lumber? There is no mention here of who shall be providing materials."

I scanned my own messy handwriting. Over the past, Jesus, it had really been *months* now, I'd developed a standard layout to keep track of where the materials were coming from, who was getting paid, how long the work should take, how long the work would probably *actually* take, etc.

And I was missing a line.

"Ugh." I rubbed my face. "Let me think, where was I supposed to get that from?" I glanced back to my desk, picking through my notes. "If anyone has a surplus of wood, tell me now or forever hold your peace."

There was a rustling of reports behind me. "Nothing from me, Mistress."

"I mean, I don't think there's any extra, but I'm bad at math."

"Uuughh." I knocked my head on my desk. "I'm gonna have to go through it all again." I could already feel the headache coming on. "Reports back. Dee, Dum, I'll have to talk to you later. We need those ships."

"No prob, boss," Dee said.

Dum chuckled. "Always been bad at numbers."

I gave a laugh. "Missed you two." It was nice to have my original crew back together, even though it looked like I'd just doubled my workload by accident.

"Mistress," Rel said. "Now that you've drawn up the basic schedules, I should be able to fix the rest."

I shook my head. "There might be other mistakes. I thought I was tracking all the projects but if I let something like that slip, I might have to redo everything."

"More like, 'I'm gonna redo everything anyway,'" Electra said.

I turned to glare at her. "Well, maybe if you'd finished calc two you could help me out."

"You don't need *calculus* to balance a budget." Electra shook her head, laughing. "You just won't let me help."

"Because you'll mess something up."

"Why don't you just, I dunno, invent double-entry bookkeeping or something." She shrugged. "That's, like, an Isekai staple."

"What even is that?" I raised an eyebrow. "You don't know basic math, but you expect me to have an encyclopedic knowledge of random medieval accounting techniques? I can't just google random smart-sounding words that the audience won't bother to look up."

"Also . . ." Ishanti raised her hand. "We already have two-entry book-keeping? It is, as you say, quite a basic method for balancing budgets."

I turned back to Electra, tapping my foot. "Next you're gonna tell me to invent the overshot waterwheel."

Electra tilted her head. "Aren't we standing in one of . . ."

"Exactly," I said. "Keep talking."

She huffed. "Okay, well, even a broken clock is right twice a day. You really need to offload some work if you're making simple mistakes like that!" She glanced over at Rel. "Besides, don't you want your suave minion to help you out?"

I gave a small laugh, glancing over at my first and most faithful follower. "I rely on her too much as it is."

Rel blushed. "It's nothing, Mistress."

"'Sides, you can't worry about other people's workload but not your own."

I rolled my eyes. "Sure I can—I'm the boss." I waved it off. "Besides, it's not like I have anything else I *have* to take care of today. Right? Maarin, everything's going good with communication mirror production, right? We'll have those rolling soon."

"A-ah, uh, well."

I sighed. "Maarin. You're killing me here."

Electra giggled. "Careful, she might kill *you* if it's bad news."

"I only do that to people who personally disappoint me." I turned to face my pet enchanter, hands on my hips. "You aren't going to *disappoint me* are you, Maarin?"

His face went bone white, eyes darting back and forth. Electra smacked him on the shoulder. "Relax, she's joking, man." She paused. "At least, I think she's joking. Em' isn't really in the habit of offing her lieutenants, unlike most villains."

"I've never had lieutenants before," I said.

Somehow, he got even more pale. I sighed. Okay, the joke was clearly played out. "Just tell me, Maarin. I need an accurate assessment of our production line."

"Well, w-we managed a few prototypes," he said. "Unfortunately, making th-the multi-connection part f-fully automatic is beyond me. The enchantment doesn't bend so easily, and layering a second on top, to swap out the 'address rods,' as you call them, destabilizes the whole thing and almost took the functioning prototypes with it!"

I quirked my lip. "So what do we have now?"

He rubbed his arm. "Three sets of one-way m-mirrors, and then th-three more that c-can connect to each other, but you need to manually switch the connects at a central location."

"Range?"

He shrugged. "The single-connection mirrors sh-should work anywhere on the island; the materials you provided were very high quality."

"That alone is worth it." I folded my arms. "Focus on getting me more of those for the time being. Waiting on *the Little Mistress* to get back from the capital is too long to wait for news. I'll think about the other problem."

"But Empress." Electra grinned at me, waving the sheaf of papers in her hand. "Weren't you going to work on this?"

I frowned. "I can do both. Especially now that I've had a nap."

"Sure, like there aren't still *huuuge* bags under your eyes." Electra laughed. "You're so out of it you didn't even notice 'Shanti's been carrying around that bird for the last, like, three days."

I stepped back. "No way." I looked over at Ishanti. "That can't be true."

The princess opened her mouth, pausing for a second, before looking away. "I would prefer if you did not call me 'shanty' as if I were some kind of song performed by bawdy sailors."

Electra grinned. "Whatever you say, 'Shanti."

Ishanti huffed.

I slumped against the desk. "I seriously missed the venomous hummingbird? I thought you said the cage was just finished."

". . . I had it in a simpler wrought iron affair." Ishanti glanced away. "But I felt it lacked gravitas."

"You haven't looked up from your desk in flipping *days,* Empress."

I opened my mouth to reply, when the door to my office burst open again. I glanced down to see a child, Rel's little mini-me, standing in the entrance, breathing heavily.

"Uh-oh," Electra said.

"Attack." The tween pointed out towards the farm. "Monsters and bandits. Golden eyes."

Ishanti sucked in a breath.

I turned towards her. "This wouldn't have something to do with your pet having gold feathers all of a sudden?"

"I . . . wish I could say no." The princess hunched in on herself. "I have no knowledge, only bare rumors, but if the Seneschal has deployed one of the golden against us . . . it means he is finally taking us seriously."

I looked out the window. In the distance, I could just see a plume of smoke beginning to rise at one of the outlying farms. Meanwhile, here I was going over reports and trying to make sure we had enough wood to build a ship, instead of focusing on the enemy at our gates.

"Ah," I said. "I've let myself get complacent." I nodded once. "You're right, Electra. I really should have someone else handle some of these reports for me."

The blonde blinked. "Okaaay? Why do I get the feeling that I'm gonna regret that?"

"Simple, isn't it?" I shook my head. "I've let myself get so distracted running everything that I got slowed down. It's been half a month, and I couldn't spare the time to mop up the rest of the bandits in the jungle." I turned, kicking my desk hard enough to send it sliding an inch. "Moron!"

"Hey, there's no need to be so harsh!" Electra said.

"No, no. You were right," I replied. "Savor it, Elenore. You finally won an argument."

"I . . . win plenty of arguments?"

I smiled. It wasn't a nice smile. "Well, you're losing this next one. So get ready to move out." I huffed, gathering up the last of my papers. "Fucking Seneschal, thinking he can just 'take me seriously' all of a sudden."

Behind me, my allies shuffled, no doubt trading glances at my sudden change of behavior.

Really, though, it had been building for a while now. I'd been so focused on the next thing to build, the next project to set in motion. I'd been too obsessed with my city on the hill, so much, in fact, that I'd forgotten the reason I'd started building it in the first place.

". . . Where are we going?" Electra asked.

"Once more into the breach."

CHAPTER 19

Grave Import

In the end, I did what everyone kept whining at me to do and set up a basic bureaucracy. *Not* because I couldn't handle it.

I'm sure future generations would come to curse me in triplicate, but for now, Ishanti, Rel, and I assembled a simple system to track resources and labor, to make sure everyone got paid and all of the projects had the materials they needed.

Then, we were off.

"All set, boss?" Dee asked.

I stuck my head out the front of the wagon. "All set back here, too." I grinned at Dee and Dum, the two practically falling off the driver's seat. "Sure we don't need a bigger wagon?"

"Can't find one big enough for his fat ass," Dee said.

"And if yah could, wouldn't fit his fat head!" Dum replied.

I laughed along with both of them at the simple joke. "Ah, it's good to have you two back, just like old times."

"The best."

"Hey!" Electra leaned out the front of the covered wagon, hands on my shoulders. "What am I, chopped liver?"

I sighed. "No, but *we* could certainly use some time apart." I smirked up at her. "They say absence makes the heart grow fonder, after all."

She giggled. "Then you'd better keep me close; wouldn't want you catching icky feelings, Empress."

"Please, I'd have to be deaf and blind."

Normally, a jab like that got her all huffy, but this time Electra just smirked back at me. "I get it, I get it. I'm just not your *type*."

I shrugged, sending her staggering back into the wagon. "Much better." I turned my attention back to the boys. "Let's get this show on the road."

With a crack of the reins, the cart started down the road away from Lady's Port. I'd considered doing some big send-off; it would be good for morale, but I didn't exactly want to *advertise* that I was going on a sabbatical.

I assumed Seneschal Hawkwright would learn about it soon enough, but I wanted him to think I was going after the remnants of the Adventurer's Guild still hiding in the jungle.

I *was* going after them, but not personally. Efficient delegation is an important tool in any would-be Empress's arsenal, after all. Rel would be leading our militia to stamp them out before they made any more trouble.

And before they could support that golden-eyed individual the Seneschal sent after my head.

"What are things like in Silverwall?" I asked. "I heard they closed the Miner's Gate, but not much else."

"Not good, boss," Dum said. "The guard came down on the docks like a sack of hammers. Weren't too happy you slipped them the first time."

"Curfews, patrols, random searches," Dee added. "Deep hells, they're not even taking bribes at the gate anymore!"

I frowned. "Will that be a problem?" Naturally, Electra and I planned to hide, but that wouldn't help if the wagon was thoroughly searched.

"Naw." Dum shook his head. "We gots ourselves a friend in the guard. Eloncio is one of Mama's. He'll let us through, jus' as long as we don't make any more trouble for him."

I chuckled at that. "I shall be the absolute soul of discretion," I said. "And did you hear anything about the inner walls?" That was where the palace sat, along with my target.

"Like the rest of the city, just more guards." Dum shrugged. "They don't have enough bodies to cover all of Silverwall, but they have enough that gettin' through the inner walls will be . . ."

I tapped my chin. "Random searches and patrols in the city proper. They're using the uncertainty to make up for their lack of numbers. And with a secure fallback point behind the inner walls, no other group can easily strike back."

Dee shrugged. "Seems like what they're doin'. It's not hard to move round the city once you get inside. Just never know when a bunch of silver spears gonna swing around the corner."

I nodded. "That's all I need. Thanks Dee, Dum."

"Heh." Dee smirked. "She thanked me first."

Dum snorted, shouldering his brother. The two of them started playfully jockeying in the driver's seat. Though, I didn't know if I could call it *playful* if they were rocking the wagon back and forth.

I gave them both a whack to the back of the head. "Don't break our ride."

"Sorry, boss!"

That taken care of, I ducked back into the wagon. It would be a day and a half ride back to Silverwall. We weren't in a horse-drawn cart for *speed*. All that extra time meant I had ample time to refine my plans.

"Sure this is gonna work?" Electra asked. She tapped the lid of one of the coffins filling the back of the wagon. "Why would the people in that rich inner wall commune place want a bunch of fancy coffins?"

"Rich people want fancy everything." I ran a hand over the lacquered wooden surface and ornate metal fastenings. Making all ten of these had taken some doing, but luckily, metal and wood were things we had in abundance. "It's Dee's plan, anyway. Supposedly he has a contact on the inside who works for a mortician."

"Sure you want to trust Dee's advice?" Electra giggled at the thought. "Those boys might have arms thick as tree stumps, but their brains are too!"

I rolled my eyes. "Dee has a good head on his shoulders. If he knows someone inside the wall, he knows someone inside the wall. All that matters is getting past the guards."

"Yeah, well, if it were that easy, someone else would have done it by now."

I sighed, nodding. "I'm worried about the inner wall, but as long as we have a way into the city, we'll have options." I reached into a belt pouch. I'd worn my power armor, freshly recharged, for this job, which meant I had my old utility belt, a standard for every hero and villain. "Plus, we have this!"

Electra giggled as I waved the long-range communication mirror back and forth. "The old ones didn't get good reception from Silver-wall back before the enchantments started failing and we had to ditch them," she said. "What makes you think *that* will do any better?"

"Why don't we check right now?" I flipped it open.

I'd fashioned my last communication into a mirror compact because it felt more comfortable to carry. Now that feature came standard, making it easy to turn the mirror 'off' when it was shut in order to save power. I didn't really understand how the whole magical battery thing worked out, but fortunately, industry was built on the backs of delegation and distribution of labor.

When I opened the mirror itself, it reflected my face for a moment before going black. From experience, I knew that the paired mirror would be vibrating slightly to show that the paired enchantment was active.

Maarin was such a useful friend to have.

A few seconds later, the other mirror opened, darkness giving way to an image of Rel's face reflected back at me. For some reason, the mirrors showed the images backwards, Rel's bangs sweeping down towards the left side of her face, instead of the usual right.

Just an idiosyncrasy of magical communication.

When Rel saw me, her face broke out into a smile. "Mistress!" she said. "I didn't think you would check in so soon."

I rolled my eyes. "Don't worry, I'm sure you haven't had time to burn the place down yet. I just wanted to make sure the mirrors worked."

"Of course, Mistress." Her smile grew a bit sly. "Did you also . . . want to see me, maybe?"

I chuckled. "Of course, how could I resist checking in on my favorite minion?" I flicked my eyes to the side. "Especially now that I have this one to deal with."

"Nyeeeh!" Electra stuck out her tongue.

"How have things been?" I asked Rel.

"It has only been a day, my lady." Rel tilted her head. "But the changes you made were well received. The new managers are all well liked, and they care about making sure their crews get the right materials." She huffed. "And the right pay. Don't worry, though, Ishanti and I have them well in hand."

I nodded slowly at that. Creating managers, along with a simple paperwork system, was necessary to keep things running while I was away. Of course, if I knew one thing about bureaucracy, it was that it would be completely entrenched by the time I got back to Lady's Port, and it would answer first to Rel and Ishanti, if only because they were the two actually managing it.

"That's . . . good," I said. "I trust you."

Rel smiled wider. "I won't let you down, Mistress."

I laughed. "I know you won't. I trust you." I knew I'd just said that, but it bore repeating.

Especially when I was telling it to myself.

"In any case," I continued, "I'm glad to hear that things are working well. I'm not sure how often I'll be able to contact you once we're in Silverwall, but I'll do my best to stay in touch."

"You don't have to call about only business, my lady." Rel bit her lip, looking to the side. "It would be nice just to hear from you."

I smiled, and a knot of tension in my chest eased. "I'll see about adding a . . . nightly call . . . to my schedule."

"Thank you!"

I gave a little wave and a goodbye before shutting the mirror with a flick of my wrist.

"Looks like you miss her already."

I looked over to see Electra grinning at me.

I rubbed my face. "I'm worried."

She blinked. "About what?"

"About giving them so much power." I sighed. "They'll be the ones running things now. By the time we get back, all of the reports will go to them. It would be trivially easy for them to control what I see. Sure, I'd puzzle it out eventually, but . . ." I shook my head. "I think it's why I didn't want to share my workload before. I don't play nice with others."

Electra shrugged. "I mean, sure, but, like, would either of them do that? Ishanti's not gonna bite the hand that feeds her, and Rel is . . ."

"Is Rel," I finished. "I know, it's stupid and irrational, but I still worry, then I hate myself more for worrying."

"Why?" Electra asked.

I leaned forward, resting my forehead against my palm. "Because . . . because I used to think people trusted me, too, back when I worked at Aegis." I saw Electra's eyes widen before she schooled her expression. "Yes, I'm sure it was in my profile." I'd worked for the heroes before I'd started down the path of supervillainy.

"You don't talk about it much." Electra twiddled her thumbs, looking up at the ceiling. "Kinda figured I didn't wanna poke the elephant, you know?"

"I do." I sighed. "In any case, I thought people trusted me, and then I realized that it's not trust when one side holds all the power." I turned the mirror over in my hands. "I've trusted Rel once before, and it worked out. I . . . I *hate* that I'm worried about trusting her again."

"Or maybe you're just worried?" Electra waved a hand. "In any case, we all worry about stuff, Em'. One good choice doesn't just erase a lifetime of issues."

I huffed. "No, I guess it doesn't." I raised an eyebrow at the blonde. "And what else did your company-mandated therapist tell you when you were lost and full of doubt?"

But the hero just smiled at my dig, leaning back on the stack of coffins. "Keep trying to make the right choice, and eventually it'll all work out."

I looked back down at the mirror. I suppose it made a great deal of sense. Trust was not a single choice, after all.

"Yes," I said at length. "Yes, I believe I can do that."

CHAPTER 20

Eyes Turned Skyward

We'd stopped a ways from Silverwall in the predawn hours, so I could set one last plan into motion. Fortunately, my skill to summon demons was multitudinous in its application. While I could always pull out a hammer in the form of a horde of lesser demons, I'd found the best uses tended to be in the form of a scalpel.

The cart sat by the side of the road, while Electra and I were a dozen or so paces deeper into the jungle. The cloyingly thick foliage broke for a second at a ridgeline before plunging down towards the distant ocean.

"So, another day, another demon, Em?"

I glanced over to Electra with a fond smile. "Can you imagine ever saying something like that to me, back on Earth?"

"Oh, for *sure.*" She giggled. "It's just, you'd be the demon."

"And you the hero sent to banish me back to hell."

A wind blew in off the sea, lifting my hair behind me. I leaned into it, feeling the cool air caress my face.

"Last chance to back out," I said. "Everything up until this point can be argued away. Saving people from gang violence, creating an asylum for refugees, growing a technology base so that you could get back home. All of that is well within the purview of a hero." I spread my arms. "But now, we're about to attack the head of a foreign polity on its own soil. No amount of fast talking will make that mark disappear from your record."

Electra gave an easy shrug. "In for a penny, in for a pound, right?" She folded her hands behind her head. "Besides, I'm starting to get it now."

I raised an eyebrow. "Get what?"

"Why you tear it all down," she said.

I chuckled. "Careful." I knelt, pressing my hand against the soil. "Don't let your boss hear you talking like that."

"You know, I'd be more worried, but it feels like we're not gonna be going home for a very long time."

"In for a penny," I repeated, "in for a pound."

I took a deep breath, activating my summoning skill.

Like I'd realized before, my magic was built around preparation and support. In the heat of the moment, I would be stuck with whatever demon I could convince to come out and lend a tentacle in return for what I was offering. Really, it wasn't any surprise that most young demonologists ended up bargaining away their souls.

When it came to direct combat power, I hadn't found anything better than my hobblefiends and blightbats. They were good for fodder and scouting, and anything more intelligent tended to want blood sacrifices or X number of virgins or some nonsense. Blood demons, not the nicest people in the world.

Not the worst, though!

"God, why does it feel like you're thinking something really evil right now, Em'?"

I smirked at Electra's question. "Because I am." Slowly, the ground beneath my hand began to glow red, expanding outward like ripples in a still pond. The circle grew and grew until it encompassed the entire clearing, waves of flickering light growing higher and higher until they looked like waves of blood in truth.

"You're . . . *not* actually summoning some evil city-killing demons, right?" Electra asked.

"Of course not." I shook my head. "Assholes like that expect payment upfront, and then they'll go and eat the entire city anyway." My smile grew wider. "Now, demons that don't like fighting? That just want a few days out in the real world in exchange for some easy work where nothing is trying to kill them?" My cute little lumpy baby coal imps came to mind, or my gryphon, or my jellyfish harvesters. "Well, you'd be surprised what you can do with a little ingenuity and a *lot* of preparation."

The glow turned a deep red, and for a second it felt like we were sinking beneath the waves.

"Starting to feel like a blood sacrifice here, Empress . . ."

"Don't be ridiculous," I said. The circle flashed once, as something *other* tore its way into this reality. "I would have tied you down first."

Electra looked up and *up* at my newest friend. She tilted her head. "It kinda looks like a space skywhale."

I stood up, dusting off my palms. "Skywhale, maybe, but essentially that's what it is."

"*Groouoo . . .*" my new skywhale crooned softly.

It was large, big enough to take up most of the ten-meter clearing. It had a curved underside, like a blue whale, and two large, almost wing-like flippers. Its skin, though, was pale and clear, like a vase filled with murky liquid. In its depths I saw flickers of constellations, patterns that pulsed in some facsimile of a heartbeat, hidden by the light of day. Really, more than anything else, the beasty looked green, since its skin took on the hue of the jungle canopy behind it.

It craned its elongated neck down towards us, as if it was looking at us with its eyeless face. A wide mouth gaped open. "*Gruuuoooo . . .* "

I giggled. "Oh, Llen would just have a field day with you."

"He looks . . . happy to see us?" Electra said. She tilted her head. "We're a bit far from the ocean, though."

"*Gruooouuu . . .*"

I patted the side of his neck. "Don't worry, big guy; we'll get you moving soon enough. First, just hold out one of those fins for me, will you?"

It bobbed its head, holding out a long fin at its side. It had to keep it folded or it would have knocked over a stand of dense green palms that ringed the clearing. With a hum, I wandered over, pulling a harness out of my bag. Well, I said harness, but really it was just a few lengths of leather with a complicated mount on the bottom. I threw it over his big old fin where it met his translucent torso.

"Empress, are we really gonna cart this big boy down to the ocean?" Electra asked.

"Look, can you just stop asking questions and help me get this part set up?" I replied. "We don't have all day."

"Ugh, whatever." She hopped over to the other side of the fin, and we quickly got the harness strapped into place. The rest of the leather assembly hung down from beneath his fin in a mess of straps and buckles, but we weren't quite there yet.

Finally, I took out a compact cylinder from my bag, about as thick and long as my own head, and slotted a backup communication mirror into the top of that. It snapped securely into place. I'd designed it with this special mirror in mind. It was one of Maarin's extra-strength ones, but built to my *exacting* specifications.

It had to match the final lens perfectly, after all.

With that, I slotted it gently into the harness dangling from the demon's wing. As long as he kept his wing out straight, the harness would keep it snug and steady.

"Alright." I patted him one last time. "Off you go."

"*Grooooooo!*"

"It's just gonna walk all the way out to the sea by itself?" Electra asked for the third time.

In front of us, the demon shifted, planting two more muscular limbs beneath itself and folding its fins—gently—against its torso.

"Why, Elenore." I took a step backwards. "Whoever said anything about the sea?"

"*GroooOOOOUU!*"

It jumped, casting itself into the air with a rush of wind that sent us both staggering backwards. The moment the beasty cleared the canopy, it spread its fins wide, catching the currents and slowly but surely winging its way higher. In under a minute, it vanished into the sky above, its translucent skin blending perfectly with the unbroken blue.

"Now for the moment of truth," I said. I pulled the matching communication mirror out of the bag. I flipped it open, activating the enchantment.

The screen lit up with the image of two women standing in the middle of a forest clearing, one black-haired and one blonde. The black-haired one was holding something in her hand.

"Fuck yes!" I pumped a fist in the air. "I *knew* I got the magnification right!"

Electra craned her head over the mirror, and the Electra in the mirror did the same. "Um, Em', what the heck is that?"

I grinned. "During the Renaissance, Sir Isaac Newton invented a telescope that was able to magnify up to forty times, while staying small enough to sit comfortably on his desk," I said. "While everyone else was obsessed with making longer and longer tubes with more glass lenses, Newton made one that used burnished copper mirrors."

Electra's eyes widened. "Copper like we've been buying by the shipload."

"Useful for more than just wire." I laughed, punching the air again. "How's *that* for standing on the shoulders of giants!"

"But how does it work with the mirror?"

"Well, obviously I didn't make my little telescope times-forty or anything. I just want a clear picture of the ground, not this solar system." I waved a hand. "So I added an actual glass lens that *flips* the light, then projects it onto the concave mirror I stuck in the top of the telescope. Add in a bit of enchantment to make sure it all stays perfectly aligned—because believe me, figuring out that part was a *bitch*—and *voilà*." I held out my brand-new spy mirror. "I Mac-Gyvered us up a drone."

"Oh."

Electra looked like she was still catching up, so I decided to spell it out for her.

"My new friend here is some kind of filter feeder. It flies through the air all day and subsists off of mana microorganisms in the sky or something. It'll follow us to Silverwall, then stay floating above the city, giving us our very own eye in the sky."

Her eyes widened. "We'll be able to see the inner city before trying to break in!"

"More than that," I said. "With this we can plot out guard patrols, find areas that are less frequented to hide in, *and* if we're lucky, we'll even be able to find Seneschal Hawkwright if he sets foot outside."

"Oh," she said again. She turned back towards the mirror, which was still showing a somewhat smaller but still recognizable image of the two of us standing in the jungle clearing. At the edge of the mirror, I could even make out part of our wagon on the road. "I'm beginning to understand why people didn't like picking fights with the U.S., you know, before supers started popping up."

"Well, I mean, mine doesn't shoot missiles." I waved a hand. "Maybe next generation. Then I can sell it to overseas investors in exchange for preferential oil rights."

Electra rolled her eyes at me. "Hey now, *you're* the one who's trying to depose the head of a country to get a new figurehead installed in his place."

"He's just the Seneschal of a city," I said. "Hardly even a head of state."

"Feels like you're kinda missing the point here, Em'."

I sniffed. "Well, he bombed me first."

The Hearse Right Here

In the mirror, I watched a wagon covered in a dusty white tarp wind itself down the cracked clay road. My viewpoint would fly over the wagon before looping back around. The commanding view was only cut by the thick canopy of green flanking the raised berm of the roadway.

"Now I finally know what it feels like to be the United States of America," I said.

Electra pulled her head back into the cart. "You already made a drone joke," she said. "Still, I can't believe the thing is invisible."

"How else would it survive hell?" I waved a hand. "They're the magical equivalent of herbivores, so their best defense is not to get caught at all."

"So they just eat magic?" Electra asked.

"Well, it *is* hell, so they also eat smaller demons that happen to wander into their jaws." I smirked. "Never turn down a free lunch."

"I thought there was no such thing as a free lunch?" Electra asked.

"Sure there is," I said. "Just make something else pay the price."

"Like what?"

"Here." I waved a hand, summoning a little off-white ball of fluff and pushing it over towards Electra. "I have no idea what this demon is called; it's basically a floating cotton swab."

"*Pruuuuu . . .*" The barely sentient ball of cotton warbled as it bounced off Electra's stomach. It started to float towards the back of the cart as its momentum wore off, before Electra scooped it up.

"Aww, isn't it just the cutest?" She hugged it to her chest. "This thing isn't secretly going to give me demon cancer or something, right, Em'?"

"No, it's basically a magical piece of plankton," I said. "They float around on the mana currents in hell, subsisting on . . . hot takes and bad vibes, or something equally asinine, until something with a mouth comes by and gobbles them up. They're a favorite food of the invisible skywhale."

"Is that what we're calling them now?" Electra smooshed the little cotton ball in her hands, then began stretching it. It continued to squeak in her grip without expressing anything approaching distress.

"I mean, do you have a better name?"

"I liked space whale," she replied. "Slick, evocative, a real A-plus, like my PR team would have told me." She gave a laugh. "I didn't get a lot of A-pluses, you know?"

"Make the corporate drones earn their salary," I replied. "They were the ones who signed up to manage superheroes."

She giggled again. "And I guess you felt the same way back when you were a corporate drone working for Aegis?"

I shook my head. "I was in accounting."

"Gotta use that big brain for something."

"Yeah." I leaned back on my bench. "Like figuring out how much the CEO was underpaying me to afford her second yacht."

"Oof." Electra gave a sympathetic wince. "Is that why you went all evil?"

"Don't be ridiculous." I waved off her concern. "They were actually paying over market rate; their dividends were just better. It took more than the communist manifesto and some back-of-the-napkin math to push me over the deep end."

Electra sat down on her bench, still holding the cotton ball to her chest. "You never did mention why you quit."

"I got canned, actually, towards the end of the whole Cipher incident."

She blinked once, before her eyes widened. "Oh!"

"Yeah." I nodded. "Not to say I wasn't getting into some trouble before that; I had family problems that I thought were unrelated, but it turned out . . ."

"Am I about to get the whole scoop?" Electra leaned forward. "They say your file is so classified that only Wonderman has access to the unredacted version!"

I shoved her. "Stop treating my tragic backstory like a corny prequel movie."

"Right, sorry."

"Literally the worst." I rolled my eyes. "My younger brother got caught up in the whole Red Diamonds mess, and I had to do some things to bail him out."

"And that's when you found out that . . ."

"I'd rather not talk about the rest, if it's all the same." I tried for a laid-back smile, but the old wounds still stung, even after all this time. "Gotta save some material for my memoires."

Electra laughed, but the unanswered question continued to hang in the air between us, stifling any further conversation until we made it to the final stretch of road before Silverwall. When the sound of the wheels switched to cobble, that was our cue to hop into the coffins.

The inside of the simple wooden boxes was unfurnished except for the lacquer—and they weren't pine either—but hopefully the stack of unalive boxes would be our ticket past the outer gate.

"See you on the other side!" Electra said. Then she pulled the lid of her coffin shut, and I did the same. In the darkness, I heard the sound of wood on wood as Dee hopped into the wagon to stack some of the other coffins on top of our own. Given that the guards could see our classes if they could get a look at us, this type of subterfuge was necessary, even if it wouldn't stand up to a thorough inspection.

"'Ey there, 'Loncio!" I heard Dee call.

"Never thought I'd see the day when *you* boneheads went straight," came the answering reply.

How fortunate, I thought, that we weren't going to have a thorough inspection.

I let out a breath as the cart slowed to a stop. Dee and Dum exchanged a few words with the gate guards before their friend in the guard, Eloncio, hopped into the back of the wagon to check the merchandise. From what the boys had told me, Eloncio was another one of Mama's orphans. The matron had apparently helped raise half the street rats in Silverwall, and she did her best to get them into some kind of paying work, on either side of the law.

Eloncio made a show of shuffling through the coffins as he checked them; I could tell by the sounds he made. Before long though, he hopped out of the cart with a 'looks good enough to me,' and the rest of the guards waved us through without another word.

"When you get off your shift, 'Loncio?" Dum asked. "I'll buy you a pint, for old time's sake!"

"Eh, long day today," came the reply. "Check in at the Winking Rodent, usually go there when I'm feeling like slumming it."

"That shithole didn't burn down?"

"Not yet!"

And then we were through the gate.

Past the thick wall, the sounds of the city rose up around us. It sounded much the same as it had before we left. Were the people more worried? How the hell was I supposed to tell? The only time a crowd sounded different was when they started chanting in unison, and at that point, you usually had bigger problems.

The cart slowly trundled down the main thoroughfare of the city in fits and starts. Silverwall still utterly dwarfed Lady's Port in size. If the shadowy Seneschal mobilized the population—hell, even if he just turned out the guard—he could easily march to Lady's Port in two days, perhaps only one if he pushed it, and overran us with pure numbers.

In that regard, the jungle worked to *our* advantage rather than our opponents'. The road was wide enough for two wagons to squeak past each other, if you were wary of the slope, but mustering a thousand men and marching them down that road? It would not be particularly quick going, and as I'd just discovered, you'd be surrounded by the jungle on all sides, with who knows what waiting out of sight. More and more, I was beginning to realize *why* the northern part of Vecorvia was so isolated. It was just simply easier for the capital to leave Silverwall to its own affairs, unless things grew so out of control that they *needed* to march an army north through the dense, monster-filled jungle.

No wonder one of those ever-distant continental powers never managed to conquer this little tropical 'paradise.'

I was drawn from my thoughts as we pulled off the main road and away from the crowd and voices. The ride grew progressively bumpier as we took twists and turns deeper into the city, until I found myself bracing my arms against the walls of the coffin. Fortunately, I wouldn't have to ride the stupid box out of Silverwall.

At least, not if I was alive.

I let out a breath of relief as the wagon came to a final stop. I heard voices, some money changing hands, and then finally—*finally*—Dee and Dum pulled the rest of the coffins off of mine and let Electra and me out of our erstwhile ride.

"Finally." I sucked in a breath of . . . slightly fresher air as I hopped out of the cart and into the stables. "Felt like I was riding to my own funeral."

"I'm surprised you never pulled that trick off, actually," Electra said. She mussed her hair, but it was getting a bit long to spring back into its usual spikes. "The funeral thing, I mean."

I smirked. "It's on my bucket list." I glanced around the dingy set of stalls we found ourselves in. "So where are we, anyway?"

"The Winkin' Rodent," Dee said. "Figured we'd meet 'Loncio here and talk about our next move."

I eyed him. "You really trust Eloncio, huh?"

Dum shrugged. "He's one 'o Mama's. We do right by each other."

Dee chuckled. "When we can."

"When we can."

I shrugged. "I've trusted worse people for worse reasons," I said. "Let's go inside, though . . ." I glanced at the rest of the Winking Rodent inn. "Maybe we should stay away from the food and drink."

"Awww." Dum shuffled his feet, trying his best to look like a petulant child despite his hulking six-foot-five frame. "Why? I heard they dun even put rats in the stills no more."

I pinched my nose. "On second thought, it's an order. We're going somewhere else for food."

"Thank god for that," Electra said.

Dee and Dum grumbled but followed the two of us dutifully into the inn itself.

They say never judge a book by its cover, but in this case, the cover really did tell the whole story. The inside of the inn was just as ratty and rundown as the outside, with uneven floorboards and rickety, splintering tables. Electra stumbled when her foot caught a buckled timber.

I grabbed her by the arm before she ate a mouthful of splinters. "Try not to make a fool of us before you even open your mouth."

She pushed herself to her feet. "Knew you cared, Em'."

"That's not—" I shook my head. "Whatever, let's just grab a table."

There was a surfeit to choose from, as the only patrons of the Winking Rodent were a drunk snoring over by a battered bar and a mangy dog snoring even louder next to a cold stone hearth set into the far wall.

"On second thought," I said, "Dee, Dum, see if you can't find some chairs that will hold you up first, *then* we can all take a seat."

It took some doing, and some shuffling around, but eventually we were all seated at a table near the bar. I would have argued for closer to the dog, but I was clearly outvoted in this instance. The innkeeper wandered out of the back room.

He sized us up with two beady eyes. "Drinks?"

Dee and Dum turned their most ferocious pouts on me again.

"Ugh, fine." I waved a hand. "One round for each of you, and pay for it yourself. I'm not covering beer expenses."

Lady's Port was . . . solvent, but only because internally I controlled all the resources, and up until I left, I'd been essentially paying people in company scrip.

At least one good thing would come of setting up a bureaucracy.

Dee and Dum settled down with their big pints of beer—a dive like this had to have *some* selling point—and eventually Electra and I caved and bought some bread and cheese. It wasn't the worst meal I'd ever eaten, and that was about all I could say for it.

From time to time, I would check my mirror, taking in the flow of people on the streets of Silverwall. My 'skywhale' was gliding high enough above that I couldn't pick out individuals anymore, but it gave me what I needed most: an overview.

If I looked closely enough, I could even see where my old, burned-out warehouse still sat, alone and abandoned, right in the middle of the old docks.

I smiled. It was always nice to come back to an old friend.

At length, Eloncio finally showed up, sharing a quick round of greetings with the boys and grabbing a beer of his own before taking a seat.

He took a massive gulp of the frothy brew, before pulling a face. "Ain't the same since they started fishin' the rats out."

I saw why they got along.

CHAPTER 22

Just Business

After the boys and Eloncio worked their way through another round of truly atrocious beer, we finally got down to brass tacks.

"What can you tell me about the city?" I asked.

Eloncio shrugged. "'Bout the same as always, just worse."

I nodded. One didn't co-opt a bunch of disgraced former adventurers if things were going great at home. "Can you elaborate on that?"

"Lots more patrols." He cracked a lazy smile. "Captain Maria wasn't too happy you gave her the slip."

"Pity," I replied.

"She cracked down on a lotta the gangs dockside. Closed the old Miner's Gate too. Put a big squeeze on the little people." He took another swig of beer. "'Course, Arlo kept his nose right clean, nabbed up all he could when we cracked down on the other gangs."

"Bastard." I rolled my eyes. "He left me holding the bag for the Adventurer's Guild as well. It shouldn't surprise me that he did the same to everyone else."

"Told ya he was bad news, boss," Dum said.

"There, there." I patted him on a massive shoulder. "You most certainly did. Fortunately, we used him as well." I had a town of my own now, with working electricity and cell phones, so I thought the real winner was pretty clear.

He grinned happily, and I motioned for Eloncio to keep going.

"Not much else to say, after that," he told me. "The one-day riots hurt a lot of the guilds as well, 'course, but plenty got back on their feet." He finished off his beer with one long pull. "Lots outta work in the meantime, though."

"More recruits for the Tarnished." I drummed my fingers on the table. "I imagine he's the only game in town, at this point."

"More or less," Eloncio said.

Electra nudged me. "That's what happens when you work with criminals, Em'! You can never trust them to hold up their side of the bargain."

I rolled my eyes. "I'm a criminal, El."

"Yup." She giggled. "Though, in your case, you always end up going above and beyond."

I sighed. "I don't know if I should be pleased you have such a high opinion of me, or simply appalled." Electra just shrugged as I returned to the matter at hand. "What about the inner city? Do you get up there much, as a guard?"

"A time or two," Eloncio said. "Made second, after all, so sometimes I get to patrol around the fancy houses."

I raised an eyebrow. "I don't suppose you can just crack open a door for us?"

He shook his head. "Always a captain or higher running the important shit up there. Senny keeps 'em good and bought, too."

"Senny?" I tilted my head. "The Seneschal?"

Eloncio nodded. "Guard works for the Duchess, but we answer to Senny."

I hummed. "Well, I suppose it was too much to hope that we could simply buy our way in." I turned my gaze back to the guard. "Though, that does beg the question: why are you helping us?"

"Aww, don't be like that, boss." Dum leaned forward. "'Loncio's good people."

"I don't doubt it." Still, my gaze did not wander from Eloncio's face.

"Practically grew up together, me and your boys," he said. "Mama kept us all alive, and that's a debt worth more than gold."

I chuckled at that. "She's picked up a new crop of orphans who fled the city with us." And more that suffered from bandit raids and monster attacks. "You should come visit. I'm sure she'd love to see you."

He gave a wan smile. "Might be hard."

"Yes," I said. "And that brings me to my last question. Why were we able to get into the city so easily?"

"Lady's Port don't exist, far as Senny is concerned." Eloncio shrugged. "We search anyone coming up from the south, 'course."

"But it's hard to be at war if you can't even admit your casus belli . . ." I stroked my chin.

"Casa's belly?" Electra asked. "I don't remember that from high school Spanish."

I flicked her on the nose. "Stop being obtuse," I said. "Anyway, it's just another reason that the Seneschal is trying to take care of this in the shadows, which means we will be better served by doing the opposite."

Eloncio raised an eyebrow. "And what's that?"

I smirked. "We're going to blow this little shadow war wide open." I turned my gaze towards the window, where a second wall with silver crenelations was visible in the distance. "If we're lucky, maybe we can catch a few more . . . physical objects in the explosion."

Dee chuckled. "Been a while since we lit something good and on fire."

"Okay, but seriously," Electra said. "What's this Kansas berry stuff?"

I fixed her with a withering glare.

"What?"

Thankfully, I was saved from answering when the door to the inn flew open. It hit the wall hard enough that one of the boards splintered off, hitting the dirt floor with a muted thud.

The five of us glanced over in unison as a small group of men and women walked into the room. I counted ten in all, each one with a metal band wrapped around their upper arms.

"Speaking of Arlo's Tarnished," I murmured. I turned towards my two hulking brutes and their guardsman friend. "None of you are particularly inconspicuous." Over by the bar, I saw the innkeeper peek out of the back room before wisely making himself scarce.

"Ah." Eloncio nodded. "Probably caught wind of me when I started heading down."

With a sigh, I pushed myself to my feet, throwing my cloak over my shoulder so that the smooth panels of my power armor were on full display.

I wasn't the only one with some obviously enchanted equipment, though. The leader of this little squad had a craggy mace in his grip, made of black stone that glistened like a soap bubble. I didn't know what it did, but safe bet was you didn't want to get hit by it.

"Gentlemen." I glanced over the group. "Ladies. To what do I owe the pleasure of this visit?"

The head thug blinked. "What?"

I snorted, looking over my shoulder. "Hey, Electra! Found someone you can talk about casus belli with."

She pouted. "That's not very nice. I thought we were friends!"

"I never said I was a very good friend," I said. "In fact—"

"Oi!" The man took a heavy step forward. "The fuck are you on about?"

"Oh, sorry." I turned back in his direction. "I thought you were going to be staring off into space for another minute." I smirked. "You seem like the type."

Electra giggled behind me. "Empress! You're *embarrassing* him."

I waved her off. "NPCs don't feel emotions."

The man took another step within arm's reach, raising his club to his shoulder. "Listen here, you—"

I placed a hand on his chest, fingers wreathed in the shadowy magic of my Demon-itize spell. "It's been a while since I've used this skill." I smiled up at him. "Want to help me remember how it works?"

He paused, swallowing heavily.

"Now then," I continued. "Why don't you tell me why you're here? Use small words, I'm sure that's your strong suit."

"Um."

One of the women behind him snorted. "Sunken hells, Creeg."

The now-named Creeg worked his jaw silently. I couldn't exactly see behind him—clearly the only muscle he didn't exercise was the one between his ears—but I heard when another man stepped forward. "We got a message from the boss," he said. "How's about you let Creeg go, and we can give it over?"

I raised an eyebrow up at Creeg. "How many men does it take to send a message?"

"I don't . . . know?"

I sighed. "At a certain point it's not even fun anymore," I said. "I'm saying that I can kill you and still get a message just as well, moron. Get with the program here?"

"If you kill him, we'll rip you to pieces," the woman said. It was really annoying not being able to see these people. Creeg's broad shoulders and barrel chest took up essentially my entire field of view. I don't know why he chose to wear only pants, but ostensibly it had something to do with the tropical heat.

"How about this then: you give me whatever this 'message' is, and *then* I'll let your friend go."

There was a moment's pause, during which Electra and the boys pushed themselves to their feet.

Creeg looked increasingly uncomfortable, which really did show how long it took thoughts to penetrate his skull.

"Or," I said, "I can blow him up and we can skip to the part where we fight to the death?" I grinned up at Creeg. "If you're all so eager."

"Arlo wants a meetin' with ya!" he blurted out.

"There, was that so hard?" I raised a finger as he opened his mouth. "No, don't answer that. Better question is, why are you all here, then?"

I heard an awkward shuffle. "We're . . . supposed to make sure you come quietly," the woman said.

I smirked. "And how's that working out for you?"

"We can still kill you all," the man said. "If you think you're hard enough."

I shook my head. "No, see, I've done this song and dance with your boss before. I have better things to do than pander to his ego."

"You don't—"

I hauled back my arm, servos whirring. Then I slammed my fist into Creeg's sternum so hard I felt a rib crack. He flew backwards, almost taking out the woman as he hit the ground in a tangle of limbs.

I caught his fancy hammer out of the air before it could hit the ground.

"So here's a message for my old friend Arlo." I rested the hammer on my shoulder in a copy of Creeg's stance. My other hand still held my

Demon-itize skill like a shadowy glove. "If he wants to talk so bad, he can come here, tomorrow, without the whole goon squad. Then we'll talk."

The man and woman, both with weapons that looked a great deal less important than my shiny new mace, shared a long look.

"*Or*," I said, "you can try to take us out, now that we're ready for you, after you've already lost your trump card." I spun the mace once in my grip. "If you think you're *hard* enough."

On the ground, Creeg wheezed.

The woman ran a hand through her short brown hair. "Uh, yeah, we'll just . . ." She pointed down at the gasping man. "Take him and go."

I smiled at them. "Oh, by all means! I wouldn't want to be *unreasonable.*"

I watched silently as two of them hauled Creeg's hulking form up by his armpits and dragged him from the Winking Rodent. The battered old door creaked shut behind them with a note of quiet finality.

With a nod, I tapped the mace against my shoulder once again. The handle felt cold even through the material of my glove. I released my skill before checking my spy mirror. The skywhale was a little higher up than before, but I'd told it to stay above me most of the time. I watched idly as the group of Tarnished thugs retreated down the twisting road-ways of the south side of town. It looked like they were heading back to the old docks, which would make sense if Arlo still had his base in the area.

I flicked the mirror shut, slipping it back into my utility belt. Then I turned back to the table. Eloncio, I noticed, was still sitting, even though Electra and my boys were on their feet. I made no mention of it as I returned to my seat, a dozen schemes bubbling away at the back of my head.

"Now then." I smiled. "It looks like I have more business to take care of in Silverwall than I thought."

And I did so hate *unfinished* business.

CHAPTER 23

Call Me Maybe

We moved to a different inn after the Tarnished crashed our party.

The boys got two rooms for our little group, and Electra and I took the one with a window we could jump out of. Hopefully things wouldn't come to that, but as they said, it wasn't paranoia if they really were out to get you.

Electra poked one of the ratty, straw-filled mattresses as we entered the room. "Don't suppose you have a waterbed in that utility belt of yours." She pulled a face. "Or some Raid."

"Forget that." I took a step forward and the floor creaked beneath my foot. "I'm worried that I'm about to fall through the floor. The place is not rated for power armor."

"Speaking of, Empress, why haven't you been wearing it, like, every day?" Electra asked.

"I need to be smart and flexible." I smirked. "Power armor slows you down, no matter how well made."

She tilted her head "Then why break it out now?"

"Sometimes, life needs you to be smart and flexible, like a consummate mastermind." My armor whirred as I raised my gauntleted fist. "And sometimes it needs a bit of good old-fashioned *brutality*."

Electra giggled. "God, you're such a giant ham."

I sighed. "Everyone's a critic."

Electra gave the mattress one last suspicious look before straightening up and examining the rest of the room. "Well, I'm gonna get this place set up in case we get jumped." She gave me a sneaky grin. "Don't you have a call to make?"

I frowned. "I'm not in the habit of micromanaging . . ."

Electra burst out laughing. "Em', you've been micromanaging liter-ally *everyone* for months now."

My scowl deepened. "That's hardly fair."

"We kicked you out of town so you could take a vacation." She kept snickering. "We're literally on a vacation so you can execute a villainous scheme. Because infiltrating a city is better for your blood pressure."

I felt my cheeks growing hot. "I don't see how—"

"Gosh darn it, Empress. Call the girl already."

I huffed. "Fine. Just don't forget to bar the door."

She dragged the lone chair over, jamming it under the handle with a pointed look.

I turned and walked to the corner, pulling my own communication mirror out from my pocket and flipping it open.

I felt the casing of the mirror grow warm for a moment as the enchantment activated, communicating with its twin all the way back in Lady's Port. Maarin was already earning his salary.

After a moment, the darkened surface of the mirror resolved into Relia's face. Her eyes lit up as she saw me, and I found myself smiling despite myself.

"Mistress! You made it into the city?"

I nodded. "Our old friends in the Tarnished gave us some trouble, but it looks like no one else is expecting us."

Rel frowned. "Trouble?"

"Arlo wants to have a meeting so he can threaten to expose me to the law, try to browbeat me into compliance and demand repayment for slights I never committed." I waved my hand. "You know, the usual."

Rel's face twisted into a frown, eyes flashing. "Do I need to send more people?"

I sighed. "I'm not here to start gang war two: electric boogaloo," I said. "Besides, don't you have your own problems?"

Rel mouthed 'electric boogaloo' before shaking her head. "Mistress, I would bear any burden for you."

"That doesn't answer my question."

"Things are difficult here, but Ishanti and I can make do with less." She paused, glancing away. "Give me a command and I will follow it."

I sighed. "Yes, because taking on more than I could chew wasn't the whole reason you all kicked me out of town."

"That's not . . ." She bit her lip. "I am poor at this."

"Running Lady's Port?" I raised an eyebrow. "I should hope not. It's your whole job description."

"Mistress—"

"Tell me how 'difficult' things are, Rel," I said. "Honestly, I've only been gone for a few days."

She let out a breath. "I'm bad at speaking over you, Mistress."

I let my lips curl up into a smile. "Well, maybe that's also part of your job description."

She let out a light laugh, ducking her head.

"Now, the town?"

"Yes, my lady." Her eyes flicked back towards the mirror. "Anything you ask."

I paused again, blinking even as she took in a steadying breath. "There were more bandits in the jungle than we anticipated," Relia said. I almost missed it, instead taking in her face as she looked off to the side. Her eyes were sharp, focused. "We rooted them all out, as I said, but many of them managed to scatter."

I focused back on the moment. "Scatter *where*? How much jungle is there on this island?"

"They didn't scatter into the jungle, Mistress." Rel shook her head, brown locks curling around the edge of a wry smile. "Many of them went back north . . ."

"Towards Silverwall." I bit my lip. "So we're stuck here."

"If they returned to the area around Silverwall, yes. They'll have blocked your retreat."

"And if not," I said, "they'd do so the moment Mr. Seneschal realizes I'm not in Silverwall, which will happen about five seconds after he checks in to give his deniable assets new orders."

"We figured out what some of those orders are, at least."

I raised an eyebrow. "Oh?"

Rel nodded. "There is a woman with golden eyes: she is in control of the bandits. Some of the men and women who surrendered said she is flighty and irrational, but stronger than she should be."

"Physically, or her class skills?"

"Yes," Rel replied.

"Great, exactly what we need." I rolled that thought over in my head. A golden-eyed woman, twitchy, probably sent directly from Silverwall. "But what makes her special . . . ?"

"Mistress."

I waved it away. "You said you've figured out their goals."

"It's like Llen suggested," she said. "They intend to send the migrating monsters south and overrun Lady's Port." She paused. "But more than that, we found cages."

I tilted my head. "They're catching monsters?"

"We freed several strongmaws and sent them running south, along with other monsters. They might be for use as bait . . ."

"Or they're catching them to release them all at once," I finished. Rel gave a grim nod. "They'll create a flood of monsters heading south, multiple waves even."

"The jungles are less dense in the northern parts of the island," Rel said. "There should not be as many monsters, according to Llen."

"Forgive me if I don't bet on that making the difference." I blew out a breath, leaning back on the straw mattress. "And even if it does, then a bunch of bandits can come mop us up just in time for some guardsmen from Silverwall to come down and restore order. Nice and deniable."

Rel looked down. "Yes. I've focused on finishing the outer wall, and making some simple earthworks, but we only have so many people."

"And not nearly as many combat classes," I said. "We managed to defeat them in detail because of the jungle, but that won't matter in a traditional . . . engagement . . ."

From the corner of my eye, I saw Rel looking at me quietly as my mind whirled. Of course, in a conventional fight, we were at severe disadvantage. How fortunate, then, that my opponent also didn't want to see this conflict escalate into a conventional war.

"Instead of moats and trenches . . ." I said. "How do you feel about hunting me some more hummingbirds?"

"Mistress?"

"Those glades are always so immaculate." I ran a finger along my chin. "Almost as if nothing wants to step inside."

Her eyes widened. "I'll speak with Llen about that idea immediately."

"You do that." My smile grew. "Also, I'm going to need you to march some men out into the jungle the day after tomorrow and have them camp there for a day."

". . . Where do they need to go?"

"Out of sight," I said. "But never far from mind. Just make sure they are seen on the road towards Silverwall."

She tilted her head.

"I just need some plausible deniability," I said. "That's all."

Rel blinked, then a small smile flickered across her face. "The Miner's Gate was shut, Mistress."

I examined my nails. "That's the thing about gates: you can always make a new one."

"Be careful, Mistress," Rel said. "You don't have many friends left in the city."

I smiled. "I'm sure I'm not the only one who wants a new gate. It will be nice to have something to talk about in my meeting tomorrow with Arlo." I stretched my arm over my head. "Now, unless there was something else, I think I need to get my beauty sleep."

I started to close the mirror.

"Lady Via!"

I paused. "What?" I tilted my head, opening the mirror again. "If there was something that important, you'd think you'd lead with that."

"I-I tried to!" She took a deep breath, hunching over herself. "I tried to, but I am not . . . good at this."

"At what?"

She swallowed. "I meant . . . what I said earlier, my lady," Rel said. "Give me the command and I will obey." She rested the tips of her fingers against the mirror. "Order me to reach through this mirror and touch you, and I will be there."

One thought filled my mind to the exclusion of all else.

"You've been reading Ishanti's books."

Rel's face turned a full, brilliant red. "I-I-I— Th-that's—"

I coughed into my other hand. "Anyway . . . that was a bit direct, but—"

"I was told to be direct!" she shouted.

"If you were told—" I stopped. "Relia."

She continued meeting my gaze, flushing bright and brilliant red. "I meant what I said." She let out a breath. "Mistress, I . . ."

She looked down, shoulders wiggling.

I slowly raised my other hand to pinch the bridge of my nose. I felt almost dizzy, pulse rushing in my veins.

"I . . ." I stopped, words failing me. After a moment, I tried again. "Why did you wait until I was halfway across the island?"

"You were so busy! I didn't want to add more difficulties . . ."

"I . . ." I shook my head, heart beating rapidly in my chest. "I have . . ." My thoughts sputtered in circles.

In the mirror, Rel's face slowly crumpled.

"I am sorry, my lady, for overstepping."

"Rel, wait that's not what—"

The mirror went dark in my hands.

I stared at my own reflection. For some reason, it felt so much more accusatory than staring at a blank screen.

"This is why I never fucking FaceTime."

There was a creak as Electra opened the door, peeking her head inside. I had a moment to take in the wide grin on her face. "Sooooooo? How'd it go?"

I was on my feet in an instant. In one stride I'd crossed the room, gauntlet clamping down on Electra's shoulder like a vice.

She blinked as I dragged her through the doorway and shoved her against the wall. "Uh, that bad, huh?"

"*You* were the one who told her to hit on me?"

Electra shifted in my grip. "I . . . don't think that's a productive question."

"You idiot! I'm planning a revolution here. I'm building a city. I don't have *time* for this. *Madre de dios!* I haven't even—"

"What?" she asked. "You haven't been hit on before."

I shot her a withering glare. "Of course I've been hit on before, you imbecile. I've gotten enough dick pics to know not all men *should be so proud of their fucking package.*" I sucked in a deep breath before letting it out. "I just . . . haven't been in a serious relationship. Ever."

"Man, that's, like, super flipping depressing," Electra said.

"I'm twenty-two!" I shouted. "And I almost took over the world! Several times!"

"I think we're maybe getting a *teensy* bit off track here?" Electra took a long step to the side, away from my hand. "I noticed you didn't seem super upset that *Rel* was the one to ask you out."

I turned away, face hot. "That is not material."

"Yeah, like, I think you should maybe call her back, Em'."

I looked down at the communication mirror in my hand. ". . . Tomorrow."

"Oh *hell* no!" Electra stepped forward, pointing at me. "I'm not letting this devolve into some B-movie romance plot! You call her back right now, missy! If you're feeling messed up, just think of how bad *Rel* feels after you rejected her!"

"Oh, fuck me."

"I mean, isn't that kinda sorta, y'know, the end goal here?"

"Shut up." I flipped the mirror open. "It's my job to be the witty, smart one."

Electra sputtered. "Then what am I here for?"

"Comic relief."

The mirror lit up.

Relia was looking at me again, face carefully neutral. "Yes . . . my lady."

"Relia," I said. "Let's . . . have a talk. A real talk."

She sucked in a breath of air, looking up at me through her lashes with something that might have even been hope.

"I think I would like that . . . Mistress."

CHAPTER 24

Say My Name

We should talk," I said again.

I had some trouble coming up with the right words to express the odd, stretching and tightening *feeling* forming in my stomach.

It wasn't like I'd never been hit on before. Oh sure, after that whole debacle with Aegis Corp that catapulted me into my villain career, I'd had to block all of my socials. Prior, I'd gotten the same irregular stream of truly cringe DMs as any other woman on the internet, but . . . I'd just never received the attention of someone I . . .

Actually liked?

Cared about?

Appreciated in any way at all?

Okay, foibles of the internet aside, none of this was helping me quantify the emotions stewing inside me right now. That seemed like a problem.

"Mistress."

On reflex, I huffed. "You could at least call me Via, if you're coming onto me."

"Coming . . . on?" Rel asked.

"I mean, what else would you call it?" I shook my head. "Approaching someone over the phone, while they're in a different city no less? It's not kosher, you know, bad etiquette. And if I said 'yes' to your interest, what would we even do? I'm behind enemy lines; it's not like we could hop over to the coffee shop for a quick date. Not that there's even a coffee shop, because I'm so busy that I haven't even had time to invent coffee yet, but here we are, basically worlds apart! It's like you're asking me to be your girlfriend from a different school!"

"My lady." Rel blinked once, eyes slowly shuttering before opening again. "I do not think I understand what you're trying to say."

I bit my lip. "It's just . . . this is a first, okay?"

Rel's expression softened as a look of understanding crossed her face. "It is for me as well, Mistress."

". . . Why'd you have to wait until now?" I wasn't whining. Just because my voice was a little pitchy sometimes didn't mean I was whining when I asked a *perfectly* valid and reasonable question. "I wasn't lying when I said I was so busy right now."

"That's true; you've been very busy," Rel replied. She swallowed once, before her expression firmed again. "I'm sorry that I haven't been able to help more."

I let out a breath I hadn't realized that I'd been holding. "Well." I shrugged my shoulders. The movement was jerky, awkward. "You've helped a lot."

Honestly, I probably would have drowned under the paperwork if not for Rel. The fact that she and Ishanti had built a bureaucracy around me still—ugh, off topic. Focus. "Still," I said. "You understand why—"

"I understand that I have spent more time speaking with you now than I have in the past month while you were in Lady's Port." Rel swallowed. "I am sorry for interrupting, my lady, but it needs to be said. You have not had time for anything or anyone until now, when you have *left* the city."

I paused for a moment, then ran a hand down my face. "If you're going to talk back to me like that, you really should be using my name." It felt so weird having an argument with someone who was bowing and scraping to me. "Fine. I've been busy. Maybe even a little too busy, you know, a tad overstretched. But it's not like I'm less busy right now!"

"Yes, you are . . . Lady Via."

I groaned. "That's not better."

Rel shrugged, tugging on a lock of her brown hair. "I'm sorry, but neither is you putting off this conversation because you have to check projected crop yields again."

"Did I do that?"

"No," Rel said, "but I think it says something that you don't remember, Lady Via." She met my eyes. "You have spent a great deal of time assessing crop yields."

"Food is important," I said.

"Yes, but we cannot spend every minute eating."

"Well." I put on a smirk. "You clearly haven't met some people from back on *Earth*."

"Lady Via . . . please."

"Fine. Fine; I'll stay focused." I sighed. "I don't . . . fuck, I'm so bad at this. I'm not trying to ignore what you said I just— It's been a while, okay?"

"Yes." A smile curled at the edge of Rel's lips. I found myself looking at it. "You've been busy, Lady Via."

"Exactly." I let out a breath.

"You're less busy now, though," Rel continued. "Do you think you will have a lighter workload when you return to Lady's Port?"

I shook my head.

Rel sucked on her lower lip. "Also, Lady Via, I could not live with myself if something were to happen."

I said nothing for a long minute, chewing over what had been said. For once, words failed me.

After I didn't reply, Rel seemed to slump lower in the mirror. "You . . . can reject me, my lady. I know that I am hardly worthy to serve you, let alone—"

I shook my head, an almost convulsive motion.

". . . Lady Via?"

I looked back to the mirror. As mentioned once or twice, even if only in my own thoughts, my scruffy little minion had cleaned up into quite a respectable young woman. Her light brown eyes were wide and expressive, looking at me with an expression that sent my heart fluttering in my chest.

No one should be looking at me like that.

"How old even are you?" I hated that my voice came out closer to a whisper.

Rel tilted her head. She did that a lot. I liked the way it made her straight-cut bangs list across her forehead. "This year I will be nineteen summers?" she said, voice questioning.

I pressed a hand against my face. "It matters, okay. Don't . . . don't worry about it."

Nineteen? How was she turning nineteen? She'd been thin as a stick when I'd picked her up. Granted, she'd shot up a couple inches after I started feeding her and the boys better, but that wasn't the point.

"I'm just . . . so busy," I tried again. "But . . ."

"You spend so much time focusing on making sure everyone else in Lady's Port is taken care of," Rel said. "Would it really be such a crime to focus on something else for once?"

"If it was a crime, I'd already be on board."

Rel gave a short giggle. I sucked in my lip at the sound. "You claim that you were some kind of criminal, back on your world. I find it harder and harder to believe, Lady Via."

"Still with the Lady." I slapped my cheek once with my free hand. "Are you hitting on me or preparing high tea?"

"I shall . . . try to stop, if it means so much to you?"

"I should hope so." I nodded once, firming my expression. "I'm not interested in spending time with someone who constantly acts like my inferior, so you'll have to shape up."

"Oh . . ." Rel sagged again, before she took in my expression. "O-oh?"

"I have very high standards," I said. "Which is why things never work out, but . . ." I looked off to the side. "It . . . wouldn't be a crime if you called me more often to talk about things." I felt proud for keeping my voice so steady. "I wouldn't mind."

If nothing else, she was right that I had more free time now. How fucked was that? I'd been running myself so ragged I literally had more time to myself on a deep cover mission in a hostile city than I did in the seat of my own power.

What kind of villain didn't give herself time to enjoy the fruits of her victory?

"Maybe a change of pace . . . won't be so bad after all."

Rel smiled, eyes crinkling in a way that made me want to smile back. "I promise I won't disappoint you!"

I huffed, tossing my hair. "You'd better not." I fixed her with a sharp look. "If I get back and my town is burning down because you spent too long chatting with me . . ."

"That would never happen." Rel straightened, meeting my gaze head on. "I know how to delegate my duties, unlike some people."

"Hey." I scowled playfully. "Watch it."

"Of course . . ." Rel's smile shifted into something sly. "Anything for you . . . *Via*."

The screen went black, leaving me blinking at my own reflection a second later. "That bitch hung up on me!"

My head snapped up when Electra giggled. It was only then that I realized she'd never left the room after telling me to call Rel back.

I jumped to my feet, pointing a finger at her menacingly. "Not a word out of you!"

"Oh, not from me, no siree bob!" Electra giggled again. "*But, Rel, I'm so busy.*"

"I said not a word!"

"But *Via*," she simpered, "those are *your* words!"

I growled. Never mind that my conversation with Rel had been enough to boost my Little Mistress class up a whole level. The class was definitely a BDSM reference, but I could never let Electra know that.

Instead, I took a step towards her, floor creaking under me ominously. El had the temerity to laugh even louder.

"Oh but *Via*." She placed a hand against her mouth. "What will Rel think of you laying hands on another woman?"

"You know what they say." I grabbed her around the arms, power armored gauntlets clamping shut like manacles. "Out with the old."

"Em'?" She started squirming for real when I picked her up. "Empress?!"

"You know," I said as I took a step towards the window, "people always seem to forget how strong I am in my power armor."

CHAPTER 25

Dig Yourself a Hole

I did not end up throwing Electra out of the window.

Call me a puritan, but I tried not to throw away the people I actively needed in my schemes, because it set a bad precedent. Well, no, the bad precedent was already there. I just wanted to move past the generational villainess trauma that mandated I mistreat my underlings for no good reason.

"Where'd you even find this forking drill?" Electra muttered.

I bopped her on the back of the head, shooting another surge of electricity from my suit's battery into her skull. "Less talky, more drilly."

Instead, I mistreated them for perfectly valid and responsible reasons.

With a grumble, Electra got back to powering the electric drill I'd cobbled together. Now, when I said drill, I'm sure you pictured something that *I* would use, like a handheld drill for driving screws into pre-bored holes. No, this was a mining drill. The head was bigger than Electra's, and it was powered by running a charge through a tightly wound copper spool, forcing the drive shaft to spin.

Electra was using it to dig us a hole under the wall.

Not the fancy interior wall—too many guard patrols for that—but the outer wall. You'd think there would be guard patrols there too, but turns out if you burn down a good section of the old docks area and evict pretty much everyone else, you're left with a lot of buildings leaning up against the outer wall that make a perfect staging ground for a tunnel.

"How does it look?"

Electra glanced over her shoulder. "Are you sure you can squeeze through this?" she asked. "I mean, are you hecking sure *I* can squeeze through this, because these hips don't lie."

"Not without Photoshop, anyway." I rolled my eyes at her indignant 'hey!' "You're only breaking up the stone and loosening the soil. Our new friends will be digging the actual tunnel." I reached over, scratching the head of my newest demonic acquisition.

The dire mole, working name, came up to the middle of my thigh while it sat back on its haunches. It had a big mouth, full of grinding teeth for chewing on gravel, and two big, shovel-like mitts that it called paws. Really, with hair that was smooth on the surface and bushy and warm once you stuck your fingers into it, they would make *excellent* pets.

Once you got past the whole, you know, demon thing.

"And why am *I* the one drilling a hole when you have a bunch of hellbadgers to do it for me?"

"Language," I chided.

Electra sputtered, a clod of dirt flying into her open mouth before she spit it out. "Wh—am I supposed to call them, heckbadgers?"

"That might be better than dire mole, actually." They only looked like moles a little bit. They didn't have the weird tentacle nose thing, and they had eyes.

I gave the newly re-christened heckbadger another pat. "To answer your question, the reason I'm not having my friend the heckbadger or his buddies do it is because I'm afraid they'll start trying to eat the wall. And also since I don't offer pay in human souls, I have to be a bit more flexible in my agreements." I paused. "Actually, it's helping me level a decent amount too."

"Munchkinnery at its finest." Electra gave a happy nod. "At this rate you're going to unlock a third class and take out the whole city by yourself."

After she dislodged a big chunk of clay with the drill and pushed it out of the widening hole, a second heckbadger waddled over and started munching on it. That was the deal: they help me dig a hole, and in return they get lots of free food that they didn't have to excavate themselves.

Apparently, real-world soil is very mana nutritious.

"Don't sell yourself short." I flipped open my spy mirror, taking in a view of the city from above as my invisible cloud skimmer continued to circle. "I'd need you to power up my armor; the lack of proper charging infrastructure really is a wrench in my plans. Take a quick break; there's a patrol coming along the top of the wall, don't want them to feel any vibrations."

Electra pulled back, wiping the sweat from her brow. "This thing isn't that powerful, is it?" She shook the drill once, dirt cascading off it.

"Stone carries waves differently." I shrugged. "In any case, it's not worth the risk. They'll be past momentarily."

"Then maybe you can take a turn with the drill?" She held the handle, which, again, was little more than copper leads wrapped around a durable drive shaft.

"I already told you, I can't power it because it won't plug into my armor."

She huffed. "You're the one who's designing all this so-called infrastructure, why aren't you making it backwards compatible?"

I sighed. "One day, I'll sit down and explain replaceable parts to you, and why it was such a revolution in the process of industrialization."

She raised an eyebrow at me. "Why wouldn't screws be replaceable?"

"Why not"—I nodded to my slow friend—"why not indeed." But the only standardization in this fantasy world was when my family of forge imps decided to make all of one thing the same size. There was only so much I could do in such a short period of time.

Electra stared at me for a moment, to see if I was going to elaborate, before she shrugged. "Speaking of parts," she continued, wiggling her eyebrows, "what about yours and Rel's?"

I slapped a hand across my face. "That was a truly terrible segue."

"You're blushing!" I could hear the smirk in her voice. "You're really blushing, aren't you? That's so cute! Oh, I knew you two would be perfect for each other."

"I am *not* talking about this with you," I said.

Electra giggled. "Who else are you going to talk about it with, then? Or are you going to go over your feelings when you call Rel again tonight?"

I grumbled, glancing away. "I'm just . . . worried."

"Huh? Worried about what?"

"That this relationship will . . . get in the way." I looked back at the mirror. The patrol had passed our section of wall, but I didn't tell Electra to get back to work just yet. "I'm essentially the ruler of an enclave deep within hostile territory, engaged in a shadow war with my far more powerful neighbors."

"So, business as usual then," Electra said. "You know, for you."

I ignored her.

"I am just not . . . certain that I can be both the leader I need to be and a partner at the same time."

She snorted. "What are you, the female lead in a classic sci-fi?" She turned back to the hole. "They're gone, right?"

". . . Yes." I eyed the back of her head.

"You can be a girl boss and have a girlfriend, Em'." With a crackle of ozone, she powered up the drill again, blue lightning flicking off her sleeves as the head of the drill dug back into the earth. "It's not rocket science, and you *do* rocket science."

"I wasn't aware you were such a connoisseur of turn-of-the-millennium films."

She giggled again. "Wonderman *loves* them, oh, my god. Every time it's his turn for movie night he picks something from the aughts. It's, like, practically hilarious."

I folded my arms, returning the spy mirror back to the sealed pouch on my utility belt. "What would you suggest I do, then?"

"I mean, do you like her?"

I bit my lip. "I don't know that I like anybody."

"I mean, that's fine you know, if you're wired like that," Electra said. "But it kinda seems like you like her. She's your fav, right?"

"I don't have a favorite." I rolled my eyes.

"Suuuuuure."

"Fine." I huffed. "Out of all of you, Rel is definitely my favorite minion."

"I'm sure the boys will be crushed."

"Yes, well, I stole Dee and Dum from a rival gang after I killed their boss." I paused. "Actually, now that I think about it, they went along with me rather easily, in retrospect."

"Probably wasn't a very good boss?" Electra shrugged, dislodging a particularly nasty rock. Two of my three heckbadgers got into a tiny scuffle for it, but the one with red markings on his light brown coat came out victorious. "They had the chance to stab you in the back and didn't take it, y'know?"

"I do . . ." I sighed. "Thanks for reminding me to let them know where this tunnel is, once we find them again."

"Sure it's worth it?" she asked. "Their big ol' butts won't even fit!"

"Be that as it may." I paused, a part of me wanted to ignore the previous conversation. I'd been closer to death, over the course of my long career as a villain, but never so viscerally as when a noose drew tight—too tight—around my neck.

I rubbed beneath my jaw. Time had healed the bruises and rope marks, but it had not dulled the memory of the sensation.

"So . . . you're suggesting what, exactly?" I asked, returning to the previous topic. "Go with the flow? Let nature 'take its course' or some trite nonsense?"

The dirt beneath the wall shifted, allowing for a sliver of light to poke through from the far side of the wall. "There we go!" Electra leaned back, clambering out of the hole as she brushed the dirt from her hands. "I mean, would it be so bad to not have to be in control all the time?" She asked back. "Seems kinda exhausting."

"It's the only reason I'm still alive."

"Hey." She slugged me in the shoulder, before hissing, shaking out her hand.

I raised an eyebrow. "You forgot about the armor, didn't you?"

"I forgot about the armor." She rubbed her knuckles. "Anywho, you got friends now, don't you, Em'? You don't always need to be on top of everything!"

I sighed, gesturing for the heckbadgers to get started with the hole. "Maybe not."

"That's the spirit!" She slung an arm over my shoulders, and for once, I didn't feel the urge to shove her off a cliff into an erupting volcano. What can I say, Electra had that effect on people.

Together we watched as a trio of heckbadgers munched their way through the guide tunnel Electra had dug, widening it to the point that the two of us could easily crawl through.

"Well, no point in wasting time." I hopped down the slope, peering through the four-meter-long tunnel under the wall. The dirt was a bit loose, but we'd avoided the supports, so with any luck, it wouldn't catastrophically collapse while I was beneath a hundred tons of stone.

Electra could make her own way.

"But what about our heart-to-heart?" Electra followed after me. "We were, like, having character development or something."

"I prefer the development of my character to happen at the expense of someone else's," I replied. "So let's go see what Seneschal Hawkwright has in store for us, hidden away in his domain."

"You know," Electra said as she crawled through the passage after me. "That explains so much about you."

On the other side, we quickly dragged a few thick fronds over the mouth of the tunnel and covered it with underbrush. Exit successfully made, we quickly vanished into the jungle just before the next guard patrol rounded this section of the wall.

"So anyway, how are we gonna find where all those mercenaries are hiding?" Electra asked. "It's not a small island, you know."

I flicked out my spy mirror once again. "That's why we brought air superiority." Holding the mirror closer to my lips, I spoke again. "Circle inland and pass over any areas with high concentrations of people."

Electra let out a low whistle as the sky skimmer obeyed my command, winging away from Silverwall high above to scout our way to the target. "How'd he hear you? 'Cause I know the mirrors send sound, but isn't that taped to his belly or something?"

I smirked as my Safe Words skill leveled up again. It was incredibly useful, knowing that your orders would always reach their destination perfectly intact. "See, that's the thing," I said. "It's magic."

CHAPTER 26

Spawn Camping

The sound of snarls filled the air. Dozens of figures carried wood and water, fodder and food to an encampment much larger than any of the ones we'd found skulking around in my part of the jungle.

Spotting them had been child's play. The camp was like a wound when seen from above, a gash in the greenery that exposed the red soil of the northern part of the island. It was within easy walking distance of Silverwall, closer even than the lava tube mines that covered the volcanic plains only an hour north.

The reason for that was clear.

"That's a lot of people," Electra said.

I nodded. "And not just soldiers or mercenaries." They had people with the look of miners as well, cutting down trees or tending to cages. "It looks like I've finally provoked a real response."

Electra snorted. "Yeah, you think?"

"Still," I continued, "the thought of all of these monsters stampeding through my town all at once . . ." From the corner of my eye, I saw Electra shiver.

"Sounds like something you'd pull," she said.

"Once or twice."

I made a quick count of the cages. "It looks like they already have at least forty or fifty smaller monsters, like those strongmaws always lurking around the town."

"Over a dozen midsized ones as well." Electra shrugged. "Probably big enough to tear down a palisade if they get mad enough. Like, IDK, if they were all stuck together in boxes for the past month and a half."

Of course, neither of us had yet mentioned the elephant in the room.

With a bellowing roar, the walled cage at the center of the camp shook. It was made from wood and stone, maybe fifteen or twenty meters high, and I could still see the tips of the monster's spines as it tried to tear down the walls of its prison.

"I can't imagine they're planning to hold that for long," I said.

"Well, yeah, but this isn't really enough, is it?" Electra looked up and down the valley. The hill we stood on offered a commanding view of the camp, while its lush undergrowth kept us protected from prying eyes.

I turned back to my spy mirror. The skywhale had found this camp right away, but since then, it had circled over a few more sites that looked similar. "This is just the biggest one."

"Ah . . ." Electra glanced over at the mirror. "Well, heck."

"Look at the bright side." I flicked the case shut. "It looks like only this camp has a monster big enough to tear down a wall if it really gets going." I shook my head in disbelief, "*Dios mio*, how'd they even manage to catch it and keep it in place?"

Electra shaded her eyes. "I see chains." A small smile flickered over her features. "Not surprised that you missed them, down there."

"Ha-ha." I rolled my eyes. "Even from here I can see that's the same type of monster that chased me across the river when I went to catch that grove of poisonous hummingbirds. This one's almost as big, and it looks twice as mad."

I remembered my impressions from back then, all scales and spikes and *anger*. It was every child's picture of the biggest, meanest monster in the jungle, and pretty soon, it would be headed right for the town I'd built and all the people who lived there.

"You'd think it could follow you across a river, if it really wanted to."

"That would have been tricky," I said. "Fortunately, Llen told us that they're mostly just territorial. It stopped chasing the moment we got out of its range."

"Well . . ." Electra rubbed her chin. "If it's just territorial, why don't we let it defend its territory?"

I blinked, turning to look at her. "Electra, is that . . . your very first villainous scheme I hear?" She fidgeted, turning away even as a smile spread across my face. "Letting it out in the middle of the enemy's camp, actually quite a good idea."

"Stop." She rubbed the back of her neck. "I'm weak to earnest praise, you know!"

I reached up to pat her on the shoulder. "We'll make a proper villainess out of you yet."

"Like you wouldn't have thought of it," she replied.

"Actually," I said. "I was thinking something more along the lines of starting a forest fire and stampeding yet more monsters into the camp, sort of a poetic justice thing, if you will." I smiled. "Sometimes, though, simplest is best. How nice of them to build that enclosure at the edge of the camp for us."

"I mean, it *is* pretty loud, isn't it?" As if on cue, the monster roared again.

"It probably doesn't smell nice either. Still, that's our plan of action. Now just let me check some contingencies."

Electra smirked as I swapped the spy mirror for my long-distance communication one. "Want me to give you lovebirds some space?"

"If it means you'll stop being completely insufferable," I shot back.

She raised her hands in surrender. "I'll start scouting a way into the camp."

"You do that." I still waited until she was out of earshot to flip the communication mirror open. It was annoying that I had to carry so many, but I just hadn't had the time to set up a call center—or the manpower, for that matter. After I got back to Lady's Port, and we had enough mirrors for it to actually matter, however . . .

I left that train of thought behind as the mirror lightened, showing Rel's face. "Mistress!"

"Rel." I felt my lips pull into a soft smile, unbidden, before I schooled my expression. "I wish I had time for a social call, but I need to check in. Did you march some of our men into the jungle this morning like I asked?"

Rel nodded, a pleased smile spreading across her features. "We even found a small group sent to spy on us and took them out." She leaned a little closer to the mirror. "I made sure to miss the one who was running away with my knives."

"Excellent." I returned her smile. "They saw who was with you, though?" If Seneschal Hawkwright and the rest of Silverwall thought I was still in Lady's Port, I'd have to limit the skills I used in our attack.

"Actually, Mistress, we had someone dressed up as you."

"What?" I blinked. "Who?"

"Oh, I'm sure you know her," Rel said. "It was my little helper Elaine. Once we dressed her up as you, no one could tell the difference."

For a moment my mind stalled, before I remembered the little girl Rel had running errands for her, complete with a copy of Rel's distinctive hat. A little girl who couldn't have been more than fourteen years old and ninety pounds soaking wet.

Completely unacceptable.

"Rel." I fixed my minion and maybe more with my sharpest, sternest glare. "I do not approve of using children in that manner at all. In fact, I am very disappointed in you!"

Rel immediately tried to backpedal. "Mistress, she was completely safe. In fact we had—"

But it was too late.

"No!" I slashed a hand through the air. "This was beyond the pale, Rel." It took all I had to hold back from stomping my foot like a petulant child. "I'm *not* that short!"

"—guarding her and." Rel stopped speaking midsentence. "What was that?"

I was not pouting. It was a glare. I was very good at glares. "You heard me. I'm not that short! You shouldn't have to get a child to pretend to be me."

"She . . . has a class for it?" Rel said.

That was enough to make me pause. "She does?"

Rel nodded. "It's called Mini-me, and comes with a variety of disguise options." She flicked her eyes to the side, lips curling. "Though, when she pretended to be you, it wasn't very mini at all. So . . ."

"Relia!" This time I did stomp. "I'll get you for this."

Her smile widened. "I look forward to it, my Via."

I stopped again.

This time, Rel's panic was even more palpable, as her cheeks went bright red. "Ah, uh, only if such a title is . . . um, a-a-acceptable for you, my lady. If not—"

"Rel," I said.

"Yes, Lady Via."

"Just . . . give me a moment." I took a deep breath. "I won't lie; my first response was to tell you never to call me that again." It had been a knee-jerk reaction, but after seeing Rel start to wilt, I was glad I'd crushed it. "But we're trying new things here. Aaaaall about trying new things." I flashed her a smirk. "Preferably when I'm not about to assault an enemy base in the middle of the jungle. Understand?"

"Yes, Mistress."

"Good." I nodded. "You can try the nickname out again tonight. Sound good?"

"Yes, Mistress."

"Excellent." I winked at her, feeling a little bubble of giddiness as her blush deepened. "I'll talk to you later."

"You're about to assault an enemy camp, Lady Via?" Despite everything we'd just discussed, her voice held more than a little bit of trepidation.

"Yep." I gave her my best smile. "See you when I get back. I promise."

At that, she smiled back. "Of course. I'll . . . see you tonight, my lady."

With one last nod, I closed the mirror.

"Man, if I'd known you were this cute, I would have seduced you to the side of justice *ages* ago."

I snapped the mirror behind my back, glaring at Electra. She had the gall to laugh at me.

"You're not my type," I said. "And anyway, I clearly would have seduced you to the side of evil, like I *did*."

"We're attacking an enemy base to stop their evil plan by releasing a caged monster they keep in a box," Electra replied. "Every part of that sounds pretty heroic to me."

I huffed. "The devil, as always, is in the details."

Electra laughed. "Those are your job, Em'. I'm just the muscle."

"At least we're all on the same page, El." I rolled my eyes. "Tell me you found us an approach and you weren't spotted."

"I'll do you one better." She grinned. "They only had one sentry at the north side of camp, and I already knocked him out." She held up a finger, a silent burst of electricity showering down around her. "I've got some cool new skills, too! Though not, like, summon-six-billion-demons cool or anything."

"Hopefully we won't need quite that many," I said. "Still, excellent work. You'd think they would keep a better eye on that thing."

"It looks like most of their people are watching the south."

That made me smile. "So my distraction is already bearing fruit? This day just keeps getting better and better. Lead the way."

With one last nod, Electra and I switched into business mode, quickly working our way down the slope. For those who've never been in a battle between supers, there's just a level of focus, of understanding, that comes with familiar territory. Electra and I had clashed dozens, if not hundreds, of times during my reign as the most successful—and glamorous—supervillainess in the continental United States. We knew each other's tricks, how we moved, how we struck.

It was almost too easy to infiltrate the camp. My own armor made subduing wandering mercenaries rather simple. I grabbed them, Electra knocked them out, and before we knew it, we were already crouching behind a couple of messy tents and lean-tos, only a few meters away from the gate to Mr. Spiney's enclosure.

Electra and I shared a glance as we got a closer look at the guards in front of the massive steel portcullis. There were four of them, all armed, standing in the open in front of the gate. No way for us to sneak up on them.

This close, we could also get a good look at the monster itself—something I hadn't been able to do thus far.

What struck me was how long and sinewy it looked. The beast had a long, sharp muzzle, like an alligator's, with wicked serrated teeth poking down over its lower jaw. Big amber eyes with slitted pupils glared at its captors, and spines nearly as long as I was tall (which was, as I'd discussed with Rel, *very* long) ran the entire length of its spine, to an absolutely wicked-looking thagomizer on its tail.

In case it wasn't clear, that meant it had even more spikes on its tail to slam people with.

After taking in the scene, Electra jerked her thumb towards the guards. I raised an eyebrow, pointing at the gate. She thought about it for a moment, before nodding.

Well, guess it was my turn then. How nice of Rel to provide me with an alibi that put me so far from home at exactly this moment.

With a wave of my hand, I summoned a small army of hobblefiends. "Fly, my pretties!" I saw the guards turning to look towards me just in time for the first wave of hobblefiends to crash through the tents and jump on top of them.

The guards managed to hold off most of them, just like Delia had managed, even as the rest of my demons wreaked havoc in the camp itself. That being said, if our goal was the monster, my tiny lumpy sacks of anger and teeth wouldn't be quite enough.

Luckily, as I'd grown in levels and in strength, I'd increased the size of my mana pool and the number of demons I had access to.

Lucky for me, I mean. Not for the guards, as the second wave of hobblefiends, with a few gryphons mixed in, managed to overrun the gate before spreading to cause chaos in the rest of the camp. I'd be a bit more worried about the screams, but once a bandit, always a bandit. The miners and laborers, who'd been confined to the edges of the camp, had already fled into the jungle.

That was one way to deal with a monster attack.

"Free the other monsters!" I commanded them. Meanwhile, Electra and I quickly gained the gate, just in time for a small band of mercenaries, bedraggled and looking for orders, to stumble into a whip of magic lightning that sent them twitching across the ground.

"You know," she said, "this used to be a lot harder."

"Sometimes," I replied, "the hard part is in the preparation. The *doing* is what's easy."

"I feel like that explains so much about you." Putting one hand to the gate, she drew on her power, quickly magnetizing the portcullis in a way that would never occur in nature. With a keening whine, the metal spikes buckled, then shattered in an ear-rending screech. With a flick of her wrist and a burst of lightning, she deflected the metal fragments harmlessly.

"And *that*," I said, "is why I always hated fighting you."

Electra grinned at me as I tried to figure out how to undo the chains holding Mr. Spiney down without getting eaten.

Then, Mr. Spiney lunged forward into the hole where the gate had been. Its long neck stretched out into the open, chains groaning and creaking before snapping like twigs, first one at a time and then faster and faster as it gained more room to maneuver its massive bulk and—

"I think we should run now."

Electra nodded. "Got a ride?"

"Yes." I reached over, picking her up. "It's called power armor."

We made it to the jungle just as Mr. Spiney ripped off the last of the chains and made his displeasure *very clear* to anyone and everyone who'd decided to stick around.

CHAPTER 27

Falcon and Falconer

You utter imbecile!"

Seneschal Hawkwright glared at the captain of the guard, his steel-gray eyes narrowed into slits.

"Are you always so utterly incompetent or did you make an especially determined attempt this time? Did you, perhaps, invite the enemy directly into the heart of the camp, to do whatever they wished? No?"

Across from him, guard captain Maria hunched her shoulders under the withering barrage. She stood in a salute, fist pressed against her chest, unwilling to move while the Seneschal continued to scream her head off.

"Well, Captain?" He stalked forward, stopping only a few feet from the woman. "I should like an answer for this failure, this . . . *travesty*!"

"We did not invite them into our camp, Seneschal," she said.

"You didn't? You didn't!" The man threw up his hands. "How lovely, you didn't invite the enemy into your camp." He took a deep breath, pressing his fingers against the sharp bridge of his nose. On his hand, the ducal seal glinted in the low light of his chambers. Duchess Ivey was present in the room, but only in body. She hadn't moved from her seat in the twenty minutes Hawkwright had been yelling, sitting close to the fire as a physician attended to her fretfully.

Hawkwright, of course, paid her as much attention as the Duchess spared the rest of the room as he continued to lay into the guard captain.

"How then," he asked, voice low, "did a group that couldn't have numbered more than ten manage to destroy one of our largest camps? Months of work, wasted in an hour, and the only answer you have for me is 'we didn't invite them inside'?" He shook his head. "How did they *enter*? How did they do so much damage while *your men* were guarding the camp, when you knew that they were coming?!"

Maria swallowed. "We posted more sentries to the south, watching the road and the coasts," she said. "After hearing news of a group closer to Lady's P—"

"Do not call it that!" Hawkwright slashed his hand through the air. "It is a squalid stain on the face of our republic, nothing more."

Maria paused for a moment, eyes flicking left and right. "After a group of enemies attacked our sentries closer to the enemy's . . . . camp, I gave orders to redouble those watches, and to keep close eyes on the jungle as well. They saw nothing."

Hawkwright paused, turning back to glare at her once again. "Nothing?"

Maria shook her head. "Not a whisper, Seneschal." She glanced down for a moment, before taking a steadying breath. "After piecing together testimony from the camp, the best I can determine, they were attacked instead from the north, where our perimeter was weakest."

Hawkwright said nothing for a long second, combing spidery fingers through his sharply pointed beard. "The north . . ." he said. "Still, that does not answer how an entire camp full of guards and mercenaries were so thoroughly routed."

"Demons, sir," Maria replied.

Hawkwright's countenance grew tense, drawn like a string about to snap. "*She* was there."

"The best as I could determine, Seneschal."

"By all the hells in the deeps." He picked up a goblet on the edge of his desk, fingers clutched knuckle white around the stem. He took a long pull, before gently, almost delicately, setting the cup back down on the wood without a drop being spilled. "And then," he muttered, "with a horde of demons running amok through the camp, your men were distracted for long enough to free the Direspine."

Maria jerked her chin in a rough approximation of a nod. "That is what I have determined."

Hawkwright snorted. Catching a sleeping Direspine with a prepared group was one thing. Having one free to rampage through a disorganized group of men, setting loose other monsters as it went was entirely another. There was a reason such massive beasts still roamed the jungles of Vecorvia: putting them down was more trouble than it was worth.

Hawkwright turned to face Maria once again. "And how did she evade your sentries?"

Maria paused, glancing to the side.

"Answer me, Captain!"

She bit her lip. "I don't know, Seneschal."

"What?"

"I said I don't know," she repeated. "I sent runners. There is no trace of anyone passing through the jungle, no one on the road that wasn't stopped and questioned. No ships, no caravans running down the coast . . . nothing at all!"

"A high-level scout, then," Hawkwright muttered.

"I had my dual classers investigate, sir," Maria said. "They found nothing either."

Hawkwright stilled. "It must be a traitor then."

Maria said nothing, eyes locked on the floor.

"You have a traitor, Captain Maria, in your ranks." Hawkwright turned to face her fully. "One that not only allowed the enemy to pass unseen, but no doubt aided their passage and obscured their trail." He clenched his jaw so hard his teeth creaked. "Perhaps they've even vanished south, back to that pisshole of theirs."

Maria said nothing.

Reaching out, Hawkwright grabbed Maria's chin, forcing the woman's eyes up to meet his own. "Did you reach the same conclusion?"

"It . . . seems the most reasonable."

With a muttered curse, he shoved her away. Maria staggered, one hand half rising to the hilt of her sword, before one of the Seneschal's guards took a half step forward from the wall.

Maria swallowed again, forcing her hand back to her side.

"Find the traitor. Whatever it costs."

Maria nodded. "Yes, Seneschal."

"Consolidate the rest of the monster camps. Make them impossible to target, build fortifications if you have to. This alone will set us back weeks or more, I will not countenance another successful raid."

Maria looked away. "I am not sure if I have the men, your grace . . ."

Hawkwright raised a brow. "Oh?"

"Between scouring the ranks for the traitor and increasing the forces necessary to guard a giant camp in the middle of the lava fields, I don't have the forces."

Hawkwright waved a hand. "Take them from the outer city."

"Sir—!"

"That is an order, Captain."

Captain Maria lowered her hand. "Understood . . . Seneschal."

"Good." The man nodded once. "Now get out of my sight. Next time, perhaps you will have better news for me."

With one last salute, Captain Maria nearly fled from the room, the thick oak door slamming shut behind her.

Hawkwright, with controlled motions, returned to his desk, sinking into the overstuffed leather chair behind it. He took his goblet up once more, fingers trembling in barely repressed rage.

"I have half a mind to dash your brains out against the wall, Duchess," he said. "Your niece has caused me no end of trouble."

A dry, wheezing chuckle came from Duchess Ivey's lips. "Of course." The woman's voice came in a whisper. "Please allow me to sympathize with your troubles, my dear Seneschal. It is truly so difficult . . . to maintain your grip on this city you've stolen, with wealth that is not your own, opposed by the enemies of your own . . . creation—"

He growled. "Enough."

"No . . . no." She shook her head slowly. "How like a man, to seize all he desires, and then complain that it is no longer to his liking . . ."

"I said *enough*!" He hurled his goblet at the wall. It hit the marble plinth above the fireplace with a ringing chime, before thudding against the thick carpets. "Guards."

Then the man paused. He let out an annoyed huff. "Get the Duchess out of here."

He said nothing as the physicians wheeled Ivey from the room. Only then did he lift his head. "Did you think I wouldn't notice you skulking about?"

From the shadows stepped a woman with golden eyes, the two nearest guards flinched away from her in surprise, but Hawkwright waved them off for the moment. He had last seen her nearly two months ago, when he dispatched her to *handle* the problem of Lady's Port to the south. That she had returned . . .

"You've done a poor job," he said.

"Aww, don't be like that." She shuffled forward from the edge of the room, one hand picking at the skin of her opposite wrist. "Haven't I been working hard? I got so many monsters for you, didn't I?"

"Only because you failed in your primary mission." He turned away, slumping back in his chair. "The Devil of Lady's Port sent you running with your tail between your legs."

"One person can only do so much." The woman spread her arms, lips twitching into a lopsided smile. "She got a bunch at her beck and call now."

"And *you* wasted all of your dust."

"Hey, now." Her eyes narrowed. "I only used it 'cause I wanted to finish the jobs you gave quick."

"And yet you failed in both regards," Hawkwright replied, "so here you come to beg for more."

The woman said nothing, but her eyes glimmered hopefully in the half darkness. This alone—her abject desire for more heaven dust—was all the reason Hawkwright needed not to touch it himself. Still, such tools could be useful, but only until they became more invested in their next dose of the drug, instead of following orders. It was Hawkwright's own fault for assuming Mornia could carry out a longer mission.

Something his foe had no trouble accomplishing.

Hawkwright frowned. "If that devil woman did not already know my plans, she will certainly have grasped them now."

"So send me to—"

"Be silent." Hawkwright shook his head. "The last time I sent you anywhere, you did nothing but cause more problems than you solved. No."

Now that he'd been struck once, there was no doubt that another blow would soon follow. Hawkwright had been too focused on the offensive campaign; he neglected to attend to his own protections. No longer.

He waved the guards forward. "Your aid has become a hinderance."

The woman blinked as two sets of hands clamped down on her shoulders. "Wh—Hey! What are you doing? You need me!"

"I assure you." Hawkwright turned away. "I do not."

Mornia had time for one last scream.

CHAPTER 28

Pieces and Players

Really?" Electra asked.

"No, really." I gave a shrug. "It was actually a hell of a time filling out paperwork the one time I flew to El Salvador. No one ever told me the abbreviation for the United States was EEUU," I said, sounding out the vowels.

"But what does that even stand for? Like, Estados doesn't have two *Es*."

"Look who's flexing her high school Spanish."

Electra laughed. "Took French, actually."

"Suddenly, you remembering Spanish makes much more sense."

"Doesn't it just?"

"Anyway, *mi mama* knew, but couldn't tell me why. Turns out when the subject noun of an acronym is plural, you double the letters, so Esta*dos* Uni*dos*?" I waved my hand "E, E, U, U."

"Wild." Electra pushed open the door to the inn where we were staying. "But why?"

"Hell if I know." I shrugged. "Anyway, that was the last time I ever flew commercial, so I never needed to fill out the paperwork again." I followed after her, and she pushed the door shut quickly.

"Wait." Electra leaned against the wooden door. "What do you call Mexico in Spanish, then?"

I raised an eyebrow. "What are you talking about."

"Well, because it's the United States of Mexico, isn't it."

"*Mexico es Mexico,*" I said. "*Todo no es complicado.*"

"I thought you didn't speak much Spanish," she replied.

"More than your two years of high school French."

We waited for a long moment.

The two of us had taken a meandering, circuitous route back through Silverwall, affecting nonchalance every step of the way. But if we'd been made, now would be the perfect time for our pursuers to pounce.

After a few moments of Silence, Electra and I relaxed in truth. "Looks like we're goo—"

"Sea and stars, what did you fuckers *do*?!"

We both spun. I sank to a knee, Electra slipping behind my more durable armored form as both of our arms came up.

In the middle of the room, Eloncio blinked as he tried to look up at the red laser sight hovering on his forehead. Behind me, I heard the crackling *pops* of lightning dancing across Electra's fingers.

"Uh . . ." The guard who'd smuggled us into Silverwall raised a finger. "Forget I said anything."

I tilted my head back, sharing a glance with Electra. She shrugged. With a huff, I stood, shaking out my arms as I walked deeper into the room. "You should know better than to sneak up on people like that."

Eloncio gave a maudlin sigh, returning to his seat at the stereotypical fantasy bar. "Heed your own council." He tilted back his mug, taking a long pull of the piss-weak beer this place served. Dee and Dum loved it too, which gave me rodent-related worries. "Every guard in the city was called up at midday. Had to turn my entire unit out to hear of some attack against labor camps near the lava mines."

He gave the two of us a sideways glance.

"Labor." I pulled up a chair. "Right."

Electra waved over the innkeeper from the back room. The man was old, tottering, and hard of hearing, but he served both of us mugs of water quickly enough, which Electra purified with a few quick jolts of electricity.

At least the water was clear. Peasants and tradesmen wouldn't pay for visibly tainted water, no matter what amateur historians on twitlock said.

"You've heard about what those camps were for?" I asked Eloncio at length.

The man looked down at his half-empty mug. "Only that I'll be going out to guard them."

I raised an eyebrow. Doubling down on security certainly made sense after Electra and I rolled one of the monster hunting camps over. I was expecting yet more mercenaries to plug the gaps, but it was nice to hear that there wasn't an unlimited number of adventurers-turned-bandits for Seneschal Hawkwright to exploit.

Aloud, I only said, "Bring some long spits. A friend told me it helps feed captured monsters without losing a hand."

Eloncio finished the rest of his beer with a single drink. "Should I thank you for the warning or for landing me stuck in the mess to start with?"

"How about this." I reached up, patting his shoulder with a smile. "Thank me for not attacking whatever camp you were sent to guard."

He stared at me for several seconds, visibly working his jaw, before letting out another sigh. What a cheery guy. "There's only gonna be one camp."

I blinked.

"How'd Hawkwright tell you all of this without mentioning the monsters?"

He shrugged. "You don't join the guard 'cause you like knowing the fiddly details of your work."

"No, I imagine not." I bit my lip. "Still, that complicates things. Thanks for the information." I took a sip of my own water. "Tell you what, we'll let you know before we make a move, huh?" I nudged his elbow. "That way you can get you and your friends out."

He rubbed his face. "Right into the jungle."

I shrugged. "Any port in a storm?"

"You outworlders have the strangest sayings." He pushed his mug down the counter and stood. "I won't be able to help you anymore."

What went unspoken was 'I won't help you attack the camp full of monsters I'll be living in,' which, you know, fair enough. He barely knew us, and he'd already smuggled us into Silverwall as a favor to some old friends.

You had to know when to push people, as a villain, but also when to let them walk away. So I just smiled, sipping at my water. "Don't worry, we'll be able to figure out the rest for ourselves. Just keep your head down, and we'll make sure you keep your head to yourself."

For some reason, that didn't seem to calm him down. Still, he just gave a jerky nod before walking out of the bar, leaving me and Electra alone with an old man who I really hoped was as deaf as he acted.

The door thunked shut for the second time since our return.

"Man," Electra said, "wish we could go back to swapping stories from Earth."

"We knew they would respond," I replied. She gave me a look, and I rolled my eyes. "Oh, I'm sorry, I keep forgetting you come from the other side of the fence. When you hit someone, they shore up their defenses; it doesn't matter if they're cartel . . . or a local head of state."

"Somehow," she said, "I feel like you have more experience with both."

"Most accomplished supervillain in the continental United States."

She gave a short laugh. "Never thought that would help calm me down." She rolled her shoulders, shaking out her messy blonde hair. "So, what's the plan, boss?"

"First, wait for Dee and Dum to get back," I said. "We need more information. Eloncio told us a lot, but I need to know how *many* guards are being pulled out of the city, and where they're coming from."

"You think the twin peaks will be able to figure out more stuff than the guy who's literally in the city guard?"

"You heard the man." I spun a finger around the rim of my glass. "You don't sign up because you want an in-depth breakdown of city security. I'm hoping the boys have a few other friends in the city who can give us a clearer picture."

"And then once we figure out their defenses," Electra continued, "we hit the camp again."

I paused, turning to look my ally in her sharp blue eyes. I decided to delegate a bit.

"We won't be hitting the camp."

She blinked. "We won't? Wasn't the plan to take the rest of them out, so that they couldn't overrun Lady's Port?"

"That *was* the plan." I drummed my fingers on the table. "Past tense." I waved her closer. "Let me teach you a thing or two, my apprentice."

Electra snorted. "I think Aegis gave me enough training on this sh— this stuff already, thanks."

"Must be why I keep beating them." I rolled my eyes. "Listen up, do you want to be part of the planning or not? *Dios de mi vida*, you and Rel were *just* convincing me to share some of this stuff, weren't you?"

"Well, yeah." She blinked. "I didn't expect you to start offering advice like a villainous fortune cookie."

"Never consume an energy field larger than your head."

"What?"

While she was blinking at me in confusion, I flicked her nose. Electra jerked backwards, arms pinwheeling as she almost fell out of her chair.

"Villainy is all about the show," I said, cutting her off as she regained her balance. "But any good stage performer will tell you the importance of misdirection."

She huffed, crossing her arms. "Well, yeah, obvs. But you didn't have to hit me."

"You'd be surprised how many of my victories were based on that obvious observation." I leaned over my cup. "When you're the under-dog, you can never meet your enemy's strength with your own. Again, completely obvious." I gave a self-depreciating smirk. "The trick is forc-ing yourself not to care."

"Huh?" Electra blinked at my non sequitur.

"If your enemy has more power than you, more resources than you, more knowledge and expertise than you, the only thing you can do is *not care*. Once you're unshackled from worries about what you'll lose or what they'll gain, you can rearrange the board however you like." I took a drink of water. "Kick it over again and again, while they scramble to put the pieces back in order."

"That's a pretty cynical way to look at it, Em'." Electra leaned over. "Besides, don't you have people you care about now?"

"That's why I used to work alone." I shrugged. "But yes, the real world always gets in the way. I certainly wouldn't trade my kingdom for a bowl of pottage. Returning to the matter of the camps and monster hunters, if Eloncio's information is true, that means that Seneschal Hawkwright is very invested in this little project of his." I waved a hand. "So, it's time for us to stop caring about it."

She narrowed her eyes. "Including all of the monsters that they're going to send to stampede over Lady's Port and flatten it into the ground?"

I folded my hands beneath my chin. "If you could defeat the villain or save yourself, which would you choose?"

"Wh—the villain, of course, but you're not the one who—"

"The trick about arranging the board," I said, "is that any piece can be the king. What your opponent thinks is your king could be just another sacrificial pawn." I took in Electra's aghast expression and laughed. "Not Lady's Port, moron. No, you've rubbed off on me too much for that." My smile deepened. "But I told you, didn't I, about all the times I appeared just to get you and the rest of Aegis to look at *me*, while my robots or allies of convenience did the real work in the background?"

She blinked at me for a moment, before groaning. "We already played bait, Em'."

"And it turned out so well the first time."

She grimaced, rubbing her hand against her neck. "Yeah." Her voice came thick with an emotion I couldn't identify. "I guess you could say that." Before I could say anything, she met my eyes again. "What was it you said," she asked, "don't care?"

I gave a wan smile. "Don't care, and least of all about yourself." I leaned in, cupping a hand around my mouth. "You want to know a secret?"

Electra nodded.

"That's why most villains fail while I succeed. They care too much about themselves, the only thing they cannot surrender." I showed my teeth. "And that's why no one can imagine, even for a second, that I might."

She blinked, eyes fluttering in surprise. She shouldn't have been so shocked. It was the same trick I'd pulled on the Adventurer's Guild, and even then, that was far from the first time I'd 'sacrificed' myself.

It was just the first time I'd done so while relying entirely on someone else. Relying on Relia.

Then a heavy knock came to the door of the tavern, and for a moment I thought Dee and Dum had finally made it back. The door was shoved open and a group of men wearing familiar tarnished armbands filtered into the room.

I laughed. "Arlo!" I raised my mug of water. "What perfect timing, we were *just* talking about you."

It was a lie, of course, except in the way that mattered most.

CHAPTER 29

Do Unto Others

Just talking about me?" Arlo gave an affable chuckle as he walked inside. Behind him, four tough-looking men filed in before finally closing the door. I counted two level 15s and two 10s. "Should I be troubled?"

"All good things, all good things." I waved him off. "But really, how have you *been*? Oh, my god, it's been an age. I hear you basically run things around here these days!"

For having become the ostensible head of all organized crime in Silverwall, Arlo looked much the same: black hair going gray at the temples, a sharp widow's peak, a loose tunic, and a bartender's rag tucked into his belt. His thick mustache was impeccably groomed, but other than that, he had no affectations of wealth. No chains or jewels, nothing but an unadorned band around his left index finger. You could almost mistake the silver for steel, if not for the tarnished surface.

"It's a job." The man shrugged. "One of my boys said you wanted to talk on your ground." He spread his arms wide. "So here I am."

"How kind." I hummed, kicking one leg idly against the bar. "You know, I thought about setting up the whole room again, get the big round table, the sconces, maybe find a vindictive redhead, you know, just runback our first meeting." I wrinkled my nose. "It felt a bit crass." Instead, I pointed to the bar stool next to me, even as Electra rose to her feet, taking a step to the side.

Arlo grinned. "Well, I didn't come all of this way just to turn back around."

He settled into the stool next to me as the elderly innkeep tottered out with a round of drinks before disappearing into the back of the inn and shutting the door behind him.

You get what you pay for.

Arlo and I took a drink, while the other five ignored theirs. On the balance, I trusted Electra and myself to carry the day if there was any chance at victory at all, but I'd much prefer if things didn't come to blows until Dee and Dum came back.

Arlo smacked his lips. "Ah, wish I could go back to the days when I didn't care if rats fell into my still."

I looked down at my own mug for a long moment, before pushing it a bit farther away from me. "Does the crown not agree with you?" I asked.

"Crown?" He raised a thick finger to his bare temple. "I think you have me wrong. Besides, last I heard any news from the south, it was you who had set yourself up as Lady of the port."

I tiled my head in acknowledgment. "We've both done well for ourselves, but only one of us stayed here." I dragged my gloved finger across the splintered bar. "That is, of the three that once met in a seedy bar like this."

Arlo chuckled.

I smiled wider. "It's not as grand as you imagined."

He paused, taking another sip of his beer. "Now, what makes you say that?"

"Because I know you." I rested my check on my palm, leaning against the bar. "We're of the same kind, you and I; I knew it from the first time we met. I bet you did too, and that's why you took a bet on *me*."

"And what kind is that?" he asked.

I raised an eyebrow. "Do I really have to say it? The kind that's never satisfied."

He chuckled, looking away from me. "I think the two of us are woven from different thread."

"If that were the case, we never would have made it this far."

He shrugged. "Gulls on the same beach can ride different winds."

"Funny; in my homeland, we say 'birds of a feather flock together.'"

"Sounds like a strange place."

"It would have to be, to make a girl like me."

Arlo took another sip of his drink, stewing. I continued to lean on the bar, idly dragging my gauntleted fingers across the wood. I didn't miss the way his eyes tracked along the smoothly curved and polished black surface of my power armor. There was nothing like it in this world; it made him wary.

I just smiled. "Of course, if you were *really* satisfied, would you even be here?" I tilted my head coquettishly. "Unless there was something you wanted."

"All I wanted was to hear what you were doing in my city," he replied.

"Just passing through. You know, to the city with the fancier wall." I buffed my nails, affecting a surprised pause. "Oh, not to imply you didn't control all of Silverwall, Arlo! Just . . ." I shrugged.

He didn't reply to that right away. Instead, he drained the rest of his tankard and set it back down on the counter. The man had a good poker face, but I could see a hint of tension running along the side of his jaw, teeth clenched tight.

"You've always talked like the tide rushing in." He inclined his head. "I guess it wouldn't hurt to hear what you have to say."

"Great!" I perked up. "First off—"

"If you can give me a reason to trust you."

"Me?" I placed a hand on my chest plate. "Arlo, I think you're forgetting just who was hung out to dry, last time I was in town."

"That's exactly why I don't trust you." He pointed a single thick finger at me. "Because trade places, and I'd be spitting mad. Mad enough to come all the way back to Silverwall just to settle some old grudges."

"You wound me." I smiled, letting my eyes grow slitted. "It was just . . . business, after all."

He chuckled, easy demeanor returning. "You're a good liar, little lady," he said. "There are a lot of words I might have believed from those pretty lips, but not those."

I tutted. "I never took you for a poor businessman."

"'Tis exactly because I'm a businessman that I know you're lying."

I clicked my tongue. He'd backed me into a corner on this one. Perhaps revenge for getting under his skin.

I shrugged, spreading my arms wide. "In truth, I hate your guts, Arlo."

He nodded his head. "And now it comes out."

"But really, chasing me out of Silverwall turned out to be a favor in the end," I continued. "After all, I've done quite well for myself. And you're right, I have come back to town to settle some old grudges." I waved a finger between the two of us. "But not this one—not yet at least."

He stroked his spruce mustache, eyeing me with those cold, dark eyes. "I don't believe that either," he said. "But it will do, for now."

I gave him another smile. "How kind."

"So, what mad little scheme have you cooked up this time?" Arlo asked. "There are naught more guilds in Silverwall. We've burned the lot of them out."

"You mistake me." I leaned on the bar. "I'm not interested in the part of the city *you* control."

His eyes widened a hair. "Ah, you're here to end this little war of yours."

"Is it really a war, when one side does all the winning?" I asked.

"Ah, but the Old Hawk hasn't even turned out the militia yet, let alone the guard." Arlo smirked, the edge of his mouth curling up along his cheek. "That tiny little town of yours would already be crushed if he cared to stand up an army."

"And I imagine he already would have," I said, "if he had full control of this little city of his."

Arlo chuckled. "You think too much of me." He waved a hand. "I've never been one to make waves. It's bad for . . . business."

"I imagine that Seneschal Hawkwright has myriad worries, but he would be a fool if you weren't one of them." I shrugged. "I just want you to worry him some more."

Arlo hummed. "You know, I heard a rumor. Something about those work camps in the jungle, where they dig and dig but not a piece of ore returns."

I smiled. "A good rumor, I hope."

"You want me to raise some hell in the outer city, draw out the rest of the guard, so you can knife the Old Hawk in the back."

I hummed. "That's certainly something I *could* do."

"See, little lady, I already told you," Arlo continued. "War? It's bad for business. I don't see a reason I should risk my neck for yours a second time." He ran his fingers around his throat. "Consid'ring what near happened last time."

At my side, Electra shivered, her hands curling into fists.

"Oh, Arlo, Arlo, Arlo." I reached out, patting him on the shoulder. For a second, I considered offering him all of Silverwall, but I didn't think he would swallow that lie. "War's already on; the only thing that matters is being on the winning side."

He stroked his mustache again, rubbing a palm against his stubbled chin. "Now that is some good sense. But I think I see things differently than you."

"Most do." I sighed. "Such is the burden of my genius."

He snorted. "Now, what's stopping me from picking my own winning side? Sea and stars, what's stopping me from dragging the two of you in front of Hawkwright right now?"

"The crown really does *not* agree with you." I shook my head. "What a shame."

"What, don't think I can do it?" His four thugs stepped forward. "Do you really think I don't have more people outside?" He placed an arm on the table, "Or that it wouldn't matter if you let me get so close to you?"

I raised an eyebrow. "You know what I do to petty gang lords who get within arm's reach, right?"

"I know all about your skills, little lady, but ones like that have their own drawbacks." He smiled. "You'll find it hard to turn me into a demon." I tightened my grip on his shoulder, but his smile only widened.

I tutted again. On one hand, I believed him. There was a lot Electra and I didn't know about classes, and with Arlo's resources it would be easy enough to counter my most directly dangerous skill. This close, he probably thought he could gut me before I summoned enough demons to turn the tide.

On the other, he was mistaken if he thought my ability to turn people into demons was my only advantage.

"Do you really think I'd let you this close if it wasn't to my advantage?" I asked.

Arlo blinked.

Then I started to squeeze.

The servos in my power armor gave an airy whirr as I shoved Arlo against the counter. He jerked once in surprise, muscles straining to no avail. His other arm lashed out, a maw of playing cards flying from his sleeve.

I twisted. The cards caught my shoulder, but they didn't even scratch the enamel. With a twist, I broke through whatever skill he was using and shoved his face against the rough wood of the bar.

Our mugs fell to the floor with a clatter.

Another quick step to the side and I placed myself behind him, anchoring my hold and twisting his arm. I caught his other hand as he tried to drive a knife into my eye, gauntlet tightening in a vice grip around his wrist. My movements were quick, certain, and with a huff I lifted, pinning him fully against the bar, legs off the ground, not a hint of leverage to speak of.

You didn't become a successful Villain without learning some hand-to-hand.

Credit where credit was due, he twisted his wrist even as I put him in the hold, sinking into the gap between armor plates at the wrist. Of course, the lining was made from a cut-resistant shock absorbing gel, so it didn't do much more, but it would have sucked to face him when I didn't already have him half in a joint lock.

I twisted my arm, and the knife rang once as it hit the ground before I kicked it away.

Behind me, Arlo's men were just starting to shout when Electra put herself at my back, already glowing with blue-white lightning.

"Wanna see how you match up against *my* skills?" she asked. Oh, I used to hate that heroic bravado, but it felt quite different when the heroine was on my side.

"Now then." I readjusted my grip, further pinning Arlo down. "You were saying something about dropping me off for that . . . *Old Hawk*, was it?"

Truth be told, I wasn't the biggest girl. On flat ground, I'd have trouble keeping him still, but the wooden bar was sturdy and provided me an effective prop to rob Arlo of any possible leverage.

"Alright." Arlo squirmed. "Alright! You've made your point."

"Have I? Have I really?" I circled my fingers around his wrist. "I would have believed a lot of words out of those lips," I parroted his earlier remark, "but not those."

He glared at me over his shoulder. "What do you want, you mad bitch?"

I smiled. If I had one regret about being stuck in Lady's Port for so long, it was that I hadn't had the chance to be properly villainous for far too long.

"Sound more contrite, Arlo. Here, let me give you a *hand*."

I squeezed. The servos in my gauntlet let out the most satisfying whine as they ratcheted tighter.

Arlo howled as the bones in his wrist popped.

Broke.

Every muscle in his body went taut, then the man slumped over the bar, panting.

"Not a step!" There was a crack of light and the smell of ozone as Electra shouted.

Arlo turned his head to glare at me again, breath leveling out.

"I was willing to forgive you for running me out of town," I said. "I was willing to forgive you for summoning me like you were some king, not just the luckiest slumlord; hell, I was even willing to forgive you for the bad manners of showing up unannounced and trying to intimidate me." I paused, taking in a deep breath.

"But a second betrayal? Well, my homeland has another saying." I leaned close to his ear and whispered, "Do unto others as they do unto you."

I stood up, tossing my hair. "Now get your boys out of here, before I rip your lying throat out."

I heard a shuffling of feet behind me. Arlo remained silent.

"What?" I asked. "Worried I'll kill you?" I tightened my grip on his wrist once again. He grunted as the pain hit him. All those pesky little nerves, grinding against each other. "I promise you that I am much more inventive than that."

I could feel the adrenaline soaring in my veins. If Arlo decided to fight it out, then we'd be in real trouble, and this time I didn't have an exit strategy.

Then there was a ringing in the back of my head as my second class leveled up.

"Fuck." He spat. "Get out of here, you useless sacks of meat! Fuck!" The veins in his neck bulged as he ground his teeth. "Now!"

I grinned. How's that for the power of some convincing words? Just like I said, villains only cared about themselves, forever and always.

"And the rest," I said.

Arlo just jerked his head towards the door before slumping back down against the wood. I didn't even bother to turn as four sets of footsteps started towards the door. I could hear them hesitating, but in a moment, they were gone all the same.

"Electra, check that everyone's cleared out."

She moved to the windows, doing a quick perimeter sweep with practiced efficiency.

"One's right around the corner, no sign of anyone else."

"Send him running."

"Got it." There was another crack of electricity.

And then it was just us, Arlo, and the deaf barkeeper in the back.

"Excellent." I hauled Arlo off the bar, tossing him through a battered set of chairs. He hit the floor, cradling his broken wrist with murder in his eyes. "We're done here," I said. "Let's get moving, Electra."

She glanced at me, but we were both in super mode right now. She nodded, falling in behind me as we quickly gathered our few belongings and slipped out the back.

"What about Dee and Dum?" she asked as we slipped down the nearest road and out of sight of the inn.

"They'll figure out what happened. Unless Arlo got to them first." I shook my head. "I suspect they're fine. He wanted to take our measure before trying to stab me in the back."

"And leaving him alive?" Electra worried her lip. "What, is this some other 7-D chess thing about rearranging the board again?"

I turned, raising an eyebrow at her. "You think today was a failure?"

She snorted. "Don't give me that. You were blindsided, or we never would have ended up in that situation to begin with."

I sighed. This is why I didn't work with people—eventually they started to figure me out. "I would have preferred to do this with Arlo's help," I said. "But this wasn't a defeat."

"Oh?"

"What I needed from that man wasn't his allegiance," I said. "It was some chaos and mayhem." I smirked at her. "Do you think he feels particularly peaceful right now?"

She blinked, before rolling her eyes. "You're pulling that out of your a—out of your butt."

I chuckled. "Maybe half of it, but he'll make a mess for us to use all the same." The current situation was far from ideal, but I thrived on chaos, and I trusted my ability to pick my way through better than anyone else. "Now come on, I only broke his wrist, not his spirit; we need to go to ground before he can rally the rest of the Tarnished."

She giggled. "The two of us against the whole city, huh?"

I grinned. I couldn't help it.

"Just like old times."

CHAPTER 30

Relegate

Unfortunately, events are falling out faster than anticipated."

Despite the early hour, Mistress Via's face was still shrouded in darkness. Only the light from her own communication mirror lit up the curve of her lips and the sharp lines of her cheek bones. Rel still didn't quite grasp the concept of the mirrors, the wonder of captured light. It remained yet another miracle.

In the back of Rel's head, her Dream Sequence skill chimed in, *S-she's waiting for y-you to say s-something . . .*

Rel coughed. "Yes." She cleared her throat. "Llen thought that Hawkwright would just take advantage of normal migration patterns to drive monsters towards Lady's Port, but to hear that he's capturing them outright . . ."

"I need you to focus more on our defenses." Via shifted, her back pressed against roughly cut stone. "I'd come, but getting out of Silverwall right now would be a bit . . . tricky."

"Then surely I should come to you, Mistress."

Y-yeah. Lady Via needs our help.

Via rolled her eyes, whites flashing in the scant light. "Did you miss the part where the whole city is locked down?" Her lips twitched into a wan smile. "It wouldn't surprise me if they have a small army watching Lady's Port as well, after what happened last time."

"We put their sentries to flight before—"

"Doing so again isn't useful." Lady Via's expression hardened. "Right now, Hawkwright still thinks he can win with these indirect attacks, but if he decides to just raise the militia and march the guardsmen down to Lady's Port instead of bothering with all of this monster stampede nonsense . . ."

Rel ducked her head, pulling on a strand of her dark hair. "I thought you said he wouldn't do that because of . . ." She stopped speaking when she made the connection.

"Because of Arlo?" Mistress gave a wry chuckle. "Yes, well, if I hadn't just emasculated him in front of his most trusted guards, maybe that old man would have made some trouble for Hawkwright. As it stands now, I'd count myself lucky if he didn't volunteer for the militia himself."

B-but as long as M-mistress is still in S-silverwall . . .

Rel nodded once, unhappy. "But as long as you remain within his reach, he will try to capture you himself."

"Got it in one!" Lady Via grinned. "Really, I'm not even mad that he decided to betray me. I was just hoping it would come at a better time." She sighed. "Now everything is so . . . complicated."

"All the more reason I should be at your side, my lady. Danger or no."

"And leave who running my town, exactly?" Via raised an eyebrow.

Uuuwwww . . . Dream Sequence gave a discontented moan. It was a perfect summary of Rel's own emotional state.

"Ishanti—"

"Can manage the defenses and our own militia on top of everything else?" A second brow joined the first. "And here I thought you were so upset with me for trying to take on too many responsibilities."

"W-we've done a great deal to streamline all of our efforts!"

"Great. Capital." Lady Via shook her head. "You're going to need it, because it's crunch time." She ran a hand through her hair. "I'm a bad boss, but I need you *there* right now."

UUUUUUUUWW . . .

Rel wilted. "I . . . understand."

"Good." Lady Via sighed. "Don't worry about me, I've gotten out of worse scraps before."

"The entire city is hunting you!"

Via only smiled. "One city? My darling, you should see my track record."

This time Rel did blush. Via laughed quietly.

"You . . . talk differently now."

"Do I?"

Rel nodded. "To me."

Via tilted her head.

From the background, Rel heard Electra chime in with a muted "*She's got you there.*"

Rel stiffened.

She h-heard everything?

"Sorry, Rel." Via noticed her embarrassment, because of course she did. "But privacy is hard to come by right about now."

"Where are you, Mistress?"

"Hmm?" She smirked. "Hiding in a graveyard." Rel blinked in surprise. "As for your other question," Via continued, "I tend to get . . . tunnel vision about the things I care about."

"You don't say," Electra muttered.

Via punched the other woman. "I suppose this is just one more of those things."

"Oh."

After a moment, Lady Via sighed. "I would love to spend more time focusing on this." She made an abortive gesture to the space between Rel and herself. "But unfortunately, time is also in short supply right about now."

Rel swallowed. "I understand, Mistress."

It still stung, but the pain was eased by the direct admission that Lady Via *cared*.

"How many mirrors do we have?"

Rel straightened, running a quick hand down her arm. "Nearly a dozen. Maarin has . . . perfected a system to allow different mirrors to connect to each other, but it is complicated. And it requires a person to manage the connections."

"Yes, setting up a grapevine was always going to be the hardest part of this endeavor," Via muttered. She looked up, meeting Rel's eyes. "How does his solution work?"

"Each mirror can be bound to an object, like a token of some sort," Rel said. "Then, you can put those tokens in contact to make those mirrors connect directly to each other."

Via nodded. "Like we'd already figured out how to do."

"Right," Rel replied. "The problem was that there was no way of knowing when two people wanted their mirrors to be connected, especially if we are to make many of them. Maarin has figured out how to ensure that all of the communication mirrors are connected to a central scrying disk, or something like that. When someone wants to use a mirror, they'll open it."

"Then they'll show up in the central disk, and someone can connect them to the right mirror?"

"Exactly, Mistress."

Via sucked on her lip. "Remarkably similar to the way operators used to work back on Earth, but that's convergent evolution for you." She tilted her head back, looking upwards.

Rel waited, still Lady Via made no move to explain her meaning, apparently lost deep in thought. Often she and Electra would make references to their shared outworld heritage. Rel wished she could share that with her Mistress, but she did not know these things.

With a deep breath, Rel let the feeling of frustration go. There was much, much more at stake, and—

"I'm going to need you to make something complicated," Via said.

"For the mirrors?"

"Yes." The woman nodded. "This is the real reason I need you in Lady's Port. You are the only one I trust to be able to implement them." She pinched the bridge of her nose. "Also, we're going to need a lot more than a dozen mirrors. This battle with Silverwall won't be decided on a single axis."

"How many mirrors?" Rel asked.

"How many feathers do we have?"

"Ah, quite more than we anticipated."

Via cocked her head. "How many have you killed?"

Rel shook her head. "Ishanti and Llen determined a method to harvest the feathers without killing them."

"How does that work?"

"Well . . ." Rel shrugged. "Ishanti took one as a pet and realized that they shed feathers quite often. It is just a question of not . . ."

"Getting poisoned and dying."

"Yes, that."

Via gave a laugh. "About time something broke my way," she said. "Repeaters are more important; make sure we can communicate from Lady's Port to Silverwall. After that, start handing them out to everyone in charge of multiple work groups or squads. If we can get more granular than that, do it."

Rel bit her lip. "Understood." That would be very many mirrors.

"I don't know if I will make it back"—Rel's heart caught in her chest—" before Hawkwright marches on you, so I'm going to be relying on you quite a lot."

"I wish you could rely on me to be by your side . . ."

Via smiled. "I forgot how cute you are when you're moping."

Rel huffed, looking away, but she couldn't stay mad for very long.

She k-keeps complimenting us!

Rel had long since gotten used to having another voice in her head. Still, sometimes she wished she could lie to herself a little longer.

"There's one last thing I need," Lady Via said.

Rel sucked in a breath. "Name it, my lady."

"Have the boys checked in?"

Rel nodded. "Once; they are posing as merchants."

Via shook her head. "Better than I hoped. Tell them to keep their heads down and avoid the Tarnished if they can. I'll approach them with those plans I mentioned, and then hopefully they can get out of town before things get too hot. They'll need a sloop to pick them up."

"Mistress, you need all the help you can get."

"I have this dunderhead." She pushed Electra, still just out of view of the mirror. "That's more than I usually get."

Electra poked her head of spiked blonde hair in front of Lady Via. "Don't worry, I'll get your girl back to you in one piece."

Rel nodded. "Please."

"I'll be fine, thank you very much." Via shoved Electra back out of view. "We'll talk more after I get out of this town alive."

"You do have a plan for that, right, Mistress?"

Lady Via shrugged. "Ostensibly, Hawkwright doesn't know I'm in his city, so it shouldn't be too difficult."

Rel frowned. "Unless Arlo . . ."

"Well, if he decides to team up with the law, then I've already lost. Right now, our only advantage is that Arlo wants to avoid drawing attention almost as much as we do."

"Don't *jinx* us!" Electra hissed.

Lady Via tossed her hair once. "We're already trespassing in a grave-yard, Elenore."

"Yeah, but during the day; it doesn't count!"

Via made eye contact with Rel, as if to say 'look what I have to put up with.'

"And if Arlo *does* tell the guard you're in Silverwall?" Rel asked.

Via hummed, drumming her fingers against her lips. Rel found her eyes drawn to them, taping with just enough pressure to leave dimples along Lady Via's mouth.

"I have an idea or two. There are three ways past the walls, after all."

Rel blinked, eyes jerking up. "Three?"

Lady Via grinned. "Over, under, or through."

Rel sighed in relief that her staring had not been noticed. That aside, though, when her Mistress was only willing to share a few words, Rel knew the plan would be dangerous. "Please, take care of yourself."

"I already said I would," Via replied. "Now, unless *you* have some-thing to share, the two of us need to catch some shut eye. It's going to be a late night."

Via shook her head. "Sleep well, Mistress."

"Good night." The woman's lips curved up into a devilish smirk. "Or maybe 'good morning' is more appropriate." Then, with a click, the mirror went black. A second later, it shimmered once, before reflecting Rel's face back like a perfectly normal mirror.

Rel gently closed her own mirror, the small circular case sitting lightly in her palm. She clenched her fingers tightly against the metal, knuckles turning white.

"That cannot be good for the enchantments."

Rel's head snapped up, and she was halfway to her feet before she saw Ishanti standing by the door. Rel sank back into the chair behind

Via's desk. She had been using the room in her Mistress's stead, and the creak and crackle of the Lightning Mill had masked Ishanti's approach.

"How long have you been standing there?"

Ishanti pondered that question for a moment, turning to look at the hummingbird perched on her raised finger. Where its feathers had been a deep emerald green, the edges had lightened to gold since Ishanti had taken it into her care.

"Not long." The pale woman's voice was quiet, with a princess's decorum. "Enough to hear you planned to leave Lady's Port." She ran a hand through her long, silver hair. "I admit, it is heartening that both of my . . . benefactors are so willing to delegate power. It is a trait that the good Seneschal never embodied."

Rel paused for a moment, before shaking her head. "How is your little friend?" She gestured towards the bird.

"He is doing well." Ishanti raised her other hand to the humming-bird's beak. It jabbed its head out, easily piercing her skin. The woman didn't flinch as a drop of blood welled up from the skin, and the hum-mingbird eagerly lapped it up. "Ranger Llen was correct that they gained their venom from the flowers." She pulled her hand away, and the tiny creature did not pursue, content to sit silently on Ishanti's fin-ger. "And quite intelligent as well."

Rel nodded. "Smart enough not to bite the hand that feeds them." She paused, eyes flicking to Ishanti. "Figuratively."

"Yes, it has quite the parallels to my own situation." Ishanti gave a vague smile. "I find it deeply amusing."

Rel frowned. "Our Mistress would never—"

"I put little stock in what men and women 'would never' or 'should always' do." Ishanti met Rel's gaze, eyes flashing. "For such claims turn invariably false. For now, I am grateful for your lady's patronage and intend to repay it fully."

Rel rose to her feet, slowly. "But you still think you've traded one cage for another."

"Betimes." Ishanti gave a languid shrug, earlier fire leaving her. "But then, I am well used to cages, and much prefer this one's shape." She reached out again, this time ruffling the hummingbird's chest, her finger nearly as large as its whole body. "Do you think my little friend feels the same?"

Rel shook her head.

"Ah, what a pity." Ishanti turned. "I find most comforting the knowledge of where one stands. I would share it with my pretty jewel."

"Why did you come to see me? Rel asked.

"Why, to see where I stand, of course," Ishanti replied. "It seems we will be fighting a war, after all."

"*We* will be fighting," Rel said. "You seem less invested."

"Did I not already explain myself?" Ishanti raised a brow. "Perhaps it is you, Relia, who does not know where she stands."

CHAPTER 31

Cross Purposes

The moment the sun set we slipped out from under the pilfered tarp.

"We have two objectives," I said. The damp air swallowed my voice as it tried to slip between the surrounding tombstones. "Disrupt our enemies' operations and set them against each other in the process."

"Okay, uh." Electra pushed herself upright a beat after me. "I know this is important and all, but I'm pretty curious where you came up with this graveyard idea."

I looked down at the tarp that Electra was busy shoving under the nearest bush. "Is it really so inventive? People don't like to go into graveyards, ergo, they're a great place to hide."

"I mean, there are a lot of good places to hide, right? I just wanna know why you picked this one."

I rolled my eyes. "We're kind of on a clock here, Electra."

She huffed, brushing the dirt off her pants. "It's just we've been learning so much about each other recently!"

I huffed. "My uncle slept in graveyards to hide when he was a kid. It's how the *coyotes* smuggled people up to the U.S. boarder. He told me about it when I was in high school."

"Really?"

"Really." I nodded. "It was for a report I was writing, or some stupid school project like that. They people up during the night, and during the day you camp out in one place no one ever goes except for during funerals."

"That's . . . uh, darker than I was expecting."

"Do you want all sunshine and daisies?" I rolled my eyes. "I didn't turn to a life of crime because I was a happy, well-adjusted individual from a good Christian family."

"What else did you learn from your uncle?" Electra asked.

I smirked. "Never trust the cops. It's a lesson that's served me well in two worlds now."

Electra laughed as the heavy air dissipated. "It's a favorite of yours, I know."

I smiled back. "Let's just say I know where my antiauthoritarianism comes from. Now, any other questions?"

Electra shook her head as the two of us slipped out of the graveyard. Silverwall was quieter at night, and the streets were black as pitch. It formed a striking contrast with my own little town, where electric lights allowed people to be out until the small hours in the morning.

A small advantage, but one we sorely needed.

"I took some time to look over the city through my spy mirror." I pointed up. "Our skywhale is high enough up that you can't get good detail, but fortunately, I already knew where to look."

"Oh?" Electra asked.

"From the way Arlo acted, it's pretty clear he doesn't have complete control of the outer city. In fact, I'd hazard a guess his territory doesn't extend very far south of the main thoroughfare that cuts Silverwall in half."

"So you were paying attention to the parts he *does* control." Electra nodded in understanding.

"I knew I brought you along for a reason."

"Hey, I got my start in RICO stuff, yanno, before I got picked up by Aegis Corp." She hummed. "If the Tarnished only control the northern half of the city, why did we have to sleep in a graveyard, though?"

"Better safe than sorry." We took a turn away from a small group standing in the light of a guttering torch. "And also, would you want to walk another three miles in the dark instead?"

"Point." Electra grumbled to herself. "I can barely see the nose on my face."

"You can always see you nose; your brain just ignores it most of the time." I ignored her muted shout. "Anyway, I'm sure they have passwords and lookouts, but it's pretty clear when one part of town gets a lot more foot traffic than it really should, especially in the bad part of town."

"Yeah, satellite surveillance is kinda OP," Electra replied. "So what are we hitting?"

"No idea." I paused at an intersection, focusing on my mental map of the city as seen from above. It was not a simple task. "This way."

"You don't know?"

"They didn't exactly put a sign on the roof. I told you what data I'm working with, El."

She worked over that statement in her mind as we took a few more blind turns before finally slowing as we crept down a dark street just a hundred meters or so from our destination.

"They're kinda bold, ain't they?" Electra nodded her head towards another group of men. There were quite a few of them, near a ring of torches in the middle of the street, and we could hear them cheering and shouting from here.

It was hard to tell from here, but if we got closer, I was sure we'd see tarnished metal bands on their arms.

"Arlo was right about one thing: they own this part of town."

"So what's the plan? I don't think we're gonna have much time once they realize we're here, Em'."

I nodded. "That's why we go in hard, sow as much chaos as we can . . ."

"And ride the confusion before the guard shows up."

I glanced over my shoulder. "Look at you, thinking like a proper villain now."

Electra nodded, but even in the dark I could make out the conflicted expression on her face. "If we go back to Earth," she said, "will we go back to playing these cat-and-mouse games with each other, Via?"

I paused, licking my suddenly dry lips. "If?"

"Oh don't give me that." Electra shook her head. "You have a lot going on here. Heck, so do I, and neither of us are the type to leave things half finished."

"Too true," I murmured. We edged closer to the light, voices turning into whispers. "What brought this on? Just because we've been learning about each other?"

Electra shrugged, the fabric of her cloak rustling in the wind. "You said it best. We work well together, it's just . . ."

I hummed in acknowledgment. "We're also very good at working *against* each other."

"Yeah. But we could do a lot together, not just on this world, you know?"

"Now you're talking like a proper light novel protagonist."

She sighed lightly. "I think we all know the main character of this story, Em'."

"Flattery will get you nowhere." I paused. Any closer and we were liable to be overheard. "I don't think your friends at Aegis would be so keen on me joining up."

"I wouldn't ask you to join Aegis, jeez." She shook her head. "Forget I said anything."

"No, no, it's too late for that now." I turned to look at my erstwhile enemy turned ally. "I'm just surprised is all. What we're doing here is pretty villainous as well, after all."

"So maybe I've changed some too—sue me," she said. "I just wanted to know if you would change as well."

I looked up at the moonless sky. "We've had this discussion before, haven't we?"

"Usually you try to tempt me over to the dark side. Figured I'd try the opposite this time."

"Tell you what." I chuckled. "After we fix everything here, after we create a foundation that won't just collapse the moment we vanish, then you can ask me that question again."

She grumbled. "Seems like a cop-out to me."

"Villain, remember?" I replied. "I'm good at running from the cops. Now . . ." I turned back towards the fire.

"It's a deal."

I paused. "Hmm?"

"After we fix whatever mess is wrong with Silverwall, with this whole island and whatever sick experiments they're doing to Ishanti's family or whatever it is, I'll get your answer."

"I guess heroes have to be ambitious." I fought back against a smirk Electra wouldn't even be able to see. "I don't hate it."

"Great." She started forward again. "Now let's break some heads."

I laughed, no longer worried about stealth. "And here I thought you were trying to convince me to be a hero." As I raised my hands, a wave of my favorite demons appeared before me. Now that I could level my skills again, it felt almost easy to assemble my favorite legion of hobblefiends, coupled with bigger gryphons and nimble blightbats for air superiority."

"Whatever." Electra raised a hand of her own, just as the men in front of our target started to turn and peer into the darkness. "Strike Twice!"

Twin bolts of lightning hit the ground, throwing the low-level thugs to the ground with a massive *boom.*

"Let's get to work, my pretties!" I cackled as I raced forward with a wave of demons, before breaking over the heads of stunned thugs and cutthroats.

If the Tarnished didn't know we were here, they sure would now.

I hardly needed to contribute, but I couldn't help but want to stretch my power armor. I caught a man's fist, grunting as he pushed me back a step before I socked him across the face. A blow that would send a normal person to the hospital didn't even knock him off his feet.

Then a gryphon swooped out of the sky, bearing him to the dirt with claws and a razor-sharp beak.

I shook out my hand. Fortunately, my armor was designed to match superhuman strength; what a pity for me that any two-bit gangster could push a few levels and suddenly be as strong as your average C-list hero back home.

On Earth I wasn't able to summon literal demons, so I'd call it a wash.

Electra came up to my side, fingers still sparking with lightning both magical and mundane. "That's all of them."

"Looks like it." I turned towards the warehouse that was the target of our attack. "Did anyone get away?"

"One or two, I think I saw," Electra said.

"We're already short on time. Just blast the front off the building."

Electra tilted her head. "We're not even gonna go inside?"

"I'd love to loot it down to the studs, but they don't even *have* studs in the walls here." I waved my hands. "Plus, how would we carry our loot?"

She shrugged. "Suit yourself." She lowered her center of gravity, before launching off another thunderbolt at the worn brick edifice. It blew a steaming hole in the wall, before the roof crashed in with a shuddering groan.

Water rushed out of the building, forcing Electra to take a few steps back. I glanced down as a river washed past my boots, running first clear, then increasingly red.

Small wooden chits bumped against my heels, mixed with oddly decorated playing cards. "A gambling den . . . bathhouse?" I asked.

"I've seen weirder," Electra replied. "So . . ."

I nodded. "Let's get out of here." I looked back at my small army of demons as we moved. "Give the guards a scare when they show up."

Electra didn't say anything, but I could feel the discomfort radiating from her. She still identified with the law. To be fair, the guards of Silverwall were surprisingly uncorrupt; they simply served a corrupt regime.

Too bad I didn't accept 'I was just following orders' as an excuse.

We jogged back into the night just as people were starting to stick their heads out of their windows. I lead the way, doing my best to mentally keep track of our location. Without even discussing it, we circled back around for another look at the scene of our attack. With practiced efficiency, we climbed up onto the roof of a nearby tenement house, wood creaking beneath me all the while, just in time to see the guard make it to the scene.

By the looks of it, the Tarnished had made it there first. I'd felt a few more of my demons vanish while we'd moved, but the gang had called it quits. Maybe they wanted the guard to bleed instead of them.

A squad of ten men and women and silver armor came down the street, a large brass lantern floating above them.

At my side, I felt Electra tense as they formed up to confront what remained of my unholy horde. They'd . . . probably win?

I sighed. "For what it's worth, Electra, I've changed as well."

With a snap of my fingers, the demons dissolved back into aether, leaving a confused squad of guardsmen standing alone in the middle of the street.

Electra looked at me askance. "Empress?"

"Let's get moving."

We made our way back to the street.

"I thought the plan was to set our enemies against each other." She wasn't asking a question.

"Yeah, well, it's kinda well known at this point that I work with demons," I replied. "It'll probably make the Tarnished madder if they think *we're* working with the city guard."

". . . I know we're gonna have to fight them both," Electra said.

I nodded. "But not today."

"Not today," she repeated. "Thanks, Em'."

CHAPTER 32

The Best-Laid Plans

Go! Go! Go!"

I jumped from the rooftop, Electra half a step behind.

I crashed into the Head Cracker feet first, servos whining as my legs hit the ground. I rolled, coming to a stop in front of another member of the Tarnished. My hand came up, pressing against his grieved shin as he tried to get a sword out of his sheath.

"Demon-itize!" Black tendrils of magic raced into him. He screamed for half a beat. Then he exploded, and a gryphon reared in the space he'd just stood.

I flipped the hood of my cloak back from where it caught the blood splatter. Then I stood just in time for Electra to throw a bolt of lightning into the guards in front of the Tarnished warehouse. My demons came a second later, just in time to catch the reinforcements pouring out of the doors.

We'd come a long way from just jumping people in alleys. Unfortunately, the Tarnished had adapted as well.

A spear user pushed out the front doors of the warehouse. With swift strikes, he cleared a space for the rest of his men. I hurled a demon-itize at his head, but he batted it away with the haft of his spear.

I was really starting to get annoyed by combat classers no-selling my magic.

I took two steps back, directing my newly summoned gryphon into the fray. It caught a blade on its inky-black wing, taking the blow to rip out the wielder's throat.

The spear punched through its head a moment later.

I clicked my tongue. "That was your friend, you know."

The Hoplite gave a laugh and leapt at me spear first.

I had just enough time for a curse before the tip hit my gauntlets and threw me backwards. I hit a wall, spinning away from a follow-up thrust.

"Could use a hand here, Electra!" Normally, my words would be swallowed by the din, but fortunately, I had a skill that made sure my orders were carried perfectly.

I ducked a thrust, jumping back as the spear shattered part of the brick wall behind me in a flash of silver.

Electra was at my side a beat before the Hoplite could turn. She flicked out a hand, and two thunderbolts raced out from her fingers.

"Haa!" the leader shouted. His spear spun, slowing as it hit both streaks of lightning like it was cutting through something physical. The magical electricity dissipated in a shower of sparks that popped when they hit the ground.

"Getting real tired of this sword saint B.S." Electra raised her other hand.

"How do you think I feel?"

I drew my arm back to throw another skill at the man, then he lunged.

"Fucking—" I threw up my arms, the blade of the spear screaming off the gauntlets. I saw a flash of annoyance cross his face as his skill failed to penetrate once more.

Empress's Armor 2, system bullshit 0.

"Hey, stick boy!" Electra punched. Her fist glowed blue with lightning.

The Hoplite jerked back, arcing streaks of electricity singing his hair. I took a few steps back as her next two punches met the haft of his spear.

I could feel the tide of the battle slowly grinding into a stalemate with my Crowd Source skill. The Tarnished Hoplite kept Electra and me from adding our weight to the main push of the demons, and without a heavy hitter, my hobblefiends and gryphons couldn't take out a well-prepared group of combat classers.

He took a leap back and counterattacked with a wall of pinpoint thrusts. I found Electra and myself pushed back from the front of the warehouse and my army of demons growing perilously thin.

Electra grunted as she batted a thrust aside with a burst of electricity. "Looks like they were more ready than you thought, huh, Empress?"

"Faster than I wanted."

I took a step forward, catching an overhead blow against crossed arms. The man raised an eyebrow; I tried to get a grip on his spear, but he yanked it back before I could and replied with a kick to the stomach. I let out a gasp, even as my armor gel took the worst of the impact.

Electra threw an arc of lightning at him. It bought us a second to breathe. "Think he'll let us get away?"

"Not likely." I summoned another pair of gryphons. They were the beefiest demons I had and were always down for a scrap. I didn't have the time to bargain for something better suited to the current challenge. "Charge me up."

"I'll be running pretty low on *actual* electricity after that."

I popped the emergency charge port on my shoulder as the Hoplite made short work of my first gryphon.

Her hand slapped my arm, and my armor beeped once as it went from power-saving mode to fully charged.

Another spear thrust killed my second gryphon.

My gantlet unfolded into a death ray. The coiled emitter vibrated against the back of my hand before spitting out a beam of supercharged, one-size-fits-all death.

For the first time, the man's eyes widened. His spear snapped up, glowing a sharp gold as he activated a skill of his own. The tip of the spear hit the plasma beam. An explosion bloomed from the point of contact, painting the alley a blinding white. I shielded my eyes with one hand.

At my side, the death ray whined once before powering down. With a flick of my arm, it folded away.

"Sheesh." Electra waved away the smoke. "Why don't you use that all the time?"

"When I'm running on battery power, a couple of shots is enough to drain the suit," I said. "Someone blew up my generator."

"Could have been anyone," she replied.

Despite the banter, neither of us took our eyes from the smoke.

Slowly it cleared, revealing our opponent still standing on his own two feet. "Oh come *on*!" It was a struggle not to roll my eyes. "What are they feeding you people?"

Electra chuckled, her hands rising into a ready stance once again. "Might want to upgrade your kit, Em'."

At least the man hadn't emerged unscathed. He was breathing heavily, clutching his shattered spear. I saw a streak of blood on his cheek, where a bit of superheated metal had flown past and cut him open. While the magic of this world was powerful, its material science lagged just a few steps behind my own.

Electra hummed. "Do you think *he'll* run away?"

I raised my hand, fingers glowing inky black. "He will if he knows what's good for him."

His eyes flicked to his spear, then back to the two of us.

I fired my skill.

The Hoplite blurred backwards, taking out a few more hobblefiends as he went.

"Nice." Electra walked out of the alleyway. "Now let's finish this."

I glanced down the street. "We're out of time, unfortunately."

She followed my gaze, catching sight of the distinctive silver-embossed armor of the city guard. "Dang. I liked it more when inevitability was on my side."

"We could probably take them both," I offered.

Electra shot me an aggrieved look.

"Yeah, yeah." I waved a hand, turning back towards the alleyway as I summoned one more wave of demons. "No messing with the law unless we have to."

Electra followed after me as we broke into a jog. "You know most of them are just doing the best they can."

I looked at her over my shoulder. "I'm sure most of the Tarnished are doing what they think is best as well."

She grumbled, picking up the pace. "Is this even working, Empress?"

Normally, it would be a struggle to keep up with the more physically fit hero, but power armor made it a breeze. "I'll let you know after we hit the location."

"They'll probably be ready there as well."

"Yes, that's what I'm hoping." I smirked. "Besides, haven't you noticed?"

"Noticed what?" Electra asked.

"Arlo hasn't shown his smarmy face since I handed his balls to him two days ago, despite the fact that they could definitely use another elite to help shore up the defenses."

"I mean, he didn't look very combat-oriented when you bent him over a table."

"Hopefully the rest of the Tarnished have a few more high-level classers like him, instead of people like that Hoplite." I looked up at the overcast sky. It drizzled lightly this morning, and the cloud cover had only thickened since then. "It's all moot. I can't use the spy mirror to pick out new targets without making our sky skimmer fly so low people might be able to see it."

Electra mulled that over. We slowed, flipping up our hoods as we mixed back into the crowds of people filling the streets of Silverwall. The city continued to move despite the gang war waged entirely by two women. I could see the tension and worry in their faces, though, especially as we wound closer to our next target on the north side of the city.

Well, you couldn't make an omelet without breaking a few eggs.

"The response time of the city guard is getting faster," Electra said after a few minutes of silence.

I nodded. "This time, maybe they'll finish the job for us. Arlo's probably lost his informants and toadies in the guard as well."

"I don't know, the demons also make it pretty obvious that you're here as well, don't they?"

"Hoisted by my own petard." I gave a wry smile. "Yes, it's probably clear I'm in the city now, but what makes it so strange is that Hawkwright hasn't done anything about it. He's refusing to change focus." That made it especially frustrating that our efforts against the Tarnished were already running into serious opposition.

If Hawkwright brought more guards back from the jungle to reinforce the city, we could turn around and hit his monster camp again. If we managed to scatter all the monsters, it could put an end to his ambition to create a stampede to overrun Lady's Port before the end of the migration season. The old man clearly knew that, and while mid-sized squads of guards eventually responded to any disturbance Electra and I caused, the number of patrols on the streets remained nearly zero.

"So much for upending the board," I muttered. "I expected him to care a little bit more about his own skin."

"Not sure why he would." Electra nodded her head towards the massive inner wall. Even in the overcast light, its silver-capped crenelations gleamed against the stone. "He's safe up there."

"And we're still down here." I shook my head. "Just a bunch of mangy dogs biting and nipping at each other while the master sits inside the house."

"Sure would have been a lot easier if Arlo had decided to play nice, huh?"

"Yes," I replied. "It sure would have."

We slowed to a stop as we neared our next destination. Electra tugged my sleeve and pointed to a lookout hunched over on a nearby roof.

"Well, let's get to work." I flicked back my hood. He hadn't seen us yet.

"I don't have enough electricity to charge up your get-out-of-jail-free card this time," Electra said.

"Then let's not need it." I shook out my hands. "Quick in and out before those pesky guards get here this time."

"Hey, look at the bright side." Electra sank to one knee, lining up a shot on the lookout. Magical lightning was surprisingly silent until it was released. "If the guards are here, they aren't at the camp."

"They aren't *somewhere*."

The man on the rooftop must have caught sight of the actinic blue glow of Electra's skill. He raised his head in our direction just as Electra released the bolt of lightning. It hit him full in the face with a dull *crack*.

The man toppled over backwards without making another sound.

I bumped her shoulder. "Lucky shot."

Electra grinned. "Always is."

CHAPTER 33

Rain Parade

I put the sheaf of stolen parchment bearing the design of my 'call center' into one of the few remaining coffins and closed the lid. "Thought I told you boys to get out of here days ago."

Dee shrugged, pulling the large wooden box back into the wagon. "We had to finish sellin' our stuff, boss."

"Sure you did." I rolled my eyes. "That's why there are exactly two coffins left?"

"Kept those actually," he replied. "Thought the both of ya might want to get out."

"Electra and I dug a tunnel. North side, covered it with some branches," I told him. "That's our escape route."

He gave a worried look, massive nose scrunching in concern. "Sure you wanna stick it out, boss? Friend at the graveyard said he wanted all the coffins, 'n more, if we had em. Things ain't goin' too well around here."

I shared a glance with Electra. "Why not?"

"Seneschal's been clamping down, plus all the people gettin' sent off to work in the camps. After the Tarnished took over all the guilds . . ." He gave a helpless shrug. "Not a lot a work, 'less you wanna catch monsters."

I frowned. Now that he mentioned it, the last few days, people had been looking worn down, restless. I'd just attributed it to the rain and my own battle with the Tarnished, but to hear that things were difficult all around . . .

"Sides, boss . . ." Dum came over, giving my right side a wide berth. "You ain't looking too good either."

I shook off the stray thoughts. There would be time to go over that new information later.

"What, you mean Dave?" I patted the ten-tentacled demon currently cuddling me beneath my cloak. His eyes blinked up at me, flickering through several different colors. I thought that meant he was enjoying himself, but my ability to understand my demons wasn't foolproof. "Dave's a good boy, aren't you, Dave?"

Dave bobbed once, wiggling.

I nodded. "Dave is gonna be a valuable member of our community going forward and should be treated with respect."

Electra leaned against the cart to avoid the rain. "Can't believe you named the thing Dave."

"What, me?" I pressed a hand against my chest. Dave wrapped one of his smaller tentacles around my pinky, eyeballs as small as my knuckle staring up at me, but I ignored it. "I didn't name anyone; he told me his name was Dave."

"No shot."

"Well, technically, his name is In'xra-Dved'nkthsskkshnuva, but he tells everyone to call him Dave." I wiggled my finger against the tentacle. "Don't you, boy?"

Another happy wiggle, complete with a wave of blinking. He'd been much happier after I got him out of the wet and under my cloak. Apparently, it didn't rain very much in hell, and the misty drizzle that blanketed the street irritated his many eyes.

"He could be saying anything." Electra pouted. "I don't even know if I believe *you* know what he's saying."

"Oh, Elenore." I flashed her a winsome smile. "That's the point. No one knows what he's saying. That's part of our deal after all."

"What was this deal again?"

Dee pushed another coffin towards the edge of the wagon, flipping it open.

"Time for you to go now." I pulled Dave off of me and set him inside the wooden box. "Remember, you will be the head manager of my new communication department. In return, you can listen to as many conversations as your little secret-hoarding heart desires."

He flashed a particularly aggressive pattern of reds and yellows at me.

I nodded, scratching him under his central eye. "That's right; any secrets you hear are not to be shared with anyone."

Eyes blinking, pupils going wide.

I placed my hand on my chest. "Not even me. The knowledge will be yours to keep until the end of days."

He bobbled happily, before reaching up to close the lid of his own coffin.

I clapped my hands once. "Well, he seems happy enough."

"I can't believe you're handing over control of our mirror phones to a literal mind flayer." Electra shook her head, droplets of rain flying off her drooping spikes.

"He's not a mind flayer, whatever that is," I replied. "Dave's species gets stronger by acquiring and keeping secrets, the more valuable and less well known the secret, the better. That's why I was able to strike such an advantageous deal with him!" I raised a finger. "Also, they don't have to eat, which is good, because last I checked we were struggling to preserve enough food for the winter."

"Okay, absolutely zero of that fills me with confidence."

I pinched the bridge of my nose. "Fine, I'll use small words. Dave like secret. Dave no like sharing secret. Any secret Dave learn Dave very incentivized to protect big strongly." I waved a hand. "It's exactly the same as an internet privacy policy, except the terms are actually enforced by a binding oath."

Electra tilted her head. "Incentivized isn't a small word."

"Fuck you."

"What's this oath anyway?"

I sighed. "Didn't I just explain it? Dave is bound not to reveal any secrets he learns while serving under me, not even to me. He was really happy when I brought up that clause, even offering to give up his vacation days in return for that addendum. I told him he could have both and he practically summoned himself."

Electra blinked. "You give demons vacation days?"

I raised my eyebrow. "Do I look like a thin-skinned billionaire who threatens people's job security if they don't work unpaid overtime making my faulty, overpriced products? I give everyone vacation days. Also, is this really the time for this conversation?"

"Uh." Dum raised a hand. "What's this about vacation days?"

"Nobody reads their schedules." I shook my head. "Do you even know how much I'm paying you now?"

Dee and Dum shared a glance.

I planted both hands on the small of Dum's back and shoved him back towards the front of the cart, while the servos whirred in my armor. "Time to go. Give all of that to Relia as soon as you get back, got it?"

"We hear you, boss." Dee pulled his brother up onto the driver's seat of the wagon.

Electra walked over. "You two gonna get out of here alright?"

Dum shrugged. "Lots a carts going in and out of the gates today."

Dum nodded. "They're sendin' more people and supplies to the huntin' camp."

"You'll blend right in," I murmured. "Now if only they would commit some of those people to the problems on their own doorstep."

"Drawing them into a fight not really working, huh, Em'?" Electra nudged my side.

"It's enough that the city guard finish the fights that we start." I flipped up the hood of my cloak.

Electra gave an aggrieved sigh. "If you say so."

"Come up with a better idea then." I turned to look at the boys. "Are you going to see Eloncio on the way out?"

"Not sure," Dum said. "He mentioned he might be back on gate duty today. S'why we were waiting."

"I'm sure that was the only reason." I ignored their denials as I turned over a new idea in my head. With Dee and Dum heading back to Silverwall, I was running precariously short on allies, so perhaps it was time to make more direct use of my enemies instead. "If you do see him, tell him that Electra and I will be hitting the camp again in . . . the next seven days."

"Be sure to pass it on, boss."

I nodded, waving for them to get on with it.

Dee snapped the reins, and the two horses pulled out of the muddy stable and onto the streets of Silverwall. Electra and I left the other direction, blending into the sparse crowd of people rushing through the rain.

For a while, we moved in silence. Now that I was looking, I could see the worry that shrouded the people of Silverwall. It wasn't the thickening rain. Hell, the men and women of the city were doggedly continuing to work despite it. The quiet war between me and Hawkwright was taking its toll on the city, and the Seneschal seemed more than happy to let his citizens pay it.

Electra nudged me. "Your plan is falling apart, Empress."

"I'm working on it." I took in the bone-deep weariness and haggard features of the people around us. "Evaluating alternative courses of action."

"Is that why we're attacking the monster camp again?" She turned to look at me, blue eyes flashing in the gloom. "I thought we were supposed to draw Hawkwright's attention away from that."

"I said I'm *working on it.*" I let out a deep breath. "And no, we won't be attacking the camp again." I tapped the case holding my spire mirror. "Even before the clouds rolled in, it was too well defended."

"Then why'd you lie to the boys?"

"Think about it." I tilted my head slightly as we turned down a narrow street. "We show up in Silverwall to talk to Eloncio, and within a day we get ambushed by Arlo and his gang."

She caught on quickly enough. "You think he flipped."

"Maybe." I shrugged. "It's also not hard to puzzle out who we are, since anyone can see a person's class if they try. That's why I've been working so hard to keep us out of sight during the day."

"But?" Electra asked.

I nodded. "*But* people *did* find out we were in town. I'm hoping that people find out about this plan as well."

"So much for drawing them into a fight with each other."

"Like you said, it's not working." I glanced over my shoulder, before pushing open a battered door frame. "Plans adapt."

Electra shut the door behind us. "This scheme is a lot more touch and go than I remember."

Inside was an empty room. The floorboards and stairs to the upper floor were broken, but the roof still kept out the rain. It was where Dee and Dum had been hiding out for the last few days; hopefully it would allow us to fly under the radar for at least one more.

"It's always been touch and go." I pulled over a battered stool. "Like any performer, the trick is to make it look as easy as breathing."

She scoffed. "What, you're saying you were always one slip-up from getting caught by Aegis?"

"Of course not, but I'm not working with my normal support network either. When you have all the time in the world to plan your heist, build your tools, and set up your getaway strategy, things will go a bit more smoothly than"—made a nebulous hand gesture—"this."

Electra nodded in understanding as she took her own seat. "Things would be a lot easier if we didn't have to defend your town."

"It's your town too."

"I just work there." She rubbed her eyes. "Jeez, I'm tired. I know crashing in this place is better than drowning in a graveyard, but still . . ."

"Out of charge?" I asked. From my long and storied history of fighting Electra, I knew that she was indefatigable while hopped up on even the smallest amount of electricity.

"I was holding onto a bit, but the mist made it too hard," she replied. "Not as bad as salt water, but ugh." She shook her head. "There's a reason I hate the rain. Please let it stop soon."

"I don't think that's going to happen." I looked towards the shuttered window and watched streaks of water run down the wall. "It looks like this might be the start of a monsoon."

Electra groaned. "How'd you figure?"

"All the people we saw on the street looked pretty prepared, don't you think?" I shrugged. "Sure, no one likes getting soaked, but it was very business as usual. Plus, island. Islands have rainy seasons."

"Please, just be wrong for once in your life." Electra put her face in her hands. "I hate, hate, hate the rain."

"Maybe you'll get hit by lightning again." I smirked. "Remember when I trapped you in a rainstorm that one time?"

She laughed. "I thought I was a goner, and then!"

"Boom." I made an explosion with my hands.

Electra laid her head back against the wall. "I dang near fried every piece of electronics in that construction site and you along with them."

"Fortunately, it was after I added the extra insulation." I winced, even though now the defeat was mostly a pleasant memory. "The static when I peeled myself out of that suit made my hair stand up for a week."

"No, really?"

I nodded, and Electra laughed again.

"You weren't the only one; I got reamed by Marvelous *and* Wonderman for reckless endangerment!"

My smile took on an entirely different cast. "Of course, that was the last week of Marvelous's career."

She gave me a weird look. "One day, you're gonna have to tell me what went down between the two of you."

"One day." I looked back towards the window, noting the fading light. "But not today."

Electra blinked as I stood up. "What? Aw, c'mon, Em, we were *just* talking about how much I hated the rain."

"And I said that to the people of Silverwall, this is business as usual." I held out my hand. "So why should it be any different for us?"

"You're busting my—butt." She grabbed my hand all the same. "I thought we were changing plans!"

"I'm evaluating." I pulled her upright. "Almost got you to curse, Electra. Better be careful, those corporate lawyers are gonna start making noises about brand safety."

She pulled a face. "Somehow, it still creeps me out how much you know about Aegis."

"I've always been good at my job." I smiled. "Now come on, let's keep pushing our luck until we get caught."

Electra ran a hand down her face. "Knock on wood."

CHAPTER 34

Deals in the Dark

Maria shoved the criminal against the rough wood of the inn's table.

She'd taken down blackguards and cutthroats in places like these, but Maria still took no small pleasure in paying back the weeks of discomfort. She had chased after shadows, tested her blade against demons and criminals alike causing mayhem in the streets, lost close friends to the brutal shocks of this gang war. Now, finally, she could bring it to an end.

It was always a triumph to bring the wicked to justice, but Maria would be lying if she said that this one wasn't a *personal* victory as well.

"Here is the leader of the Tarnished, Seneschal." She leaned forward, pressing Arlo's face against the grain. "My men will turn this building inside out and find any other Tarnished that might still be in hiding."

Hawkwright turned and regarded the struggling man in Maria's grip. The low light of the inn cast the hard lines of his face in shadow, making him look gaunt. Hard amber eyes took in the way the Tarnished thug thrashed against the table. He ran his fingers down the sharp point of his graying beard.

"Events must be transpiring poorly for you indeed." Hawkwright trailed his fingers across the polished mahogany as he circled the table, feet silent against the carpet. "You've been bled so dry that a single detachment of guards was enough to subdue and capture you in the heart of your power." He cast a hand at the cheap plaster walls, the crumbling material revealing unfinished timber beneath. "And hiding in a heap of refuse like this? Did you truly think we did not know your face even now?"

The man grunted, squirming against Maria's grip. She was higher level than him, with more attention to her physical stats besides. She lifted him the slightest bit, before slamming his lying face back down once again. "Be still."

Hawkwright tutted. "Don't damage him overmuch, Captain. It would deprive the headsman of his duty."

"Yes, Seneschal."

"Still, excellent work." He walked to the table, running a single gloved finger against the wood and coming back with splinters. "I did not believe your reports that this man could be so easily subdued. Events must be going out very poorly *indeed*."

"It was an honor to carry out the raid," Maria said.

Arlo thrashed again. "Be an honor to gut you, gormless bitch!"

Hawkwright sighed, waving a hand.

Maria rabbit punched Arlo with an armored fist, sending his head bouncing off the surface of the table so hard it cracked.

The man grunted and lay still, breath coming in pained rasps.

"Bring him over here," Hawkwright said.

At the Seneschal's words, Maria pulled Arlo back and threw him onto the floor. She hoped he would try to get up so she could have the pleasure of breaking a leg. Sadly, the criminal had a sense of self-preservation after all. He stayed there, face pressed against the stained and warped wood.

"Dogs should know their place." Hawkwright folded his hands behind his back, looking down at Arlo. "I've heard it said a pup that disobeys may be corrected, but old hounds are not worth the effort. What do you say?"

Arlo's face contorted in rage. "Causing you problems, am I?"

"You've caused me no end of troubles, dog." Hawkwright took a seat at the cracked table, picking up an amber bottle and poured out a finger of dark liquid. "This swill is almost as offensive as you are."

"Should I fetch you some of my better spirits, yer grace?" Arlo grunted. "'Pologies for not making ready for your *visit*. I've just been busy workin' my fingers to the bone trying to fix your mistakes!"

Hawkwright gave a disappointed expression. "In fact, better spirits sound quite excellent." He ignored the rest of Arlo's outburst. "Captain, find out if this establishment has anything serviceable, though I doubt there will be any food worth the name.

Maria directed two of her men to fulfill the Seneschal's request. Arlo glowered up from the floor as they found two bottles that were actually labeled, as well as a small plate of fine cheese.

Hawkwright chuckled as the food and drink were set before him. "It seems the hound keeps the choicest bits to himself." He tossed the old brew from his glass, letting it splash to the ground, before refilling it with the higher-quality liquor. The man took a sip. "Serviceable, if I must. Now, please do elaborate on what 'mistakes' you think I made." He took a small cut of cheese, and popped it into his mouth, chewing deliberately.

Arlo blinked once, but the old card shark was a crafty one. He understood Hawkwright's meaning after a scant few seconds of silence. "You know the Lady's in Silverwall?" He bared his teeth. "Why in the drowned hells are you giving her the run of the place?"

"The 'run' of the city, was it?" Hawkwright chuckled. "She's certainly done her best to distract me from what really matters."

". . . What really matters?" Arlo struggled against Maria's grip. "She's tearing this place apart."

Hawkwright continued as if he hadn't heard the other man. "She can run through the streets and cower in the slums; it makes little difference to me."

Maria held back a grimace at those words. She'd lost the right to complain the first time she'd failed to bring in the so-called Empress.

"In a week, her little town will be wiped off the face of Vecorvia, and events will return to their natural order." Hawkwright chuckled. "In truth, I might even thank you, filthy rat that you are. Had you not kept the woman preoccupied, she might have made an actual problem of herself."

Arlo growled, trying to rise.

Maria forced him back down once again.

"Which is why," the Seneschal continued, "I am entertaining your current existence. I did not need to come on this little raid, of course. I could have just as easily given the order for your throat to be slit open in your sleep." He took another drink. "But you've done well enough to keep her occupied, and even drove off that blasted woman once or twice. That makes you potentially useless to me, and I find myself curious as to what you might be able to accomplish with the initiative."

As captain of the city guard, Maria couldn't let that stand without a rebuttal. "My lord Seneschal, my men and I would be more than enough to capture the fugitive without resorting to this *trash*!"

Hawkwright waved a hand. "And if you failed again, as you have before, she would be left free to strike at the inner city. Or else run amok in our hunting grounds."

Maria shook her head. "While we are stretched thin, if I was simply allowed to consolidate—"

"That big camp outside the city, huh?" Arlo shifted beneath her boot. "I heard that she's planning to attack it this week. Somethin' about . . . drawing your attention away from the inner walls."

Maria twisted her lips into a scowl.

Hawkwright clapped his hands. "See, Captain? The dog has already proven to be of some value. Now, if you would let him up, perhaps we will even be able to converse as civilized beings, without resorting to such crass language."

"Yes . . . sir." Maria stepped back, returning to a parade rest. Arlo coughed once, sucking in a deep breath of air.

The gang leader looked up, running a hand through his mussed hair. "So, my *lord Seneschal,* I take it you want me to handle the woman who's been bothering you for so long?"

The other man laughed. "There, Maria, you see? The old dog can learn new tricks after all."

Maria said nothing, folding her arms as Arlo gingerly pushed himself back to his feet. The man wasn't young, but she made no move to help him.

"Oh, aye," Arlo said. "I can learn a trick or two, for the right incentive."

Hawkwright chuckled again. "My dear guttersnipe, your continued existence is the incentive."

Arlo shifted, muscles in his shoulders tensing.

Maria took a step forward, hand clamping down on his shoulder.

Hawkwright continued to smile pleasantly as he ate Arlo's food and drank his wine. "I believe you misapprehended the situation. I am not offering you a choice. I will dictate orders to you, and you will carry them out."

Arlo grunted. "And what's stopping me from just joining up with that bitch and making you eat those words?"

Maria's grip tightened, but Arlo ignored it.

"Perhaps this is a waste of time, after all." Hawkwright sighed, setting down the now-empty glass. "Any poor fool could see that the bridges between the two of you have been irreconcilably burned. By all means, throw yourself at her feet. It will save me the cost of the noose."

"Rat bastard."

Hawkwright's fingers tightened around the cup, leather gloves creaking. "Captain Maria, should that man speak without permission again, relieve him of his tongue."

"With pleasure, sir." Maybe that would be enough to put an end to this whole farce.

Arlo stiffened, but to his credit, he seemed to know the difference between idle insults and a genuine threat.

"Here is what you shall do for me, dog." Hawkwright turned back to his meal, trying the other bottle of spirits. "Ah, this is a much better vintage, truly." He cleared his throat. "Where was I? Ah yes. You have held your own against the so-called Empress of Lady's Port. This time, you will be taking the fight to her. Should you manage to kill her and her compatriots, I will have no further interest in your affairs. Should you fail . . ." Hawkwright finished his glass. "I will have no further interest in your affairs. Do you understand me?"

Arlo clenched his fists, before relaxing. "Fair enough. Like you've said, I gave the girl as good as I got, but she's a slippery one."

"That is why *I* shall be providing initiative. We have our own eyes in the city." Hawkwright looked at Arlo once again. "Though, I would like to know where you learned of the attack on the camp."

Arlo gave a savage grin. "One o' the guards who smuggled the Empress into the city let me know." Maria jolted. "Turns out he has two masters, and neither of 'em you."

Hawkwright stroked his beard. "See, Maria? Had I given the order to you, our quarry would have heard before the end of the day."

Arlo chuckled. "Tell you who, if you let me know which one of my men gave me up."

"Now, now, that is hardly germane to the current conversation." Hawkwright's answering smile was a sharp thing that Maria didn't like the look of.

"Sir, but a spy—!"

"That will be all, Captain. Should I need your input, I will ask for it."

Arlo shook a shocked hand off his shoulder. "He means shut up, bitch."

Hawkwright paused. "I am more than capable of disciplining my own subordinates."

"'Pologies." Arlo gave a guileless shrug. "Was just getting the hang of this new working relationship we got."

Hawkwright raised an eyebrow. "Quite."

"So, you'll let us know where to hit her, yeah? That's good. 'Course, I don't have that many fighters left, between fighting your battles for you and getting nipped by your guard dogs."

Hawkwright waved a hand. "Your men will be released with you. Understand, of course, that I am not offering clemency. Should you fail to fulfill your end of the bargain, I will be much less . . . reasonable."

Arlo snorted but gave a nod all the same.

"You'll find I'm much less ambivalent about those who betray me."

"Must be a long list," Arlo replied.

"No." Hawkwright's thin lips stretched back into a smile. "It's very, *very* short."

". . . Right." Arlo rubbed his hands together. "All that's well and good, but if you want to be *sure* I knock the girl, a little bit of help wouldn't go . . . amiss."

Hawkwright raised a brow.

"Just making a point, Lord Seneschal." Arlo spread his hands. "I could give you my word and this and that 'bout the job, but you've already made it clear you think my word is shit. So, a little bit extra from *you* would go a long way."

"I'll not send any of my men to work with this two-faced bastard," Maria said.

Hawkwright sighed. "What did I say, Captain?"

Maria paled, taking a step back.

Before she could so much as apologize, the man raised his hand. "No matter. It is rude to air out such discourtesies in front of a retainer."

Arlo chuckled. "See, Maria? I'm a retainer now."

Fear and anger warred in Maria's breast, binding her lips shut.

"In regard to your earlier question," Hawkwright continued, "this should suffice for 'support' in your endeavors." He reached into the coat of his doublet, pulling out a small, thumb-sized vial of fine golden powder.

Maria's breath caught.

"This substance will enhance the skills of one who inhales it." Hawkwright's smile was ghastly. "For a short time, anyway."

Arlo whistled. "That so? Never heard of such a thing."

"Indeed. We have worked very hard to keep it that way." Hawkwright's smile grew. "There is a reason that Silverwall remains almost entirely independent from the Senate. I have worked very hard to maintain *that* state of affairs as well."

He handed the gang leader the vial. "Now then. That does about take care of everything. We shall be in touch."

Arlo blinked. "Hoh? Gonna summon me to your fancy inner city?"

"Perish the thought." Hawkwright turned away. "But my guard captain has already made clear her stance on our liaison."

Maria swallowed. "Sir . . ."

"If none of her men will work with you, Arlo, then Captain Maria shall be your point of contact." Hawkwright met her gaze with his steel gray eyes. "Understood?"

Maria ducked her gaze. "Yes, Lord Seneschal."

"Excellent." Hawkwright clapped once. "I will leave you to see to the particulars. I want his ilk out of my dungeons by the time night falls."

"It will be done, Lord Seneschal."

"As for you." Hawkwright looked over his shoulder at Arlo. "As soon as we find that woman's bolt hole, you will be informed. Strike quickly, so that she cannot escape."

Arlo smiled. "It'll be my pleasure, Lord Seneschal."

CHAPTER 35

A Call Away

First time doing a video conference since the pandemic." I tapped the mirror once; the small screen wasn't made for this.

Electra laughed, leaning over my shoulder to get a better view of the mirror. "Used to have a call every Tuesday."

"God, don't remind me."

"My lady?" Rel's face peeked in from out of frame. "What is the 'video conference'?" Her voice was partially blocked out by the sound of rain, but I could make it out clearly enough.

"Something I will *not* be recreating in this world, if at all possible." I shook my head. "An utterly awful outgrowth of self-important middle managers."

"I know right?" Electra scrunched her nose. "You wind up in a fantasy world and the best future you can come up with is generic capitalism?"

"Another staple of your Isekai not-novels?" I cupped my chin. "Imagination should never end where experience does. Now, show me what *our* imagination has accomplished."

At that, I managed to get a small smile from Relia. "As you wish." She pulled back, shifting the mirror so that she was holding it in front of her, face pointed outward.

"Trippy. Kinda like a wide-angle lens," Electra said.

"How a mirror sees the world . . ." It was clearer than I thought, even with the occasional droplet fogging the glass. These mirrors were flat as I'd been able to make them, so the light came through clear enough to see Dee, Dum, and Ishanti standing next to the new facility I'd designed. The walls still looked rough, and the path leading up to the door was yet unpaved.

But my little town had been completed it in record time.

"You're grinning, Em'."

I took a breath. "So what if I am." I pushed Electra back. "And the interior? Was Maarin able to enchant all of the structures it needed?"

Ishanti stepped forward. "It looked as though he would fall short, but late last night he had a burst of inspiration, to hear him say it."

"Incredible." I was still smiling. "Three days, and in the pouring rain no less."

"Aww, we're used to it, boss," Dum said. "An' we had a nice dry spell yesterday where near everyone pitched in to get it done."

I shook my head. "Where did you find all the lumber?"

"We stopped building ships." Rel tilted the mirror back, revealing the large, antenna-like pole rising from the top of the building, made of . . .

"Is that a mast?"

"Four, actually," Rel replied. "While you were overtaxing yourself, you told the shipyard to make too many. They served perfectly here."

I squinted. "With a crow's nest on the top?"

"A hummingbird's actually." The mirror snapped back down to Ishanti as she stepped forward. "Maarin said it would increase the connection between the mirrors. Also, the number of hummingbirds has increased rather exponentially."

I shared a look with Electra. "Exponentially?"

"It's mating season, boss." Dum scratched the back of his neck awkwardly. "'S why all the beasties in the jungle are migrating in the first place."

"And mating season means eggs, right." I nodded. "Do they really get their venom from the flowers?"

"Indeed," Ishanti said. "Fed with normal flowers, they are harmless—if rather aggressive—birds."

I sighed. "It'll keep the facility safe."

"Been calling it the Mirror Nest, boss."

I gave Dum my least impressed stare. "Mirror Nest and Lightning Mill, huh?"

Electra punched my shoulder. "Yeah, well, you wanted to name it 'call facility one.'" Rel tilted the mirror back towards the Mirror Nest.

Now that I looked closer, I saw that there were actually flowers set on small platforms going up the central masts, woven in between metal bands covered in runes. Maarin's work. All I cared was that the enchantments functioned. The four masts formed a pillar that was almost three stories tall, plenty of surface area for the man to use, and it gave the structure a mysterious air, shrouded as it was with rain and mist.

The rest of the building didn't really live up to that idea. It looked like nothing so much as half an egg protruding from the rough ground. Between that and the leftover lumber and stone scattered around it, I could see why they'd started calling it a nest.

Still, form was second to function here. I just needed it to work.

"Let's take a look inside."

"Yes, Lady Via."

Rel and the others shuffled into the building, revealing a wide circular room, with the four masts descending down through the ceiling to anchor solidly against the floor. The beams were set so that there was a small space between them; for a human it would have been claustrophobic, but for my tentacled friend Dave, it looked like a perfect fit.

"How are you settling in?" I asked the eyeball octopus.

From his spot between the masts, Dave waved a tentacle, eyes blinking cheerily.

"Happy as a clam." I smiled. "Where's Maarin?"

"Sleeping, boss." Dee walked over to the central pillars, patting the symbols carved into the wood. "Had to put in a lot of work to get everything running right, practically collapsed after . . ."

I waved a hand. "Does it work?"

Dee and Dum shared a look. "Uh, Maarin says it does."

Dave wiggled up and down, eyes blinking all at once.

"Neat, it works."

"How, exactly?" Ishanti asked.

I grinned. "The first set of mirrors only had one connection; it was perfect for the situation we found ourselves in, but I'm sure you've noticed it's unwieldy to have separate mirrors for each connection."

"I keep mixing mine up," Rel admitted.

"Now, it looks like Maarin has finally refined his proof of concept into something usable," I said. "See the ring of disks around the central pillar?" I pointed, not that it helped. Within Dave's reach, there was a circle of indentations in the floor, each about the size of a petri dish. Seven small disks sat in the first of those indentations, though there was room for dozens.

"It looks like he made them from melted amber. Inside each is a hummingbird feather, and each mirror is linked to one of those disks. If one of you could activate your new mirror?"

There was a shuffle as Dee pulled out a newer mirror, flipping it open. The leftmost disk buzzed once when it sat on the floor, and Dave swept it up.

I laughed as Dee swore, almost dropping the mirror as a host of eyes appeared in it. "Now, tell Dave who you want to talk to."

"Uh, call my brother."

The eyes blinked once, then Dave picked up another disk, placing them both in a slot carved into the nearest mast. Each mast had several vertical slots carved into their surface, each one big enough for two disks to be placed face to face. The moment Dave did so, Dum's mirror buzzed in turn.

"And voila! Instant connections to any mirror on the network. The disks talk to each other directly, and the pillar 'boosts' the signal so that we can talk as far away as Silverwall." I couldn't stop myself from grinning. "Honestly, I'll have to go over the enchantments with Maarin later. His first draft was much less refined than this."

"Boss, he said he managed the other thing too."

My eyes widened. "Excellent. Dave, show the boys the map, if you will."

Dave wibbled gleefully. Taking the two disks out of their little cubby, he moved them over to the fourth mast. There, the slots were sized for just one disk, and they all connected to the same place. I couldn't see their mirrors directly, but I knew when the connection was made.

"Uh, boss?" Dum tilted his head. "Why are we looking at the clouds?"

I rolled my eyes. "Because you're connected to our skywhale, who's *above* the clouds."

"Why do we wanna do that?"

I sighed. "I admit, not the most useful at the moment; I conceived the idea before the monsoon rolled in. But once the clouds break, we'll have instant oversight of any region within range of the tower."

"Okay, that's pretty cool," Electra said. "But also a bit . . . uh."

I waved her off. "We can talk about proper oversight later. For now, there's only one skywhale, and only I can tell it where to go."

"Still." Electra shifted.

I turned to look at her. "We need every advantage we can get, El."

She grumbled.

"Tell you what." I gave her a pat on the shoulder. "You can write the protocol for it."

She pulled a face. "Oh, so *now* you start unloading paperwork on other people."

"You asked for it." I turned back to the mirror. "Now that we have our call facility in the Nest, I need more mirrors: at least one for every squad leader and every scout. Can you do that?"

Rel shared a glance with the boys. "It should be . . . possible, Mistress. Now that we have a surfeit of feathers, the main bottleneck is Maarin. In the next few days, we should be able to produce at least a dozen such mirrors."

"Good. Get it done, and get ready," I said. "I've heard that as soon as the rains end, the monsters will start to move. I imagine Hawkwright will launch his attack at the same time."

"That's what Llen expects as well, Mistress."

I nodded, before pausing. "The hummingbirds don't migrate, do they?"

"No, Mistress." Rel turned the mirror back towards herself. "They stay in their groves all year."

"Yet they don't get trampled, and now we have a bunch of them." I stroked my chin. "Enough to expand that grove we'd already built, right?"

"Yes, we've already planted several of the flowers closer to the sea."

"But if we could expand them . . ." I could still remember the first trip Electra and I had taken to the hummingbird grove, when a massive panther-like creature had died just from stumbling into the glade full of flowers. "I'll need to talk to Llen next. There's been a change of plan for our defenses."

"Of course." Rel nodded. "And now that communication has been taken care of, there is no reason—"

"Relia, you aren't coming back to Silverwall," I said. "My decision hasn't changed."

"But, Mistress!"

"Hey, boys." I raised my voice. "Could you get back into Silverwall, now that Eloncio's not on gate duty anymore?"

I heard them shuffle. "Probably not, boss. They barely let us out, with all the trouble you've been causing."

"There you go." I fixed Rel with a hard look. "I understand that you want to support me. That's why I need you exactly where you are."

She turned her head away. I sighed.

A tentacle crept up into view, wrapping around Rel's arm and giving it a squeeze. She jolted as Dave blinked up at her, mismatched eyes squinting in sympathy.

"See? Dave agrees with me."

"And you're taking his word over mine?" she asked mulishly.

I shook my head. "I'm standing by my own decision." She didn't reply. "Relia. What Electra and I are doing right now wouldn't benefit from just one more person. We'd need an army to tilt the scales more in our favor."

"Then come home, Lady Via." She looked at me, eyes wide and beseeching. "Come back to . . . back to us."

Back to me, she didn't say.

My next words caught in my throat. This time I looked away, avoiding Electra's gaze as well. It would be so easy to say yes. All Electra and I had done was give Arlo a bloody nose. If we left now, maybe I could add to the defenses around Lady's Port, maybe I could make a difference in the battle we all knew was coming.

But the *chance*. If I could just get to Hawkwright and end this entire farce . . .

At the end of the day, I was bad at relationships, and this was why.

"I'm sorry, Rel," I said, "but that's not going to happen."

She slumped.

I straightened my spine, taking a deep breath. "Hand the mirror off to Llen; there's still work to be done."

Electra placed a hand on my back. "It wouldn't kill ya to take the easy way out for once, Em'," she said. "We could use a rest."

I shook my head once, a single convulsive motion. "I'll rest when I'm dead."

CHAPTER 36

Reliant

Rel watched Dee leave with the mirror.

Her arms hung heavy and listless at her sides. She wanted desperately to reach out, but Lady Via wasn't here to touch; she was only a reflection in a looking glass.

Dream Sequence moaned and whined in the back of Rel's head, tying itself in knots. *I-I-I don't like this . . .*

Rel said the first words that came to her mind. "Can we take the city instead?"

Ishanti and Dum turned to stare at her. The big man scratched his bald head, wiping away lingering traces of rain. "Ah, little tricky, that . . ."

Ishanti, as always, was more direct. "Impossible. Even if a surfeit of guards allows us breach the walls, we will still be outside the defended inner wall."

Rel's stomach twisted. "And wind up caught like rats on a sinking ship." Just like Lady Via was right now. "Maybe if we bypass the walls entirely—"

"On what, flying kites?" Ishanti shook her head, long silver hair whirling. "Do you think they lack archers and ballista? Do you think the monsoon itself will not drag us from the sky with the storm's own spite?"

"We have to do something!" Rel slammed her hand against the wall of the Mirror Nest.

No one else had a suggestion.

Dave, Mistress's newest demon, pulled himself out of his little nook in the center of the room. Rel watched as he wiggled across the floor, before laying one tentacle against her thigh. His eyes blinked out of sync, taking on a sad purple hue.

Relia sighed. "Thank you, Dave." She reached down, finding a piece of skin to scratch. Dave was cool to the touch, and the eyes on either side of her finger crossed happily before rolling back in their sockets. It startled a laugh out of her.

"Your problem," Ishanti said, "is that you cannot make a decision independent of your Mistress."

Rel's head snapped up as if she'd been struck.

Dave wibbled, going a deep red as he reached for her retreating hand, but Rel was already past him. "What did you just say?"

"I believe you heard me," Ishanti replied. "But if I must, I shall repeat myself."

"I make decisions on my own all the time."

The princess simply raised a brow. "Do you believe I haven't surmised the nature of that skill? The one that allows you to perfectly predict your lady's desires? Who, I wonder, is truly making your decisions."

W-why y-ou! Dream Sequence gave an angry squeal.

Rel squeezed her eyes shut for a long moment. "I am the one making my decisions," she replied. "I simply trust in something other than myself."

"Trust in others is fickle." Ishanti hummed. "Would that end better for you than it did for me?"

Rel crossed her arms. "Is that what this is about, then? You're worried that Lady Via will betray you like Seneschal Hawkwright did?"

"More that I fear her arrogance will deliver me, and all of her adherents, into his clutches." Ishanti turned towards the open door, where the steady beat of rain drowned out any other sound. "You would not be acting as such if you did not fear the same."

Rel shook her head. "I trust my lady. She will . . . she would let me know if I was needed."

Now if only she could convince herself of that.

"Actually, Miss Rel." Dum took a step forward, floorboards creaking under his massive feet. "Not sure she would."

Rel flinched.

Dum shrugged. "She looked rough, last I saw her. Miss 'Lectra too. Been running ragged trying to stir up a gang war with the Tarnished."

"There you go." Ishanti waved a hand. "Your lady, the object of your utmost devotion, is beset on all sides, and here you stand fretting about orders."

Rel's eyes narrowed at the other woman. "Yet you just claimed my devotion was the problem."

"I claimed your inability to decide was the problem," Ishanti replied. "If you wish to pledge your life to this woman's altar, then I can hardly claim she's done nothing deserving of it. What I find so galling is that when someone threatens all that she stands for and created, you instead stand *here*, paralyzed by a face in the looking glass."

Rel looked away, biting her lip. "What should I do then?"

"Is it not plain to see? Make a choice on your own for once."

Rel shook her head. "And go directly against what Lady Via needs of me?"

"Come now?" Ishanti took a step forward. "You know as well as I do that we have become self-sufficient. The people of Lady's Port know what is at stake, and you are not the lynchpin holding it all together, as your Lady once was."

Rel wrung her hands before turning towards Dum. "Did she truly look so terrible when you saw her last?"

The massive man shrugged helplessly. "Not good. The deeps know I woulda stayed if I could, but . . . y'know."

"It is so hard to say no, when she is standing right in front of you." Rel nodded once.

"How fortunate, then, that she is not here at present," Ishanti said. "Which is the cause of our current troubles."

Rel rounded on her. "And how strange that you're so invested in this. Is it because you'll be the one in charge if I leave?"

Ishanti blinked. "Do I seem so self-deluded? Your mistress is the keystone of this entire settlement. I must state plainly that Seneschal Hawkwright stands poised to sweep her into his clutches, and with her, all of us as well." The woman shook her head again. "When you board a vessel, you inquire after the health of the captain."

Rel raised an eyebrow. "Do you think the captain is unsound?"

"I would be more sanguine should the first mate rise to her own station."

Rel let out a hiss of air, then nodded. Careful self-preservation made sense to her. It wasn't like she wanted Lady Via to fail either, though hopefully for less selfish reasons.

S-still . . . Dream Sequence chimed in, *Can we r-really—*

Sometimes, it was better to ask for forgiveness than permission.

There was one last snag. "None of this matters if I can't get into Silverwall," Rel said. "You said you couldn't smuggle us back through the gate."

Dum grinned. "Ah, well, 'Loncio might not be at the gates no more, but it's not like that's the only way into Silverwall."

"They'll be watching the jungle too," Rel said.

"Didn't stop you last time, did it?" Dum shrugged. "Maybe if we knock over a few more scouts, they'll stop sending 'em. And me and my brother've gotten real good at makin' our way through the jungle."

Rel pointed towards the open door. "In the rain?"

"Not worse than we've done before," he replied. "An' it'll make it easier to sneak past any lookouts."

"As long as there are few enough of you," Ishanti added. "A large party will find itself mired down, even though the distance to Silverwall is short."

"A day and a half on a wagon, more than that on foot." Dum tapped the side of his nose. "But once we get there, Lady Via showed me a way into the city."

"How?"

"She dug a hole under the wall, and then hid it. Bet it's still there."

"In the pouring rain?" Rel crossed her arms. "If it hasn't collapsed, it'll be completely flooded by now."

Dum chuckled. "It's . . . probably fine?"

"Are you willing to bet on it?"

Ishanti took a step forward. "Are *you* willing to bet that Lady Via will survive without you? If so, you need simply remain here."

Rel hunched her shoulders. "So I should trek through the pouring rain, dodging enemy scouts, and hope that a flooded tunnel is still open in order to save Lady Via?"

Ishanti spread her arms. "Would she do the same for you?"

Rel slumped. "In a heartbeat."

"Hmm." Ishanti turned to go.

Rel said nothing as the door shut behind her, leaving her alone with Dum and Mistress's newest acquisition. Speaking of, Rel turned to Dave. "What do you think?"

He shifted, tentacles coloring in alternating bands of red and blue. Indecisive as she was.

"Do you think the tunnel will have collapsed?" Rel asked Dum. "I don't think it will be as easy to get back out again."

He shrugged. "Might not be big enough for me to fit, but a little thing like Miss Rel? Easy as a breeze."

Relia let out a shuddering breath. "Okay." She ran a hand through her hair. "Okay. I can do a little swimming." It would be worth it, if Mistress needed her help.

Dum squeezed her shoulder. "Meet you at the gate."

Rel nodded, then turned to Dave. "You won't tell Mistress, will you?"

Dave scratched his head with a tentacle and gave a perfect shrug.

A startled laugh leapt from her lips. "Tell her what indeed."

CHAPTER 37

Back and There Again

It'd been three days since I'd last spoken with Rel, and getting the Mirror Nest set up was the only thing that had gone well in that time.

"Were we followed?"

Electra glanced away from the window. Rain trickled through the narrow gap in the shutters, wetting her cheek. "Doesn't look like it, but . . ."

I grimaced. "We don't have any detection methods."

"Yeah, tell me about it." Electra turned back to the narrow gap. "Not like we have anywhere else to go."

I knelt, floor creaking beneath my power armor. "We're being hunted. Systematically." Our only saving grace was my second class. Little Mistress had leveled steadily from parsing the motives of the people around us. I'd caught more than one tail with newly unlocked skills and pumped quite a few stat points into my summoning.

It might not be enough.

"That's why we're in this rats' nest?" Electra kicked a broken brick away from the wall. "We hit this place more than a week ago."

I let out a huff of laughter. "The villain always returns to the scene of the crime."

Electra grumbled. "That's advice for law enforcement, Em'."

"Let's just hope they don't have gritty detectives in Silverwall." I looked up. "We'll have to move again soon, though."

"Where?" Electra pulled the battered shutters all the way closed. "Back to drown in a graveyard?"

"I don't know." I wormed my gauntleted fingers beneath a shattered floorboard. "I just hope the rain is good for something."

Electra snorted. "Yeah, those poisonous flowers had better be sprouting like *weeds*."

The board came loose in my grip. "That's what they do, I've been told." Beneath it, I didn't see waterlogged mud like I expected. Instead there was more wood, sealed with rough plaster. "Hello there."

"What's up?" Electra glanced over.

"I think we might just be about to figure out how this bathhouse was so profitable," I said.

"Thought it was the gambling."

"Yeah." I reared my fist back. "I did too."

It took two blows to break through the wood and plaster. A flare of magic announced the feeble defenses of the structure fracturing and proved my first instinct right. People in this part of town didn't have money to waste on structural stability.

"Here, help me with this." I yanked at the wood, quickly widening the hole as Electra shoveled broken planks out of the way. More excavation revealed the hidden floor to be a ceiling. No doubt there was a surreptitiously hidden trap door somewhere else in the bathhouse, but sometimes brute force was a skeleton key.

Electra peered down into the hole. "You take me to the nicest places." We could make out the barest hint of a floor in the dim light, but nothing else. "Think it's a smex dungeon?"

"Child." I rolled my eyes. "Why don't you go find out?"

"Nuh-uh." Electra shook her head. "You're in full armor. I just have a few scraps of metal over normal clothes."

"You have a reactive skill," I replied.

"True!" She raised a finger. "*But,* when we were hummingbird hunting, you promised that you'd let me toss you into danger instead."

I frowned. "You really are a child."

"My PR agent said I was one at heart." She shrugged. "And in brain. Now, am I gonna have to throw you down the hole?"

"And people say *I'm* the villain." I shot her a glare, but I flicked on my shoulder-mounted flashlight. "Geronimo."

I landed against the packed dirt floor a moment later. Standing up, I turned to cast the flashlight beam across the narrow room. I saw shovels and piles of stone, but other than that, it was empty. The sound of the rain faded to a distant patter outside.

"Anyone down there?"

"Just me!" I took a step to follow a trail of moisture in the dirt. It didn't come from the rain, though; instead, it led me to the mouth of a narrow tunnel leading off into the distance. My flashlight disappeared into darkness framed by rough-cut supporting beams. "Interesting."

"Oof!" I glanced over my shoulder at Electra dusting herself off. "What's interesting?" With a flick, she threw a caged mote of electricity into the air. Actinic light bounced off unadorned walls. In the opposite corner of the tunnel, I saw a rickety wooden staircase leading back up to the bathhouse.

"It was a front," I said.

Electra tilted her head. "I mean, yeah? Isn't that the whole point? The bathhouse was just a front for a gambling den."

"I'm sure that's what everyone was supposed to think." I pointed towards the tunnel. "Seems like Arlo decided to get a little more clever than that."

Electra leaned over my head. "Secret passage. Neat!"

I shoved her off.

"Where do you think it goes, Em'?"

"Good question." I turned back towards the tunnel, arm raised as I tried to picture the layout of the city above. "Say, when you were looking out the window, could you see the inner wall?"

"Would be kinda hard to miss." Electra threw another crackling bulb of light down the tunnel. It lit up rows and rows of supports before sputtering out. "We're pretty close."

"Close enough to dig a tunnel under it, even."

Electra blinked. "This is going under the wall?"

"Unless it takes a right angle just out of sight, there's nowhere else it could be going." I scratched my chin. "We're, what, a hundred, two hundred meters from the inner city? It would take some doing, especially if you had to hide all the dirt, but it looks like our boy Arlo was already planning to take over Silverwall."

"Maybe that's why he blew you off."

"Oh please. Don't underestimate my skill at pissing people off," I replied. "Besides, this whole kind of double bluff never works." I waved a hand. "Hawkwright would have sniffed out this operation sooner or later."

"Might have been a lot later, if we'd kept distracting him instead of the Tarnished." Electra smirked. "Or even if we'd just packed up and gone home."

"Rub it in, why don't you." I turned to face her. "In any case, I think I've found out where we're going to hide for the next couple of days."

She blinked. "What, in the tunnel?"

I rubbed my face. "No, dummy. We finish the tunnel. Then we pay a little visit to Hawkwright."

"Finish the tunnel?" She peered into the darkness. "Is this a 'just the two of us, we can make it if we try' kind of deal? Cause—"

"Oh, shut up." I rolled my eyes. "I can summon the heckbadgers. If we're quick about it, we might even be able to swing back to where I stashed the power drill."

"I'm out of charge, remember?" Electra asked.

I shrugged. "It's raining; maybe you'll get lucky and be struck by lightning."

"Of course! If we just rely on luck, I'm sure it will go great." Electra nodded. "And how do we get out after, exactly?"

"Cut off the head of the snake and the body dies?" I offered.

Electra gave me a look. "I thought you always planned for the worst, Em'."

"I'm kinda running out of plans here." I sighed.

She continued staring.

"I'll work on it, okay?" I shook my head. "It would be a lot easier if I could get a look inside, but with this cloud cover . . ."

"Don't tell me your plan is actually to wait for a lightning strike." Electra winced. "You know how much I hate the water."

"So that's why you never followed me to Hawaii." I tapped my chin.

"Well, yeah." She gave an awkward laugh. "You and Riptide."

"Playing it safe." I nodded. "But we don't have the time to be careful. We're gonna have to take a gamble sooner or later, Electra." I pointed towards the tunnel. "You really think we can wait for better odds than *this*?"

"Starting to sound like sunk cost fallacy to me." Electra crossed her arms.

"You would know, little miss hero."

"Okay, first." She raised a finger. "It was my *job* to go after you every time you popped up. Second, you do not get to compare me protecting innocent people from your rampages to charging headfirst into danger without even the start of a plan."

"I do my best thinking on my feet."

She scoffed. "Oh sure, try to sell me that after you've spent the last half a year telling me that it's all about the prep work, all about the pieces getting into place, all about knowing everything that you and your enemy can do." She fixed me with a dead-eyed stare. "Go ahead, try to convince me you were lying the whole time."

I huffed, looking away. "I liked you better when you just went along with anything I said."

"Is that all it took to get on your good side?" she asked.

"I never claimed to be complicated," I said. "Look, we have two options here. We can go forward or we can go back."

"Reductive as always, Em'."

I slammed my fist against the nearest support. "*Carajo,* will you shut up for one fucking second?"

Electra leaned back against the wall of the tunnel, making a zipping motion with her lips.

I took a deep breath before pointing down the tunnel. "Forward. We try to take out the man in charge and hope to get out afterwards in the confusion." I pointed towards the staircase leading out of the basement. "Backwards. We give up and hope to hell that we can get out now while everyone is looking for us. Point is, we don't just get to take our chips to the cages and book a loss.

"Sometimes, the only way to get out of the game is to go all-in on one last hand."

Electra didn't say anything for several seconds. Finally, she took a deep breath. "Is that another one of those little things you've practiced, waiting for a moment like this?" she asked.

"Yeah, every night in front of a mirror. Thanks so much for the chance to pull it out of my back pocket." I threw my hands up in the air. "What do you want from me?"

Electra chewed her lip for a second. "If I decided I'd be more useful back in Lady's Port, what would you do? Would you walk away with me?"

I drew myself up to my full height, such as it was. "No."

Electra covered her face with one hand. "Well, crap."

"And here I thought you couldn't swear," I said.

She pushed herself off the wall. "You know what I want, actually? I want you to stop deflecting."

I raised an eyebrow. "What, is this an appeal to—"

"No." She shook her head. "No, no, no. Now it's your time to shut up. I gave you your thirty seconds, now it's my turn."

I opened my mouth.

Electra glared daggers at me.

"Fine." I took a step back. "You have the conch."

"The conch?" She shook her head again. "You know what? No, again. I'm not even going to touch that." She groaned, rubbing her face. "The way I see it, you were right when you said we only had two options, but this is what *I* think they are."

She pointed to the tunnel. "We make the wrong choice, say damn the torpedoes, and if we're even the slightest bit unlucky, a lot of people die." She pointed towards the stairs. "I make the right choice and put myself in the best place to protect the most people." She swallowed. "And one person I care about a lot, *lot* more than I should . . . almost definitely dies."

I said nothing.

"So tell me, Empress." Electra spread her hands. "What should I choose?"

Before I could muster up a response, though, the door at the top of the stairs flew off its hinges. It hit the far wall with a bang, and Electra and I spun just in time to see a man with a familiar silver armband walk down the stairs.

He wasn't alone.

"Well, well." Arlo gave both of us a grin as the rest of his gang filed in behind him. I counted at least two dozen. "Almost thought you weren't here, if not for the shouting."

I took a step back towards the tunnel. "Guess we figured out what our choice is."

"Guess so." Electra shifted to cover my side. "Fun talk."

"The best," I replied.

Arlo scratched his beard. "What's that, not gonna try to talk *me* around? Spin some yarn about how now that we're all here, we can finish this here tunnel that I've already been working on and take the fight to the real villain or some such rot?"

I let out a wan laugh. "Seems like you've laid out all the relevant points, old man."

"Ah, but see, I wanna hear it from you." Arlo leaned forward, grin growing wider. "So go on, girly, convince me. I'm listening."

"Oh, Arlo." I shook my head. "Give me a little bit of credit? We both know your mind was made up when you walked in here."

"And what makes you say a thing like that?" he asked.

"Because your mind was made up the moment you tried to ambush me the first time around." With a wave of my hand, an army of my own stepped into being. "All the rest was window dressing."

He chuckled. "Kill the blonde one, but bring me the girl alive."

I settled into a ready stance as the Tarnished pulled out their swords and clubs. "Hey, Electra."

"Yeah?" She tilted her head.

"It was a good run, wasn't it?"

Lightning danced over her knuckles. "The best."

Then three people crashed through the hole in the ceiling.

CHAPTER 38

Rel Look

Rel hauled herself from the tunnel with a gasp. Her fingers grasped weakly at the muddy floor of the building, stumbling away from the flooded hole beneath the wall. Her sodden clothes dripped icy cold water on the ground.

She shivered, walking back over to the tunnel just in time for a massive hand to stick out of the water, waving frantically.

"Shit!" Rel grabbed Dum's hand, pulling hard. He almost pulled her back into the water. She firmed her stance and grunted, lifting with burning thighs.

Dum broke the surface, sending a wave of muddy water over the edge and soaking in to Rel's already soaked boots. Rel slumped as the both of them took a second to catch their breath.

"Thanks, Rels." Dum blinked the muck from his eyes. "Thought I was a goner."

"Still stuck?" she asked.

"A bit." He grunted, shifting his shoulders. "Think I should be able to . . ." He let out a huff of air, thick muscles in his neck standing out in stark relief. With a quiet squelch, the dirt floor over his back cracked. Rel grabbed the man's hand again, and a moment later, they were both on dry ground once again.

"Thank the rains for that last point of strength."

Rel gave jittery laugh. "Rains're why you almost drowned."

He shrugged. "The sky gives and takes."

"The sea takes and gives," Rel finished.

"Right." With another grunt, he pushed himself to his feet. "We're in. Not so sure about getting back out though."

The two of them looked back at the tunnel, which was now half-collapsed in Dum's wake. The man's massive shoulders had managed to break through the muddy ground, but at the cost of their escape plan.

"I'm sure Lady Via can dig another?" Rel shrugged.

"So, we gonna track her down, then?" Dum gave a significant glance to the tightly wrapped pouch guarding their communication mirrors.

Rel's hand went to the strap. The oil cloth had already shed most of the water, but she made no move to unwrap it. "We should . . . survey the city first. Mistress might be hidden or otherwise preoccupied, I wouldn't want to . . ."

The hulking man snorted. "Let her know we're here?"

Rel swallowed. "Not yet."

P-probably wouldn't want us to be anyway, Dream Sequence grumbled.

Rel winced. Her skill had been less than helpful since her decision to leave Lady's Port. She was done being a passive actor in her own life, regardless of what her skill thought.

Regardless of what Lady Via thought.

"Any idea where to start?" Relia asked.

"Might try to find 'Loncio." Dum shrugged. "He usually got an eye on the tides round here."

Rel raised an eyebrow as she vainly tried to wring the water from her hair. "Isn't he guarding the monster camp? Why didn't we check there?"

The big man rubbed the back of his neck. "Barely got a word to him last time. Don't think it'll be easier, coming from the south instead."

Rel nodded. "So we check the barracks instead."

Dum opened the door to the shack. "After you."

Rel sighed, looking out at the misting rain that hadn't broken since they'd left for Silverwall. "At least we didn't waste time getting dry."

Dum chuckled. "Sounds like sommat boss would say."

Rel's stomach twisted in a knot, and she stepped out onto the street.

The first stop was to purchase a new pair of rain cloaks. No matter the material, half swimming through a muddy tunnel would soak even the most water-resistant fabric. Rel and Dum shared a glance as the spinster they visited nervously counted out coins before all but throwing the fabric at them.

There were fewer faces than Rel remembered in the north quarter, but those who remained gave the duo a wide berth. It set the hairs on the back of neck standing up despite the rain.

"We should hurry." Rel tugged the hood of her cloak down lower over her face. Anyone looking at her could see her class if they wanted, but the people on the street looked so skittish she doubted any would risk it. "We're standing out too much."

They picked up the pace, winding closer to the nearest barracks. Despite moving closer to the center of Silverwall, the people on the streets grew no more friendly nor more numerous. If anything, figures would catch sight of Dum's hulking physique through the rain and then turn and vanish down another street before Rel could even make out their faces.

"More skittish than last time," the man murmured.

Rel paused when they came in sight of the barracks. "That would be before Mistress started a gang war?"

He grunted in response.

Perhaps most telling of all, there were no guards at the barracks. The training yard stood empty, and none emerged to challenge them as Rel and Dum approached the building itself. Relia was about to ask her companion to force the door, but paused.

She tried the latch and found it open.

The two of them shared another glance.

"I doubt we'll find your friend here," Relia said.

"Wanna see what got left behind?"

Rel nodded, stepping quietly into the building.

Within was as desolate as without, but her eyes caught tracks on the dusty floor. She pointed, and Dum nodded, falling in step behind her as Rel picked her way deeper into the bruilding.

The bunk rooms themselves lay empty, and none of the prints went towards them or the armory. Instead, every footprint led towards the sergeant's quarters at the back of the building. The two of them paused at the soft candlelight that spilled through the half-open door.

Rel held up three fingers.

Dum slipped a club into his hands.

Two fingers.

She placed her other hand on the wood.

One finger.

"Arlo? You fucking back yet, you—"

Rel froze as a woman yanked the door open, a half-empty bottle of wine clutched in her off hand.

The woman took a half step back, armored boots clanking against the floor. "Who the fuck are you lot?"

Behind Relia, Dum gave out a booming laugh. "Little Maria, that you?"

The woman's face twisted into a frown. "The hells are you?"

"Aww, don't be like that." Dum pulled back his arm.

The woman threw up her arms just in time for Dum's fist to plow into them. With the sound of breaking glass, the guard flew across the room. She landed with a stagger, the remains of her skill flickering into nothing around her gauntlets.

Rel lunged in the same moment the woman went for her sword. "Cut!" A blade of will leapt from her lips, forcing the woman to block. Rel's knives flashed out a beat behind.

With a growl, Maria threw her hand out. A glowing chain flew from splayed fingers. Rel threw out a blade. It knocked the chain away. Rel stepped into the other woman's guard, binding their blades just in time for her knife to curve back around and take the guard in the back.

"Guugh—!" A gasp tore from the woman's lips.

Rel felt her Knife to Meat You skill grow in the back of her mind. She pushed the feeling aside even as she pushed Maria back a step. The strength fled the other woman's limbs.

A second later, Dum was there. He tore Maria's blade from her grip, yanking her hands behind her back with his massive grip.

The woman sagged, breath coming in pained rasps as blood painted the back of her tunic a deep crimson.

Dum tilted his head. "Get a lung?"

Rel shook her head. "Her cuirass protects her chest." The dagger protruded lower from the woman's back. "If we don't get her to a healer, she might still die." Gut wounds were nasty things, and the back wasn't much better. When she was a girl, she remembered seeing men slowly sicken and die from such blows.

Dum took that bit differently. "Hear that, Maria?" He wrapped a hand around the sagging woman's neck. "If you don't tell us what we want to know, you might die. Now wouldn't that be a cryin' shame?"

Maria raised her head up, glaring at both of them.

Rel stepped forward. "Do you know where Lady Via is?" If she didn't, then they'd come here for nothing.

The woman's eyes flickered, before her expression firmed, but that was enough for Rel.

"You do know." Rel palmed another dagger. Still, the threat of a bare blade did nothing to move Maria. Rel let out a deep breath. How would Lady Via handle a situation like this?

S-she'd find out what she could. Dream Sequence stirred in the back of Rel's mind. *Already found—found something, didn't we?*

Rel nodded. "She's not here," she said aloud. "Otherwise, there would be more of your men. You haven't captured her yet, or *you* wouldn't be here either." It made sense to her, and Maria's deepening glower all but confirmed it. Rel took another step forward, putting her face to face with the wounded woman. "Tell me where she is and what you're planning."

"Go drown in the river." Maria spat. It landed on Rel's cheek.

Rel slapped her, cracking the woman's head to the side, before wiping the glob of saliva from her skin. "Should we torture her?"

Dum grunted. "Usually doesn't work on guardsmen. Lotsa warrior types get pain resistance."

Rel nodded. "Back to looking for Eloncio, then."

Dum's eyes glinted. "And little Maria, here?"

Rel flicked her dagger over her fingers. "Mistress has never shied away from getting her hands dirty."

"One less sword driving them monsters forward, I say."

"Bloody seas." Maria spat again, bloody spit splattering across the floor. "Where does she find you little maniacs?" She lifted her head to glare at the two of them. "And Eloncio too? Piece of pig shit probably spying on me for the Tarnished as well."

Dum chuckled. "He always liked to play both sides. Why d'you think he joined the city guard?"

"For better reasons, I'd hoped." Maria jerked once in Dum's grip, to no avail. "Guess I was wrong."

Rel raised her knife to the woman's throat. "Loyalty is earned. I lived my entire life in Silverwall, and this city did less to earn mine than Lady Via did in a week." The edge of the blade cut into the skin and a single blood-red bead ran down the glimmering metal. "I wonder what this city did to earn your life."

She shifted her grip slightly.

It was entirely different, to kill like this, close enough to embrace. Rel did not know if she was ready for it, but that had never stopped her before.

"It didn't."

Rel paused at the woman's words.

"Silverwall didn't buy my life," Maria continued. "It shit on me and spat on me, but I clawed my way out of the gutter all the same, only to get shit and spat on all the more."

"What a sad thought to end your life with."

Maria nodded, heedless of the blade at her neck. "It really is, isn't it?"

"It makes me sad," Rel said. "You never had someone reach down and lift you up, like I did. But that alone isn't enough to stop me."

Maria looked up into Relia's eyes. "If I show you where she is, will you let me live?"

"If you take me to my lady, I will do more for you than that."

"Fuck." Maria let out a hollow laugh. "Fine, let me see the woman who inspired that kind of loyalty."

Rel turned to look at Dum. "Can you stabilize her if I pull the knife out?"

"Got some potions and a poultice," he replied. "Should do."

Rel sheathed her blade. "As long as it keeps her alive long enough for all of us to find what we're looking for."

CHAPTER 39

Friends Like These

When in mortal peril, chaos is your ally and there is no time for doubt.

I had just enough time to identify Dum's massive silhouette falling from the hole in the ceiling. "Get 'em!" I roared. My demons charged, and the first still-surprised Tarnished fell beneath a wave of claws and teeth. "Looks like you're stuck in here with me, Arlo!"

"Don't just stand there, lackwits!" Arlo flicked his wrist.

I ducked as a trio of cards spiraled over my head, and they thunked into wooden supports behind me.

Unfortunately, he rallied the rest of his goons before the fight could snowball in my favor, and they came loaded for demons. I summoned a second wave, bigger demons taking up the space I'd gained. "Hem them towards the door." My skills pinged as they ensured my orders were heard. "Don't let them spread out."

"On it!" Electra took a step forward, lightning-wreathed fist shrieking as it caved in a man's cuirass. With a vanguard of gryphons, Electra held the left side down on her own. Meanwhile, Dum and a slight figure that could only be my Relia alongside him hemmed in the left.

Who else would be so willing to disobey my direct orders? Not that I was in a position to complain.

I took a few steps back from the scrum, instructing my weaker hobblefiends to harry the flanks instead of just charging in blindly. I winced as the Tarnished chopped one of my gryphons to bits.

The Hoplite from before stepped forward, spear glowing as he cut into the middle of my horde. I sighed. As always, I was at my best in commanding from the rear, where both my skills and intelligence could shine. But of course, if you want something done right . . .

I jogged two steps forward just as a glowing spear thrust skewered another gryphon. I ducked around its disintegrating body. "Remember me?"

The Hoplite jerked back, but this close, the length of his spear was a liability. He bumped into the man behind him, and I stepped in close and swung. The man blocked my fist with his haft. The wood held, grain burning a bright blue.

He grunted, arm lashing out.

I blocked. Despite my servos, the blow nearly pushed my arm back into my face. This close, he couldn't slip back, and I snagged his weapon.

He jerked to the side. I dug in my feet.

"Little help here!"

A hobblefiend clambered up my armor. I saw the Hoplite's gray eyes widen when the little demon threw itself at his face. He killed it with a punch.

I spun, flipping the spear in my grip. The servos in my armor snapped the wood, and I jumped back just in time to avoid getting clubbed in the face with what was left of his spear.

"Demon-itize!" My lone offensive skill shot from my fingers in a black lance.

The man ducked. Of course, that only meant my attack hit the Tarnished standing behind him.

One more demon for the horde.

I cackled, firing off another dozen shots with my dwindling reserves. Many were blocked, but each one that hit a target was a surefire kill. "What's the matter, Arlo? I thought this was an ambush!"

The man pulled back up the stairs, watching as Electra and Rel picked apart anyone my demons managed to separate while I distracted the rest from the front. Maybe if it was just Electra and me alone, he could have cut through and killed me in time, but with two more people on my side to pick up the slack, the situation was quickly tilting in my favor.

He swore. "Damn the cannons."

I stiffened as he reached into his jacket and pulled out a golden vial. "Electra, shiny!"

Her head snapped up as he stoppered it. "Hey, asshole!"

Our friendly neighborhood Hoplite tackled her into the ground just in time for Arlo to take a deep snort of the golden dust inside the glass vial.

I pinched my nose. "Always some random fantasy bullshit."

The fighting slowed when Arlo started laughing maniacally. As a villainess of some renown, I rated it a solid 6/10; he lost points because it was so cliché.

Oh, and the glowing gold eyes, double-plus cliché, not impressing the expert judge.

"Damn," he said, "that's the good stuff." He rolled his wrist, and a brace of cards flew from his sleeve, spiraling lazily around his forearm. They glowed the same color as his eyes.

I should have just killed him when I had the chance back at the stupid inn. He didn't even get into a fight with the city guard for me. What a fucking joke.

I glanced over as Electra slipped to my side. "Looks like a trump card."

She was talking about hero slang for last-minute powerups that all supers kept in their pockets. A trump card like Arlo's was something external that would probably wear off if given enough time.

"He has more of it, though."

"Bait and hook?" she suggested.

Arlo started to walk down the stairs, cards snaking out of his sleeves.

"Sounds like our best bet." I waved my demons forward.

Arlo responded by launching the cards circling his arm in a shotgun blast.

"Duck." I stepped forward, catching the first barrage on my armor.

My demons didn't have anything like that. Half of them died, leaving room for the rest of the Tarnished to spread out. I glanced at my forearms before turning my glare back to Arlo. "You scratched my armor! Piece of shit, do you know how hard this will be to buff out?"

"Ah, 'course, 'course." Whatever magic drug he was on, it chilled him way the fuck out, which was a problem. "Next time I'll aim for your face."

I shifted my stance. "Big strong man, scarring up a pretty woman like me." I flicked my eyes to the side. "Rel, Dum. Over here. Bring your friend."

Arlo laughed again. "Just paying you back for before."

"Need you all to buy me some time," I whispered to my remaining demons. Then I raised my voice. "You mean when I beat your ass like a drum?"

His face twitched. There we go.

The last gryphon cut him off with a screech. It leapt, spreading its black wings wide. Oh sure, it died a second later, but in the meantime, the rest of the hobblefiends managed to get one more of Arlo's boys, and I could see the irritation plain on his face as the last of my demons finally dissipated back into the ether.

I inched back towards the open tunnel, pulling the rest of my team along with me. I tapped Dum, nodding my head at the support right next to him.

"That's enough running away." Arlo's voice lost its playful edge as he started forward. "I see you made friends with the Knight Captain. Thanks for saving me the trouble of running her down after."

I glanced over at the woman hanging from Dum's grip. She looked battered, but her armor did match the rest of the city guard. "Well, you know how it goes. I'm *great* at making friends."

"Dammit, Arlo—" the woman started. Dum put a hand over her mouth.

"Don't worry your little head, Maria. I was gonna kill you anyway." His smile turned nasty. "Even if yah didn't switch sides."

"Not that this cliché bit of dialogue doesn't make for some lovely worldbuilding," I cut in, "but we have places to be. Now!"

With a roar, Dum turned, punching out the wooden support at the mouth of the tunnel. Electra blew out the matching support with a burst of lightning. We ran as the ceiling started to groan before . . . stopping.

I slowed to a stop when the tunnel didn't collapse behind us. When I looked back, Arlo had moved to the mouth of the tunnel, an insufferable smirk on his face. "Was that supposed to do something, love?"

"Ruin my dramatic timing, why don't you." I reared back my fist, punching the wall hard enough to shatter stone. The tunnel groaned again, cracks spreading up to the ceiling. While everyone else ran, I took a second to smirk at Arlo. "Bye, bye, birdie!"

His face twisted into a glower. "No you don't!"

I raced down the tunnel as Arlo blasted after me, cards boosting him through the air.

I could hear chunks of rock falling from the ceiling behind us.

The light cut out almost immediately, but I kept sprinting into the darkness even as the crashing stones raced up behind me. A wave of dust blew past me, landing heavy on my tongue. Fuck.

I staggered, coughing, before throwing myself forward in one last desperate lunge. I hit Dum—no one else had such a massive back—and he caught me with one massive mitt, dragging me farther.

Someone screamed.

Then the rumbling stopped.

I lifted my head, coughing again as I breathed in more rock dust. "Nobody—" I gagged, spitting to the side. "Nobody move," I whispered. "Don't want to bring the rest of the tunnel down."

Someone swore violently. I recognized the voice.

"Arlo, that you, old boy?"

The stream of profanity continued until Electra summoned an actinic ball of blue light over her palm. I quickly cast my eyes around the remains of the tunnel, quickly picking out Rel, Electra, Dum, and our other passenger, the guardswoman. All of them were unharmed, just caked in dust and breathing heavily.

When I turned, I saw Arlo was much less fortunate.

"Took a nasty fall there, huh, old man?"

Arlo hissed and spit at me, fingers scrabbling at the dirt. Meanwhile, both of his legs were crushed beneath the collapsed remains of the tunnel. Apparently whatever benefits he got from that golden dust didn't protect him from several hundred tons of rock.

"I'll kill you for this." His eyes flickered weakly between their normal brown and a dull gold.

"No." I knelt on his wrist, catching the other one in my hand. "You won't."

The man glowered silently at me as his blood began to pool over the rocks.

"We've had this coming for a long time, haven't we, Arlo?"

He struggled once more, but his fading strength wasn't a match for my power armor. After a moment, the man slumped, and the gold faded from his eyes. "Fucking depths. Thought I really had you this time."

"Fool me once, shame on you; fool me twice, shame on me," I said. "I'm not giving you a third chance." I reached down, gripping him tightly beneath the chin.

"Heh, fair e—"

I twisted my wrist with a sharp *crack.*

Arlo slumped.

I let out a breath. Then I reached into the front of his shirt, pulling the thin glass phial from his shirt. The dust glowed gently in the darkness of the tunnel, still three-quarters full when I tucked it into my utility belt.

Then I stood and faced my retinue. "Now," I said. "We have a fight to finish."

CHAPTER 40

Rise of the Wretched Mole People

First, can we, like, move away from . . ." Electra pointed at Arlo's corpse. "Y'know."

I rolled my eyes. "We need to see how far the tunnel goes anyway."

Electra tossed her little ball of light. It didn't go very far. "Um."

"Well." I sighed. "I guess that answers *that* question." I turned to Dum, Rel, and the guardswoman. But something caught my eye as I turned. "Electra, get that light over here."

She peeked over my shoulder as I placed my hands on the shattered rocks. Mixed in with the simple stone were worked bricks, thick and polished smooth.

"We're under the wall," I said. "Arlo built a tunnel all the way under the inner wall."

Electra let out a low whistle. "How long d'you think *that* took?"

"On Earth, I'd say months, but with skills?" I shrugged. "They could have started long after we left Silverwall and still made it this far." I frowned, annoyed that Arlo had a knife poised at the back of Seneschal Hawkwright and still chose to fight with me instead. "They must be going wild up there." The wall would have cracked at least, and maybe a whole section could have collapsed.

It meant we were on the clock.

"Means we have options, yeah?" Electra asked.

I turned back towards Rel and Dum. "Depends on what resources we have, as I have some I wasn't expecting."

Rel hunched. "Mistress, I—"

"You disobeyed my direct orders coming here," I said. "How did you even get into the city?"

"We used your old tunnel, boss," Dum called as he settled the guardswoman against the side of the tunnel.

I raised an eyebrow. "That's too small for you."

He grunted. "Wish I'd known that first off."

"At least you didn't drown." I rubbed my face. "And Dee?"

He shook his head. "Dun' worry. He stayed behind ta keep an eye on things."

I sighed again. "Like you both should have done. I needed you there for a *reason*."

Rel flinched, but then she stiffened her spine and met my gaze head on. "So you could get caught?"

I blinked at the pushback.

"Was that part of your plan, Mistress? Getting drawn into an ambush and probably killed in the basement of a bathhouse?"

"I wasn't going to be *killed*." I crossed my arms. "At worse, Arlo was going to cart me off to this woman here." I pointed at the guard. "Thanks for bringing her, by the way, I'd like to convey my gratitude."

"You're changing the subject," Rel said.

"Am I?" I asked. "Usually I don't discuss important matters with an enemy in our midst, but I understand that many of my decisions have been questioned recently."

Rel clenched her fists. "You *taught* me how to distract people like that, my lady. Don't think it will work on me!"

I glared. "Apparently I didn't teach you well enough."

"Just what are you so afraid of?" she all but screamed.

"You were safe, dammit!" I slammed my fist against the stone hard enough to crack it. "And now you're here, in just as much danger as I am, and I don't know if I can get you out of here alive!"

Rel said nothing for several seconds, long enough for the dust to finish settling. "How did you think I felt, Mistress, with you trapped in this city?" She pressed a hand tight against her chest. "You would have me worry about my safety but disregard your own."

"Life isn't fair," I said. "I gave you an *order*—"

Electra coughed. "There you go deflecting again, Em'."

"Shut up, you're supposed to be on *my* side here!"

"Hey, hey." She raised her hands. "I'm not on anybody's side. Just, ya still haven't answered why you're so worried about little Relia here, when our butts are already in the fire."

I glared. "We had a fallback route and a choke point, even."

"I mean, it's not like we haven't been in worse spots, but like . . ." She gave a helpless shrug. "Getting bailed out there is pretty preferable, doncha think? 'Specially when they coulda just brought the tunnel down on *us.* "

"Mistress." Rel looked at me, dark eyes shining in the low light. "Why do you not want me here?"

I slumped.

"Via?" Rel reached out a hand.

"Because I can't protect you." I looked up, meeting her gaze once more. "It's been so long, so, *so* long since I had to take care of anyone other than myself. I get neurotic about it." I looked around the tunnel. "As everyone here is aware."

Electra and Dum shared an awkward glance, but for once they both stayed blessedly silent.

I rubbed my face, before pushing myself upright. "I can't *not* care about you," I said. "That surprised me most of all. Even now, I'm driving myself frantic, trying to figure out a way to get you out of this city, even though I know I *can't* run away."

Rel's hand clasped my shoulder, pulling me a step closer. "My lady," she said. "Let me care about you as well."

I snorted. "It's not that easy."

"Isn't it?" she asked. "I'm not some princess to be locked away. You gave me the confidence, the ability to stand on my own, so let me stand *beside* you, not behind you."

"You're my minion." I pulled a step back. "You're my responsibility."

"And you are mine." Rel followed. "My lady, I *know* you would give your life for me, for your people. Do not deny me the same level of devotion."

I slumped. "Fuck." This was why I worked alone. I tried to be above it all, lean into my persona, but in the end, I always got attached.

But maybe it was time to stop lying to myself.

"Fine." I ran a hand through my hair. "Fine. Fine!" I waved my hands when Rel took a step closer. "I'll try. There's nothing to do about it now. Though, I would have preferred it if you let me know you were coming."

Rel looked away. "You would have told me to head back."

I couldn't help but laugh. "And you would have listened?"

"You . . . know how to handle me, Mistress."

"Apparently not well enough," I said.

"Jesus, Em'." Electra took a step forward. "Quit being so harsh already! She did bail us out. You said it's fine, so let's move on already."

I quirked my lip. She was right, but there was one more thing I just couldn't forget. "What if they'd been a minute later, Electra?"

"Well, they probably wouldn't have?" She gave a grin. "I'm . . . pretty lucky these days."

I paused. "Of course." She'd been smug for a while now. "You have a new class."

"Yep." She popped her lips.

I raised my eyes to the stone above us. "It would be nice if people told me things." I held up my hand to forestall any reply. "No, no. Far be it from me to need to know the capabilities and decisions of my allies before we all wind up in a buried tunnel." I raised my chin. "I notice that none of you are worried about being trapped underground; could it be because I shared my own?"

With that, I walked past them, towards the end of the tunnel. "For now, we focus on our goal. Everything else can wait until after."

If there was an after.

I let my Safe Words skill lapse. "Let's move, people." From the corner of my eye, I saw Captain Maria shake her head as our words suddenly became intelligible. "Knock out the good Captain. We don't need anyone seeing this next part."

After all, whether or not she understood what we were saying, the very existence of my communication mirrors was a secret that I wanted to keep for as long as possible.

"Wait!"

I turned.

The captain struggled with her arms held behind her back.

I faced her. "What?" I spread my arms. "In case you haven't noticed, I'm a little busy here, and I'm running perilously short on patience, not to mention the fact that we are slowly creeping towards suffocation."

She grimaced at that, but Silverwall was a mining city, so the threat of suffocation was clearly one she was familiar with.

"I want to speak to you," she said.

I pinched my nose. Why did everyone wait until we were stuck underground to *talk* to me?

With a flick of my wrist, I summoned a pair of heckbadgers. "Got some overtime for you, boys. Get us a tunnel back to the surface; don't break out until I tell you to."

The guard shifted back on her heels. "I thought you didn't want to suffocate."

I smiled. "Your old friend Arlo dug this tunnel all the way under your vaunted inner wall."

The woman stiffened at that, glancing back over her shoulder.

"Makes me wonder what he planned to do with it after he finished up with me. You know, if he maybe had any designs *after* your whole army marched south to deal with my little port."

"He couldn't have taken the inner city," she replied.

I pulled out the golden vial Arlo had used to boost his powers. "Not even with this?"

She flinched.

I tucked the vial back into my belt pouch. "Seems like you've been betrayed." I straightened up, brushing dust from my armor. "Anyway, excuse me if I don't have much time to chat; I have to finish this stupid war your Seneschal started."

She swallowed once. "And me?"

"Well, if you're a good girl, we'll just put you to sleep for a little bit." I smiled at her again. "Who knows, maybe you'll even be lost in the confusion."

"Even if the Tarnished could sack the palace, you four certainly can't!" Her voice echoed off the stone. "If anything, you should be planning how to get *out* of the city."

"That's a lot more digging," I said. "Tell you what: you give us a nice easy escape route, and we'll consider it after we finish handling your boss."

She cast her eyes around the dimly lit tunnel. "And the rest of you are just going to go charging to your deaths?"

I was a little proud that even after my reprimand, none of them broke ranks.

Rel did flick her gaze over to me.

I sighed. "We'll finish our conversation later, but for now we're in this mess together, and the only way out is through."

She nodded.

Maria laughed, one harsh, sharp sound. "I'd heard you inspired loyalty, but maybe all of your followers are just suicidal instead."

"Loyalty?" I asked. Behind me, the heckbadgers continued to dig. "You mean like how Arlo was loyal to you? Or maybe how the guard who let me into the city was loyal? Or perhaps do you mean about how all the guards on the Tarnished's payroll were loyal?" I scoffed. "Don't run your mouth about things you don't understand, 'kay?"

The woman glowered up at me.

"Done?" I asked.

"Why are you doing this?" she asked.

"Why am I—" I shared a much-aggrieved look with Electra. "Why do people always ask me that? Aren't my motives clear? Transparent even?"

"I mean, not *really*, but you're pretty straightforward for a supervillain." Electra shrugged. "Also, pretty sure you just told her that you wanted to be left alone."

I snapped my fingers. "Exactly. I'm here because I want your boss to leave me and mine the fuck alone. He's proven incapable of that, so I'm here to take my complaints to him directly."

Maria looked down at the ground, a long strand of brown hair slipping free to hang over her tanned face.

"Somehow I doubt you're about to have some revelation about your loyalties," I said. "But I'll let you sleep on it. Electra?"

"Gotcha." She placed a hand over Maria's head. "Time to go night night!"

The woman flinched, then with a spark of blue, she slumped over.

Electra knelt to check her pulse. "We're good. Don't know how long until she wakes up, though."

"Probably sooner than average, given how the system works." I passed a hand over my utility belt. "I don't carry zip ties. Dum, you're on prisoner duty."

The big man nodded.

That done, I pulled out my communication mirror. When I flicked it open, I was met with black. There was no image of Dave's slowly blinking eye or even of my own reflection. Instead, it was as if the mirror was held in complete darkness.

Electra peeked over the top of my head. "Huh, don't think we've ever had no service before."

I snapped it shut with a frown. "The repeater is on my skywhale."

"And it's all the way over the monster camp." Electra took a step back. "Meanwhile, we're here, underground."

"Things could be going very badly, right now."

"Yeah, well, that's why you set things up to run without you steering the ship, ain't it?"

I glanced over my shoulder, towards Rel. "Half the people I left in charge are here now."

She shrugged. "Once we get out of this tunnel you should have a signal again, right?"

I clicked the mirror shut. "After we get out of this tunnel, we're going to be very, *very* busy."

She looked over her shoulder as well. "Aha, yeah. Y'know, being deep in the enemy's stronghold is usually like that."

"The collapsed wall will also draw the rest of the guards in the city to our very spot."

Electra didn't reply for a moment. "Think we should dig a little farther?"

"This section of tunnel is perhaps about six feet high by five feet wide. And it's only a few yards deep. That's not a lot of oxygen, Electra, and we have five people breathing it."

She pulled at her collar. "Already getting a little stuffy."

"So whatever the situation is above ground, we're just going to have to roll with it."

She gave a light chuckle. "Carpe Diem and all that." She bumped her hip against mine. "Why the long face, 'Em? We've been in worse spots."

My lips twitched. "I suppose we have." Usually on opposite sides, but there was some camaraderie to be had even in that.

Then the heckbadgers stopped digging. One of them turned, chuffing at me.

"Right." I nodded once. "Show time!"

CHAPTER 41

Riot Out of Luck

We busted out of the ground at a sprint.

The darkness of the tunnel gave way to complete chaos, shouting, screams, and more dust in the air than in the *underground tunnel*, surprisingly, but I digress.

"This way!" Electra shouted.

We darted from the smoke and dust into the open air, and a glimmering row of guardsmen materialized right in front of us.

"Out of the way!" I pushed my armor harder. Ducking my head, I crashed through the closest man, taking him in his stomach with two folded elbows. Clearly, he wasn't expecting someone as small as me to hit like a truck. A second later, Dum crashed through the hole I'd formed in the line, widening it enough for the rest of us to slip through.

"Stop them!"

"Time to toss our party favor!" I shouted over my shoulder.

With a grunt, Dum spun around. He threw Maria like a boulder at the disoriented guards. They caught her, damn stat boosts. Then the man on the left slipped on a piece of rubble, and they tumbled in on themselves like shiny silver bowling pins while the rest of the confused guards had to choose between pursuing us or helping their comrades.

To say nothing of the wall.

Electra ducked down the nearest street, but even the row of well-appointed houses couldn't hide the rising cloud of dust and the hole in the inner wall that caused it. A whole section had gone down, so wide maybe five people could walk through it side by side. Right now, more guardsmen rushed towards the site of the breach while nobles and well-to-do merchants looked on in bewilderment.

And, I noticed, more than a fair bit of worry. I could feel it thrumming through the air, like a dissonant chord. A weakness: Hawkwright had kept the people here so insulated from his secret war that they were struck dumb by the disaster.

I was good at exploiting weaknesses.

I sucked in a deep breath. "They breached the *wall*!" My voice cut through the air in a shrill scream. With my class, I could put just the right amount of terror behind every word. "The Tarnished! The Tarnished broke through! They're coming to kill us and steal all of our precious heirlooms!"

Electra shot a glance at me, mouthing *Heirlooms?*, but I could *feel* the impact my words were having. Let me tell you, the threat to their money was hitting a lot harder than the one to their lives.

Probably because these people had never known true danger a day in their lives.

"They're here for the silver! They're here for the gold!" I screamed at the top of my lungs. "Quick! They're breaking through! Lock up your safes before they break in your doors!"

I heard a shifting as people started to look at me, murmuring among themselves. They didn't believe, but then another man, tall and thin, came around the corner from the other direction. "The wall is down! The wall is down!"

His voice joined mine, and like a chorus, they formed a unison greater than the sum of their parts.

I grinned as I heard other people start to repeat my words. 'The tarnished,' 'broke through,' 'the wall'! They grew louder and louder, and when the next person started to run . . .

That was the pebble that kicked off the avalanche.

"Now *that's* how you start a riot." I cackled, nudging Electra to follow the crowd. Naturally, they ran towards the perceived safety of the castle. We followed along without a single person looking our way.

Well, except at one of us. I cast a glance at my largest follower. Even now, the men and women around us gave Dum a large berth, casting fearful glances at him as though he were about to turn on them as one of the 'poors' in their midst.

"Dum." My voice carried directly to his ears. "I need you to split off. Sow chaos, get the whole inner city into a riot if you can, then get the hell out."

He grimaced. "Uh, how'm I gonna do that second part, boss?"

"You know," I said. "They usually leave the main gate open in the middle of the day, don't they? Think you can do it?" It really was his best chance of getting out of here alive. I was forming an exit strategy already, but there was no way it would work for four people.

I wasn't sure if it would work for three.

He gave me a hard look before glancing back in the direction we were going.

"I'll give it my best shot."

Little Mistress leveled up, and I put the points into my physical skills. I was going to need all the edge I could get in this upcoming confrontation, because there was no way that Seneschal Hawkwright left his home undefended, and I was just about to send away my best muscle.

"Godspeed, you big lug." I gave him a shove to the side, and he broke off. The stampede had grown so thick he actually had to shove his way to the nearest street. Then he was out of sight, and my eyes were filled with the castle ahead.

Seeing as it was shorter than the inner walls, this was the first time I'd laid eyes on it. The building was simple, less ostentatious than the manor houses surrounding it, with four squat towers and sturdy stone walls decorated with yet more silver.

If nothing else, Silverwall continued to live up to its name.

I could see a low gate, with two men standing in front of it. Their armor was richly appointed, and unless I missed my guess, entirely ceremonial. Even from here, I could see the trepidation in their eyes as a mob bore down on them. Already I heard people clamoring for the gates to open, that the hounds were loose in the city, and dammit the Duchess had better protect them.

"Follow me, we're slipping around the side."

Rel and Electra fell in step behind me. We were to the fence fast enough that we could still slip through the gathering crowd, with a few power armor–assisted shoves. Now, more and more people joined the press, and I could see the mob slipping fully out of my control.

That was fine. I'd spent the last few weeks trying to whip up a riot; I wasn't about to complain when I finally managed one.

We went around the side of the castle's outer fence. The squat building itself didn't have any parapets, and hopefully all those within would be too focused on the mess out front. Once we reached the far side of the castle, I grabbed two of the wrought iron bars and bent them outward with a whine from my armor's servos.

"Right, let's go." The three of us raced across the castle's lawn and pressed up against the gray stone walls.

Electra looked up, eyes tracking the murder holes and archer's nests. "Think they can see us?"

"Not unless someone sticks their head out." I started along towards the nearest door. "Almost wish it was still raining, but we made it through all the same."

"If it was raining, there wouldn't have been so many people out and about," she replied.

I blinked. "True." I glanced up at the sky, noting how the clouds had well and truly broken. "It looks like the monsoon is over." I grimaced. "Probably bad news for us."

"How d'you figure?"

"The ground might still be muddy, but now that it's stopped raining, Hawkwright could send word to let the monsters loose any day."

"Uh . . . um Mistress?"

I turned to look at Rel. The woman ducked her head. "The jungle easily drinks that much water. The rivers will be full and near overflowing, but the ground will be solid enough within the day."

"Well, fuck me." I looked back towards the castle. "At least the river's to the north of us."

"Didn't you build a bridge over it, Empress?"

"Not one we can't collapse." I frowned. "Let's get inside first, quickly now."

Electra tested the door. It was a smaller one, set low enough that I had to duck to enter, some kind of servant's entrance. Fortunately, it was left unlocked.

"Guess no one expected to be put under siege today." Electra grinned as we slipped inside. I looked around the narrow passage, quickly pushing us farther into the castle. Everyone had been drawn to the other side of the castle, and these outer rooms and ways sat empty. That suited my purposes perfectly.

I found empty room with naught but a rickety wooden table and half burned candles and we slipped inside. Relia barred the door behind us.

"Plan?" Electra asked.

I took a deep breath. "Don't get caught, find Hawkwright, take care of him, get the hell out again."

She winced. "Seems rough."

"I'm working on it." I ran a hand down my face. "Rel, I don't suppose you were ever in this castle, were you?"

"No, Mistress." She shook her head. "My mother was a successful ship captain for a time, but not so successful as to be invited by the Duchess."

"So we're flying blind." Electra leaned against the wall. "Any ideas?"

"I'm *working* on it." I sighed. "We have one more objective though." I pulled out the vial of golden dust from my belt. "If we find out where this stuff is kept, we need to burn it all."

"Yeah . . ." Electra replied. "Never good to leave something like that with your enemies."

"Just a whiff of this turned Arlo from an ineffectual combatant into a juggernaut." I swirled the dust around, watching how it glimmered against the glass. "That means it'll be somewhere secure; can't have the help getting ideas."

"Not sure how it'd work on a Maid or a Cook."

"Arlo was a Card Shark," I said. "If it did that to him, it'll give anyone enough of a boost to be a nuisance. Tower or dungeon, I'd bet."

Electra nodded. "My vote is tower. Gets damp around here. Keep something like that in a dungeon, and it'll turn into slurry if you're not careful."

"Makes sense." I fished my mirror out of my pocket. "Right. I'm going to bring the skywhale back to Silverwall, now that the clouds have broken. Then I'll need to check up on things back at Lady's Port."

"Hey, maybe Ishanti knows a thing or two about the layout of this place." Electra grinned.

"One can hope."

I flicked the mirror open, giving Dave a small smile as he blinked at me happily.

"Hey, buddy," I said. "Yeah, I'm still alive. Listen, can you tell my spy plane to loop back towards the city?"

He flickered a few different colors, eyes shifting from bright orange to a deep red.

"What do you mean he's heading south?" I blanched. "They're on the move."

Electra blinked. "The monsters?"

I nodded.

The blonde looked at me, then around the small stone room we sat in. "Well, shit."

I couldn't help but laugh. When the goody two-shoes started cussing, you knew we were up the creek.

"Hawkwright must have left an order for them to start the stampede the moment the rain stopped or something." I grit my teeth. "Not good. Tell him to come back anyway. I need him overhead."

"Not keeping an eye on the monsters?" Electra asked.

"We know which way they're going."

She gave a stiff nod. "Right."

"Put me through to Ishanti," I told Dave. "The defenses need to be ready."

Dave burbled something I didn't quite catch.

"What?"

The mirror flickered, and suddenly I was staring into Dee's face. "Boss! Thank the tides! I thought my idiot brother got himself lost."

"Dee?" I felt my stomach twist into a knot. "Dee, where the fuck is Ishanti?"

He blinked. "She left already, boss."

"Left?"

"Yes . . ." He blinked rapidly. "Just yesterday, said she got an order direct from you, and sailed south t'wards the capital."

I squeezed my eyes shut. A dozen curses vied to explode from my mouth, but in the end, I think Electra said it best.

"Well, *shit.*"

CHAPTER 42

Onwards and Upwards

I stilled at the news of Ishanti's betrayal.

Across the room, Rel looked completely poleaxed, like someone had broken her legs off and she was just waiting for gravity to catch up and slam her into the ground.

I was, in a word, furious.

"Dee," I said. "Muster the militia, and get everyone inside the walls. They kicked off the monster stampede."

His eyes widened.

I continued. "You and Llen are in charge. If Ishanti shows up again, keep her out of my town until this whole mess is over."

"She was . . ." Dee looks pained.

"She was lying." I nodded. "Make sure the people in charge know, but for now, we have bigger fish to fry. It takes about a day and a half for you to walk from Silverwall down to Lady's Port, I imagine a horde of monsters will be there by nightfall."

Dee grunted. "At the latest. But, boss, why'd they start the migration now? River's running high enough that even a boat'd have trouble crossing it."

"I don't know what they're planning to do about the river." Which worried me most of all. "Assume they have a plan."

"Right."

"And—fuck. The hummingbirds. Did you set everything up?"

Dee looked pained. "Thought so. I'll send a runner out to check."

"Be quick about it. After that, focus on the plan."

"Boss," Dee interrupted just as I was about to close the mirror. "Will you be back in time?"

I quirked my lip. "Don't count on it." I snapped the case shut. Straightening, I looked at my two remaining companions. "Things," I said, "are not preceding according to plan."

Rel took a jerking step forward. "Mistress, I—"

I held up a hand. "Save it for after. You've made your bed, now we just have to figure out who's gonna be lying in it."

Electra blew out a breath against her bangs. "Like, for real. We're in kinda deep now, Em'."

"Circumstances have changed." I nodded. "Our current course of action has not. We find Hawkwright, find the source of the gold dust, and remove them both."

"That's a euphemism for killing, right?" Electra asked.

"Let me put it this way: we are no longer in a situation where we have the luxury of taking prisoners, even if we wanted to." I crossed my arms. "Lady's Port is about to get hit with a massive attack while four of our heaviest hitters are missing. We have to trust they'll hold."

"Gonna be a mess afterwards." Electra nodded. "Well, alright then. Guess we're cutting off the head of the snake."

"We're close to a tower already. We'll start there. Now let's move; that riot will only keep the inhabitants of the castle busy for so long."

As if summoned by my words, the door to our hiding place opened and a boy walked inside. He had messy hair and wore a kitchen smock with an empty wicker basket propped against his hip. He didn't even notice us until he was two steps from the pile of root vegetables stacked in crates against the far wall.

The door thunked shut.

Blinking, the young man looked at the three of us. "Uh . . . pardon, yer ladyships."

I pinched my nose. "Electra."

"Got it." She hopped off the crate she was perched on and strode over with a big friendly smile on her face. "Hey, kid, how about you take a nap for us, cool?"

"A nap? I—" Electra put a hand on his shoulder, and with a quiet zap, he slumped to the floor.

"Most useful skill I ever got."

"Put him against the wall." I moved over to the door. "Quickly. We're on a timer now."

"Don't think you have to be too worried about a kitchen boy taking a nap in the cellar." Electra gave a giggle as she propped him against the nearest crate.

"Forgive me for not wanting any more distractions." I pulled the door open. The hallway was empty of any more wandering kitchen hands. "On me."

The three of us slipped deeper into the castle, pausing only at intersections. The layout was confusing, perhaps even on purpose, but we finally found our way out of the servant hallways and into the main corridors. Rich blue and silver carpet served to muffle our steps. Most of the castle was still worried about the mass of people pressing against the far gate; Electra and I managed to subdue the few servants or guards who stumbled across us. Hawkwright's fancy little castle even had enough drawing rooms and side halls to stash the unconscious victims out of sight.

That changed when we made it to the base of the tower.

A thick wooden door blocked our way. With banded steel and a grate at eye level, it formed a secure checkpoint. I shared a silent glance with Electra before sidling up and trying the handle. Locked.

The clink of metal alerted someone inside. "Heh?" I saw the tip of a nose press against the grate. "Whos'ere!"

I swallowed a curse. "Food from the kitchens." I tried. "Cook thought wiff all the excitement, you'd like a bit."

"Cook fuckin' hates me." The man's voice deepened. He pressed his face against the grate to try to catch a glimpse of me. "Come where I can see you."

"Worth a try," I said. Rearing back, I punched my fist through the flimsy pig iron, sending the man crashing back into the room. I heard a shout; more than one guard, then.

With a snap of my fingers, I summoned a few demons into the room, and the shouts turned into screams. "Get the door open!" I shouted at my minions. Demons, however, were distractible creatures at the best of times. I yanked twice at the hole in the door, before giving it up for a bad job. "Over here, idiots! The handle!"

Electra let out a loud sigh. "Oh, gosh darn it all."

My head snapped to the side. Two women had just rounded the corner, one clearly a noble, the other perhaps her maid. They saw us, heard the screams, and the noblewoman immediately turned and ducked back around the nearest bend.

"Stop!" Rel's Cutting Words skill carved a gash into the stone a second too late.

"Fuck." I said. "*Now* we're on a timer." I kicked the door again, denting the wood, but it didn't even splinter. A few seconds later, the metal latch and deadbolt rasped as one of my hobblefiends finally managed to piece together what I wanted. I yanked the door open to find what was left of the two guards posted inside, both fully deceased, and a clockwise staircase spiraling up the tower itself.

"There." I pointed to the ceiling about two stories up. "Trapdoor."

"Let's hustle!" Electra started up the stairs. "C'mon, Rel, might need some knifework soon."

The woman glanced at me, face still lined with worry. I merely nodded. "I'll bring up the rear."

Shouts of surprise and alarm followed us up the tower, nipping at our heels. Electra put her hand against the wooden surface of the trap door, pushing once. "Locked as well." She shot a worried glance over her shoulder. "Any ideas?"

I opened my mouth. Then the trap door opened from the other side. I saw a flash of metal greaves as Electra's head snapped back up.

"Oh." I could hear the grin in her voice. "Lucky." Her hand snapped out, catching the guard around the ankle. With a *crack* of thunder, he flew across the room, landing out of sight with a crash.

"Go!"

The three of us piled into the next room, triple teaming the last remaining guard. I swiped a set of keys from one of their belts and bolted the trapdoor shut behind us.

"Where to next?" Electra asked.

I gave the room a quick once-over. Another banded door led back to the castle proper, second or maybe even third story. The rest of the room was more richly appointed than the base, with a desk and a shelf pressed against the castle's outer wall. A slim wooden staircase led up to a proper door, and . . .

I paused, drawing closer to the staircase. The highest steps had golden flecks embedded into their lacquered surface. At first, it looked like decoration, and the rest of this place had more than enough accents to make it blend in.

But all the flourishes in this castle were silver.

"Up again." I turned to Electra. "Looks like you're lucky after all."

She grinned. "Pretty useful sometimes, isn't it?"

"Rel." She snapped to attention at my call. "Are they in the tower yet?"

She nodded. "Sounds like it, Mistress. Not sure how long the trapdoor'll hold."

I glanced at the larger door. So far, no one was pounding on it, but it was only a matter of time. If someone else had the keys . . .

"Dump the shelf on the trapdoor and shove that desk over there. Hopefully that'll buy us some time."

Electra raised an eyebrow. "And what are you doing?"

I spun the keys around my finger. "I'm about to figure out why he kept this tower all locked up."

This time, I didn't need to bust the door open. It took just a few seconds to find the right key. The door to the next floor was made of finely lacquered wood, so deep brown it was almost black, and it opened silently on its hinges.

The last room of the tower was dark. Where the lower two floors had been lit with lamps and torches, this one was kept cool, almost damp. I slipped inside, letting my eyes adjust to the dim blue glow of a lone magical light, pulsing gently on a stand in the center of the room.

Plants covered the ceiling, climbing vines and rows of mossy undergrowth with small flowers barely larger than my pinky. Four columns ringed the room, wrapped in yet more ivy. The air had a smell to it: mossy, with just a hint of *dust*.

Golden moths fluttered from flower to vine and back again. After my eyes finished adjusting, the moths almost seemed to glow themselves. Occasionally, a thin wisp of gold would spill from their wings.

More damning was the row of golden vials against the far wall. There were three full, each stoppered with a small piece of cork, but the rack holding them had space for many more.

"So, whatever these moths are, you farm them for this drug, huh?" I stalked across the room, opening the small box that rested on a side table next to the vials. Within were more documents, some old and weathered. If I had been hoping for a deeper explanation in the process, I would have been sorely disappointed.

Instead, they were medical records, or close enough. Diagrams, health progress, or rather, degradation. They implanted the moth pupa into . . . the Duchess by the looks of things. That was part of their life-cycle, without which they wouldn't hatch properly.

But, of course, parasitic relationships always had a cost. In this case, it came from the health of the host, who would slowly wither away. That explained why Seneschal Hawkwright was so desperate to get his hands on Ishanti.

I put the papers down just as Rel and Electra came up the stairs.

"Bought us some time, Em', but we gotta move quick." She glanced around. "What's this?"

"Our target." I passed her the notes.

"Heh, lucky!" She went over the pages, and the smile vanished. "Wow. This is . . . *dark.*"

"Don't worry, we're burning it."

"Cool, but, uh, how are we going to get out of a burning tower when all the exits are surrounded?"

I looked around again, catching sight of a slim ladder leading up to the ceiling, the only other exit from the chamber.

"Don't worry." I placed a hand on the pouch containing my spy mirror. We'd be needing my little skywhale pretty soon. "I have a plan."

Don't Knock It Till You Try It

Y ou're sure?" I asked the mirror.

My skywhale gave a mournful hum. In the mirror's surface, I saw the tower we currently stood within. The demon circled above, lower to the ground than usual, but still high enough to be well out of sight.

Besides which, the guards had their hands full at the moment. The streets of the inner city were packed with panicked throngs of people. It looked like Dum had done his job; I hoped he'd be able to make good on his escape.

Less certain was ours.

"No. It'll be fine. Just keep your eyes open for a little snack, and then don't stop for anything until you make it all the way back to Lady's Port."

Another groaning hum echoed through my fingertips. "Well." I smirked. "I won't exactly have much time to talk after."

I clicked the mirror shut and turned. "We ready to go?"

Electra and Rel had broken down the furniture and grabbed a torch. I wasn't sure how well the plants would catch—too green—but some of the leftover dust should prove a strong enough accelerant.

From experience, I knew power-enhancing drugs burned the weirdest colors.

"Ready when you are, boss." Electra called.

"And not a moment too soon." Below our feet, the shouts had only grown in volume. Now, I heard the steady crashing of a battering ram as they tried to break down the door. It seems they didn't keep spare keys outside. "Light it up, then we're getting out of here."

She grinned, setting off a small flame with a spark. Girl Scout that she was, Electra quickly built the ember into a full fire, letting it spread to the hand-carved furniture we'd vandalized. The vines were a different matter, leaves popping and curling at the base of the nearest pillar. With a shrug, I pulled one of the golden vials from a pouch. The others clinked against each other as I pressed my back against another column.

"Bombs away."

I tossed the vial into the fire. It shattered. The fire *whooshed*, a sudden gout of heat and light that forced me to cover my eyes. When I opened them again, that half of the room was alight and the flames were spreading fast.

I grinned. "Right! That's what we're here for."

"One out of two isn't bad." Electra shrugged. "Don't think they'll let us go looking for Hawkwright."

The corner of my lip quirked up, and we climbed the ladder. The last door in the tower *wasn't* locked, so in a few minutes, we were on the roof. It was a small circular space with raised crenelations that looked more decorative than functional, not that I'd ever built a castle.

"We gotta move quick, because I can already feel the stones heating up under my feet." I took a long length of rope out from my utility belt and I tossed it to Rel. "Tie yourself and Electra up in that, leave as much slack as you can on one end."

Rel nodded. "Yes, Mistress!" She made quick work of the rope while I peeked over the parapet.

I saw people craning their heads out of the windows to look up at the tower as smoke started to seep from between the cracks in the stone. I gave them a cheery wave.

"Fire!" I heard someone shout from below. "They set the tower on fire!"

Yes, as a matter of fact, we did.

"What's the plan, Em'?" Electra asked. "Is this some magic teleport-y rope or something?"

"Wrong setting, Electra." I took my communication mirrors from my belt pouch. The new one that could connect to any other mirror, I handed to Rel. "Listen up: you're in charge of communicating with our people back home. They need to know when the stampede is going to hit, and which way the monsters are going. Don't drop it."

She blinked at me, cupping the mirror with both hands. "Mistress, I—"

I silenced her with a finger to the lips. "This is your chance to fix the mess you made."

She nodded, passing me the end of the rope.

"Electra! Keep an eye on what's happening down there."

She snorted. "Do you want me to get hit by an arrow?"

"Only in the mornings." With a flick of my fingers, I summoned a small demon made of fuzz, barely more than algae really. It warbled as I tied the other end of the rope around it.

"Lady Via?"

"You know," I said as I finished my knot. "Lots of my demons can fly, but most of them can't really carry more than one or two passengers." I tossed the little ball of fluff into the air, where it lazily floated off on invisible currents of mana. "Especially not if they're wearing such heavy armor."

"Shit!" Electra ducked back from the parapet in a clatter of arrows. "Looks like they have a few bows down there after all!"

"Don't worry." I heard a crash from below as they finally broke through the doors. "You should be out of here fast enough that it won't matter."

"You'll . . . wait, don't you mean—"

The skywhale swooped down, its massive transparent body casting refractions of the sky above. I saw a glimpse of its insides as a mouth opened wide and snapped up the fluffy little demon I'd tied the other end of the rope around.

Skywhales loved eating those things.

"Give the boys my best," I said.

I had just enough time to laugh at the betrayed expression on Electra's face before the rope snapped taut and yanked her and Rel off the rooftop.

"I'm supposed to be the heroic sacrifiiiiiiice—!" Electra screamed. Then, they were too far away to hear, rapidly shrinking specks as the skywhale climbed back into the cloud cover. A few wayward arrows missed by miles.

I glanced into my spy mirror, watching Silverwall fall away below, my two dearest friends hanging from beneath the skywhale. Then the rope clasped in its mouth hit the spy scope I'd spent so long painfully assembling, and it snapped loose.

I caught one last beautiful glimpse of the horizon, sun touching the water, before it shattered against the ground. The mirror in my hand went dark, before it returned to being a normal mirror.

"Good, that's taken care of." I nodded to myself.

Below, I heard, "Douse it! Put the fire out! Put it out!" That sounded like it would keep them busy for a while.

You might think this was the perfect time to make good on my own escape, but that sounded like a lot of work. I did have a few demons that could carry me away, but given how quickly Arlo's thugs had chopped apart my gryphons, I wasn't so sure I'd be able to make it out of arrow range, let alone clear the wall, before my mount was sniped out from under me and I fell about three stories.

My armor was good, but there was still a squishy human in here.

I patted the mirror in my hands once. "You did a good job." Still, there was some unfinished business for me to take care of. I pulled a vial of golden dust from my belt, weighing it in one hand, a mirror in the other.

"Check the parapets! Make sure the fire hasn't spread."

I raised my eyebrows. That sounded like a familiar voice. Not the one I was hoping would show up, though. I let out a sigh.

That meant I had some more work to do.

As the smoke wafting out of the tower turned to steam, I tapped out a long golden line following the circumference of my mirror. Slowly, I spiraled inward, leaving my own little yellow brick road until the entire contents of the vial were used up.

I'd seen what happened to Arlo when he used it, and honestly, I wasn't looking forward to going batshit insane. Oh sure, if my willpower was strong enough and all of that. Maybe Electra could have stayed in control, but I knew myself well enough to know that I should never be trusted with unlimited power.

Much less whatever this was, shimmering golden in the palm of my hand.

I looked up as the first guardsman hauled himself up onto the roof of the building.

He jerked back at the sight of me, sword practically leaping from its sheath. "One's up 'ere still!" Poor man almost tripped back down the ladder when I waved my fingers at him.

I leaned back on the crenelations, unbothered as another three men climbed out of the trap door. They eyed me warily, blades bare, but unwilling to make the first move. Really, who could blame them? If I saw the insane outworlder who'd been running circles around me for the past few days standing before me with a mirrorful of glowing dust, I might have second thoughts as well.

Finally, another figure hauled herself up onto the parapet. She was dirty, face streaked with soot and dust, arm bandaged up. Guard Captain Maria glared at me from across the narrow expanse of stone.

I raised the mirror slightly, like a toast in her honor. "Captain, so good to see you again."

She blanched at the sight of the dust.

What can I say, I have a knack for putting people off balance.

"Who would have thought that we'd end up here, only a scant few hours after I saved your life." I shrugged. "But that's just how the story goes, isn't it? Time and time again, my generosity is betrayed with treachery." I snorted. "And people wonder why I became a villain."

"I received no kindness at your hands, blackguard." She drew herself upright, somehow managing to look *almost* impressive despite her bedraggled state. "Throw down your arms and surrender, or I shall treat you with far less."

"Not so much as a clever retort?" I shook my head. "I can see why Hawkwright gives you all the shit jobs. Man's probably sitting in his solar, deciding how many lashes to give you for your failures."

If I wasn't looking for it, I would have missed how her eyes flicked to the rightmost tower, the one that stood taller than the rest, with arching windows on its highest floor.

Good to know where my target was hiding.

Still, she rallied. "I have no more words for you than this: Surrender! You know not what you hold." Maria took a step forward. "I'll not ask a third time."

"I think I understand well enough." I looked down at my reflection in the mirror, distorted as it was by waves of gold. "Remember, Via, this is your brain." My soft whisper disturbed the dust, washing it over the rest of the mirror.

"Kill her."

"And this is your brain on drugs."

I pressed my face to the glass and *inhaled.*

CHAPTER 44

Power Trip

My hand caught the first blade and I laughed. "Fools!" I shoved him back, inhaling deeply. "I am—" The world spun around me, my vision swimming.

But I felt like I could run a marathon.

He pulled back. I clenched my hand around the blade. No, I was monologuing, stop moving. I snorted, slamming my foot down on the parapet. "BE STILL."

He froze, glowing sword still clasped in his hand.

"That's new!" I giggled. "There you go, just stand there!" I patted the man on the cheek. I took a step, then the stone under me crumbled and I almost tripped. "God!" I caught myself against the wall, parapet . . . thing. "What happened to building codes? Oh, wait, I just stomped so hard it shattered the stone."

I looked up, grinning at Maria and the other guards. "Strong stuff." I giggled again. "Get it? Strong. Because—"

"Get her already!"

The other two charged.

I raised my other hand—oh wait, I'd never lowered my first hand that was—and spread my fingers wide. "None of *that now*."

Claws ripped from the air, catching both men.

"So *easy!*" I clenched my fingers tight, and the demons clawed them apart. The blood looked almost gold as it ran across the stones. "Man, why don't you all use this stuff?" I laughed again. "It's insane."

Maria took a step back.

"None of that—" I paused, tilting my head. "Wait, I already said that one. Need to work on my one-liners. Note to self: work on my one-liners!" I waved my hand. From each claw or arm in the air, a full demon bounded into reality.

They tackled Maria before she made it two steps.

"There we go." I crouched down next to her, my golden eyes reflecting off her breast plate. Pretty. "You just stay still . . . now."

I could feel my pulse thrumming in my ears as I leaned down, placing a hand over the golden circles. "Pretty."

She struggled, but honestly with, like, a couple tons of demons on each arm, it was pretty futile. She should know that. "What you're doing is pretty futile, you know," I told her.

She growled. "So are you."

"I know you are but what am I. Now—" I stood up. "Usually not a biiiig fan of executions, but given my track record with leaving people in this city alive . . ." I waved a hand. "I mean, you didn't even leave me alone for a day."

"I thought you might be different from the rest of the scum in Silverwall." She glared up at me. "But you turned out to be an even bigger monster."

A pulse of white-hot rage ran through me. "Oh, spare me the sanctimonious bullshit!" I slashed my hand through the air, and my demons did the rest, leaving one more body on the top of the tower.

I spun around, facing the first guard. "There, see?" I grinned at him, before it grew into another laugh. "You're—you're the lucky one!"

He swallowed, muscles in his neck convulsing. "I don't feel very . . . lucky."

I glared. "Did someone give you permission to speak?"

He shook his head.

"Good boy, stay there while I finish this." I took two steps over to the edge of the tower. Glancing over the edge, I snorted at my earlier timidity. If one or two gryphons would be shot out of the sky, I would simply summon a hundred.

"Unlimited POWER!" With my shout, a host of gryphons poured out of the abyss and into reality, lashed to my will. "Fly, my minions. Fly!"

Cackling, I stepped onto a gryphon's back as it winged off the tower. The shouts and screams of those below sounded like music to my ears, and I laughed only louder as the wind whipped my hair. My only regret in the entire world?

The distance between the towers was too short for a proper villainous monologue.

My hoard of gryphons crashed through the far tower's window in a symphony of broken glass. Shards shimmered like silver, shooting across the room. A tide of black feathers and twisted beaks overwhelmed the few remaining guards with barely a thought. Frantic nobles tried to flee, and they too were caught up.

All this before I dismounted—no, *alighted* from my own conveyance onto Seneschal Hawkwright's map table, idly kicking aside the carefully crafted castle representing the city of Silverwall.

Villainy is *all* about presentation.

"Ladies and gentlemen." I spread my arms in an elaborate bow. "Thank you for joining me for the festivities this evening; I assure you we have a *wonderful* show in store for you!"

They looked at me like I was absolutely insane. "Right, so!" I paused in my script as some of my demons started to melt, dissolving into gold slurry in time to the pounding tempo in my head. "Well. That's probably not a good sign."

Hawkwright pushed himself to his feet at the far side of the room, bald pate glinting in the sunlight. "The dead woman shows herself at last."

"Moi?" I pointed to myself. Then I blinked away the gold at the edges of my vision. "No, wait, sorry. I'm in the middle of a monologue. You can wait your turn." I cleared my throat. "Now! For my next trick, I'll need a volunteer from the audience. What's that, no one wants to participate? Well." I turned back to Hawkwright. "Come over here."

He physically struggled against my words, before taking a step back. "No."

Something snapped inside me. I growled. "That's not very nice. That's fine, I don't mind doing things from here."

"And *I* don't appreciate you wasting my time." He raised his chin. "You've abused the Ash of Creation. Just from your eyes I can see it burning you out from within. Whatever you hope to accomplish here will end in *nothing*."

"Ash of Creation is a really fancy name for this super drug you killed people to make." I took a step forward, crunching the carefully sculpted map under the heel of my boot. "And from one dead person to another, you don't have room to talk."

He glared, narrow eyes flashing. "*All* your efforts have been useless. Your minions may have escaped, but they flee to their death. Your pitiful village will be overrun by the monsters you failed to disperse, the guardsmen you could not defeat will raze the ashes and put every single one of your followers to the sword, and you will die here."

I laughed, long and loud. I could hear gold ringing in my ears, taste it upon my tongue.

"I may die." My words echoed off the walls, reverberating deep into my bones. "But that just means the people I care about will live."

"For the last time." He took a step forward. "Your cause is wasted, no matter the outcome here."

"No." I stepped forward as well, grin stretching so wide across my face it threatened to rip open my cheeks. "Because *my* life is just one more thing I'm willing to trade."

I lunged.

His hands came up, glowing with some skill.

I punched through his guard, through his chest, fist smashing out his back in a rush of golden light that pounded against my skull.

Boom. Boom. Boom.

"Practically businesslike." I shook my head. "We just sat across the board from each other, not even playing the same game."

I turned around, staggering once. The room pulsed golden around me, lights flashing in my eyes. "Now then, you lot were Hawkwright's closest supporters, yes?"

A wave of denials washed over me, the words flashing across my eyes. I staggered.

BOOM. BOOM. BOOM.

"No." I raised my hand. "Speak the truth."

From trembling lips, an older man spat. "Y-y-yessss."

I nodded. "Normally, I'd be more circumspect, but it turns out I am perilously low on mercy or forbearance. Kill them all."

And the room was awash with gold.

Oh, that wasn't just the blood anymore. Most of my demons were . . . melting away. That, that wouldn't do. Deep in the sinking, pulsating morass of my brain, I decided that I didn't want that.

"We're not quite finished." I raised my hands; they felt heavy. "Drive everyone from the castle." My demons rose again. This time, I felt the power rushing out of me like a physical torrent.

I staggered, armor catching me before I could fall. "Ah that's not . . . so good." I sank to the ground, catching myself against the wall. The room still glowed gold, but sickly, shimmering like spoilt honey. It clogged my throat and lungs. "Go." I rasped.

I felt as my demons went.

I began to shiver, teeth clattering together. I clenched my jaw, forcing the shivers to migrate down to my chest, shoulders jerking uncontrollably.

"How—how uncomfortable." Pins and needles ran down my arms. I hated it. I could still taste metal on the back of my tongue. Ah, of course, blood. I should have realized that sooner. I thought I was having some trip-induced synesthesia.

"Ar-armor." I coughed once, swallowing back the blood. "Contingency mode."

A beep.

I allowed myself to go limp as my power armor moved me into a fetal position, chin pressed against my knees. My hands folded in front of my ankles, wrist-mounted weapons opening up. I let out a shuddering breath as the joints locked into place.

At least I wouldn't have to leave my armor behind again. Put . . . way too much effort into it to just hang it out to dry.

Ugh, I was absolutely covered in sweat. What a horrendous way to die.

CHAPTER 45

Rel Aid

The castle dropped away beneath them. For a moment, it felt as though the rope would split Relia in half and send her giblets raining down to the ground below, but her stats proved high enough, and a moment later the pain eased, leaving Relia to soar over the roofs and towers of Silverwall.

She gasped for breath. A hail of arrows followed them, and Rel frantically slashed one from the air, but the rest fell short.

She was treated to the sight of Lady Via disappearing in a rush of gold.

Then they were past the inner wall, past the outer wall, and sweeping over the dense jungle canopy.

"Uffda." The rope binding Electra and Rel together creaked as the blonde woman shifted. "That's gonna bruise!"

Rel twisted, glaring upwards. "How can you. Be so. Blasé!" Her words came out in tight gasps as the rope continued to constrict her middle. "We've left her for dead!"

Electra waved her hands. "Don't go jerking around! This thing's got the rope in its mouth."

Rel stilled as the rope creaked ominously. Above them, the skywhale gave a rumbling groan that reverberated through Relia's bones.

"It . . . caught the end of the rope in its mouth?" Rel asked.

Electra nodded. "Via told it to eat the little puffy demon she tied the rope to."

They were hanging by a literal thread.

"We should . . ." Rel stiffened as the rope swayed again.

"Here, let's climb up." Electra offered her hand. "I don't think I can lift both of us, but if you get up *here* and we pull *together . . .*"

Rel looked at her own hands. One was clenched around the rope that kept her aloft, the other wrapped tight around even more precious cargo: the mirror Lady Via had entrusted to her. With careful motions, Rel tucked the communication mirror into the clever pouch inside her vest and cinched it shut. Then she took the other woman's hand.

With a grunt, Electra heaved her up, putting them face to face. The blonde woman grinned. "Come here often?"

Rel groaned. "Please, just climb."

Hand over hand, the two of them hauled their way up the rope. Rel fought the urge to squeak every time it so much as shifted, but soon enough they were at the demon's mouth. It groaned and grumbled at them as Electra boosted Rel over the flat expanse of its nose.

Rel pulled Electra up after her, and a moment later, the skywhale spat out the other end of the rope—noticeably devoid of any other demon that may or may not have been considered food.

"Poof fluffy." Electra wiped at the corner of her eyes. "We hardly knew ye."

Rel grunted. Then she made the mistake of looking down again. "Oh, oh bottomless seas."

"Hmm?" Electra glanced over her shoulder. "Oh, yeah, it's kinda disconcerting, isn't it?" She patted the skywhale's translucent skin. "Kinda looks like we're sitting on nothing."

Rel forced her eyes shut, fingers digging into the smooth and nearly invisible surface of the creature's skin. "How is this worse than hanging from a rope?" She felt the rope around her middle shift and almost screamed again.

"Relax. I'm just tying us in!" Electra raised her voice to carry over the rushing wind. "Didn't think you'd be afraid of heights, but I guess that makes sense, huh?"

"I didn't know one could be afraid of such a thing!" Rel pressed herself tighter against the demon as the rope tugged and shifted around her.

"I'll have to remind Via to take you flying more often," Electra replied. "There, done." She placed a hand on Rel's shoulder. "We're all tied in, just take a deep breath and try not to look down."

Rel nodded, pushing herself upright. The wind tugged at her hair and clothes, so fast and cold she had to shield her eyes as she slowly opened them again. Her other hand locked tight around the rope at her waist. It helped to ground her.

Even though the ground was so far below.

From the corner of her eye, she could see the horizon dipping away from her. The ocean sparkled to the west, still so vast—or perhaps even more so from her great height. Relia's breath caught, torn between terror and wonder.

Electra laughed. "Via would have some quote for you, like 'Once you have walked with your eyes turned skyward' or something." She put a steadying hand on Rel's shoulder once more. "Just focus, hear me? We've still got some work to do to make Via proud."

"Right." Rel took a deep breath. Her eyes tracked down for a moment before snapping back to the white line of the horizon. "Do you think she will survive?"

Electra quirked her lip. "I mean, I've never won anything by betting against her." She pointed to the west. "Either way, we have bigger problems."

Rel's eyes tracked over, looking at so far a distance she didn't even feel like she was truly looking *down*. Along the coastline, plumes of dust rose from the jungle, and even from this distance, she could see a path carved from devastated trees, leaving a thick scar of brown visible in the emerald green.

"The stampede," Rel said.

Electra nodded. "They're moving fast, too. Didn't Llen say we'd probably have a full day?"

"The strongmaws and smaller monsters must be fleeing in terror," Rel said. "They're racing ahead, and the larger monsters are following in their tracks."

"That could be a problem then." Electra thumped the skywhale twice. "Hey, buddy! Think you can get us a closer look?"

The whale let loose a deep groan, banking to the right. Rel latched on to the harness as the world tilted on its axis.

She refused to close her eyes.

The wind nipped at her cheeks as they flew closer to the sea, hours of travel by foot racing by beneath them as fast as she could breathe.

"Do you still have the mirror Via gave you?" Electra asked.

Rel nodded, pressing her hand against the pouch in her vest. "What if I drop it?" she shouted back over the wind.

"Don't!"

Rel swallowed around the lump in her throat, but if she left it unused it would be the same as if it slipped her from fingers.

"Get us right over them!" Electra shouted to the skywhale. They still had a way to travel before they arrived over the column of monsters, but by now Rel could pick out some of the larger members, hulking behemoths of the jungle replete with spine and claw.

"Did you even slow them down?" The words slipped from her lips unbidden, snatched away by the wind.

Electra looked over her shoulder. "What?"

"Did you even slow them down!"

The blonde's face twisted into a grimace. "Doesn't really look like it!" She scanned the stampeding horde, before her lips parted in a sigh of relief. "They didn't catch the spikesaurus rex again."

"The what?"

"The big spiny guy!" Electra gestured with her hands. "You know, the huge one that everyone's so scared of."

Rel's eyes widened. "They had a jungle king, a *direspine*?"

"Not anymore!"

Rel sighed. "The smallest mercy."

"Hey!" Electra turned back to her, a smile on her face. "Sometimes that's all you need. Now get the mirror out already!"

"Ah, right." Slowly, carefully, Rel reached back into her pouch and withdrew the mirror. She handled it with both hands, popping the clasp and holding the top of the mirror open against the wind.

An eye appeared in the circular surface of the mirror. It widened, going through a dozen happy shades.

"Dave!" Rel rubbed her throat. "The monster stampede is coming faster than we expected! I need you to connect me with Dee."

Dave blinked, eyes going a worried, sickly green.

"Quickly!" Rel shouted.

The mirror's surface flickered like a pond. It rippled once, twice, before the image resolved into Dee's face.

The massive man looked haggard, his jowls all but drooping under the strain of running Lady's Port. Still, his face lit up when he saw her. "Little Rel! You made it out?"

Rel shook her head. "Lady Electra and I did!" She looked to the side. "Mistress stayed behind to cover for us."

At once, Dee's face darkened. "My . . . brother?"

"He split from us," Rel said. "He has to escape the city on his own, but . . ."

"No." Dee shook his head. "If he's in Silverwall, he'll know how ta get out."

Rel nodded. The three of them were born and raised in the slums of that city. She hoped it would be enough, because right now, as Electra said, they had *much* bigger problems.

"The stampede is coming."

"Aye." Dee nodded. "We see the dust kicked up. We'll be ready."

"The dust is rising from the rear!" She looked down. They were nearly overhead. "The front runners have already raced ahead. They could reach the river within an hour!"

He grunted in surprise. "Already?"

Rel cast her eyes back to the horizon. She could see where the front of the stampede disappeared back into the underbrush, before the larger monsters knocked more trees aside to make way. "If not sooner," she replied.

"We'll be ready," Dee said. "Can you do anything to stop them?"

"Electra?" Rel asked.

The woman worried her lip. "Might have a skill or two, but against this many?"

"Drive them away from the coast!" Dum shouted. "Send them inland."

"Right!" Rel's heart leapt in her chest. "Our defenses."

"What defenses?" Electra shouted.

"You'll see! Now get us to the river; we need to turn the stampede, drive it eastward along the riverbank."

"Turn the stampede, she says!" Electra rolled her eyes. "Just get to the front, she says! No one ever says *how*!"

"What happened to a little luck being all we need?" Rel shouted back.

Electra growled. "Oh I'm gonna do it! I just reserve the right to complain!" She patted the skywhale. "Hear that, buddy? We need you to get us back to Lady's Port as fast as you can!"

The demon let out a rumbling moan, flapping its long not-wings once. Still, even as fast as they flew, it would be hours before they made it back.

"That's it, buddy." Electra rubbed her hand along the translucent skin of its back. "Remember, the hero also makes it in the Nick of Time." The world around them surged.

The wind ripped Rel's breath from her lungs as they raced ahead, so fast she could barely keep her eyes open. "Get ready!" she shouted to Dee. "We'll be there!"

He nodded once, closing the mirror. It took all of Rel's focus to stow it safely away again. She tucked her face into her arms, even as Electra started to laugh.

"How are we going so fast?!" Rel could barely hear her own voice over the roaring wind. She felt like she stood in the path of a typhoon.

"That's my second class!" She could hear the grin in Electra's voice. "Herowin!"

"What?!"

"Now let's get a little lucky!"

Somehow, impossibly, the wind kicked up behind them and pushed them even faster. The air itself howled around them like a living thing, screaming in Relia's ear. Below, the land blurred, then Rel realized it was only the tears streaming down her cheeks.

She was raised on the ocean, but she'd never known a storm like this.

Rel tried to speak, but it felt as though the wind shoved the words back down her throat. She could do nothing but cling to the harness as they raced against the horde of monsters down below. A day and a half on foot between Silverwall and Lady's Port. With a good horse, you could make that journey before sundown.

They reached the river so quickly Rel could scarcely believe any time had passed at all. All she knew was that suddenly, the skywhale began to slow, and when she looked down she could see the Lightning Mill, its reinforced wooden wheel churning hard and fast in the high waters of the river.

"Take us lower!" Electra shouted.

Rel blinked the tears from her eyes and picked out three lines of Electra's militia on the southern bank of the river, right in front of the wooden palisade. As she watched, the first strongmaws and twin-tailed panthers pulled themselves from the swelling river, only to be thrown back by a forest of spears in tight formation. So swollen was the river that it swept many of the wounded monsters out to sea.

But the battle was only just beginning.

More and more monsters poured from the jungle on the north bank. At the water, many of them paused, milled back and forth. Some scant few broke east, turning farther inland, but most of the monsters tried crossing the river in small groups and were easily turned back.

Then Rel caught sight of something more concerning. "They're climbing the water wheel!"

"Yeah, well, good for them." Electra turned to face the jungle. "I need to charge up for this next trick, so let me know when a bunch more of 'em show up!"

Rel nodded, heart catching in her throat as more and more monsters started to climb the water wheel. It spun, dunking half of them back in the river, but the rest clawed at the stone, sometimes even dropping down on the defender.

"Hold the line!" Rel heard a voice call as the militia pitched body after body into the river. "Hold steady!"

Rel caught sight of Dee as he rallied the spears, keeping them in formation and beating down any panther that tried to jump down from above.

If the stampede was only this, they would hold.

Then the larger monsters strode out from the jungle.

Even from on high, she could see that they easily stood at twice or even three times her height. All the beasts her mother warned her about to keep her from exploring too far from the city walls: the long and sinuous form of titan cobras, the hulking spiked spines of the broad-backed apes, the writhing legs of collosopedes.

The smaller monsters at the river took one glance back and leapt forward en masse, lest they be trampled and devoured.

"Electra! They're here!"

"Need another minute!"

In moments, the river seemed to disappear in a tide of fur and scales. White plumes like rapids formed from a thousand paws beating at the current. The stampede formed a mass so thick that you could walk across it without so much as dipping your toe in the water.

"Ready to receive!" Dee bellowed below. "Don't let them out of the water!"

The lines of militia lowered their spears.

"Forward step!"

As one, the wall of men and women drove their spears forward into the first wave of monsters. A wall of force, the product of countless skills working in unison forced them back.

But before they could so much as pull back their weapons, the next wave of monsters came clambering over the corpses of the first.

"Electra!"

The air started to crackle. "Almost there!"

The waves of monsters merged into an unending mass, pressing forward, clawing and surging over still-bleeding bodies into a forest of spears. And the spears began to break.

"Hold! Hold, damn you!"

The roar from a thousand throats drowned out the orders, and Rel could only watch as militia men began to fall. A gap opened in the front rank. Her breath caught as a row of reserves surged forward, spears glowing, to plug the gap.

But there were simply too many monsters.

Even the ones washed out to sea turned, limping back to the shore to engulf the formation from the west.

They needed to pull back to the gate, but could they even manage such a maneuver without breaking and routing?

Then Electra stood. "Look out below!" she screamed. From her pointed finger, a torrent of blue-white lightning issued forth. The *boom* struck Rel like a blow, sending her tipping backwards against the harness. It blinded her, deafened her, stole the sense from her thoughts.

When her eyes returned, the battlefield had changed entirely.

The bolt of the gods' own thunder had carved a jagged line across the northern beach, spreading into the water. It arced into the waters, and now hundreds of lesser monsters lay unmoving in the current.

As Rel watched, a frantic horde broke inland, fleeing from the river, from the thunder. Electra doubled over, gasping for air. A low laugh burbled from her throat as more and more of the monsters followed the splinter, sweeping out along the river.

"Can you do that again?" Rel shouted.

Electra shook her head, unable to speak.

The fleeing monsters curved back again, crossing the river upstream without opposition and turning to envelop Lady's Port on two fronts. Rel smiled as a torrent of glittering feathers rose from the eastern fields.

Hummingbirds, as many of them as they could move.

The entire eastern side of the city had been turned into the most expansive grove of poisonous flowers Rel had ever laid eyes on. Monsters staggered, put to sleep by the spores and picked apart by the venomous little devils, before instinct took over and they fled farther inland. Away.

"It's working!" Rel pushed herself upright. "It's working!"

"Not enough." Electra cursed, and the sound sent a lance of dread through Rel's chest. "Didn't get 'em fast enough.

Rel's head snapped back to the river. The lightning had frenzied the monsters, and not all of them chose to follow the stampede inland. Scores, hundreds, threw themselves into the river and onto the spears of the quickly regrouping militia.

Hordes climbed up the water wheel as well, until it cracked, splintered, and with a groan even Rel could hear, the entire side of the Lightning Mill fell outward, crashing into the river in an avalanche of wood and stone.

Before the waves had settled, half of the monsters poured up onto the new half-bridge spanning the southern half of the river. The militia, which used to be anchored on each side of the building, suddenly found itself exposed in the middle of its formation. Men turned, tried to hold, but the lines weren't deep enough, the ground too broken to close the gap in time.

Monsters poured into the breach like a river of feather and scale.

Men died.

"They have to pull back," Rel whispered. "They have to get back behind the walls."

Electra shook her head. "They'll never get through the gate in time. And even if they do, the Mill was part of the wall! The stampede will just tear right through!"

"There has to be something you can do!" Rel turned, pushing herself to her feet. "More lightning! The river will conduct it, buy them time to retreat!"

"I'm outta juice. No mana, no electricity." Electra slumped. "Maybe if I could get a generator but"—she pointed—"they just ripped it to shreds."

"They're *dying*."

Electra met Rel's gaze, blue eyes swimming with tears. "I know."

"Damn it all!" Rel slashed her harness, turning.

Electra caught her wrist. "You can't *jump*!"

"Watch me, I—!"

A horn sounded over the battlefield.

Then another, and another.

Rel's head whipped around, looking for their source.

"The sea!" Electra shouted.

Rel spun, mouth dropping open as a dozen ships came up the coast. Bright white sails bore the mark of Vecorvia, the golden raven of the royal family.

Then the horn sounded again, and the decks, packed full of soldiers, released a hailstorm of arrows. They hit the western flank of the horde, killing and wounding monsters by the score.

Then they fired again, and again, and again. So thick and fast the arrows came in a continuous stream.

Emboldened, the militia on the riverbank pushed forward, driving all they could back into the river.

More monsters began to turn, taking the path east, inland, away.

Then a titan cobra fell, pierced countless times by pure white shafts, and the horde broke. As one body they turned, fleeing the coast, fleeing the town, fleeing the battlefield.

On the banks of a blood-red river, the militia of Lady's Port stood, battered and bruised, line shattered like the Lightning Mill.

But still they stood.

CHAPTER 46

At What Cost

In many ways, the battle's aftermath was yet bloodier.

Rel and Electra had landed inside the city, before the skywhale took off. They'd found their way to the riverbank just as the militia finished carrying the dead and wounded through the north gate. The waters of the river ran red with blood, and corpses of countless monsters bobbed gently on the surface of the water.

Rel had spent enough time near the ocean to know that dead things on the water reeked worse than any other odor known to man.

Dee met them at the gate. "Made it just in time."

"That's me!" Electra winked, before becoming more serious. "How bad were our losses?"

"Bit over twenty dead, and almost the whole militia is wounded." He sighed. "We were moments from routing when the ships came."

Electra elbowed Rel. "Smallest blessings, eh?"

"So it seems." Rel let out a breath. "Twenty is many, all the same." The militia was small enough that twenty men was almost a tenth of its strength. If they'd had time to train more soldiers, time to build more defenses . . .

Dee's words shook her from her maudlin thoughts. "Their lives bought all of ours." He let out a breath, almost deflating. It was only then that Rel noticed he was wounded as well, a long gash running the length of his arm. It had yet to be wrapped. "Any man or woman less, and we wouldn't have held until those ships arrived."

Rel glanced through the gate towards the water. "And where did the ships come from?"

"No idea. Corvandyr, most likes," Dee replied.

"They have the royal family's sigil." Rel crossed her arms as the ships slowly shifted away from the cost in a tight loop. "Have they done anything?"

"Nothin' yet." Dee followed Rel's gaze. "Looks a bit like they're comin' round to dock at the port. Or a few of 'em at least."

"Good job only three of 'em can fit, right?" Electra asked. "Not that it'll matter much."

Rel nodded. "We should be gracious hosts then."

Dum grunted. "Let me get the rest of my people sorted, and I'll meet you at the docks."

Rel glanced at Electra. "We should both go."

"Ah well." The other woman stretched her hands up over her head. "Who wants to live forever anyway?"

They stayed just long enough to ensure that everyone would be treated, and that no more stragglers would come out of the jungle and try the palisade, before the two women turned and once again crossed Lady's Port, this time to the docks.

Rel's eyes flicked to the streetlights as they walked. None were lit, even as the sun slowly dipped closer and closer to the horizon. "If . . ." She stopped, a lump in her throat.

"Hm?" Electra tilted her head.

"If Lady Via . . . does not return," Rel managed. "Will you be able to fix the Lightning Mill? Or will the lights be lost to us entirely?"

Electra sucked her lip. "I mean, sure, I know how to make a generator with some wire and a magnet, but there's a lot more to a power plant, y'know?" She managed a weak smile. "Let's not think about that right now."

Rel nodded silently.

The wind of the ocean pushed back the growing scent of death spreading from the river. Of the twelve warships, only one had made its way to dock. The other eleven remained in formation just off the coast, out of easy arrow shot.

It did little for Rel's worry. The two of them alone wouldn't be able to stop all the combat classers on even one boat, let alone another eleven behind. For as long as Relia remembered, the royal family and the Senate of Corvandyr had paid little attention to the governance of the northern part of the island, so much so that few in Silverwall even remembered that they were part of a larger kingdom.

Now, that had changed.

The vessel sliced into port, coming to a graceful stop at the quay with a single backstroke of the oars. Ropes were thrown over, and at Rel's gesture, what few men remained on hand tied the ship to the dock.

Soldiers lowered an ornate boarding ramp, and no one spoke as an honor guard of twenty soldiers in gleaming cuirasses and white leather bracers marched off the ship.

Then Ishanti glided down the gangplank after them without a single care in the word.

Rel's eyes widened. "You!"

Ishanti ignored the outburst with aplomb; instead she glided forward down the docks like she owned it. Her honor guard fell in step beside her, and the whole parade came to a stop at the bottom of the rough stone steps leading up to the rest of the city.

"Greetings, Lady Electra, Lady Relia." Ishanti raised her head, silver hair flaming around her like a halo. "From myself and from Corvandyr."

Rel found herself at a loss for words.

"Hey, Shanti." Electra folded her arms behind her back. "Heard you flew the coop, didn't expect you to roll up with an army of all things."

The princess's brow wrinkled. "Flew the——?" She shook her head. "Regardless, the army is not here for Lady's Port, though it is fortuitous that we arrived in time to forestall the stampede." She pitched her voice to carry. "Just another sign of Hawkwright's perfidious attacks on any and all who will not bow to his ego."

Electra hummed, faint smile flicking over her face. "That's a good party line. So, what are you all here for? Not that we don't appreciate the help."

"Is it not clear? During my time assisting the outworlder called Empress, I gathered proof of Hawkwright's crimes. I presented my evidence to the Senate, and they dispatched a fleet, under the leadership of Admiral Felniv, to see the man brought to justice."

Electra made a show of peeking around Ishanti. "Is he on one of those other ships? Figured if he was leading this thing, he'd, y'know, come talk to us."

Princess Ishanti huffed. "I assured him of my ability to negotiate with my allies in Lady's Port." She reached into her sleeve, withdrawing an ornate role of parchment. "In that vein, if you have returned, then surely Lady Via has as well. I wish to present to her a town charter from the Senate, as a reward for bringing Hawkwright's treachery to light."

Electra and Rel shared a glance. "And after that?"

"After that, we shall make full speed for Silverwall, and depose Hawkwright by any means necessary." The woman gave a pleased smile. "Surely you did not think I would bring an army for such a small settlement?"

Electra shrugged. "I didn't ask what you brought the army for. But there's one little hiccup in your plan."

Ishanti raised a brow. "Oh? Do tell."

"Well, as you know, Lady Via and I went to Silverwall to uh . . . *confront* Hawkwright about his crimes." Electra crossed her arms, nodding happily. "When he attempted to kill us, working with vile *assassins* no less, we, like, took justice into our own hands."

Ishanti blinked. "What do you mean?"

Electra buffed her nails on the leather of her armor. "Oh, you know, tore down the inner wall, stormed the palace, and took our problems to the good Seneschal personally." She put on an aggrieved sigh. "Unfortunately, Empress didn't make it out, but last I saw she was pulling the place down around Hawkwright's ears."

Ishanti's eyes narrowed, but Rel could see that she quickly made the connection. The only way one person would manage to take an entire castle by herself was with the Ash of Creation. The reasons Via was forced to remain behind, on the other hand, left more open to interpretation.

"You mean to say that Silverwall has been taken from within."

"Well, I don't know if I'd say *taken.*" Electra waved her arms. "But if you march up with this army of yours, I doubt anyone left'll put up much of a fight."

"I see," the woman said. "In that case, I shall present you, her deputy, with this charter." She turned to her guard. "The admiral must be informed of this development. Time is likewise of the essence; we should take a column up the main road and see the state of the city for ourselves."

"Your highness." The soldier at her right saluted, pressing a fist to his cuirass. "I'll have the ship relay your suggestions."

"Please do."

The man jogged back to the ship, leaving three women and half a company waiting on the docks.

"So," Electra said, "how about them Saints?"

Ishanti sighed. "I did not think I would miss Lady Via's sharp tongue."

"I wouldn't count her out yet, if I were you." Electra grinned. "She's survived worse. And don't even get me *started* on the Banana Bread Affair."

"I shall refrain."

Electra's grin grew wider. "You sure? It's a real doozy!"

"Quite sure." Ishanti held out the town charter. "Now, if we could move quickly? I've just been informed we have a city to take."

"Not even gonna wait for what the admiral decides to do?"

Ishanti met Electra's gaze. "I am quite certain he'll see sense."

"Long as you know I'll be coming along," Electra replied. "Rel, too."

The princess sighed again. "I wouldn't have it any other way."

They didn't have to wait long for the admiral's reply to come from the fleet. He saw sense and would be dispatching three ships' worth of men to march on the city.

Sometimes things just went according to plan.

Night fell before they reached Silverwall. Normally it was danger-ous to travel in the dark hours, but the soldiers made short work of any monster that hadn't been swept up in the stampede.

Rel dozed for most of it, nodding off in the back of a cart as the army marched through the night.

Even still, never had a day felt so long. It was near midday when they came within sight of the city. For a moment, Rel worried they would not be allowed in, but the herald raised the royal family's banner, and the people of Silverwall threw the gates wide open.

It took Electra physically restraining Rel to keep her from racing ahead the moment they set foot in the city. Nearly a thousand soldiers marched down the main thoroughfare in lock step, the sound of their steps echoing off the buildings.

As for the citizens themselves, there were no cheers, no thrown garlands. Men, women, and children watched silently. Guardsmen, what few had not already deserted, were taken into custody. None resisted.

Somehow, they reached the castle. It lay abandoned.

The only sign of what happened were piles of golden sludge, hardened and inert, that covered the corridors. Rel could only assume they were the remains of Mistress's demons, and only time would tell why no one had returned to the castle in the day since.

It didn't take long to find Lady Via.

She lay in the remains of Hawkwright's solar, amidst the wreckage of a once fine map table. Her long black hair was splayed out over the splinters like a shroud, face half-hidden against her knees. She was curled into a ball, chin tucked against chest, arms crossed over her knees. Asleep.

Or worse, Rel thought.

Her armor, on the other hand, was very much awake.

Both of her gauntlets sat extended, weapons that Rel could make neither head nor tails of slowly sweeping the room. A red light at Via's collar blinked slowly, and Rel could only hope it meant that her Mistress still lived inside of her metal coffin.

"Well, sugar." Electra scratched the back of her head. "I think she's in safeguard mode or something. It'll probably shoot anything that gets close."

"What do we do, then?"

Electra opened her mouth, then she paused, looking at Rel. "Maybe take a page from Empress's book."

Rel raised an eyebrow.

Electra stepped up behind her, shoving her a step forward.

Rel squawked, backpedaling frantically as Via's armor chirped.

"Recognized—Relia, priority two. Deactivating."

Then, with another beep and whirr, the weapons folded away, leaving just a single light still blinking softly at Lady Via's collar.

"See?" Electra walked forward. "Works like a charm. Now c'mon. Here's hoping she's still alive in that thing."

Rel rushed past the hero, too worried to be upset. She knelt at her Mistress's side, holding a hand in front of the woman's lips and praying, desperately, for breath.

Not Done Yet

In the movies, you always woke up to the beeping of a heart monitor, everything swimming in and out of focus in a sterile white hospital room.

Well, in this setting, I guess you'd actually expect someone dabbing away at your feverish brow with a cool cloth, only to run out of the room in excitement the moment you regained consciousness.

Of course, I didn't expect to wake at all.

They didn't swim around me, because I couldn't even see the far wall in the darkness. I coughed, tapping at my arms for a solid five seconds before I realized I wasn't in my armor.

That sparked another coughing fit. Finally, I managed to get a breath in, pressing a hand against my aching chest. "Swear to god if I left my armor *again*."

I shook my head, slumping back into the bed. My entire body ached, a soreness that ran all the way down to my bones. I felt like I'd been sandblasted inside and out. Hell of a comedown from a trip, but that's what happened when you snort strange substances: you didn't always get to wake up the way you wanted.

I took a second to catch my breath before feeling my surroundings. My hands found the edge of a table next to my narrow bed, and I used it to pull myself into a sitting position. That alone made my head spin, and I found myself doubling over its smooth wooden surface. Plus side, I bumped a pitcher that was, I quickly discovered, full of water.

I considered feeling in the dark for a cup before picking up the whole thing and drinking as much of it as I could.

When I finished, I was breathing heavily again, but at least my throat no longer felt like a desert. Officially not the worst bender I'd ever been on.

With a grunt, I pushed myself to my feet. Shuffling along, I found the wall, then the door leading to another dark room. Quickly, I found an exit, stumbling out into the night.

I blinked again, my eyes slowly adjusting to the starlight overhead. The moon cast a pale glow over darkened streetlamps and quiet houses. For a moment I feared that I'd been left in Lady's Port as some cruel joke, after the town had been scoured of life.

Then, the door banged open again behind me. I glanced back just in time to see Rel rush out of the house, a frantic look on her face.

She paused at the sight of me. "Mistress." She slumped. "You're awake."

"Looks like it." I turned back to the night. "Did we do it?"

"We did." Relia walked up next to me. "Are you . . ."

I waved her off. "I feel like shit, but I'm not dying. I thought I would."

She nodded. "We found you in the castle. Fortunately, we had a deacon with us who was able to address the damage."

I blinked. "A deacon?"

Rel nodded. "Ishanti brought quite a host with her."

"So she came back." I laughed. "Where did she get to, anyway?"

"She went to the capital to rally support." Rel gave a quiet laugh. "She was . . . most confused when she discovered that four of us had already toppled Silverwall before she could arrive." My minion paused. "She was instrumental in diverting the stampede, though."

I sighed. "I guess it was too much to hope that we'd fly under the radar forever." I waved off her confused glance. "We can worry about Ishanti tomorrow. I'm sure she has plenty of things she wants to talk about."

Rel nodded.

"Did both the boys make it out?" I asked.

"Yes, my lady," Rel replied. "Dee and Dum both got scratched up a bit, but they're recovering. Just like *you* should be."

I shrugged. "Put me back to bed then." I waved at the lights. "Is there a reason the lamps are out?"

"The Lighting Mill was damaged during the stampede."

I sighed again. "No rest for the wicked."

"You have time to rest, Mistress." Rel took a step closer, hand pausing an inch from my shoulder, so close I could feel the heat of her skin through the thin fabric of my clothes. "Everything . . . everything is stable, our enemies are defeated, and our allies more than willing to wait."

It was a novel feeling, having allies.

But there was something else bothering me far more. "Why are you suddenly so formal?"

Rel pulled back her hand, fingers curling. "I . . . don't take your meaning, Mistress."

I tilted my head towards her. She stood half-hunched in the moonlight, so far from the confident young woman I'd seen her slowly grow into since we'd started building Lady's Port. Instead, she looked a mirror for the street urchin Electra and I had first stumbled upon in Silverwall, before I'd helped her stand on her own.

I took a step towards her, pausing when she leaned back. "What?" I asked. "Am I contagious? Did taking that Ash of Creation stuff disfigure me hideously? It happens to all villains eventually, or so I've been told."

"H-huh?" Rel shook her head furiously. "N-no! of course not! How could you think that?"

"What else am I supposed to think, when you recoil at the sight of me?" I asked.

"I am simply . . ." She trailed off, unsure what to say.

I took another step closer, and this time she didn't pull away. "Are you afraid I'd still be disappointed in you?"

Relia flinched.

I chuckled. "It would be a bit hypocritical of me, wouldn't it?" I reached up, placing my own hand on her shoulder. "To be so upset after everything played out so well, in no small part because of your plan?"

"I . . . I didn't *have* a plan." Rel shook her head. "I was flailing in the dark, and I was *tricked* by Ishanti, and—"

"Sometimes, the best plans involve a *lot* of flailing." I smiled. "Believe me."

Rel slumped, leaning into my hand. "She still played me for a fool."

I shrugged. "That doesn't explain why you're acting so standoffish all of a sudden."

She looked away mulishly "I'm . . . not."

"You haven't said my name a single time," I replied.

"Lady—my lady—"

"There you go again." I tightened my grip ever so slightly. "Now tell me."

She remained silent, face half cast in shadow from the building. I saw one eye sparkle in the moonlight, flicking to my face and away again. In the pale light, her eyes looked so impossibly dark, like a well I could fall into if I wasn't careful.

"I tried . . . so *hard* to be worthy of you," Rel said. "Now you say that everything is alright, but in the moment, you rejected my aid, rejected *me*, because I did not listen to your orders." Her deep, dark eyes locked on mine. "Is what you truly want just a minion who obeys your every command?"

"Ah, so it's my fault then." Despite that, I couldn't bring myself to look away. "I was cruel to you, in my anger, even though it turns out you were right. And . . . I don't know what I want."

Rel's eyes widened in surprise and confusion.

I laughed. "It seems nonsensical, doesn't it. I always forge ahead, unerring." My eyes flicked down. "I know what I need to do; I know what I *need* to *change*. For so long that ember has burned inside me, growing into a fire so bright that I lose sight of myself in the blaze." I laughed. "Look at me, waxing poetic about how I'm a such a workaholic that I forgot how to sit still."

I looked back up, meeting Relia's eyes once more. "What I needed . . ." I paused, hand shifting on her shoulder. "What I *thought* I needed was people who obeyed my orders, so I could steer us out of this mess." I laughed again, this time, lighter. "Then I wake up and find you've done a pretty good job of steering from what you've told me, you and Ishanti both."

"Ishanti acted for her own gain."

"Maybe." I shrugged. "People are allowed to have their own motivations, but I don't want to talk about her right now."

Rel blinked, eyes still locked on mine.

"You asked me what I wanted." I smirked. "Let's start with a reward, for my victory and yours."

"A reward?"

I pulled her forward. Kissed her hard on the lips.

Rel froze, arms stiffening halfway in the air. I laughed as I pulled back. "I told you pursuing me wouldn't be easy." I shifted my grip, stroking her cheek. "But you've acquitted yourself masterfully."

"Mistress, I—"

"Ah, ah!" I tapped a finger on her lips. "Say my name."

Rel gasped. "Via."

"That's my girl." I leaned forward, kissing her again, softer this time. She kissed back, hands coming down gently on my shoulders.

It felt so much more real, now that our intentions were more than words spoken across a mirror.

I pulled back, quirking my lips into a smile. "Tomorrow will bring more work," I told her. "And I will no doubt be domineering, head-strong, and grumpy more often than not. Are you up for that?"

Rel nodded. "Yes, Via. That's what I want."

I chuckled. "I think I might want that too."

ABOUT THE AUTHOR

Joseph Marcia is the author of fast-paced, character-driven narratives that stretch the definition of genre. Also known as Argentorum, Marcia cut his teeth in the wild world of online fiction. *Be Thou My Brilliant* is the second book in his Devil's Foundry series, which also includes *Be Thou My Good* and *Be Thou My True*.

DISCOVER
STORIES UNBOUND

PodiumAudio.com